Once at home in sunny [...] lived on three different [...] though her favor [...] romantic location remains the tropical place [...] America. When she's not typing away at her latest romance novel, or reading about love, Luana is either crocheting, buying yarn she doesn't need, or chasing her bunnies around her house. She lives with her partner in a cosy town in the south of England. Find her on Twitter under the handle @LuDaRosaBooks.

USA TODAY and *Wall Street Journal* bestselling author **Janice Lynn** has a Master's in Nursing from Vanderbilt University and works as a nurse practitioner in a family practice. She lives in the southern United States with her Prince Charming, their children, their Maltese named Halo and a lot of unnamed dust bunnies that moved in after she started her writing career. Readers can visit Janice via her website at janicelynn.net.

Also by Luana DaRosa

Falling for Her Off-Limits Boss
Her Secret Rio Baby

Also by Janice Lynn

A Nurse to Tame the ER Doc
The Nurse's One Night to Forever
Weekend Fling with the Surgeon
Reunited with the Heart Surgeon

Discover more at millsandboon.co.uk.

FALLING AGAIN FOR THE BRAZILIAN DOC

LUANA DaROSA

THE SINGLE MUM HE CAN'T RESIST

JANICE LYNN

MILLS & BOON

First published in Great Britain 2023
by Mills & Boon, an imprint of HarperCollins*Publishers* Ltd,
1 London Bridge Street, London, SE1 9GF

www.harpercollins.co.uk

HarperCollins*Publishers*
1st Floor, Watermarque Building,
Ringsend Road, Dublin 4, Ireland

Falling Again for the Brazilian Doc © 2023 Luana DaRosa

The Single Mum He Can't Resist © 2023 Janice Lynn

ISBN: 978-0-263-30595-1

01/23

FALLING AGAIN FOR THE FOR THE BRAZILIAN DOC

LUANA DaROSA

MILLS & BOON

For Velo. I love you.

CHAPTER ONE

THE MOST UNUSUAL sensation had pooled inside Yara since she had stepped over the threshold of the hospital. Like a fiery liquid, it surrounded her stomach and filled her chest with every breath. It took a while for her to realise what that sensation was—*nerves.* For the first time in what felt like an eternity, Yara felt nervous.

Salvador.

Her heart pounded against her chest as she thought of the man she hadn't seen in thirty years. Once they'd been inseparable—now she didn't even know what he looked like or what had happened in the three decades since she left Brasília. It was by pure chance that she knew he worked at Centro Médico Juliana Amala, the hospital that had hired her to consult on a difficult case.

Salvador Martins.

Yara shifted in the chair she sat in, picking up the glass of water they had put in front of her without taking a sip. Her fingers traced along the condensation on the outside of the glass, picking up the tiny pearls of water until her fingertips were slick. She quickly put the glass back down, not trusting herself with such a fragile object.

What on earth was wrong with her? Yara had spent the years since becoming a doctor making a name for herself as a top general surgeon and a sharp-minded diagnostician whom other doctors turned to when they were at the end of their rope with the diagnosis of a patient.

Yara was at the Juliana Amala because she needed to help a team of doctors find out what was wrong with their patient. She should not be nervous—she wouldn't be, were it not for Salvador and the host of ancient feelings his memory resurrected from the deep and dusty corners of her mind. Would he have realised it was her coming to consult on the case? Was he as nervous to see her as she was to see him?

With the way she had left things with him, she doubted that. Their friendship had blossomed into something more serious when she had left for med school in Porto Alegre, far to the south of Brasília, her hometown. During her teenage years her parents had voiced their displeasure at the kind of company she chose to keep. When it came to Salvador, they hadn't held back with their negative opinions, letting her know that, as their eldest daughter, she was expected to enter into a good marriage with a man from a good family that would be worthy of the Lopes name. Someone like Lawrence Silvia—the son of family friends, and her ex-husband of one year.

They had begun to pressure her when they realised that they couldn't dissuade her from being with Salvador, dangling the one thing in front of her they knew she couldn't refuse—her tuition for medical school. Without their financial help her dream of becoming a doctor would have ended right there, along with the approval she so desperately craved from her parents.

And for what? Once Yara had left her childhood home for good, neither of them had cared much what was going on in her life. Was their only motivation to push her so hard in one direction so they could brag to their friends about it? Only for them to realise that nobody cared about this.

By the time her sister, Bianca, was old enough to choose a path for herself, their strange obsession with status had shifted. Or had they been easier on her because she was a surprise child?

Yara didn't know, and she didn't care enough to find out any more. Though the memory still burned in her chest, she had realised long ago that she needed to make her own peace with it.

The door opened, pulling her out of her pain-filled memories, and a man she'd met in several video calls strode in with a laptop under his arm. He came to a halt in front of her, stretching his hand out.

Yara got up, quickly wiping her wet fingers on the side of her skirt before she grabbed the hand in a strong shake.

'Hello, Dr Sakamoto, it's a pleasure to meet you in person,' she greeted the Chief of Medicine of the hospital.

'Likewise, Dr Silvia. I'm glad to have you here. The team and I can't wait to get started on this,' he replied and handed the laptop to her as he let go of her hand. 'These are all the patient scans, files, exams and test results we have on Mr Orlay. The entire team is on standby. If you have any questions, just give them a page.'

He nodded his chin at the phone line on the desk. 'We turned this small conference room into your office for the duration of your stay.'

Yara smiled. 'Thank you.' She nodded as she looked around. With any luck, she wouldn't be spending too much time in this room, but rather talking to the different doctors about their theories on the patient.

As she had prepared to come to Brasília, she had asked for daily updates on the patient. Her last case had ended almost two days ago, but flying in from Singapore meant

Yara had to make the choice between sleeping or reading up on the case—and she could never sleep knowing it would leave her underprepared.

Mr Orlay had come into the hospital for a procedure on his heart that he had never fully recovered from. From the briefing material Dr Sakamoto had sent, she could see that the team here had already gone through some neurological tests, yielding a lot of different results that didn't make any sense to them.

'I'd like to see the patient before I look at his file. I need to do my own exam so I can check for any inaccuracies or potentially false conclusions.' This was usually the part where she noticed some resistance from the doctors she worked with on different cases. No one liked the outsider to come into their space, telling them they were wrong about a step in the diagnosis—even though if they weren't, she wouldn't be here.

A feeling Yara understood well. She hadn't come as far as she had without learning from her mistakes. Though her parents' unending pressure for perfection had almost broken her at times, the resilience she had to establish to withstand the expectations during her younger adult years helped her to this day when it came to her career.

Dr Sakamoto, however, took the comment without even flinching, leading her outside the office and down the corridor, where they came to a halt in front of a closed door. 'We chose that conference room due to its proximity to the patient room,' he said when he noticed Yara's gaze flicking backwards.

They were in the general wing of the medical centre, in what Yara believed to be a more secluded area. Both the floors and the walls shone at her in a soothing off-white. The absence of scuffs and marks that she often saw in other hospitals showed her the age of the *cen-*

tro médico. If she had to guess, she would say the Juliana Amala had been founded no more than five years ago. That or Chief Sakamoto had run a renovation crew through just to impress her.

And Yara definitely was impressed. This was by far one of the nicest hospitals she had been to, the space light and airy rather than functional, giving patients a relaxing environment so they could focus on healing and recovery.

The doors along the corridor they walked down were spaced out, with each bearing a name on the frosted glass panes. Someone had probably had to vacate their office to turn it into a patient room for the duration of her stay here.

A detail that made her smirk on the inside. Some hospital administrators couldn't resist the urge to impress her with strange fanfares such as this one. She appreciated the convenience, but her main focus would always be the patient, and it didn't matter how far she had to walk for that.

The Chief of Medicine knocked and opened the door a second later, leading her into the patient room.

A man in his sixties lay in the bed in front of her, the heavy bags under his eyes and the washed-out complexion hinting at the strain this mystery disease had on him.

'*Bom dia, senhor.* I'm Dr Silvia and I'm here to assist the team with your diagnosis. Are you okay with me examining you?'

'*Sim.*' His voice was raspy, no doubt from the breathing tube they had him on as he recovered from his surgery.

Yara turned to the patient and grabbed her stethoscope to listen to the patient's chest. Breath signs were shallow but there. Enough to breathe on his own—for now. According to the brief she'd received when she agreed to consult on this case, Mr Orlay had been suffering from an unexplained and progressive weakness ever since he woke up from surgery.

Listening to his heart, she could tell that his new valve was moving enough blood to keep him alive, yet he didn't have enough energy to even get out of bed to do his post-surgical physiotherapy.

Had it been something between the surgery and now that had put him in such a state? Medication they'd given him as prophylaxis? Or was this an unknown disease digging its claws deeper with each passing minute, unaffected by any treatment they tried? Something unrelated to his previously weakened heart valve?

Yara made a mental note to check the list of medication he was on and to stop anything that wasn't warranted by the symptoms she could see. Then she took a small pen-light out of her pocket, testing his pupillary reaction—normal. No sign of any neurological damage.

'Thank you, Mr Orlay. I'm hoping to get to the bottom of this. I'll be back shortly to discuss our next course of action.'

This was much better. The moment the Chief of Medicine had walked in with the information package around the patient, Yara had felt back in control and on an even keel. Diagnosing patients—that was what she needed to concern herself with. Not her girlhood boyfriend and what their reunion would be like.

With a critical patient at hand, she didn't have time to devote herself to any kind of lengthy catch-up, anyway. Her primary focus would be solving this medical mystery and then she would leave her home city behind again.

Maybe she was making too much of it in her mind. Three decades had passed since they had seen each other and, while Yara had never tried to get in touch with him over the years, neither had he. So maybe he didn't want to see her, and their brief reunion would be all about the medicine and nothing else.

Maybe it was better this way.

Salvador closed his eyes for a moment, letting the deep sigh building in his chest escape into the room. In front of him were the scans of Henrique Orlay, a patient suffering from a strange post-surgical side-effect no one could make anything of. He himself had spent the last four days scrutinising the patient's scans, looking them over with a literal magnifying glass, turning them this way and that way in an attempt to find something—anything—to help this man who seemed to struggle to hold on to life for no particular reason.

Things had turned so dire that Chief Sakamoto had brought in some famous consultant to advise them on this case. His colleagues working on the case with him had bristled at the suggestion that they were no longer deemed good enough to solve this on their own, but Salvador cared little.

All he wanted to do was a good job—for his own sake and the sake of his nephew, who had recently come to live with him full-time. The hours were already tough, and having a critical patient only made things worse. Since he'd been the one with the patient from the very beginning, he was the radiologist most involved in the case. Other people on his team could run the scans, but he'd been the one studying them all in such detail. If anyone would spot anything, it'd be him.

His phone lit up, and he looked at it, reading the reminder he had set for himself. Chief Sakamoto wanted an updated contrast MRI, but when Salvador had arrived at the patient's room earlier, the man had still been sleeping. By now, the trainee doctors and med students would have done their rounds, and he'd be able to transport the patient.

When he got to the patient's room, he found the door slightly ajar and spotted the familiar figure of Chief Sakamoto in the room, along with someone else, who had to be the consulting doctor to help them figure out the case.

Salvador stopped in the doorway, his eyes drawn to the woman. She wasn't wearing anything remarkable— a dark blue blouse and a pencil skirt—yet his reaction to her was as instant as it was unexpected. His eyes followed the gentle curve of her neck as she leaned forward to listen to the patient's heartbeat. A few strands of her dark brown hair had fought themselves out of the grip of the hair tie holding the rest of her locks in a bun at her nape.

Her lips were drawn down slightly—because of the situation with the patient, or had something else displeased her? Whatever it was, Salvador's gaze lingered on them, their shape suggesting unending softness and…and what?

He blinked, trying to rid himself of the sudden fantasy coming over him and forced his attention back into the room. What was her name again? Salvador had received the news of the doctor joining them a couple of days ago, along with the rest of the team assigned to Mr Orlay's case.

He couldn't remember her last name, though he knew her first name, as that name was permanently branded into a hidden part of his soul. *Yara*.

Even after all these years, the thought of his teenage sweetheart came with a strange sense of melancholy—as if he had lost a piece of himself when she left this city, and him, saying goodbye for the last time without his knowing it was a final farewell. The confusion and hurt had lessened over the three decades that had passed since he last saw her, but remnants of their time together still remained within him. Or rather, the betrayal he'd experienced had taught him to never let his guard down with anyone. No matter how much he *believed* he knew someone, in the end he had to remember that people changed. They did whatever was best for them and nobody else.

Just like Yara had done. Something he actually owed her a debt of gratitude for. If she hadn't cut him out of her life the way she had, he'd still chase the belief that he was worthy of more than what life currently had to offer. Thanks to her, Salvador had been able to keep his relationships casual, never letting anyone get too attached to him.

His most recent ex, Edinho, had come close to breaking through the heavy fortification he'd built around his heart. But even he had failed when it came to the ultimate test—Salvador's duty towards his nephew. Keeping Felix safe and out of trouble was the one calling that made Salvador feel worthy of his place in society.

'Ah, Martins, good of you to join us so I can introduce you to Dr Silvia.' Chief Sakamoto had spotted him, ripping him out of his contemplations over the scars dwelling beneath the surface.

Salvador's eyes drifted back to Dr Silvia, who was still facing the patient, and he watched with bewilderment as her entire posture stiffened. The gentle look on her half-obscured face melted away, into an expression he wasn't able to understand from this angle.

Surprise? Wasn't she expecting to meet the doctors on her team?

'It's nice to meet you, Dr Silvia. I'm Salvador Martins, your radiologist on the case.' He stepped forward to stretch out his hand but stopped cold when a familiar sensation washed over him.

Dr Silvia hesitated for a moment, and when she finally turned around, the ghost of something ancient came rushing at him, a sense of familiarity that was impossible. It felt as though a connection fell back into place—back where it belonged—and the sheer force of it pressed the air out of his lungs.

She looked at him, her light brown eyes wide, darting all over his body for a moment before they settled on his face.

This feeling… It couldn't be right. How?

'Yara?' He forced the name over his lips, praying that he might be mistaken. Or that he might be right. The emotions were such a whirl within his chest, he didn't know how he *wanted* to feel.

The woman in front of him gave a nod, as if she understood he needed a sign to tell him she was really her.

'Hello, Salvador,' she said, her voice coated in something he couldn't decipher.

'You two already know each other?' Chief Sakamoto looked at him with a playfully hurt expression, as if he was angry he hadn't told him.

'I didn't know you were Dr Silvia,' he said, fighting through the fog that had come over his brain. 'You changed your name.'

A quick expression fluttered over her face, something painful that she shoved away just as fast as it had appeared. 'People tend to do that when they get married.'

'They do. But you said you wouldn't.' The words came out of his mouth before Salvador could understand where they had even come from. This conversation he was recalling had happened when they were teenagers, fickle beings whose words were worth little to their adult selves.

Only Yara had been so adamant about it. Her family name had been part of her. *Lopes.* It was strange to believe she had changed her mind. Then again, the woman in front of him wasn't the girl he had used to know.

He'd do well to remember that.

Yara opened her mouth in a response that wouldn't come, for her brain had been wiped clear of any thought the second her eyes had met Salvador's in a moment that had been in the making for decades.

And in all the years she'd thought about what their reunion would be like, she'd never thought it would be *those* words he hurled at her, aiming for a weakness he couldn't know lay bare underneath her skin.

What was she supposed to say to that? That her parents had believed him beneath her, so they pressured her into marriage to a different man? One that had stripped all meaning from the name Yara Lopes to the point where she didn't know if that woman still existed? If that was who Salvador wanted to meet, it would be better for him to find out now that *his* Yara was long gone.

No one knew about her divorce or how broken it had left her. She certainly wasn't going to break her silence for Salvador. There were a lot of things she owed him, but that part of her story wasn't one. What had happened with Lawrence was one of the reasons she had avoided coming back to Brazil, choosing instead to travel the world and make a career out of it. No one could ask questions if she never spent more than a week in one place, and she could keep her secret to herself for just a bit longer.

How could she admit that her parents had wielded so much power over her, threatening her future and her dream if she didn't do as they asked? She had believed them to have her best interests in mind, despite their stooping low to force her hand. And instead of fighting for Salvador, the man her younger self had believed could be the one, she gave in to the pressure, scared to lose her spot at the University of Rio Grande do Sul if she didn't comply with their orders.

'I'm originally from Brasília,' she said towards Dr Sakamoto, who shot puzzled looks between them. 'We went to school together.'

He nodded, seemingly satisfied with her explanation, and turned his attention to Salvador.

'Ah, in this case, I trust you will take some time to get your old friend acquainted with the hospital? Introduce her to everyone in the team?'

Salvador nodded, his spine so stiff from the surprise he looked almost menacing as he towered over the already tall Dr Sakamoto. The Chief only smiled, either unaware of the tension between them or choosing to ignore it altogether, as he nodded to both of them and left.

Silence filled the room, only interrupted by the soft whirring and beeping of the monitor Mr Orlay was hooked up to. There were so many things she wanted to say to him, yet none of the words formed in her head.

How did one apologise for ghosting their teenage boyfriend thirty years after the fact?

'Can we have a word outside?' A different setting was definitely the first step.

Salvador glanced at her for a second before moving to the patient. 'Henrique, I'm afraid we have to take you for another ride to the MRI. You're still familiar with this?' He pulled gloves over his hands before showing him a syringe filled with a dark liquid.

Mr Orlay nodded with a sigh that showed just how much he'd already been probed and prodded as they tried to cure him from his mystery ailment. Yara hoped she didn't have to add too many procedures to his time here before she found out what ailed him.

Salvador had picked up on his unease as well, for he pulled up a stool for a moment so they could be at eye level with each other. 'I've got good news for you, Henry. We flew this kick-ass doctor in to treat you. If anyone can find out what's going on, it'll be her. You just have to hang in there a little longer.'

Yara wasn't sure if some colour had returned to Mr Orlay's face or if she just imagined it, but she was surprised when he managed to smile at Salvador with a tired nod.

'I'll inject the contrast agent now and then we'll take you down for the scan.' He got off the chair and injected the agent through the cannula in his hand. 'Let me arrange an escort for you and I'll see you in a moment.'

Yara had watched the entire interaction with a warm feeling pooling in the pit of her stomach, which slowly spread through her entire body. She was glad to see that the years had not robbed him of his kindness. He'd always been a caring person, looking out for the weaker people around him and helping them stand strong. Qualities she had always admired in him. It was what had once driven her to strive to be better.

She unfroze when Salvador passed her with barely more than a glance, walking out of the room and down the corridor to the nurses' station, where he ordered the MRI for Mr Orlay.

'Salvador,' she called when she caught up with him and fell silent when he turned around to face her, his eyes filled with an ancient pain she hadn't expected.

'I can't talk right now, Yara, and I'm not even sure I want to,' he said when the nurse had stepped away and they were alone for the first time.

'I just need one minute. For better or for worse, we'll be working together on this for the next few days. So, I want to take a moment to…clear the air. I know nothing I can say will make a difference, but at least give me the chance to listen to you and just…take it.'

She didn't want to insult him with empty apologies that rang hollow with the decades they had been left unsaid.

Salvador crossed his arms in front of his chest, his jaw rolling as he considered her words, and with each passing second the knot in her stomach got tighter.

This was so not how she had imagined any of this would go. Sure, she knew he was going to be angry. He had every right to be. But, knowing the kind soul beneath the gruff exterior, she also truly had thought he'd give her a chance to say what she had to say. If, at the end of that, he decided that the hurt ran too deep, Yara would let it be and work with him in any professional capacity necessary.

Though as she watched Salvador silently making the decision of whether he wanted to hear her out, she realised that not a small part of her wanted to reconcile with him. Their friendship had meant so much to her and if it hadn't been for the pressure her parents put on her they might have seen their budding romance come to fruition. Her heart had called for him even as she decided to leave, choosing her dream of becoming a physician over their relationship—just as her parents had wanted her to.

'I can't deal with this right now, Yara,' Salvador finally said, and those words cracked her chest open. Disappointment flooded her system, extinguishing the tiny glimmer of hope she had nurtured on her way here.

His gaze flickered over her shoulder and she followed it, watching as someone from their medical team wheeled Mr Orlay down the corridor.

'It doesn't have to be much. Just one cup of coffee in

between patients. We'll be working together on this, no matter how we feel about each other—so I need to know there won't be any problems.'

She was the lead physician on this case, after all, and there was truth in her reasoning. They *were* going to work together, and the tension between them wouldn't help with the patient's care, especially not if either of them was constantly thinking about the other one.

'Give me one minute of your time, Salvador,' she said when his eyes drifted back to her, his glare hard and unreadable.

The line of his jaw tightened as his chest rose in a deep inhale. 'I'm needed for the scan.'

CHAPTER TWO

THE SERENITY OF the hospital was broken and Salvador knew exactly who to blame. Though the department was always buzzing and hectic, this was the place he could feel in control and at peace with himself. Here he was the master of his own fate, working with a team of physicians as passionate and dedicated as him.

It was where he could do the most good—outside of taking care of his nephew and giving him the life he deserved. A life Salvador had had to build for himself. His parents had failed both him and his brother with their problematic life choices, going so far as to drag Felipe down with them. Salvador didn't know how he'd scraped by without any lasting damage.

Yara. Memories of her popped into his mind unbidden. She'd often invited him to her home after school, letting him stay over whenever she sensed something off around him. Those had been the days his parents had fought over debt and money, their ire so uncontrollable that their children often became collateral damage.

And she'd never asked for an explanation of what happened, just accepting him into her home and her heart without the judgement he experienced from other people from her socio-economic background—or at least so he thought, until she had left him without a single word.

He'd spent so many years wondering why, unable to move on from that intense heartache. Their romance had just begun when she left to attend medical school, but the anger and pain had been enough to dissuade him from anything serious over the years since then. If he never again felt the way he did when Yara left, his life would be much simpler and free of hurt.

Though despite the anger simmering underneath his skin, he had to admit that she'd saved his life, and she didn't even know about it. The sanctuary of her home had given him the emotional distance he had needed not to fall into the same patterns of bad behaviour his parents had perpetuated. He owed her gratitude beyond any measure that he could ever hope to repay—and yet it was pain that pumped through his veins whenever he caught a memory of her drifting through his head.

Or was the heat he felt something else? The last remnant of a dying ember that had been the whirlwind of their budding relationship? No, that couldn't be it. Their attraction to each other had only *just* emerged when Yara had left for Porto Alegre. The number of kisses they had shared could be counted on one hand. Her abrupt actions had put a stop to much else, but those precious few weeks had been enough to make him dream about a future.

Salvador pushed it all away as the door next to him opened. A junior radiologist stepped in, holding a tablet. 'Here are the scans, Dr Martins,' he said as he held out his hands.

He grabbed the tablet with a nod of thanks, glancing at the scans for a moment before turning it off and tucking it under his arm. After Mr Orlay's scan, Salvador had received two additional requests to handle. Those were the more complex cases in the hospital, where they had already gone through several rounds of different scans.

The one the radiologist had handed him was a new case, but none the less a tricky one. The symptoms of the patient were disjointed, none of them pointing in a more concrete direction—so the physician on the case had requested Salvador to walk him through the scans.

'Is Dr Douglas going to see the patient now?' he asked, hoping he'd know the answer.

But his colleague shook his head. 'He's asked us to transport her back to her room, and he would see her after his next consultation.'

Salvador nodded and pushed himself off his chair. 'I'll ask the nurses' station to page him.'

The charge nurse informed him that Dr Douglas was running a training lab with the medical students and would be able to look at the scans after the class in the afternoon. Salvador glanced at his phone, checking the time.

Part of him wanted to be too busy to indulge Yara's request for a short meeting. She wanted to speak about what had happened between them all those years ago—a conversation he'd long since lost hope would ever happen. He'd been forced to make his peace with it, not knowing what drove her away or what they could have been had they stayed.

Would they have been happy? He hadn't known who he was when they first met, only realising much later that he was both attracted to women and men. How would his sexual exploration have turned out if he had tied himself to a woman for ever at such a young age?

Or were these just convenient excuses that he clung on to because he didn't believe that he could have made someone like Yara, who had known nothing but safety and splendour, happy? When his life was streaked with the discord and chaos crime and poverty brought to anyone who came in contact with it? He remembered both the glares and the whispers following him as they walked around in her neighbourhood, unworthy to even touch her the way he desired.

But Yara was right. Like it or not, they had to work on this patient as part of a team. That meant no distractions or tension that could lead to mistakes.

Biting back a sigh, he headed for the general medicine wing, where Yara had her office. On a whim, he stopped when he passed one of the staff rooms and grabbed two packets of crisps from a vending machine before knocking on the door of Yara's temporary office.

'Come in.' Her voice sounded through the door.

Yara was staring at her laptop with narrowed eyes, the fingers of her right hand twirling a pen. The notepad next to her was already filled with annotations in a tiny script.

An involuntary smile spread over Salvador's face. He had used to make fun of her for her tiny handwriting, making her notes at school so much harder to read—and she'd been a lot more diligent about her notes than him.

'I'd offer to go over your patient notes with you, but I forgot my magnifying glass at home,' he jested before he could stop himself.

Yara's head whipped towards him, eyes wide with surprise. Being off in her own world was just like her as well.

'Salvador... Hey.'

His eyes darted to her throat when it bobbed slightly. Had she been waiting for someone else? The discomfort in her stance was apparent, and he couldn't blame her. After thirty years, he'd not thought they would reunite—or be in the position where they had to lay open the things that had happened between them. That moment in their youth when they had both realised there was more between them, followed by Yara drifting out of his life without an explanation.

Salvador wasn't sure he even wanted to know any more.

'I have a minute if you want to chat,' he forced himself to say, taking a step in and closing the door behind him.

'Sure…' There was a slight hesitation in her voice before she continued. 'Please, have a seat.'

He sat down and handed one of the crisp packets to her. 'I thought all the dry patient notes might have left you with a small appetite.'

Yara picked up the crisps and turned the packet, with its bright green crocodile, around in her hand. 'Cheese flavoured?'

'You don't like them any more?' Salvador raised an eyebrow, a frown pulling on his lips.

'No, I do like them even though I know I shouldn't.' She smirked, her eyes scanning the list of ingredients. 'They're cheese flavoured, but real cheese has never touched them.'

She paused for a moment before opening them. 'I can't believe you still remember what flavour I like. Or that I like these at all.' The snack was mostly marketed for children.

Salvador looked at the packet in his own hands for a moment. He hadn't *exactly* remembered. But rather, once he stood in front of the vending machine his hands had acted before he could even make a conscious decision, punching in the number to get this specific flavour and brand.

'How is your research going?' He didn't know what to say about the snack, so he changed the topic. How could he explain that he remembered something like that after three decades without sounding as though he still cared enough to do so?

'Good, I think. A very interesting medical puzzle. His heart surgery has thrown off a lot of the diagnosis, looking for a link where there isn't one.' She popped a crisp into her mouth, chewing for a moment. Her eyes went wide as she looked at him. 'How do these things still taste the same?'

He smiled, opening his own packet and trying one of them. The taste of artificial cheese exploded in his mouth. 'I don't know how you like these,' he mumbled.

Yara laughed, the sound of it bringing memories of a time they had done nothing but laugh with each other. They sprang to life in his head, settling heavily in the pit of his stomach.

'It's comfort food. It doesn't have to taste nice,' she said, with a smile that looked exactly as he remembered.

His gaze drifted up and down her face as he took the time to look at her in the quiet of the moment they shared. She hadn't changed much over the years, the light brown hue of her eyes still dotted with the occasional black mark and shining with the curiosity that had always lived in them. Once he'd look into those eyes and young, evolving love would threaten to constrict his chest. Now he saw her and the hurt and anger he believed to have moved on from ages ago came bubbling back to the surface.

'Are those the high-contrast scans?' Yara asked, nodding at the tablet he'd put on the desk when he sat down.

'No, this is a different patient—she's only arrived this morning from a different hospital.'

'Can I see them?' The curiosity he'd remembered only moments ago came to life in her eyes as he unlocked the tablet and brought up the scans.

'Unexplained weight loss and tiredness brought her

here through a referral after her local hospital ran out of diagnostic options.' Salvador provided the context as she zoomed in on the scans.

Yara stayed quiet for a few heartbeats, tilting her head to one side while her fingers kept twirling the pen in her fingers, as if that helped her focus on the thing in front of her. 'Ah, interesting…' she mumbled.

'What is?'

She looked at him, handing the tablet back to him. 'Can you show me the patient chart? I need to know what the doctors observed outside of the two things you listed.'

'Are you trying to diagnose the patient?' Salvador raised an eyebrow at her. He'd looked at the scans already, noticing the inflammation around the aorta. But combined with the weight loss and tiredness, it could be one of many things. General medicine would have to narrow it down.

Surely she couldn't have already diagnosed her just by looking at a scan?

He took the tablet and brought up the patient chart, handing it back to Yara, who smiled at him with a grateful nod. Her eyes darted across the extensive notes from the patient's initial examination, as well as the transfer documents.

Yara remained quiet as she read. Until she finally breathed, 'Ah, she has vasculitis.'

'You can tell that from the scans?' Salvador didn't quite manage to keep the incredulity out of his voice.

'And from the notes.' She tipped on the tablet, highlighting what she had just read. 'She has a decreased pulse in her arm. Along with the tiredness and the inflammation visible on the scan, she has Takayasu Arteritis.'

Salvador furrowed his brow. 'I don't think the medical school I went to covered this disease in depth.'

'Oh…' Her lips parted as the tone escaped her throat, the expression of intrigue washed away. 'Pulseless Disease. You see, the pulmonary arteries here?' She indicated the scan. 'It's narrow around the inflammation. The notes mention a weak pulse in her left side—a common symptom when inflammation causes the arteries to swell and narrow.'

She paused for a moment, laughing softly. 'It's a fairly rare disease. I've only diagnosed it a handful of times. Lucky this came up when I was around.'

'Huh.' Salvador looked at the scans again before looking up at Yara as a strange sensation took root in his chest. They'd been sitting here for no more than a couple of minutes and she'd managed to diagnose a patient when an entire hospital had failed at it.

The girl he'd desired all those years ago had been ambitious, and it gave Salvador an unusual taste of satisfaction to see how far she'd come—mingled with the profound hurt that she'd chosen not to share this part of her life with him without giving him a chance to fight. No, she'd selfishly taken away any chance he might have had when she ignored all of his attempts to talk to her.

And why? Salvador hadn't believed that their difference in class had ever bothered her. She wasn't a person swayed by wealth or the perception of others. Even when gossips at school were passing comments about his father's criminal record, Yara had brushed it aside, seeing him for who he was—not for what his parents had done.

Until the day she'd abandoned him, and it became clear to him that he was unworthy and could never give her the kind of life she was used to. He'd stopped trying with anyone after that, leading a life of meaningless flings that never dipped below the surface. His latest relationship had started to look different, but even Ed had left when he realised that Salvador would never let his walls down. His kind and gentle nature had had Salvador almost convinced that he could have love in his life, after all. Until Ed had told him that he didn't want children right when Felix became his full-time ward.

Though maybe Yara's betrayal was something he could be grateful for, in a twisted way. What if his need to explore his attraction to men had got in the way of their relationship? When he'd first realised the feeling inside his chest when he looked at an attractive man was the same as he'd get from the women that he tied himself to for a night, he struggled to reconcile this attraction with the person he thought he was. It had taken many years and a lot of secret one-night stands before he understood that he was bisexual—and many more to understand that it was okay to be that way.

None of that would have happened if he had stayed with Yara, and how could he know that this wouldn't have caused them problems? Yet he still hurt, and he wanted to hear what she had to say about it.

'Why, Yara?'

Small fires started underneath her skin as Salvador's dark gaze drifted over her face and dipped below her neck, watching her with an unknown intent. Yara had been the one who wanted this conversation—had wanted it soon. Not because she particularly enjoyed going over her teenage insecurities, but she knew she needed harmony in this case if she wanted to do her job precisely and fast. She wanted to leave Brasília in under two weeks, to leave the city as soon as she could, before any of her family might realise that she was in town.

Yara hadn't made up her mind whether she wanted to pay her sister and cousins a visit or not. As much as she missed seeing them, she didn't want to talk about her marriage falling apart—didn't want to hear how she'd brought dishonour on her mother and all the terrible things her neighbours would whisper about her for having a divorced daughter. She wanted to avoid encountering the kind of pressure that had led her to the fatal decision of marrying someone because the match looked good on paper and would boost her family's reputation.

Though Yara was close to her sister, Bianca had never experienced the worst their parents had to offer. With almost ten years between the two women, their parents were a lot less concerned with what her sister wanted in life. After all, they had Yara to project all their unrealistic expectations onto.

Seeing the difference in treatment the sisters had received almost convinced Yara that their mother didn't know why she was like this herself. How could she be warm and understanding to Bianca while she settled all the pressure and anxiety of a fictitious reputation on Yara? Was that simply how her own mother—their grandmother—had modelled her life for her? Yara knew her mother was estranged from her own sister, and she had never actually met her aunt.

Or had her mother seen a lot more of herself in Yara than in Bianca, forcing her to live a life that she could vicariously experience for her own satisfaction?

Whatever her reasons were, Yara had never found a conclusive answer, but she had to work hard to keep the resentment for her sister at bay. It wasn't Bianca's fault that they were treated differently.

As to why she had left... The reasons why she had decided to cut Salvador out of her life were shrouded in the years that had passed without her confronting the truth behind the extent of her parents' manipulation. How could she admit that they had threatened to take away the one thing she wanted more than anything else in her life when she wouldn't comply with their wishes?

And to make herself feel better about her choices, Yara had to believe that her parents simply meant the best for her when they pushed for a match with a man she hardly knew. What kind of parents would lead their child into a life of unhappiness for the sake of reputation? It took her many years to realise how much she'd been manipulated without noticing it.

The moment she had she filed for divorce and left her marital home in the United States one year ago.

But those thoughts would remain unspoken for ever. She couldn't answer his question truthfully, not if that meant letting him see her scars.

'I was young and very stupid—though you probably already know that,' she said, cringing as she inched as close to the truth as she dared. She couldn't tell him everything, especially not what had happened since they drifted apart or how much she sometimes fantasised about how her life would look if they had had the chance to become a real couple.

'Look, if you don't want to tell me, don't. I gave up on the idea of closure many missed phone calls ago.' His voice rumbled deep, vibrating through the air between them and seeping into her skin as he crossed his arms.

His words found their mark as Yara bit her lip, taking it with the dignity she'd promised herself she would. Because he was right. After everything they shared with each other, she owed him more than *I'm sorry I ghosted you*.

Except the truth lay buried under an amount of insecurities and self-doubt she was unable to admit to anyone. She'd spent the year since her divorce finding herself again, and the process was so new and fragile, she didn't trust anyone near it.

'We've been friends for years and somewhere down the line the nature of our relationship changed,' Yara said, finding a way to get as close to the truth as she could. 'We became closer, and I thought it was what I wanted. But when I left, I realised maybe I didn't want to be more than friends—so I panicked.'

The lie tasted bitter in her mouth, but she forced her expression to stay neutral. She had panicked, but not because she had regrets—rather, she didn't know how to be so vulnerable in front of him, how to let him in by talking about the demands from her parents.

For their brief time together here in Brasília, it was better that he believed that rather than know the full truth about her insecurities.

She finally dared to look at Salvador again. His arms remained crossed on his chest, his eyes dark and narrowed as he scrutinised her.

There had been a time when he'd trusted her implicitly, never questioning or doubting her words. But that had been before she iced him out. Though it hurt, she could understand his hesitation. She still wasn't upfront with him about it, but she gave him as much as she could—and hoped that would be enough to restore civility between them.

'You didn't want to change our friendship?' He hesitated before he spoke those words, showing how much deliberation he put into his phrasing. Though his demeanour bordered on frosty, he still cared about her comfort—a realisation that thundered through her, leaving her tingling on the inside.

'I—I thought I knew what I wanted. But then I left for med school and panicked at the thought of coming back.' That at least was true, though for other reasons than Salvador now suspected. Her parents' relentless calls and pressure had worn Yara down, making her doubt her own ability to judge someone's character. Her mother had told her about the rumours surrounding Salvador's family, something she knew he struggled with, but she never asked and he never spoke about it, either.

He would have told her if he was in trouble, no? With all the doubt filling her heart, she didn't know any more. So instead, she'd avoided him—rarely a good strategy, but it was what she had gone with.

Silence spread between them. Salvador's eyes still lingered on her, peering deep into places Yara was sure he couldn't see. No one could see those.

Finally, he shook his head and breathed out a sigh. 'You could have said that,' he said, and the low rumble of his voice affected her deep inside, so much that she didn't quite manage to read his tone.

Was it relief that gave his voice such a soft quality? Had he blamed himself all these years?

'I'm sorry, Salvador. Back then, I was too self-involved to understand the gravity of my actions. But now I do, and I know it might not mean much now, but I always re-gretted losing you as my friend.' And that was the truth she needed him to know. Everything surrounding the break-up was still too personal for Yara to talk about, but she could tell him the truth that mattered—that she had missed having him in her life.

Salvador leaned back in his chair, his arms dropping to his sides, with a contemplative look on his face.

'I appreciate your apology, though I'm not sure I can or even want to be friends again. The way you left with-out a word almost broke me, and though I moved on, I remember the devastation I felt.'

His face was an unreadable mask as he spoke those words, their meaning cutting down to the bone. Even though she knew this to be the most likely outcome, her heart still squeezed inside her chest as the hope to have her friend back was extinguished by his icy stare.

'But I'm not going to cause any problems while we work together, as long as we keep our interactions related to the case,' he continued, at which point Yara nodded.

'That's all I really wanted to establish from this conversation.'

They were quiet again, but this time it was different. The previous tension that had filled the room didn't come back. Instead, a strange familiarity settled between them as they finally spoke about what happened thirty years ago.

'When are you going to see Bianca?' he asked.

'I don't know… It depends on how busy I am with this case and where I'm off to next. Work doesn't usually take me to Brazil, so it would be nice to spend some more time here, but I don't really get to decide when new cases come in.'

Salvador snorted, interrupting her rambling response. 'So you're avoiding your sister, too? Is there anyone in the city you're on good terms with?'

Yara's eyes went wide, and it took only a second to pick up on the playful notes in his voice. 'You're teasing me,' she said, crossing her arms. 'Is that what I should expect from you now for the rest of my stay here? You making fun of me until you feel better? That really doesn't seem related to the case.' She tried to give her voice a sanctimonious edge but couldn't help the relief shining through her words.

Teasing was good. Maybe that meant he'd changed his mind about being friendly, if not about being friends.

Even though her apology was left intentionally vague, she did mean it, and a part of her wanted to find a way forward from the tension between them.

'I'm impressed with how fast you've diagnosed that patient. If you always work this quickly, we'll be done with Mr Orlay tomorrow morning,' Salvador said.

Though Yara knew exactly what kind of value and expertise she brought to every hospital she visited, heat rushed to her cheeks at the compliment.

And then he smiled at her, and the flames that had been heating her face sent sparks flying all across her body, blazing fiery trails down her spine and exploding a tiny firework just behind her navel.

'Oh, with this patient I was just in the right place at the right time. While this is a rare disease, it is comparatively easy to diagnose. The difficulty lies in ruling out all the more common diseases before dusting off the medical encyclopaedias. The challenge with Mr Orlay is that so far his diagnosis has been made under the wrong impression.' The dark intensity in his gaze became too much for Yara. She dropped her eyes onto her notes, scanning over them.

She continued, 'His valve replacement led the diagnostic team onto the wrong path. He doesn't have one condition, he has two. A weakness of the heart that led to his valve replacement, and a pre-existing medical condition which explains the symptoms that cannot be explained with post-surgical complications.'

'You mean whatever ailed him was there before the surgery, but the symptoms matched his heart defect so we didn't think anything else was going on?' His expression turned thoughtful, and she watched with a hitch in her breath as his hand scrubbed over the stubbles on his cheeks.

He looked so different from the boy she'd fallen for, but beneath the years she still saw him.

'Yes, that's what I mean. Right now, I'm eliminating all the medication he's been put under because of the surgery. Once the drugs are out of his system, we—'

The chime of Salvador's phone interrupted her and he apologised. He looked at the display and got up. 'Dr Douglas is ready for me.' He picked up the tablet, tucking it under his arm. She held her breath as he passed, not wanting the ease they had finally found with each other to disappear again. Her stomach lurched when he stopped to look at her. 'We'll catch up later. Mr Orlay's condition has had the entire team working around the clock to get some results, so I'd like to hear more about your thoughts.'

'You know where to find me,' she said with a chuckle that she hoped didn't sound as awkward to him as it did to her.

Her pulse pounded in her ears as she watched him walk away, a sight both strange and familiar. Age had only refined what had already been a handsome face, and for a moment she wished she could have seen it change over the years. Would she have spotted the subtle changes?

Yara shook those thoughts away, forcing them to the back of her mind. There would be plenty of opportunities to think about how their relationship could look like going forward.

Going by what she had seen today, he was still the same.

He was still her Salvador.

CHAPTER THREE

WHEN YARA ENTERED Mr Orlay's room, she found an unexpected guest sitting next to him. Salvador was wrapped up in a discussion with the patient, talking to him in a low voice. She couldn't understand the words spoken, but, from the cadence and the calm expression on his face, she surmised that they weren't talking about anything relating to his diagnosis. She cleared her throat to make both men aware of her presence. Salvador looked at her, and something mingling in his gaze immediately set her on edge.

Their conversation yesterday had shaken her, and the closure she yearned for was nowhere closer. He'd been distant whenever she saw him, giving her no more than a faint nod to acknowledge her.

The feeling of ancient desire still stirred through her, making it hard to think clearly. Her body remembered all too well what it felt like to lean against him, to breathe in his scent, to have his warmth seep into her. The ghosts of those memories kept creeping back into her mind, and they really needed to stop that. Any kind of romantic love they might have shared many years ago had died the moment Yara decided to put physical and emotional distance between them—a choice she'd come to regret with their unexpected reunion, but a choice she couldn't take back.

Judging by his own admission yesterday, he was not interested in her any more—be it as a friend or a lover. Not that she was hoping for any kind of reconciliation. No, she just wanted to do her job well. The sooner this was done, the earlier she would be able to leave Brazil.

'Good evening, Mr Orlay, Dr Martins. I'm doing my evening round before heading out and wanted to check on you.' She stepped closer to the bed and rested one hand at the foot of it, her eyes fully trained on the patient even though a tingling sensation in her nape urged her to look at Salvador.

'We discontinued most of your medication, leaving you only with the ones necessary to ensure your heart valve heals correctly. We've also kept you on some pain-management medication and have left instructions with the night nurse to increase your dosage. So if you are in any pain throughout the night, don't hesitate to tell the nurse.'

Mr Orlay nodded at her, the dark spots under his eyes saying enough of the kind of stress the diagnosis was putting him under. That alone was motivation enough to solve this case as soon as possible.

'*Obrigado,*' he said, his voice straining.

Yara gave him a reassuring smile. 'Of course. I'll see you in the morning.' Hopefully, whatever medication was counteracting further symptoms had left his system. She heard Salvador's whispers as she walked out of the room. The fine hairs along her neck stood on end as she sensed him following her out.

'Yara,' he called to her, and she stopped in her tracks, turning round.

He caught up with her, and the corners of his mouth twitched slightly upwards. That was his version of a smile. He had done that as a teenager as well, his lips only slightly twitching to indicate his amusement. He did smile, but those scarce full smiles were reserved for rare and treasured moments—such as when she had told him that she'd been accepted into her dream medical programme. They'd hugged and jumped up and down on the spot before he grabbed her by the shoulders and kissed her on an impulse. A kiss meant to be familial, but when their lips had come apart, both felt the world around them shift. Yara had shivered when Salvador's lips touched hers again, this kiss as charged and intimate as she had yearned it to be.

'Are you off now?' he asked, prompting Yara to furrow her brow. Not the question she'd been expecting.

'I'm done for the day, so just heading back to the hotel with some light reading for the evening.' She patted the tote bag full of medical journals she had picked up from the hospital's library.

Salvador paused, a hesitancy she couldn't quite place. His mouth opened, just to close again without his uttering a word.

'Can I drive you to the hotel? I imagine with all the travelling you don't have a car,' he finally said, and Yara got the strange impression that this hadn't been what he wanted to tell her.

Why was he offering to drive her? Was he looking for an excuse to spend time with her? The thought brought the relentless heat back into her veins, and she pushed it away. Nope, under no circumstances was she allowed to indulge those thoughts. Salvador was *not* interested in her in any way—couldn't be after she'd left him like that.

No, he was just being polite, for the sake of their professional relationship, as they worked on this case together.

'My hotel is just a short walk down the road. I booked it for its proximity to the hospital,' she said.

'Then let me walk with you. Just to be safe.' Genuine concern shone through his words, fanning the flames Yara had been trying her best to ignore.

These ancient feelings were getting way too out of hand. They had just managed to get into a place where they could be relatively comfortable with each other—after finally talking about what happened. Or rather, Yara had spoken while he had just taken it all in. This thought had followed her around all afternoon as she tried to focus on her work with the patient, poring through lab results and online databases in the hope that some missing piece of information would provide the context she was currently lacking.

Salvador hadn't actually said anything. He'd told her that she could have confided in him all these years ago and then...he'd changed the subject.

'Sure, if you think that's a good use of your time.' She tried to sound light-hearted, but her voice held a note of the uncertainty she'd been carrying around since their conversation earlier.

'Chief Sakamoto would be cross with me if I didn't make our VIP doctor feel welcome and taken care of,' he said, and as he walked back with her she felt his proximity with every step of the way, her body responding to an invisible pull as if he was a magnet and she no more than tiny pieces of metal—unable to resist.

'You're as dutiful as ever, Salvador,' she replied, and watched with satisfaction as the corners of his mouth twitched in the tell-tale sign of amusement.

They stepped outside the hospital together, and Yara took a deep breath as the warm air enveloped them. Summer was almost over, bringing the temperature down to a more bearable degree.

'I missed the heat,' she admitted as they started walking. 'I spend so much time in countries with a much more reserved climate, I don't get to enjoy the sun enough.'

'Right, you're one of those people that actually *enjoy* torturous heat.' He looked at her with raised eyebrows when she gasped at his words.

'I tell you, once you spend some time away from Brazil, you'll learn to appreciate the abundance of warmth and sunshine. I spent two months in London on a series of cases and I don't think I saw the sun once.' Her overdrawn dramatics had the desired effect when the corners of his lips twitched upwards, the hint of a smile lingering on his lips.

'Maybe one day I'll get to test that theory of yours.'

'Is your family still keeping you rooted here?' Yara had wanted to ask this question ever since he left her office earlier in the day—ever since she noticed that he hadn't shared anything in return.

The paranoid part of her brain worried he might have caught on to her omissions, but how could he have? The things she kept to herself were the pieces of her life that would go with her into the afterlife—her parents' undue influence over her life, the demise of her marriage, how she *really* felt about Salvador years after she'd left Brasília.

None of these things had ever crossed her lips.

'In a sense. My parents passed away some years ago, at which point I stepped in to help Felipe and his girlfriend with their son.' He spoke slowly and deliberately, as if he put a lot of thought into the selection of his words—a caution that didn't surprise Yara.

His family had always been something difficult for him. His brother, Felipe, had used to get into a lot of trouble at school, leaving Salvador as the older sibling to deal with the fallout. Back then, Yara hadn't thought much of the things he needed to do for his family, thinking it was only right that he'd help them. After all, she understood duty to one's family more than anyone. It was that kind of obligation that drove her away from Salvador and into a marriage doomed from the start.

'Felipe had a child?' That was something she hadn't expected. Her mother had, on more than one occasion, called his brother a delinquent, and that image stood as a stark contrast to the one of a devoted father.

Salvador remained quiet for the next few steps, looking straight ahead with a blank expression. Finally, he nodded. 'His name is Felix. He's currently staying with me while Felipe...'

He left the sentence unfinished, and Yara didn't dare ask for more details. She'd only ever heard snippets of the lives of Salvador and his family when her sister called her, but she never engaged with the information too much. Talking about Salvador had the uncomfortable side-effect of bringing up ancient feelings that were wrapped up so tightly with her memories of him that she couldn't separate one from the other.

Why was he telling her that? Felix had been in and out of his care for almost all his life. Felipe had met his girlfriend at one of his usual dives, and it didn't take long to hear the news that they were having a child. The moment Salvador had heard of that, he'd started to worry about his unborn nephew. It had been a long time since Felipe had anything resembling a stable life and he was a frequent visitor in the local jail. Bringing a child into all that wasn't going to end well.

Salvador had once believed that his brother had pulled himself away from the bad crowd when he became a father, finding a legitimate job to keep his new family fed.

But after their parents died ten years ago, he watched as Felipe fell back into his old habits, going into business with dangerous people—the same people that had landed his parents in that boat accident.

Meanwhile, Salvador had worked hard to lead an honest life and to shed the reputation and legacy of his family's name. Even though it hurt, he distanced himself from Felipe for his own mental health as well as to shield his reputation as a doctor.

Until his brother got himself into such trouble that his son came into the line of fire. For the sake of Felix, Salvador had let his brother back into his life, and sure enough it hadn't been long until the authorities had placed his nephew under his care.

Salvador was fiercely protective of Felix and keeping him on the right path in life—so much that he didn't tell anyone about him outside of a handful of people he trusted implicitly. So why were these words pouring out of his mouth as if he couldn't help himself with Yara? Probably because he really couldn't. She'd been his confidant for so long, the information simply slipped out. He used to tell her everything, after all.

'This walk seems all right,' he said as they came to a stop in front of the hotel. 'I won't have to worry about you walking back and forth from the hospital on your own.'

Yara looked at him with an unreadable expression, her head slightly tipped to the side. 'You were worried about my safety?'

Her question took him by surprise. When he followed her out of Mr Orlay's room, he hadn't been quite sure why. She'd said that she was leaving, and all Salvador knew was that he really didn't want her to go just yet. He listened to her apology yesterday, a moment he'd been waiting for since she cut him out of her life without a single word. But instead of the closure he'd been expecting, it brought something else back to life within him—something dark and hungry that demanded to be fed. That something mingled with the resentment he still carried around, filling his veins with a fire that both enticed and devastated him.

Salvador realised that he had moved on from the pain, but he hadn't moved on from the *idea* of them. Despite the pain she had wrought on his life when she left after everything they had shared together, his flame for her had continued burning in a hidden corner of his heart.

A fire he had to put out straight away—though they might have been linked in a romantic sense thirty years ago, things were different now. She was Yara *Silvia* now. Married to someone else. The old affection stirring inside him had been inappropriate back then, but was even worse now as his target was a married woman.

A married woman he was still furious with.

'Of course,' he said despite himself. He could be accused of many things, but being a liar wasn't one of them. He had been worried about her, just as much as he didn't want to leave just yet. Something about her presence was…soothing.

'But since I have seen for myself that you'll be fine on your own, I'll leave you to your evening.' His feelings for her were getting too loud in his head, and he needed to remove himself from the situation. They were inappropriate for a lot of reasons.

'You want to come in and have dinner?' Yara nodded towards the hotel entrance, and he narrowed his eyes for a second.

Dinner was the last thing he wanted with a married woman that had—within no more than a day and a half—coaxed his old affection for her out of him again. Except he really wanted to have dinner with her, despite the hurt and anger still burning in his veins. Was that part of moving on? Letting those sparks of raw emotion travel through his body when he was near her until they burned out? He struggled to understand the need for closeness bubbling up within him as it pushed against his desire to be left alone after all Yara had put him through.

Why was he interested in a dinner with this woman when she had left him so broken, he had never truly healed?

He glanced at his phone. 'I can't do dinner. I need to pick Felix up from practice soon.' Disappointment flickered over Yara's expression—a sentiment he found mirrored in his own chest. 'How about a drink instead? I'd like to hear what you've been up to throughout the years.'

'Okay, let me just drop off my bag. I'll meet you at the bar?'

Salvador nodded and left the lobby to sit down at the bar, its dark wood gleaming in the dim light. Two weary patrons sat on one side, speaking in hushed tones, so he picked the chairs on the opposite side to sit down on.

Yara appeared a couple of minutes later, taking the seat next to him and sending a shock of awareness down his spine. Her proximity made him react, as it had when he'd first realised that his feelings for her had changed— that he wanted to be more to her.

Her smile was tentative, showing a hesitancy he noticed within himself as well. He'd been so shocked to see her yesterday. After three decades, he hadn't thought he'd ever see her again—or that all the affection he'd felt for her would roar back to life at the first sight of her.

'It's weird to be back,' Yara said as their beverages

arrived. 'I thought about what would happen when I see you… Funny how reality always turns out to be so different.'

'You thought about meeting me again?' That possibility hadn't even crossed his mind, but it made sense. Had she known he worked at the hospital she was consulting with?

'Dr Sakamoto sent me the profiles of everyone on the team so I could see the people I'd be working with before I accepted,' she said, as if reading his thoughts.

'Ah, so you saw my name and knew a reunion was impending.' Yara had presented herself as a lot more collected than he had during their first meeting, and now he knew why. Though Salvador had to acknowledge that he had known her name, too. If he'd looked her up he would have recognised her instantly. He just hadn't cared enough about the consulting doctor to do so.

'Does your spouse travel with you?' he asked. Maybe if he heard her speak about her partner, he could create some additional distance. Nothing better to dampen the fire than the woman of his attention gushing about someone else.

But instead, Yara went rigid in her chair, her eyes trained on the glass of virgin caipirinha on the counter in front of her. He sensed her distress the second he'd said those words, and a moment later he understood why.

'No… I'm actually divorced.' And judging by her reaction, this must have ended in contention.

Not something Salvador had a lot of first-hand knowledge of. While his parents had led chaotic and volatile lives, they'd somehow stuck around. Though how good that had been for their personal development was questionable. Their bad habits and addictions had fuelled one another, leading to the accident that had ended up with both of them dead.

An eventuality Salvador had come to expect the moment he became old enough to understand what kind of self-destructive energy their marriage contained—and the darkness that was contained in the Martins DNA that he had fought so hard to escape.

'I'm sorry to hear that,' he said, not wanting to pry any further. Maybe the wound was still fresh.

'Thank you.'

Salvador watched as she took a sip from her drink, her manner calm and collected, but he still knew how to read beyond the exterior she wanted everyone to see—how her eyes were slightly widened, thoughts racing as she kept her composure intact.

'How has travelling the world been for you?' he asked, changing the subject.

Yara took another sip, her eyes closing for a moment longer than a blink would be, and when she looked back at him a smile lingered on her lips that tugged at a deeply buried place in his chest.

'It's been really great, actually. I get to see so many places around the world and meet so many talented medical professionals.' She chuckled, a genuine sound that vibrated through his skin and nestled itself into a deep part of his chest.

'Strange. You were more of a homebody back then. Even getting you out of the door for a quick walk proved to be an insurmountable challenge.' The memory bubbled to the surface unbidden, catching Salvador by surprise as he spoke.

The reason they had initially got to know each other was because of how far teenage Yara would go to avoid walking. Their physical education teacher had asked him to collect the exercise mats strewn around the gymnasium, and when he went to pick up the trolley he'd found Yara lying in it—reading a book. When he'd asked her what she was doing here she said she was waiting for someone to push the trolley closer to the door so she could finally leave.

The utter ridiculousness of her line of thought had immediately drawn him in, and they began hanging out in the gym after lessons. It was only when she invited him to her house that he realised how different their lives were—but by then his young heart had already grown too attached to her.

Salvador would have never taken her to be one to travel much.

'I...do it more out of necessity. Someone I used to work with asked me to consult on a case in New York. That was when I was still living in Seattle. We worked on a difficult case and from there they asked me to support them on a different case at a different location.' She paused, shrugging as she took another sip of her drink. 'And that's how I built a reputation.'

Her voice remained steady, but also somewhat detached, as though these were the words she'd practised many times over to deflect people from digging too deep.

Salvador was so close to asking the question she clearly didn't want to answer, but was interrupted when she laughed quietly while shaking her head. 'I don't know how I managed to talk myself into a career like that.'

A spark flickered to life where her laugh had made itself a nest inside his body, spreading a dangerous need with every beat of his ever-increasing pulse. His lips took on a life of their own, speaking the words forming in his mind before he could take a moment to think about them—to think about what being near this woman *still* meant to him.

She was divorced.

'I can understand why people pay you to advise them—because you're brilliant.'

Self-deprecation was a shield Yara had learned to wield with expert precision. What once had been a coping mechanism in a failing marriage had become so ingrained in her personality that she didn't even notice any more.

The teams she worked with valued her contribution and weren't shy of saying so—and in a professional setting, Yara found it easier to smile and accept.

But she couldn't recall the last time a man looked at her the way Salvador did right now, eyes narrow and full of a fire she couldn't name.

'That's very kind of you to say,' she said, a shiver running down her spine.

'Nothing kind about the truth.'

Her mouth went dry, and she was thankful for the choice of a non-alcoholic drink—for she took several large gulps to calm her nerves.

What was happening? Yara had invited him to dinner because…she hadn't wanted their conversation to end. It almost felt normal again, her partial confession yesterday helping to mend the fences between them.

In truth, she had believed Salvador would see the gaps she left blank and not believe her apology was genuine. But hearing about his nephew staying with him—maybe he understood better than anyone else that some demons were not allowed to ever see the surface.

Like the lead-up to and the eventual demise of her marriage—and the reason she'd jumped at the opportunity to be as far away from her former home in Seattle as possible.

Some things would stay hidden no matter what. Or at least that was what Yara had thought. Until he'd asked a question about her ex and she'd replied with the truth.

Divorced.

Though early on she'd realised her marriage wasn't going to be one to write epic romance novels about, she never thought they'd end up getting divorced… Or that it would be so difficult to admit it.

Yara hadn't got to where she was now because she gave up.

'I think I'll still thank you, just in case this conversation somehow makes it back to my mother.'

Salvador chuckled at the mention of her mother. 'How is *Donna* Lopes? I won't even ask if you'll go to see her.'

Despite the sensitive topic, Yara joined in on the gentle laugh drawn from his throat at the mention of her mother. Growing up, Salvador had had first-row seats to the whims and demands the woman had put on her eldest daughter, and had felt her disapproval almost as much as Yara. The boy with parents of questionable integrity hadn't been good enough for the Lopes family. Though her mother had never said anything directly to him, her dislike of him had been barely veiled, and Yara would have been surprised if he hadn't picked up on it.

Hindsight made her trust in her mother's meddling look almost deranged. But whenever she went against her wishes, her mother's willingness to dangle the destruction of her dreams in front of her forced her back in line with ruthless efficiency.

'Well enough. You remember how much her interference agitates me, so I try to keep our conversations superficial,' she said.

'She used to get in your head.' He said it with gentleness, not with scorn as she'd expected. Without even trying—or knowing—he'd hit the root cause of their rift. Her parents had both meddled, pushing her in a direction she wasn't sure she should take. 'The insecure part of me sometimes wondered if you only put up with me because of how much it bothered both of your parents.'

Yara blinked at that comment. She'd never perceived him to be insecure in their friendship. Had she not been paying enough attention to him, too wrapped up in her own family drama?

'My parents didn't hold back with their hostility, I'll give you that,' she said as she looked back and remembered the scowls and thinly veiled comments launched in his direction. 'But when we met that day in the gym, my interest in you was genuine. Unfortunately, I did eventually listen to the poison they whispered in my ear. Something I regret, looking back.'

Salvador cocked his head to one side, an eyebrow slightly raised. The warmth radiating from his eyes enticed her to speak freely, the hint of his old affection for her lulling her into a sense of security as if he'd wrapped a cosy blanket around her.

'To be fair, I didn't quite understand what you saw in me, either,' he said, a self-deprecating chuckle tumbling from his lips.

'Are you kidding me? You moved the trolley over to the exit, so I didn't have to move one bit to get to my destination. That's when I knew you were someone I wanted to be friends with.' Their meeting had consisted of so much more than just that part, but she joined in with his humorous tone, and for a few heartbeats it almost seemed as though their old friendship could be salvaged, after all.

'You remember that moment?' he asked, prompting her to laugh at the absurdity of the question.

'Of course. How could I forget the moment I met you? At one point you were my best friend. I'll always cherish that memory, no matter what we might have become in the meantime.'

Yara cleared her throat as those words tumbled out of her mouth, struggling to shake the sense of nostalgic affection coming over her. Because what sparked to life in the pit of her stomach could only be described as nostalgia. There was no way any kind of *real* affection had survived the three decades they had spent apart. No, she was just yearning for lost years she couldn't have.

They were different people now, their lives no longer fitting together.

Salvador's expression turned soft for a moment, as if he, too, remembered the moment they spoke of, recalling the little details that had sparked such a deep friendship—and more. But then his face hardened, a dark presence taking over as she watched the walls around him thicken. The hint of their old connection she had sensed moments ago evaporated as if it had never existed.

'I'm glad we could talk, but I haven't changed my mind. We should keep things strictly professional, and I didn't mean to insinuate anything else by sitting down for a drink.'

His words hit with an unexpected ferocity that left her speechless for a few moments. 'That wasn't my intention. We've known each other for a long time and, while I'm not going out of my way seeking these conversations, it will happen as long as I'm here.' What was he expecting from her? That she would only ever say anything related to the case? Then he shouldn't have been the one to sit down with her in the first place.

'This is just…a lot. With everything I have going on, I just don't…' He left his sentence unfinished and glanced instead at his wrist. 'Sorry, I have to go,' he said when they both stayed quiet for far too long. He reached for his wallet, but Yara waved a hand.

'Don't worry about it. Go and get your nephew from practice. You don't want to be the parent who always shows up last, do you?'

Salvador laughed at the description of his parents. 'I can't believe you remember that small piece of information. These incidents have shaped my relationship with time in ways you can't imagine. If I'm on time, I'm already late.'

'I remember too well.' Yara joined in on the laugh, but quickly quieted. It was too easy to slip back into their old way of communicating with each other—especially when he had said he didn't want to.

Despite their banter, he reached for his wallet and took out some notes, which she swatted away. 'Seriously, go away! You bought lunch. It's only right I should get the drinks.'

Salvador crossed his arms, drawing her attention towards the lithe and impressive sight of him. Her breath caught in her throat, quickly prompting her to slide her eyes back up to his face before he could notice her checking him out. Going by the frown on his face, that effort had been in vain.

'Do you know how many packs of Yokitos I can buy for the amount on this bill?'

'Salvador, it's two drinks. You can stop being dramatic about it.' Yara sighed, rolling her eyes when his mouth formed a bemused line. 'How about I get this, and you get to the next one? Until one of us loses the game.'

'You're on, Lopes. And I'll tell you right now that I

won't end up losing this.' Hearing her maiden name from his lips sent a shockwave through her body, hitting her with an unexpected ferocity that left her breathless for a second. She thankfully managed to swallow an audible gasp, not wanting to let anything on when she herself didn't understand this reaction.

Of course, he wouldn't call her Silvia. That wasn't how he'd known her.

'I look forward to the next round,' she said, hoping that she was imagining the tone of her voice that rang with a lot more longing than was appropriate. 'So we can talk about the case,' she added.

Salvador stopped and turned his head towards her again, and a glimpse of the softness she saw moments ago came back to his eyes. 'How about dinner at Pepe's tomorrow?'

Yara's eyebrows shot up at the mention of the familiar name. 'Pepe's diner still exists?'

'I don't think you could close that place even if you tried. The community just wouldn't allow it. They'd probably continue going there as if nothing had happened,' he said, only a slight twitch at the corner of his mouth indicating his amusement. 'Pepe retired some time ago. His stepson runs it now, but you'll see very little has changed. To you, it will probably look more like a museum than a diner.'

Dinner was probably a terrible idea, especially with the wellspring of old memories mingling with the attraction that had only intensified with age. Could she trust herself to keep things only relevant to their work?

'I...' He hesitated for a moment, looking at the wall behind the bar for a moment, seemingly looking for the right words. 'Despite everything, it was nice catching up with you, Yara. Maybe thirty years is enough time to hold a grudge, and we can start over. As two people who want to find out if they *maybe* can be friends.'

Yara stared at him, her grip around her glass tightening as her pulse accelerated. It should be comforting to know that the spark of friendship between them wasn't a figment of her imagination, but instead her blood heated with each pump of her heart, sending a searing heat coursing through her body.

At least there was nothing remotely romantic about Pepe's diner, and, though her blood ran hot inside her veins, she didn't want her own lack of sensibility to stand in the way of rebuilding some of the friendship they had shared for so many years. Maybe if she gave him some time, he could grow more comfortable in talking about their past.

And what was the harm if her feelings got a bit out of hand? The case would be wrapped up by next week, and Yara would be off to whatever other team needed her help. There were several emails already waiting in her inbox.

'Okay, but only because I know you won't shut up about owing me something—your competitive spirit at its worst,' she said, her heart stuttering when his lips split into a full grin.

'See you tomorrow at seven, Lopes.' He raised his hand in a wave, and Yara summoned every ounce of will-power in her body to keep her eyes trained on the glass in front of her rather than trailing Salvador as he left.

She got up herself and made for her room, with the strange sense stirring in her chest that she was walking into the lion's den with a smile on her face.

CHAPTER FOUR

'You good?' Salvador sat down at the dining table and looked at his nephew, who was looking at his phone while piling the stew he'd made for him into his mouth.

Felix nodded, not interested enough to look up or to even answer him with anything more than a grunt. It had been like this for the last six months, ever since he'd come live with him, each conversation like pulling teeth.

Salvador bit back a sigh. He couldn't blame the boy. His life had always been in turmoil, culminating in his father's arrest, which led to the court appointing Salvador as Felix's legal guardian.

The doorbell rang and Salvador got up. Ciara, his neighbour's daughter, had agreed to watch Felix for a couple of hours. At twelve years old, he needed little supervision, but, given the fragile state Felix was still in, Salvador decided it would be better to have someone around.

'Thanks for coming over, Ciara,' he said as he let her in, grabbing his phone and keys off the side table. 'Take whatever you want from the fridge and call me if anything's up.'

She smiled at him. 'Sure thing, Salvador. Let me know if you're held up at the hospital. I can stick around.'

He froze for a moment, thinking about correcting her,

but decided against it and closed the door behind him. Whenever he called her last-minute it was usually because of emergencies at the hospital. Had it been that long since he'd gone out to meet a friend?

Not that Yara was a friend. She was... Salvador didn't know how to finish that sentence. Once she had been the person he'd thought he would want to spend the rest of his life with. Though their romantic relationship had lasted less than a month, he'd been head over heels long before that. Now all these feelings came flooding back into his system, making it hard to see clearly.

He had wanted some closure, yes. But, damn him, he *still* wanted her. Thirty years and he was right back where they had been when she left Brasília to never return, never even call him either. Why was the affection he once felt for her roaring back to life within his chest as if she'd only been gone a day? The anger remained in the pit of his stomach, rearing its head whenever his mind drifted too far.

Though she had revealed some slivers of information he hadn't been aware of. While he knew her parents didn't approve of her choice of friend, he'd never thought she would be influenced by them. At the hospital Yara had said she panicked because she didn't want their relationship to change. But what if that was only part of the truth? Had she been pressured by her parents?

He wanted her back in his life. The strange invitation to dinner he'd extended showed him as much. But why did he want to be around her? To be friends? What could his damaged self even have to offer at this point? Even friendships went too deep for him, superficial flings being the only type of relationship he could manage. There was no trust involved in a fling.

She wasn't married any more.

Those words echoed in his mind, as if they were the only reason he had restrained himself—completely ignoring all the other reasons why heeding the pull coming from her was an overall terrible idea. He didn't even know how to be with someone like her, when he'd never been with anyone long-term. Edinho was the only serious relationship he'd had outside of Yara and look how that had turned out.

No, this dinner was only to talk about their patient and giving her any information he had that might aid the diagnosis. He would not let himself spiral out of control, keeping a tight grip on the erupting heat her eyes gliding over his body caused.

But his resolve was pierced with a sharp spear through his chest when he entered Pepe's diner and saw Yara sitting at a table near the entrance, her light brown eyes lighting up when she spotted him. A small smile curled his lips before he could fight it, and the smile he got in return almost knocked the wind out of his chest.

They stood in front of each other, neither sure what to expect from the other one as a greeting, until Yara stepped forward, giving him a hug that lasted less than two seconds before sitting back down. Her scent, however, lingered in the air—bergamot and something spicy he couldn't place. And beneath it, the smell of Yara, one that hadn't changed at all.

'Thanks for meeting me. I've already ordered—'

'The bread basket?' They said the word together, Yara's eyes widening as he spoke before her face relaxed into another smile that sent a trail of small sparks racing down his spine.

That was what they had used to share during long study sessions at Pepe's. Of course she still remembered.

Why was he even surprised, when she had remembered so much else about their friendship?

'I got us our booth, too. Right next to Stanley.' She pointed at the replica of a sea creature that hung like a stuffed trophy on the wall next to them. No one they had ever asked had been able to accurately name whatever sea animal this trophy was supposed to be, looking simultaneously like a kraken and a starfish with its strange legs sticking out from a bulky head that had way too many eyes to be either.

'Stanley… That's a name I haven't heard in a long time.' Yara had chosen it, saying that the three of them hung out so much that they should introduce themselves so he wouldn't betray all of the secrets he had been witness to.

For a few moments, they simply looked at each other, the ghost of what had used to be their deep friendship hanging between them, coalescing in this space where they had forged so many memories. Until Yara cleared her throat. 'How is Mr Orlay doing? Did you see anything on the new scans?'

Salvador shook his head. 'I was looking for lesions on his brain to confirm multiple sclerosis. Anything that would bring us closer to a diagnosis. But at least the nerve conduction velocity test we did on your orders yielded some results—though I'm not sure what they mean.'

Yara nodded. 'You were looking for multiple sclerosis? That makes sense. His patient notes say he had bilateral weakness in his legs after the surgery, which was written off as fatigue.'

'I think that was a fair call, given the man had just come out of a ventricular valve replacement.' Salvador crossed his hands in front of his chest, his defensive instincts kicking in. Each one of his colleagues who had worked with Mr Orlay was on top of their game. He wouldn't let her tell anyone otherwise.

'Of course. Anyone would have thought this was because of his surgery. I'm here because we now know that it wasn't a side effect of his surgery. And since it isn't any type of MS, we needed to test the nerves along his arms to understand the severity of his weakness.' She paused for a second and the passion engulfing her eyes was a sight to behold.

Yara had looked like a pale ghost of herself when he arrived, the burden of what had happened between them lying heavy on her shoulders. The moment they spoke about their case, the Yara he'd known so well resurfaced, showing him the fire within her he hadn't been able to resist the second he'd first seen it. But he knew he had to, for his own sake. He was no longer the boy who'd fallen for Yara thirty years ago. Too much hurt had suffused their past relationship. How could he trust her when the pain still burned in his chest? Because it was *definitely* hurt that caused the heat to course through his veins.

'So all this time, we were following the wrong lead. He wasn't weak after his surgery...'

'But rather his surgery revealed a different condition,' Yara finished his thought, her hand diving into the bread basket that had appeared in front of them.

Salvador leaned back, once again impressed with her medical prowess. She had seen so much more than he could ever hope to see, and with the already growing heat inside him mingled a kernel of deep admiration of one medical professional for another.

'So, what's next for our patient?'

'I've stopped most of his medication. At this moment, I don't know what's a symptom and what's a side-effect from various medications running rampant through his system.' She frowned for a moment, waving the piece of bread in front of her face. 'He won't be comfortable, but it'll help us narrow down what's going on within his body. I asked the charge nurse to have someone page me if they see any drastic changes. But the NCV test narrows it down to a handful of potential diseases.'

Salvador settled back into his seat and was surprised when their main courses appeared in front of them. Had they been talking for so long already? The nervousness in his stomach had disappeared, leaving him with a sense of strange familiarity that he didn't know how to interpret.

They'd grown quiet for a moment but it was a different silence from the one they'd experienced in the hospital. This one was calm, easy-going, as if this brief interaction had somehow mended part of the thing she'd broken when she left Brasília—and Salvador.

Then his eyes narrowed slightly, his gaze turning dark for a moment, sending a shiver down her spine. She knew first-hand what a kind and generous heart beat within his chest—paired up with such looks, she had never stood a chance. Though those feelings were not real, she reminded herself. They were old feelings she had never resolved.

'How long has your nephew been staying with you?' she asked, to distract herself from the heat rising to her cheeks. Where was the cool composition she'd had a tight grip on only a couple of moments ago?

The dreamy spark in his eyes vanished within a heartbeat, replaced by a cold gleam, and his lips thinned into a hard line that prompted Yara to hold her breath for a second. She'd stepped over a boundary she didn't know had existed. What had happened with Felipe that he had such a vehement reaction?

'He's been staying with me for half a year now. Before that, he'd been a long-term guest on and off for another year as my brother struggled to give him a stable home.' Some of his expression relaxed, and Yara let go of the breath she'd been holding.

'What about…?' She bit the inside of her cheek to stop herself from speaking any further. Something must have happened to his brother, or Salvador wouldn't have his nephew living with him.

'Felipe is in prison,' he said in a flat tone, and Yara struggled to comprehend his words for a few heartbeats.

'Prison?' An answer that shocked her even though she had half-expected it, knowing the rumours surrounding his family and upbringing. She recalled Felipe making questionable friends, and how often Salvador himself had sought refuge in her home—to the displeasure of her parents. Even before they had become more than friends, her parents had pushed the sons of their friends onto her in the hopes she would gain interest in someone they judged *better suited*. Another manipulation she had only been able to spot many years later.

Salvador nodded, his expression veiled and unreadable. 'He started to associate with some bad people during university and soon dropped out to take part in one of those friend's "businesses". I never asked what they were doing, but at one point the police picked them up. From then on it was a litany of minor offences which have put him in prison before for a couple of months. Something big was bound to happen. I was terrified of it, wanted to pull him out of this mess…'

The instinct to comfort him kicked in. She reached over the table and laid her hand on his forearm resting on the table. His skin was warm underneath her hand and the scent of soft lavender mixed with the smells of the food around them. The touch lasted for less than a few seconds before Yara realised what she had done and pulled her hand away as if she'd been burned.

What was wrong with her that she didn't have her impulses in check? Just yesterday they had spoken about keeping their connection professional, which didn't include comforting him over the table.

'Sorry, I didn't mean to—' she started, but he interrupted her with a shake of his head.

'It's…fine. You asked a question, and I answered it.' His voice was low and clipped, and the glimpse of vulnerability she'd spotted as he spoke about his brother disappeared into non-existence. Only the heavy walls around him remained, imposing and impossible to overcome.

What had just happened? One moment she thought they might be able to restore some of their friendship again, only for him to slip further away from her. The comfort she sensed when they spoke about the past never lasted long, the shadow of her actions always looming over them.

She should just give up. They didn't have a chance, not with so much hurt between them.

Salvador was the first to break their intense stare, lowering his gaze as he reached for his drink. 'What about you? You said you don't want to visit Bianca?'

'I'm not sure. I might go to see my sister. But you know how nosy she is, and I'm not sure if I'm stable enough to withstand her overbearing nature.' Her sister and their network of cousins were a whole different challenge to Yara's stay here in Brazil. She hadn't told them she'd gone through a divorce.

Salvador raised one of his eyebrows. 'Why do you say that?'

'That's a very long and tiresome story,' Yara said, squirming under his gaze as his green eyes fixed on her.

'I…understand if you don't want to talk about it. After all, I was the one who didn't want to talk about these things.' Tension came rushing into the space between them, her breath catching in her throat for a moment before everything bled away just as fast as it had appeared.

A hint of the earlier vulnerability reappeared in his eyes, a sight so warm and enticing that the words formed in her throat before she could stop them.

'I got divorced, and I have told no one about it. It… wasn't pretty.' That was both an overstatement and an understatement of what had happened between her and Lawrence. 'It's been a year, but I just can't deal with it right now, and I know Bianca won't be able to resist the need to "fix it" when I just need some space to lick my wounds.'

To her surprise, Salvador only nodded, a solemn understanding in his eyes. 'Been in a similar situation when I became Felix's guardian. A twelve-year-old hadn't really been part of our plan together.'

'Really? Your wife left because you had to take in your nephew?' Who did such a thing, knowing the circumstances under which his nephew had come into his care?

'Ah, no, we weren't married. But yes, he left when it became clear that my brother wouldn't be released anytime soon, and Felix became my responsibility.'

The silence coming over Yara was deafening, and she blinked several times as her brain struggled to catch up with her jumbled thoughts. It was as if someone had turned off the volume on life for a second. *He?* The whirlwind the word caused inside her was disproportional to its length, forcing her own tangle of complicated feelings for Salvador into a new light she'd never even considered.

They had been seventeen when they gave in to the depth of emotion running between them, but that was three decades ago—a timeframe long enough for anyone to have their sexual awakening.

Was that why things seemed so uncomfortable between them? Not because of her actions, but rather that he'd never actually been interested in *her* as more than a friend?

The heat spreading under her skin at every intense look he shot her way turned into something confusing and disoriented as she tried to reconcile this information about him with the flood of old feelings infiltrating her system. Was she so bad at flirting that she couldn't distinguish a longing look from a neutral one?

'Wait…' She hesitated for a moment. How did one ask about this? 'You were—?'

The vibration of her phone rattled the table, interrupting her mid-sentence. She picked it up with an apologetic glance at Salvador and checked her notifications. 'It's the hospital. They're saying Mr Orlay is losing feeling in his legs and is now showing difficulties swallowing food.'

The message wiped the conversation they had just had from her brain as she shifted her mind back into doctor mode, categorising the new symptoms into the plethora of other things she had observed around the patient and his condition.

Salvador nodded without hesitation and stood up. 'Put this on my tab, Baylor,' he shouted at the man behind the bar at the far end of the diner, who raised his hand to give him a thumbs-up. 'You ready?'

'Let's go.'

CHAPTER FIVE

THEY ARRIVED AT the hospital a few minutes later, heading straight for Mr Orlay's room. As they were walking, Salvador texted Ciara to let her know he'd indeed be stuck in the hospital for a bit, to which she only replied with a winking emoji.

He hadn't wanted their dinner to end so soon, especially not the way they'd left it. Salvador was comfortable in his own skin and not interested in whatever reactions people might have to his sexuality. Most people, however, were people that he didn't have a past with. That made Yara a special case, and he found himself wanting to know her thoughts. Her reaction to his coming out to her had been instant, the surprise on her face interrupted by the emergency that had brought them here. What had she been about to say?

Being queer had lost him friends, growing up in a time far less tolerant than the one he experienced now. But there was no way Yara would be one of them, right?

There was still a significant amount of discomfort between them, the abrupt ending of their relationship hanging between them like a shadow. Salvador was constantly reminding himself to keep on his guard. The moments where he forgot about that, where he let the ease and familiarity of her presence envelope him with gentle warmth, were dangerous. He could not let himself feel any of that.

Salvador watched as Yara stepped closer to the patient's bed. Mr Orlay was much paler than he'd looked when he had finished the nerve conduction velocity test, a sheen of sweat covering his face, his chest slow to rise.

'Good evening, Mr Orlay,' she said as she approached his bedside. 'The nurse watching you paged me about your complaints. I know it's a bit of a pain, but could you walk me through it as well? I'd like to hear it first-hand.'

She smiled reassuringly as Mr Orlay went over his symptoms, showing her where he'd lost feeling in his fingers and arms. Yara went along as he described everything, her gentle touch confirming the pain points. Occasionally she'd stop, as if to commit some important detail to memory before she went back to the patient.

Watching her work unearthed a whole different dedication and talent in the medical world. Everyone Salvador had ever worked with at this hospital had been a prime example of patient care and responsibility.

It only enhanced and highlighted the worrisome connection snapping into place between them—now that the obstacle of her supposed marriage was out of the way. His brain had latched on to this information, playing it over and over in his head when it didn't even matter. Just because she was available didn't mean *he* was.

Salvador perked up when Yara disengaged from the patient, stepping back to him. 'You were watching,' she said, with a hint of amusement in her voice.

'I was.' His voice sounded a lot huskier than he intended it to be. Watching her work had been fascinating, every action taken with such deliberation and care for her patient.

'So, what do you think?'

'That you are a brilliant doctor.' The words manifested in his brain and a moment later tumbled out of his mouth with no further prompt.

Yara turned her head around to look at him, her brown eyes wide, and, despite the dim light of the patient room, he noticed a faint blush kiss her cheeks—bringing the desire he had pushed down back to the surface. His hand twitched, yearning to reach out and brush his fingers over her face. Would she be as soft as she looked?

'I meant with Mr Orlay,' she said as she pushed him out through the door so they could have their conversation out of earshot. 'What do you make of his symptoms?'

'Oh…' Of course. What else would she be talking about? They were here to see to their patient. He leaned against the wall outside of the room, crossing his arms in front of his chest and looking upwards, thinking. 'Weakness in his extremities should have dissipated at this point, but it might still relate to his surgery. Cardiac tamponade?'

Yara tapped her index finger against her cheek while following his gaze and searching the ceiling for the answer to the medical mystery presenting itself.

'Cardiac tamponade can be gradual, though after surgery I would have expected it to be rapid,' she mused.

'We could ask the cardiologist to do an EKG on him. Though he won't be in until tomorrow. I can page the on-call person in the department.'

Yara shook her head. 'I don't think it's a tamponade. Let's do a Doppler ultrasound instead and see what the blood flow to his extremities looks like.'

'Right now?' he asked, his eyes darting to the clock on the wall. The evening had already progressed way beyond what he'd expected, but what he found most concerning was how much he wanted her to say *Yes, right now*. So that their time together wouldn't end.

How strange things had turned out. Seeing her two days ago had shaken his world upside down, bringing back all the hurt and fury she'd put him through when she faded out of his life. But beneath that, he'd found all the other emotions he'd lost as well—including this deep connection they had once shared where they could say anything to each other. Salvador hadn't expected that to come rushing back when he felt the anger surge. But there it was. Tiny and so fragile, but it had survived inside his tormented self.

Yara followed his gaze to the clock and closed her eyes for a second. She hadn't realised how late it was. Mr Orlay was stable; his condition had worsened, but not to the extent that he needed immediate intervention.

'I didn't notice the time. You need to get back home to your nephew, and I have some research to do,' she said, and glimpsed the hint of an expression fluttering over Salvador's face. Was he disappointed their night was over? Or was that some needy part of her brain playing tricks on her?

'The babysitter is around for another couple of hours. We can go over your plan for the morning if you'd like.'

Her heart skipped a beat, tumbling inside her chest as if she had missed a step on the stairs. Did he want to stay with her longer? 'Okay, that sounds good. I have just the right snack.'

Yara waved him along until they reached her improvised office. She led him in, closing the door behind her, and marched over to her handbag. Smiling broadly, she took out a rectangular slab and put it on the table before taking the seat next to Salvador.

He looked at the table and then at her with a raised eyebrow. 'You carry bars of chocolate around with you?'

'*Swiss* chocolate,' she said as she reached for the wrapped bar, prying it open and breaking a small piece off to offer it to Salvador. 'I was there a couple of weeks ago for a case and just never took it out of my bag.'

'You are just as chaotic as I remember,' Salvador said as he nibbled on his piece of chocolate as if she had offered him some unknown substance he needed to analyse before putting it anywhere near his mouth.

'Glad to hear that the only thing that's changed about me is the number of wrinkles and grey hairs.' She made a joke to deflect the sudden awareness his words caused to stir in her veins, the few handspans of air between them suddenly not feeling like enough distance.

'I think they suit you,' he said in a low voice that vibrated through her every bone.

Was he…flirting with her? Impossible. The conversation they'd had at the diner came rushing back to her, the surprise at his revelation at the forefront of her mind. Salvador's last relationship had been with a man—changing her perception of their past relationship.

Had he already known back then? That would take some of the sting out of her past decision. If they'd never had a chance, her family's pressure was still appalling, but at least she could cope with the regret, knowing they were never meant to be.

If Salvador could have never loved her the way she had yearned for him to, maybe there was no risk in telling him the truth about her feelings for him—because there were no *what-ifs*. She could get this weight off her chest and absolve herself from her final regrets.

So had she been imagining the tension swirling around them ever since she came back as well?

'I have to tell you something,' Yara said, before she could change her mind.

He raised his eyes from the piece of chocolate pinched between his fingers, his expression expectant without the hint of anything else, just waiting for her to say what she wanted to say.

'I said I'd be honest with you, so…when I left for med school, I *wanted* to be with you. I still panicked and treated you in an unacceptable way. But it wouldn't be right for me to pretend that I didn't want our relationship to change. I did…want it, that is.'

Yara didn't dare to look at him. Instead, she kept her eyes trained on the bar of chocolate on the table, her fingers woven into each other to stop her from fidgeting.

'Why did you say something else two days ago?'

Her eyes shot up, not expecting the question. Why did *that* matter? If he wasn't interested in women, why would he care about whatever she'd felt for him ages ago? Yara still was sure she could tell him about her parents' influence, how she had so willingly surrendered agency over her own decisions.

'That's a lot more complicated than I can explain…' Her throat bobbed when she swallowed the lump building in her throat.

'Try me.' He pushed his chin out in a non-verbal challenge.

'I…' Yara hesitated, unsure what to say next. Telling him one piece of her truth had been hard, but the lightness following her words freed up the pressure around her chest, easing her into a comfort with him she hadn't expected—and worse, it only strengthened the irresistible pull coming from him.

'I let myself believe that my parents had my best interests at heart, and it's only been in recent years that I realised they hadn't thought of me as much as of the perfect family picture they wanted to put on their mantelpiece.'

The words bubbled forth the moment she had decided to share this piece of her as well. The warmth radiating from his eyes set her at ease, creating a glowing spark in her chest that banished the tension. It was as much as she dared to say. Even though she resented her parents for all they had put her through, she couldn't expose them as such manipulative people to Salvador. What would he think if he knew how easily they had manipulated her?

Salvador remained silent, and when she looked up to meet his gaze her breath caught in her throat at the intensity of the gleam in his dark eyes. There wasn't a trace of a smile at the corner of his mouth. No tell-tale twitch to indicate how amusing he found her past choices. His features seemed hewn from stone.

'You wanted to be with me?' he finally said, and the rasp in his voice sent signals firing to all of her nerve ends. Signals she *shouldn't* be firing because he wasn't available to her.

'Yes,' she said with a shaky voice, waving her hand to deflect any deeper digging into this. 'Now I understand I could have saved both of us a lot of pain by just being honest. I mean, I know now that you would never have been interested in me—'

'Why wouldn't I have been?' The question threw her off guard. It didn't seem to fit into the flow of conversation. Was he going to pretend as if he hadn't come out to her?

'Because you…date men.'

Salvador exhaled through his nose in an audible sigh, crossing his arms as he leaned back. His eyes didn't leave hers as he rolled his jaw, seemingly contemplating his next words.

A thought popped into her head that made her bite her lower lip. Had he not meant to out himself to her? Had this been a slip of the tongue and she was putting him on the spot? 'If I've made—'

'I'm bisexual.'

And just like that the record playing in her head scratched again, leaving her in complete silence as his words sank in.

Bisexual.

He dated men…and women.

'Oh, no…' she whispered, more to herself than to him, as the awareness of his proximity flared up again, cascading through her body and setting fire to the deepest layer of her skin.

'I struggled with it for a bit, but I can assure you it's true.' This time there was a smirk building in the corners of his mouth and amusement shone through his voice.

'No, I meant that I…' She didn't know what she meant. This wasn't going according to plan at all. They were supposed to joke about her falling for him and move on. Now everything inside her was roaring back alive, and she didn't know what was true and what wasn't. The picture in her head of Salvador changed, bending under a new reality that had been thirty years in the making.

'Does that change how you see me now?' he asked, as if reading her thoughts.

She paused, giving her brain a moment to catch up to the changing information and how it put everything she knew about him in a new perspective. After a few breaths, she shook her head.

'It doesn't change how I felt about you.'

He had never even hinted at questioning his sexuality when they were together.

'I didn't know until a few years later, though I can't

say if it had impacted our relationship or not. Since you were gone, I didn't have to explore my sexuality in the confinement of a monogamous relationship.' His words were gentle, and yet Salvador didn't show a hint of his emotions on his face as he spoke.

'It doesn't bother me, if you're asking that. I'm glad you felt comfortable enough sharing that piece of you with me,' she said after a moment of quiet. 'Maybe I would have done something similar if I hadn't got married so young…'

Her voice trailed off. Thinking about the people Salvador had been with instead of her chipped at a hidden part inside her chest, hurting more than was appropriate in this situation. After all, she had been the one to leave and give him that freedom.

'Do you still like me the way you did when you left?' His voice was a low grumble cutting through her defences and landing right in the spot behind her navel, where the force of all her feelings was accumulating.

'Salvador…' His name dropped from her lips in a nervous chuckle that vibrated through the tense air between them. He looked at her, his eyes alive with an unknown fire that sent a tremble tumbling down her spine. 'I don't know if…'

'Because it's only been two days since you came back into my life and you've slipped right under my skin, Yara,' he said, and the gravel filling his voice pulled hard on the pinch in her stomach she was trying to fight off. 'Whenever I think about you my veins blaze with anger and hurt, yet I cannot stop thinking about you to save my own life.'

'What?' Something inside Yara cracked at his words.

A thousand different scenes popped into her head, all of them depicting what life with Salvador by her side could have been like, and her heart split under the pressure of that vision, of what they had lost without even knowing. Were those visions even realistic, now that she knew about his sexuality? Or had it been necessary for her to leave so Salvador could become the man he was now?

It didn't matter at the moment, when he was getting so close that she felt his breath sweep over her hot skin.

Salvador's hand went up to her face, tracing an invisible line from the highest point of her cheek down to her chin. His thumb moved up, brushing against her lips and leaving a searing hot sensation where he'd just touched her. Her body responded instinctively, yearning to fulfil a dream she'd kept alive inside her memory for many years.

'You destroyed me when you left, and I haven't forgiven you for what happened. Despite that, all I want to do in this moment is kiss you,' he said as he brushed his finger over her lips again. 'How are you doing this to me?'

'Salvador…' This time his name was not a chuckle but a plea, and a moment later he closed the gap between them and brushed his lips against her in a kiss she had been imagining for almost all her life.

When they had started their conversation, Salvador had not expected to kiss Yara by the end of it. Her confession had thrown him for a loop, and he still wasn't sure that he had processed everything she had said. His affection for her had been a low-humming being living inside him, sent into a deep sleep over the years—but always there. He just hadn't been able to sense it over the hurt her leaving inflicted on him. But as he touched her lips, it roared alive with a frightening intensity.

He wanted to rip the clothes off her body and have

his way with her right this second. They'd lost years to meddling and insecurities, stopping them from ever realising their true potential.

Though he knew that he had ultimately needed to be on his own to explore who he really was, he still lamented the future they had never had. But she had left him broken, his trust in people's intentions never truly recovering. The walls he had built because of her abandonment were created out of steel. Nothing could tear them down, not even the woman he'd wanted so fiercely.

The scars in the depths of his soul had never quite healed. Yara had cut him out of her life without a second thought. She had told him why and the closure helped to put things into context. But the truth had not undone the damage—and a part of him wondered if it could ever *be* undone.

But despite the fury still fresh in his mind, the desire for Yara exploded through his body. They may not have a future, but maybe he could permit himself to trust her enough to fulfil a fantasy he'd carried around for years. One he could sense bubbling beneath her skin as well as she leaned into his touch, grasping at him with an urgency reflected in himself.

The way she moaned against his lips as he deepened their kiss almost made him think there was a path to repair his trust in her. The feel of her body against his blanked out all the pain and anger, and he gave in to the pull, even if it was just for a moment. Tomorrow they could go back to professional courtesy—in this moment he wanted to draw back the curtain just a little and glimpse the life they had never had.

Yara's hand came to rest on his chest as he pulled her closer into his arms, the other one grazing over his thigh, which sent a jolt of excitement through his system. He was an adult man with plenty of experience, yet a kiss and the prospect of what he would find beneath the layers of her clothes alone left him hard and aching. He wanted to have her, even if it was just for this night…

The thought lingered on the edge of his mind as his mouth left hers, feathering indulgent kisses over her jawline and down her neck.

'Salvador…' Her voice sounded airy, as if she was somewhere far away.

He smiled against her skin when he felt a shiver rock her body along with a high-pitched hiss as he nuzzled underneath the neckline of her blouse, relishing the softness of her skin.

'Salvador, your…' hearing his name from her lips in the state they were in sent another jolt coursing through his veins, bringing the need for her to an excruciating level '…your phone.'

She pressed the words out between shaky huffs that almost drove him to the very edge of existence. 'What?' His mind was murky, wrapped in a luscious cloud of her scent and the burning in her eyes that begged him not to stop.

'Your phone is vibrating,' she said and managed to bring him back to reality. His phone? Who would try to reach him at this hour?

Felix. The thought startled him back into reality, as if someone had doused him with a bucket of ice water. The air of attraction around them vanished and rational thinking kicked back in as he brought some distance between them.

Yara's eyes were wide, the fire he'd seen in them mere seconds ago extinguished.

He reached for his phone on the table and noticed the time. Just past midnight. He'd told Ciara he'd be back home an hour ago. 'I have to go. The babysitter needs to leave,' he said with a sigh and looked at Yara.

She'd retreated from him—both physically and emotionally, as he couldn't glimpse the moment they'd shared in her expression. Where the fire had burned thick walls stood now, impenetrable and devoid of any hint he could latch on to.

Regret uncoiled itself in his chest. *You stupid, stupid man.* He'd lost control for one second, and it had been enough to throw the rest of their professional relationship into the fire. Only for the fulfilment of a fantasy he knew could never become reality.

Not with his life the way it was. Not with who he was.

'You okay getting back to the hotel?'

Yara nodded, her face remaining expressionless.

He didn't want to leave. His feet remained rooted to the spot, even though he gave them the command to move. Salvador wanted to stay, to be with this woman who had slipped back under his skin as though she had never left, driving him up the wall with unresolved desire.

But *wanting* wasn't enough—and he wasn't even sure how much he truly wanted this and how much were ancient feelings stirring in his chest.

'I'll see you tomorrow for the ultrasound, yes?' His words were meant to gauge her reaction, give him some clue about what had just happened with them.

'Tomorrow, yes. Goodnight, Salvador.' She avoided his gaze as she spoke, her face blank and unreadable. Not a good sign.

Hearing his name from her lips this time didn't set his blood alight, but instead pawed at the wound he'd hidden away since they'd last spoken to each other.

What an unnecessary and difficult situation he had

just plunged himself into because of his poor impulse control, he thought as he left the office to hurry back to the one person who needed all his effort and attention right now—Felix. The one reason he should have stayed away from Yara and the ancient beast she had awoken inside him.

CHAPTER SIX

WITH A DEEP BREATH, Yara calmed her roiling nerves and pressed the doorbell. For the next couple of seconds there was silence behind the door, then she heard shuffling, followed by the clicking of a key being turned in a lock.

The door swung open, and Yara stared into the surprised face of her sister, Bianca.

'Yara, what the—?'

'I kissed Salvador last night.'

Bianca's mouth fell open, and she blinked at her several times as she struggled with comprehension.

'Right…' The word came out elongated as her thoughts caught up with her. 'Lots to unpack here.'

She stepped to the side, inviting Yara in.

Even though it had been a few years since she'd last been to Brasília, Yara found comfort in the fact that Bianca's house still looked the same. Life around her may be ever-changing, but she knew her spot on her sister's couch would be waiting for the exact moment that she needed it. Like right this moment, when she had just kissed her high-school sweetheart.

She heard Bianca potter around in the kitchen for a couple of minutes, and when she appeared through the door she was holding two steaming mugs. She handed one of them to Yara and held on to the other one, taking her seat on the couch.

'So… You and Salvador are a thing again?' Bianca asked, and Yara almost choked on her tea.

'No! Do you think I would storm into your house on a random morning if I got back together with him?' She paused, the aroma of chamomile wafting up her nose and calming some of her jumbled thoughts. 'And I don't think you can call it *back together* when we hardly dated. Mum saw to that.'

'We are Lopes women. We can't be seen consorting with vagabonds,' Bianca said with a knowing nod.

Yara sighed into her tea. 'Are you planning on being at all helpful? I need to know so I can adjust my expectations.'

'Sorry, sis. I had to tease you a bit for not telling me that you're back in Brasília.' She gave her a chiding look. 'But all right, let's have it. Why are we kissing old flames we haven't spoken to in three decades?'

'I don't know…' Yara looked down at her tea, her chest expanding with a long breath that left her body in a drawn-out sigh. 'We were talking about our time together, and I wanted to tell him the truth about what happened between us when I left for med school. It turned very nostalgic, and then he told me…'

Yara interrupted herself, masking the unnatural pause by taking a sip of her tea. She had almost blurted out the news about his sexuality as though she were some common gossip. While his sexual identity was closely linked to their relationship, she didn't feel as if she had the right to out him to anyone who wasn't of his choosing.

Bianca furrowed her brow, thankfully not noticing her abrupt stop. 'You are too far ahead of me for me to understand the story. Why are you here? And how did you end up kissing *another man*?'

She looked at her sister, the raised mug stopping halfway to her lips. In the chaos of her own inner turmoil about Salvador, his confession and their kiss, she hadn't even realised that Bianca didn't know *any* of the steps leading up to the terrible decision of kissing him. Yara was so used to her sister knowing things about her, she hadn't really noticed how that closeness had changed over the years.

Yara had spent several years travelling for work and establishing her career the way it was now to escape her marital home. She could have come home, but some remnant of the pressure her parents had put on her stopped her from confessing what had happened. Instead, she pretended that everything was fine when she spoke to her sister, and avoided Brazil even though it hurt her to stay away.

She took a deep breath. 'Lawrence and I got divorced.'

Quiet tension slipped into the space around them as Yara awaited her sister's reaction, unable to tell what it would be. She wished Bianca would have had an instant reaction—big and angry. That was something she knew how to deal with. Quiet was so much worse than anger.

'When?' was all her sister asked, her expression suddenly so serious that a shiver trickled through Yara's body.

'It was finalised last year, but we separated a few years before that.'

'When you started travelling more…' Bianca mumbled, and from her expression she could tell that her sister was putting the timeline together. 'But you struggled before you got to that point.'

It wasn't a question, but Yara nodded anyway. That

was when she'd isolated herself from her sister more and more.

'Yes. I was never in love with Lawrence. Not really. I thought I was, but it turned out that even if you want something to be true, it doesn't make it so.' For years, Yara had operated on autopilot, going through the motions as she and Lawrence led separate lives. She had thought she'd lost the ability to feel anything any more, getting too lost in a marriage that wasn't meant to be.

Until a few days ago, when she'd first had a moment alone with Salvador—and since then the air in her lungs had tasted different, fresher.

That observation had driven her into seeking out her sister today. Her feelings for Salvador morphed into more than just ancient memories and attraction, but something tangible and real—if she was brave enough to reach out and grab it.

And she needed someone to talk her out of it.

'Is that why you're kissing Salvador all of a sudden?' Bianca asked, and Yara almost laughed because even though she'd asked herself that same question, the impact was different when hearing it in her sister's voice.

'No… Kissing him wasn't part of any plan.'

'I'm still not sure why he's a part of this story.'

'Oh, right…' Another detail she'd skipped over in her desperate need to get straight to the point. 'He works at the hospital that hired me.'

Bianca put her empty mug down on the coffee table, and it was only then that Yara realised how much time had passed. The steam had stopped rising from her own tea, the ceramic mug now cool against her skin.

She wasn't any closer to finding a solution to her problem.

'How long are you staying here?' her sister asked.

'Only as long as the case lasts. Probably no longer than till the end of next week.'

Bianca nodded. 'So you don't really have enough time to get yourself into too much trouble with Salvador.' She paused with a smirk. 'Mum will not be happy about this.'

'Mum will feel nothing about this because we're not telling her,' Yara said through gritted teeth, glaring at her sister.

'Please invite me to the conversation with her when you tell her that you and Salvador ended up back together.'

'I *cannot* be with Salvador, no matter what I *want*. This was just a kiss!' Her heart slammed against her ribs, her pulse thundering through her body. The denial crossed her lips before she had the chance to process it.

The words rang in the silence between them, their heaviness settling in the pit of her stomach in the form of an icy boulder. That was the truth Yara had struggled to come to terms with over the last days. She couldn't believe how fast her desire for Salvador had re-emerged, rearing its head the second she let her guard down just a fraction. After thirty years, the spell he had put on her hadn't disappeared, but rather lain dormant in her, just waiting for a chance to erupt. Meeting him again had been too easy, their connection clicking back into place when they worked through the discomfort and awkwardness.

Maybe she had done well in leaving, giving him the space he needed to become who he was. She didn't know what their relationship would have looked like if she hadn't left. Would he have resented her for keeping him from exploring what was within him?

The idea that her mistake might have helped him learn about the facts of his sexuality was strangely calming.

'Why not?' Bianca finally said into the quiet, asking the question Yara didn't want to answer.

Yara gritted her teeth. 'I just can't. My life is not here, and he has his nephew to take care of. We can't go back and pretend nothing happened.'

'Is that really how you feel, or are those just the reasons you were able to come up with in the heat of the moment?' Her sister scrutinised her, and Yara shivered under her knowing gaze, probing into places she didn't want any light shed.

The coffee table groaned when she slammed her half-empty cup onto it with a bit too much force. This wasn't the conversation she was ready to have right now—or ever. 'I can't deal with this right now. I came here for some help, not to be talked into something I can't have.'

Bianca sat back, watching her with intent. 'I'm not trying to talk you into anything. Just trying to give you some perspective, okay? Now, sit back down.'

Yara glanced at the screen of her phone. 'I have to go and check back on the patient. We've started him on some new medication.'

Her sister recognised her words as the excuse that they were, but she nodded anyway, getting to her feet herself. 'You're off the hook for the lecture this time, but you'd better come for another visit before you leave for your next assignment, you hear that?'

An involuntary smile curled Yara's lips, and she nodded. 'I will.'

Salvador stepped through the doors of the emergency department at his hospital, and chaos erupted all around him. Nurses and doctors were shouting across different treatment bays, while monitors beeped with unrelenting intensity between heart wrenching-moans of the injured being delivered by the paramedics.

He immediately kicked into action, the reason for his visit forgotten as he realised his colleagues needed his help. He approached the trauma bay closest to him as they wheeled in an unconscious person lying still on a gurney.

'What happened? I'm here to help.' The junior doctor pushing the gurney glanced at the badge that hung from the breast pocket of his lab coat, then looked up at Salvador as if trying to confirm that he could be trusted. He couldn't blame him. As one of the high-ranking radiologists, Salvador hardly ever spent any time in the emergency department, only ever coming down here to fulfil some urgent requests of the chief.

'Bad accident on the highway near us,' the doctor explained as he started working on the patient. 'More ambulances on their way.'

'Got it.' Salvador turned around and headed to the entrance, stepping in to help the emergency department and its already thinly stretched resources.

On his way to the loading bay, he grabbed latex gloves, pulling them over his hands as the next ambulance arrived. The doors swung open as the paramedic jumped down, pulling the gurney out. Everything around him slowed when Yara's face came into focus. The paramedics' voices faded into nothing, replaced by the roaring static in his ears.

He froze as his eyes traced the splatters of blood covering her front, horror spreading through his body with each heartbeat. It wasn't until her brown eyes locked into his that he snapped out of his trance and realised that she was hunched over the patient with her hands over the wound.

'John Doe seems to be in his early forties, involved

in a car crash at high speed,' the paramedic said as he pushed the gurney towards Salvador. 'Pulse is thready, and there is a large wound on the abdomen, already packed with antibiotics en route.'

'I'll take it.' Salvador nodded at the junior doctor beside him to help him as he grabbed the gurney, looking at Yara. 'Are you okay?'

She nodded, her eyes fixed on her hands where the white gauze she held against the patient's abdomen was turning bright red. 'I was a couple of cars down in a taxi when it happened, so I jumped out to help.'

The relief relaxing Salvador's muscles was pure and beyond any words. He didn't know how he would have reacted if it had been her on that gurney. The sense of undiluted dread that had gripped him when he saw the blood on her had rendered him immobile.

I've just got her back. Those were the words that echoed through his mind as he processed the scene in front of her.

They'd shared one kiss only, yet somehow it had affected Salvador to an unexpected level—just as seeing her in an ambulance had shaken him in a place he hadn't expected.

'Let's bring him into a trauma bay so we can get Dr Silvia off our patient,' he said to the junior doctor pulling the gurney ahead of him, who nodded and rushed out of the room to get the supplies needed.

'Place your hands over hers and press down,' Salvador instructed. 'Now, slowly draw your hands out from underneath, Yara.'

She did as she was told, slipping her hands out from under the grip of the other doctor, who continued to apply pressure in her stead. Salvador reached his arm out to help her brace herself as she climbed down from the gurney and landed with a grunt on the floor.

'Okay, let's see what we have here.' He glanced at the monitors the nurse had just set up, checking the patient's vital signs with a frown. Yara appeared next to him a moment later, a gown pulled over her clothes.

'The fire department pulled him out of the passenger side of the vehicle,' she said as she circled around to the patient's head, checking the injury. 'Pupillary response is normal. No preliminary signs of brain trauma, but we should still order a scan.'

Salvador nodded and stepped forward to inspect the abdominal wound the junior doctor was still stemming. He moved his hand to the gauze and lifted it slightly. At some places, the deep wound had started to coagulate and stop bleeding, but it was too large and dirty to be cleaned and stitched here.

'Trauma Surgery will need to take care of this wound. Let's dress it up for transport.' He looked at the nurse typing on the patient's chart. 'Can you head out and see what the charge nurse wants us to do about this?' With this many patients coming in from the accident, there was bound to be a triage system set up already to prioritise which patient went into surgery first.

Salvador turned to Yara, who had finished placing a bandage around the patient's head. 'I can prep the wound for transport,' she said, and grabbed the supplies from the trolley when Salvador nodded.

He stood back as she took charge, lending a hand whenever necessary. When she'd diagnosed Dr Douglas's patient with a mere glance at the scans, he'd already known that he was in the presence of medical excellence.

What he witnessed now was her patient-care skills, working the bigger chunks of debris out of the wound and laying down gauze and bandages as they went around, saving the surgical team precious time they might need to check the patient for any internal injuries.

'Should we get an X-ray?' Yara asked, as if she was reading his mind.

He scrutinised the vital signs. The pressure on the wounds was keeping the patient from bleeding out, but the pulse was dropping. 'No, the surgical team will have to check for any internal damage with exploratory surgery. I don't think the patient is stable enough for any scans.'

Yara nodded and finished up the last bandages, before handing the patient over to the surgical trauma team, who transported the unconscious patient to the OR floor.

'On to the next one?' Salvador asked when the doors shut, and Yara nodded, a look of grim determination on her face.

CHAPTER SEVEN

AFTER TWO HOURS of lending a hand wherever needed, the workload in the emergency department returned to manageable, giving Salvador and Yara the opportunity to step away and clean themselves up.

In the rush of things, they hadn't been able to have a discussion or even acknowledge their existence to one another. The emergency had taken precedent, but now that things were quiet, Salvador became aware of the tension coiling itself around his chest once more—part longing, part fear of what the resurrection of his attraction for Yara meant.

The blood she'd been covered in while rendering first aid had dried under the gown and protective gear Yara had put on to help with the emergency. Salvador had led her to a private room Chief Sakamoto let his more senior doctors use to rest and refresh so she could get rid of the grime they'd accumulated on their shift.

Whoever had inhabited the office before it fell vacant must have spent enough time in that room, since they'd gone out of their way to make it cosy. The walls were painted in a darker grey tone that soothed any tiredness or irritation, and the couch on the far end of the corner had brought him through more than one late shift.

Though neither soothing nor comfort helped today as

he stared at the closed door of the bathroom that seemed to mock the desire uncoiling in his chest. The thought of the state of undress Yara was in manifested in his head, driving heated blood to his groin, leaving him hard and aching. Even the dirt of an emergency-department shift did precious little to dampen the flame of longing stirring his blood.

Was she telling him to follow her? Or was that just a strand of misguided need for this woman weaving itself through his mind and making him see things that weren't there?

It must be the latter. Anything else was just not possible. Chance had brought them back together, even though Salvador knew they had no future. Not when his entire life was currently wrapped up in his nephew and choosing what was right for Felix over what he himself might want. He was not meant for the world she lived in, and hearing how easily her parents had convinced her of the same thing proved his point.

But dear God, he *wanted* her. The memory of their kiss still lingered on his lips, haunting him every time he closed his eyes to drift off. It was as if she had never left—never broken his heart. How could the short span of a week have fused them together again in such a profound way that Salvador hardened at the mere thought of her naked? Even the dread at the thought of her leaving didn't dampen his desire.

Or could he dare to taste what he couldn't have all those years ago? Wasn't that what was really happening between them? An ancient attraction they'd left unfinished, and now it was back between them, taunting him every time he saw her—coming between their work.

Salvador stood up, the couch moving against the wall behind him when he surged up. Two large strides brought him to the door leading to the bathroom. The water had stopped running, intensifying the image of Yara he'd conjured in his head, all wrapped in a luscious steam as she towelled herself dry, her hands slipping over the planes of her body he yearned to touch with such ferocity that his length flexed against the band of his trousers.

His hand hovered over the door handle, an internal debate raging on for what had to be eternity, sensibility trying to best the roaring in his chest.

Then he heard footsteps shuffle on the other side of the door.

Something was strange about Salvador when Yara came out of the bathroom dressed in a pair of oversized scrubs he'd given her to change into. Her clothes had become collateral damage after she witnessed the car accident on her way to her hotel, jumping out of the taxi to help the first responders. When she had stopped the large abdominal wound with her hands, she understood this would end up in a trip to the hospital for her. There was no way to dress such a wound in the field.

What she hadn't expected was Salvador on the other side of the ambulance doors, pulling at the gurney she had sat on.

The look of horror on his face had burned itself into her memory, burying a searing dagger between her ribs that filled her with unexpected waves of heat.

He'd thought it was her blood.

But they'd had no time to talk to each other with all the chaos in the emergency department, so they'd both sprung into action, working side by side—an experience that had affected Yara more than she had thought it would. While they were already working with each other on Henrique Orlay's case, that was somewhat different, as his role with that patient was very specific. He was there to interpret scans and results, feeding into her theories. In the emergency department today, she'd seen him in a different light. She had watched and supported as he worked with the trauma team to help everyone affected by the car crash. He'd worked with them as if he had always been part of the trauma team, not missing a single beat and showing great confidence in his ability to diagnose and treat patients under pressure.

It was a side of Salvador she hadn't seen until this moment, filling her with admiration for his dedication as a doctor. When she had pursued the idea of becoming a physician, that image was what she had in mind—strong and confident, but also flexible and kind, helping wherever necessary, with no ego involved. Her years of travelling had put her in front of a lot of different doctors and teams, each of them different in how they handled things. Ego and self-importance were things she had learned to deal with early on. Teams usually didn't like other people pitching in to their work—and that rule applied even more so to outsiders.

But no one had questioned or been bothered by Salvador's presence in the emergency department as he rolled up his sleeves. They were grateful someone was there to help in a time of crisis. An emergency department environment Yara could get used to.

'Are you okay?' she asked when Salvador remained unmoving, staring at her with a veiled expression.

He stood no more than two steps away from the door she had just opened, his posture stiff and frozen in place. Their eyes met for a few heartbeats, the intensity written in his dark gaze making the breath hitch in her throat. She watched as he took a slow step forward, followed by a quick one, and a moment later she was crushed against his strong frame as he hugged her close to him. Her arms hovered in the air for an undecided second, then her body went limp, giving in to the embrace. Yara wrapped her arms around his middle, drawing herself closer as she rested her face on his chest and soaked up the warmth coming from him as his scent enveloped her with the intimacy of their embrace.

She felt his nose on the top of her head as he nestled into her hair, his warm breath grazing over her as he drew her so much closer than she thought was possible.

'You scared me,' he mumbled, and all her senses had honed in on her body's reaction to his proximity, so that it took her several moments to comprehend the words he said to her.

'I'm fine, I promise. Scarier things have happened before,' she replied, listening to the strong beats of his heart against her cheek. All the reservations and uncertainty around their relationship were gone, replaced by the unyielding and intoxicating warmth his embrace caused to ripple through her. Even so many years later, his arms around her had the same effect on her—maybe even more, as she felt his closeness inside her core.

'Not to me.' His lips brushed over her hair as he spoke, each word creating a tiny kiss that sent sparks flying down her spine, lighting a trail of fires she couldn't control. All her senses focused on where his lips connected with her body, cascading the need for more through her.

Yara lifted her head off his chest and tilted it back to look at him. A heartbeat went by, tacit understanding passing through each of them as Salvador nudged her nose with his and angled his mouth over hers, before dipping down and drawing her into a kiss. It was different from the one they had shared two days ago. This one was filled with urgency and need, no longer bound by the restraints both had put on each other as they tried to establish their professional relationship around their old feelings of affection. No, this time around they both knew what they wanted—each other.

A thought that earlier in the day had sent Yara into a tailspin, rocking her so hard that she had to seek out her sister to clear her head.

Nothing changed between them, and her mind was still the same. Yara couldn't be with anyone else right now. She was still too damaged from a loveless marriage and years of manipulation, her trust in her own abilities so broken that she didn't know how to tell the truth of her feelings from wishful thinking. Was the growing attachment for Salvador real? Or was her affection for him no more than an echo of the love she'd used to have for him, and it would fade away the moment she looked too closely?

Was that even something *he* wanted, or was he acting on old feelings bubbling back to the surface? He'd been so angry at her when they first spoke here at the hospital…

Though those doubts floated in her mind, they faded into the distance when Salvador's teeth closed around her lower lip. The gentle bite rushed a wave of heat through her, setting the butterflies in her stomach on fire. She moaned against his mouth, opening her lips to his pleading tongue.

How could she ever have believed that what she felt in her marriage was enough? Even in the early days of their courtship, their passion had never run this hot. Yara had never felt as though she might cease to exist if she didn't give everything she was to the man eliciting such exquisite pleasure from her with no more than a deep kiss.

How would that mouth feel like on other parts of her body?

That thought almost undid her, sending a tremble through her that Salvador must have felt as well, for he lifted his head to look at her with passion-glazed eyes and heaving chest. He'd lost himself in that moment as much as she had—a fact that brought the tightness in her core to a new level.

'Are you okay?' he asked, the question dispelling some of the luscious fog surrounding them.

Was she okay? Probably not. Making out with her high-school boyfriend, who she had reunited with by chance after thirty years while also coping with the new reality of being a divorcee, didn't really spell stability of mind. But for the first time in ages blood was pumping through her veins, her senses alive. She dared to give in to a need she had denied herself for far too long—even if Salvador was a risky target to give in to, he'd also been the first one to penetrate the thick walls she'd surrounded herself with. And not even with stealth, no. He'd walked through the front gate as if he was simply coming home.

His hands were still planted on her back, pressing her flush against him as he looked down on her with narrowed eyes that were filled with the same fog of lust and desire she felt inside her. Neither of them was thinking clearly, and that should be something that concerned her. But no matter how much she tried to push back on it, everything in her wanted to give in and get lost in the promise of pleasure his lips evoked.

His hands came to rest on each side of her face as he towered over her like a jaguar, looking down at its next meal after being starved for days.

Salvador grunted, taking another step forward so his entire body was covering hers as he pressed against her. His mouth nuzzled a spot behind her ear, his teeth raking downward over her skin to her neck. A firework exploded in the pit of her stomach, both because of the sensations his lips caused on her body and the intimacy of the situation. Her hips moved against him of their own accord and her eyes went wide when she brushed the apex of her thighs against his hardened length, straining against his trousers.

'This is what you do to me,' he said, to underline the truth of what she had just felt.

'Salvador…' She wove her fingers through his hair as his hands roamed over her body, finding the hem of the oversized shirt she was wearing and slipping beneath it. His fingers trailed her side, each brush stoking the fire in her core.

'This is all I've been thinking about for the last week,' he whispered as his right hand slipped to her front, palming her bare breast.

Yara instinctively leaned into his touch, writhing against him as pleasure thundered through her at this simplest of touches. She hadn't bothered to put on her bra after getting changed, thinking she'd be in her hotel room right now. Somehow, that decision had now worked in her favour.

'Me too,' she replied.

This had only been one of the many things she'd thought when it came to Salvador, but the only things she could remember were the riot of sensations the gentle brush of his fingers caused in her, and her sister's question that echoed in her head every time Yara thought she needed to put a stop to this: *Why not?*

What if she would simply enjoy what was happening in this moment without worrying about the future? Was there even a future to worry about? Before long she'd be on her way again, travelling the world to wherever difficult cases brought her. A life impossible to live for Salvador, who had his nephew to think about.

Their ideas of life didn't fit together any more, and maybe they never had. Would he have been able to be with the people he needed to be with in order to blossom into his sexuality if she had been there, holding him back?

If they both knew this was as far as things could get between them, was there any harm in giving in just this one time—as long as they were clear about their intentions?

'If we're going to do this…' Yara started, and then interrupted herself with a drawn-out sigh that tapered off in a longing moan when Salvador rolled her hard nipple between his fingers.

His mouth came back to hers, drawing her into another indulgent kiss as his other hand slipped further down, cupping her butt cheek and drawing her even closer.

'What are the ground rules?' he asked when he finally released her lips with a huff of barely leashed desire.

'This is just finishing what we started some decades ago—the purpose is not to see if we could have made it as a couple.' Salvador looked at her with narrowed eyes that made a delicious shiver rake through her body, and it took every sliver of self-restraint she possessed to think about the rules of their engagement.

He nodded. 'One time. To get it out of our system.'

As if to emphasise his point, he let his hand wander to her front, moving beyond her waistband and between her legs. His fingers traced her through her underwear, finding the fabric beginning to soak with anticipation and need from nothing more than a few heated kisses.

Salvador must have thought the same thing, for he grinned with a dangerous spark in his eyes that curled her toes inside her shoes. This man was impossible to resist, and she didn't know how she'd walked away from him the first time around—or if she would be able to do it a second time.

'Oh, God…' Her head lolled back when his fingers brushed over her bundles of nerves, shooting lightning through her. He moved so slowly, each touch happening after extensive deliberation, and she raised her hips to meet him, urging him on.

But Salvador took his time, clearly enjoying this most exquisite torture he was putting her through. 'You ran away,' he whispered in her ear as he stroked her. 'Now you have to submit to my pace.'

Her eyes flew open when he withdrew his hands from her loose scrub trousers, passing the fingers that had just been giving her pleasure over his lips with an indulgent smile that made her heart skip a beat.

'When I finally have you, Yara, it won't be in an empty office at the hospital where I can't make you scream with pleasure without worry.' With those words he retreated from her, her personal space suddenly feeling empty and aching, the ghost of his touch still lingering on her flesh.

'Meet me at my hotel later?' she asked when he turned to leave. She wanted this so bad, every single nerve ending in her body was screaming at her to throw her arms around him again, and she knew if she let him walk out without knowing, she'd lose heart and it would never happen then.

'Let me make a call, see if I can get a babysitter to stay with Felix over the weekend.'

'Over…the weekend?' Yara's heart fluttered in her chest, and she tried swallowing the dryness spreading through her mouth. She hadn't thought this would last more than a couple of hours.

'I know just the place to take you,' he said, the gravel in his voice kicking her pulse into overdrive.

'Isn't that a bit much for a no-strings-attached hook-up?' Yara didn't know why she was poking holes in the plan when she really wanted to spend more than just a weekend with Salvador. So much more that she couldn't have.

The grin on his face turned to mischief, his gaze darting all over her body before landing back on her face. 'To get this all out of our system with one time, we'll need a whole weekend,' he said, and the unbridled hunger in his eyes set off another round of fireworks in her belly as she watched him turn around and leave. 'I'll pick you up tomorrow after work.'

CHAPTER EIGHT

THEIR WEEKEND DESTINATION was no more than an hour away from Brasília. If it had been just about reliving some fond memories, Salvador could have done it within a day. But he knew they needed more time than that if they *truly* meant what they had said about getting this attraction brewing between them out of their system by just letting go of their reins.

Salvador didn't know if this was the right approach or if the unrelenting need to have her—even if it was just for one night—was clouding his judgement to the point where he wasn't thinking straight.

Because he knew Yara had been right when they had spoken about their ground rules. This was a one-time thing that couldn't have a *Part Two* or *To Be Continued*. They were bold enough to let their desire take the reins for the duration of one weekend. After that they were nothing more than colleagues, working on a case together, and once that happened, Yara would be out of his life again.

The thought of her leaving so soon after they had reunited caused a sharp pinch in the centre of his chest that he didn't dare to examine much further. Until this week when she had appeared in his hospital, he hadn't known that he wanted her back more than he was furious at her—that his love for her had not died, but rather slowed down to an imperceptible simmer that had lain dormant in him for three decades, only to roar back alive when he first touched her lips.

A complication that just couldn't happen, no matter how he felt about it. He'd unexpectedly become a father to his nephew, and it was his responsibility to guide him through his life now without treading the path the rest of his family was all too eager to walk on.

There was also the small voice inside his head that understood her reluctance from thirty years ago. He didn't fit into her world, no matter how much he distanced himself from his parents' actions, proving to the world that he was different. They might be a lot older now, but Salvador still felt those shadows looming over him. Someone from Yara's background would always gravitate towards people like Lawrence Silvia, award-winning bio-engineer at a tech company that wanted to change the face of modern medicine.

His stomach dropped when he recalled the things he'd read about Yara's husband when he'd looked him up last night. Some sense of morbid curiosity had driven him to type Yara's name into the search bar, wanting to know more about who she had been married to—who was the man worthy enough for her to change her name to his.

Now Salvador knew so much more about her ex-husband than he ever wanted to know, putting him on edge. Something he didn't want to be, not for a no-strings weekend away from home. There was nothing at stake here. She would be gone in a matter of days, ending something that hadn't even started.

Yara gasped next to him in the passenger seat when she realised where they were going.

'Are we going to Lagoa Bonita?' Her head whipped

around to look at him with bright eyes that made him want to pull over and have her right this instant.

'I couldn't let you leave Brasília without pitching up at our favourite spot.' When Salvador had bought his first car, they had taken regular trips over to Planaltina, walking around the shallow lake Lagoa Bonita that was located next to the small town. During the warmer season, the area was a popular destination for tourists as the lake was surrounded by pristine sandy dunes. The town was littered with small businesses and family-owned restaurants that appealed to both the locals who lived here to escape the bustle of the big city and also the visitors looking for a cosier experience than Brasília had to offer. Though it was Brazil's capital, much of the beauty and fun existed outside of the city's boundaries.

This late into autumn Salvador hoped that things would be calmer around here, even though he hadn't really planned on letting her leave the bed once she was in it.

'I wonder how much it has changed over the years. Do you know if they still have that small beach bar on the shore of the lake?' Yara looked at him with a sweet smile that caused his heart to leap against his chest. He remembered the bar she mentioned. They'd spent weekends there, enjoying mocktails as their friendship blossomed into something more.

'I don't know. I haven't been back since my brother's sentencing...' His voice trailed off.

Yara looked away for a moment, watching the landscape pass them by in a mixture of green and brown colours.

'How is Henrique doing?' he asked, to change the topic and bring some levity back into the conversation. Work was always the safe option for them.

'He's been very cooperative around the diagnosis. Taking him off all medication has not been easy, but he gritted his teeth through it and we gathered some useful insights. Somehow his immune system is attacking his peripheral nervous system.' She turned her head back at him, her finger tapping against the side of her nose. 'I took a deep dive into his family history and didn't find anything hereditary that could link to his symptoms. So we are down to a handful of neurological diseases that can cause this.'

'He has an autoimmune disease?' Salvador asked, and the gravity settling in between them gave him the answer. Autoimmune diseases didn't have a cure. Their only recourse here would be to teach Mr Orlay how to live with his symptoms as well as a life full of medication and regular check-ups.

'Unfortunately, yes,' she confirmed with a nod.

'It must be tough sometimes, being the bearer of so much bad news,' Salvador said after a few moments of silence as he processed the information about his patient's progressing diagnosis. 'You're brought in for the cases where the team has explored all the options and still comes up short. Which means you probably diagnose a lot of diseases that are hard or impossible to cure. They wouldn't call you in if they already knew the answer.'

'It can be hard, yes.' Yara sighed, and, acting on instinct, Salvador reached out to grab her hand with his free one, drawing it closer to him to comfort her. 'I count finding the right diagnosis as a good outcome, otherwise I would rarely feel good about my work. If I've found the right answer, that means the patient can get the treatment they need or at least some closure.'

She wiggled her fingers, weaving them through his,

and squeezed his hand. It was a tiny gesture, but so loaded with affection that Salvador's chest tightened.

'Was all the travelling hard on your marriage?' That wasn't the question he wanted to ask.

No, what he really wanted to know was how any guy could be insane enough to let this woman slip through his fingers. But he couldn't say that to her. He was already too attached to her on an emotional level. He couldn't let her know about the depth of his affection towards her. What if she left again the way she had thirty years ago? Or worse, what if she felt the same way and didn't leave? There was no way of their being together without someone giving something up—and he could never ask something of this magnitude from her. Not when he knew he wasn't nearly enough for her.

'No, I think we stuck together for so long because we found a way where we didn't have to be around each other for much of the time.' It took her so long to reply that Salvador thought she had decided not to answer his question, deeming it too much of an intrusion.

Should he even be asking? His infatuation with her already bordered on something he couldn't commit to, yet when it came to knowing Yara again—learning what he'd missed in the years they'd not seen each other— he couldn't help but dig deeper and find out who she'd become, and discover fragments of her past he hadn't known about.

'I'm sorry to hear that,' he replied, throwing her a quick side glance. Their hands were still entangled, and he felt her thumb sweep over the back of his hand, drawing small circles.

'It's okay. I think it's time I talked about it to someone, and I'm actually kind of glad it's you.'

He raised an eyebrow. 'You haven't spoken to your family about this?'

'I mentioned it to Bianca when I went to see her the other day...' A noticeable hesitancy accompanied her words, as if she was choosing them with great deliberation.

'You decided to go and talk to her, after all?' He remembered their conversation on the first day and how she hadn't planned on seeing her sister while in Brasília.

Yara laughed, but it sounded strained. Her fingers kept dancing over the back of his hand. 'I kind of needed to explain why me kissing you wasn't a problem for my marriage—since I'm no longer married.'

Salvador didn't say anything to that, though a smile stole over his lips. That moment in the conference room seemed so long ago, even though it hadn't even been a full week.

He pulled into the driveway of a house off the main street and finally put his full attention on Yara. She was looking at the two-storey house with the light blue walls. 'This looks beautiful. How did you find this place?' she asked, her eyes still roaming the exterior of the house.

'It's mine. I used to stay here in Planaltina before I got custody of Felix. Since he's in the middle of a school year, I didn't want to take him away from everything he's ever known. Not with the amount of change he was already dealing with.'

He didn't often talk about Felix to anyone, not wanting to shine a light on the criminal record of his parents and brother. But Yara already knew about that and had never judged him for the actions of his parents, and he knew it wouldn't make her think less of Felix either. No, her eyes were full of warmth and understanding.

Had he made the wrong decision to bring her here?

Somewhere that meant so much to him, to them? This weekend was supposed to be about sex and finally moving on from that phantom of a relationship that hung between them. They had this one step to complete, one they were both burning for. And then? Then Yara would leave Brasília and be out of his life again for ever. So the sympathy didn't matter, nor did the intense need gripping him whenever he was close to her. What he needed for Felix—and for himself, too—was stability, and she needed to be free to drift in and out of people's lives as she pleased. Or was there a way to combine both their needs?

Salvador pushed these thoughts away as he got out of the car. That wasn't a place he was allowed to go—ever. He would not let himself indulge in any idle fantasies just because the reality didn't live up to what he wanted it to be. This weekend with Yara, fulfilling the final step of what had been a slow-burn romance, would have to be enough. They wouldn't get a future together, so right now would have to suffice.

Yara's knees didn't quite hold all of her weight when she got out of the car and followed Salvador to the front door. They'd spoken so casually about their lives during the car ride, with her sharing things she didn't think she would—until those words had slipped right out of her mouth and into the open. The odd thing was that she felt relief to finally have admitted to an aspect of her marriage that had gone awry. That travelling the world had never meant to be such a big part of her career, but each time she had returned home she felt trapped in this farce of a marriage her parents had convinced her was what marriages were supposed to be like.

She'd come close to telling Bianca how she felt, believing her sister would understand, but her courage had thus far failed her. Even if her sister understood her, what if word got back to her mother that she'd not made the marriage she had been so keen on work? Though she knew Bianca would never betray her trust, the news might slip out.

So many years later, she still felt the pressure of carrying her parents' ideal family picture on her shoulders, weighing her down. Until Salvador had come back into her life, and all she could feel now was this burning sensation of intense longing that could only be quenched by being with him. He had not judged her for her words, simply taking them at face value and believing her.

Her heart squeezed tight when she thought about his situation and how much judgement he himself had experienced throughout his entire life. Despite his family's perilous path, he'd given up his home to take care of his nephew while his brother served his sentence. A beautiful home, Yara noted as she stepped through the door, yet something crucial seemed absent.

The entrance of the house gave way to an open-plan living room, where a large, dark blue corner couch dominated the space. An empty vase stood on the glass coffee table and that along with the empty fruit bowl standing on the granite countertop of the kitchen island gave her an understanding of what was missing—a family to make everything come alive.

As it currently was it didn't lack any beauty, but it didn't feel *alive*.

'Did you live here with your ex?' she asked, looking for the traces of the man Salvador had been attached to in the past.

Salvador put his backpack on the floor as he locked the door behind him, looking around the place as if he hadn't seen it in a while. 'Ah, no. We lived in the city.

I didn't know if Felipe would have to serve more time, but I knew my nephew would have to stay with me for some weeks until his father's sentencing. Edinho wasn't thrilled about that temporary arrangement, so when I got permanent custody of Felix we had to call things off between us.'

'He didn't want to accept Felix in your lives?' she asked, unable to comprehend this stance. If Edinho had really loved Salvador, wouldn't he at least try to make it work no matter what?

'Children hadn't been part of our plan,' Salvador said with a shrug. 'So it wasn't really a surprise for me that he didn't want to suddenly be in a relationship where a child was involved. The circumstances of our lives changed, and it was something he didn't want to commit to. It sucked, but I can understand his reasons.'

'That's such a mature way of looking at it.' Her heart cracked at the thought of him having to make such a decision on his own, as well as dealing with a pre-teen when he'd never had any children before.

'What about you?'

Yara's thoughts ground to a halt, and she looked at him in confusion. 'What about me?'

Salvador approached her with a faint smile on his face, coming close enough that she could pick up his scent of lavender and sea salt. He stopped only a few paces away from her, within touching distance.

'Did you want to have children?'

Her mind went blank for a moment, focused only on the air between them that became charged with energy, growing louder and hotter between them.

Children? That was a complicated and painful topic for Yara, and the last thing she wanted was the heaviness of her biggest regret weighing her down when they were supposed to be light—to have fun. This weekend wasn't about gaining some emotional closeness. The opposite, really—they had agreed to give in to the sexual tension that had been building between them from day one so they could finally get over it and move on.

'I…wanted to, yes. But it never happened. By the time I felt ready for children, my marriage had already deteriorated to the point where I couldn't possibly bring a child into such a situation. My parents were so clinical to each other, so focused on their perfect family picture that they didn't care about what that kind of cool detachment did to a child. I didn't want that for any child of mine.'

Salvador stepped closer when her voice faltered on her last words, laying the back of his hand against her cheek and gently stroking her cheekbone with his index finger.

'I didn't know that about your parents,' he said, his finger tracing a line down her jaw. 'Whenever I saw them at your house, they seemed like the perfect couple.'

Yara leaned into his touch, her eyes drifting close for one beat of her heart. 'They would never let anyone see the cracks in their marriage. I think that's the reason they were so adamant about who their eldest daughter picked as a spouse. The fear of what the neighbour would say if they saw me with—'

'With a ruffian like me?' Salvador finished her sentence.

With his finger under her chin now, he tilted her face upwards, grazing a soft kiss on the corner of her mouth.

Her heart slamming against her chest at the sudden closeness, she continued, 'I'm menopausal now, so I missed my window of having my own children, and I'm no longer sure if I even want to at this age.'

Ever since she'd left Lawrence, she'd thought a lot about adopting a child on her own. She'd wasted too much time waiting for the ideal timing that she lost her chance altogether. But she didn't want to be unfair to a child either. With the amount of travelling she needed to do for her work, it didn't seem fair to commit to a child when she was never settled in a single place.

Salvador stepped closer, eliminating the remaining space between them. His breath now grazed over her cheek as he angled his head down, brushing a soft kiss on her forehead. 'Strange. I never wanted children until Felix appeared in my life, and now I can't imagine what it would be like without him.'

'You don't have any regrets being forced to choose between him and your relationship?'

'There wasn't a choice. I could never abandon my nephew. After everything he's been through, he deserves some continuity and stability. I won't let anyone get in the way of that.' He said it with a finality that drove a sharp pain between her ribs, and she bit the inside of her cheek so as not to gasp.

Even though she knew it wasn't, it somehow felt as though this was targeted at her directly, as though she needed a reminder that their time together here was just about sex. It was what she wanted as well, right? It had been so long for her, the kisses they shared had been enough to open up a chasm of desire within her, just waiting to erupt from Salvador's touch.

Why were they even talking about children? That topic wasn't even near any foreplay-talk recommendations. Only this was another part of her she'd been too embarrassed to share with anyone, feeling so foolish about staying in the relationship that didn't fulfil her and give her what she wanted.

'He's lucky to have you,' Yara finally said, wrapping her hands around his midsection to pull him close against her. 'So, Dr Martins. I don't think you brought me here just to retrace my past decisions or go over yours.'

Somehow Salvador made it easy for her to share, to open up the gates on the imposing walls she had erected around herself—and that needed to stop. Sharing their innermost space wasn't necessary for that, even though it felt so right. But even though she had steeled her heart for this, words kept slipping out without a prompt, fusing her closer to the man she had slipped away from.

Salvador growled as his hands slipped around her waist to push her away from him and turn her around so her back was to him before he put his arm around her and pulled her flush against him. His lips brushed down her neck and to her shoulder, nuzzling into the silky fabric of the flowery dress she'd put on this morning for the car ride.

She shivered when his tongue darted over her skin, the fine hair along her arms standing on end as his intimate touch made the memories of her regrets sting less. This was where she was supposed to be—right in his arms, where nothing could touch her. Here she would only know affection and pleasure from the man she should have never rejected.

Her parents hadn't been concerned for her safety or wellbeing when they'd forbidden her to see him any more because of the criminal history of his parents. No, they had been worried about what people might say if their eldest daughter went out with the son of criminals.

But Salvador was nothing like them. He was kind and caring, pulling himself out from the toxic environment of his childhood home and managing to make something out of his life—even caring for his nephew in his time of need.

And now the hands of this wonderful man were gliding over her front, palming her breasts through her dress as his laboured breath swept over her ear. Something hard pressed against her, and she writhed at the anticipation of his length inside her. She moved her hips ever so slightly, grinding against Salvador behind her. The hiss escaping his throat turned into a groan that made Yara grin with delight. That she had that effect on him, even after all these years, caused such intense pleasure to ripple through her body that she felt her core contract, ready for what she'd been dreaming about.

The final step missing from what they'd had so many years ago. One night together—or rather one night spread over several hours of the weekend.

This was not at all going according to plan. Salvador had whisked her away to Planaltina to walk around Lagoa Bonita and remind both of them of the earlier days of their teenage friendship, before romantic roots had taken hold in either of their hearts. He had used to do this small trip whenever he needed to get away from his family and the damage they left in their wake. The lake north of the town was small and shallow, so the water was always warm enough to dip into if he wanted.

One day when he was sneaking away from class—his father had been taken to the police station the day before—Yara had caught him, demanding to know where he was going. When he had told her, she insisted on coming with him, not wanting him to go through any struggles alone. He'd always kept his family a secret, ashamed of their shady history and what that said about him, but even though Yara didn't know much about them, she lent him her support anyway.

Because that was exactly the kind of person she was—kind and thoughtful towards the people around her. He could see now that her upbringing had been as difficult as his, even if they grew up with a different background. Though she had made the choice to leave him, he knew the hints and machinations of her parents had driven her away from him.

Yara was a woman of remarkable calibre, and she deserved more than a passion-filled weekend—even though that was all he could give.

But the need to have her burned in his blood, circulating a dominating heat through his entire body with each beat of his heart, driving the fever pitch higher and higher.

Her butt pressing against his rigid manhood almost sent him into a red-hot frenzy, and he took a deep breath, letting his hands roam over her body, the silk of her dress cool against his heated skin.

'I was going to take you for a walk,' he whispered, despite having no intention of going for that walk any more. With one bat of her lashes, she had drawn him back under her spell.

'It'll be lovely after sundown, when the sand has some time to cool down,' she whispered, and Salvador hissed when she slipped her hand between their bodies, tracing the outline of his erection with two of her fingers.

'Skipping straight to the main event?' he asked through gritted teeth as she played with the button of his trousers.

'You know I've never been very patient. It was the one thing our teachers complained about.'

Yara pushed herself away from him and turned around in his arms, melting back into his embrace while facing him. The passion rumbling in his chest tore through his body when she locked eyes with him, a sensual smile on her lips that spoke of all the ways she wanted to have him.

Yara. The one who'd got away. The woman who had planted herself in his heart with such surety that even three decades later, the seed of it blossomed again after not even a week of being close to her. It was as if she'd never left, their connection as vibrant and alive as it had been all those years ago—his body still responding to hers with no more than instinct.

As if they had been made for each other.

'You are so sexy, Yara. Look what you do to me.' His hand slipped down her back, crushing her against him so that his full length pressed against her, twitching when he felt her shiver under his touch.

She tilted her head back in response, her fingers weaving through his dark hair and pulling his face down towards her mouth, meeting him with open lips for his tongue to explore. The last restraint on his desire snapped as their tongues tangled, taking their passionate kiss to new heights.

His hands came back to her front, finding the sash keeping her wrap dress together and pulling on it, need underpinning every move he made. When his fingers found bare flesh, he pulled away, unable to resist the temptation to finally look at her—a vision of Latin sensuality and beauty in the cream-coloured bra and panties combination she was wearing underneath.

A low growl loosened from his throat at the sight, his erection tightening even more. 'I've fantasised about seeing you like this for so long—and it doesn't even come close to what my horny teenage brain could come up with.'

Yara's eyes went wide for a moment, pink streaking over her cheeks at the unexpected compliment he'd given her, and he swallowed a disbelieving laugh. How could those words be something that made her blush? There was no way she hadn't heard these things before, was there? Or had her marriage really been just out of obligation and family duty?

It was in that blush on her cheeks as well as the tentative smile pulling at the corner of her lips that he realised how much damage her loveless marriage had caused her—how little she valued herself as a woman of tremendous beauty and sex appeal. Because Lawrence hadn't made her feel those things, she now believed Salvador's words to be no more than flattery.

One weekend might not be enough to change that perception, but he would try to give her this one thing before they had to go back to being strangers.

The look Salvador gave her made Yara feel light-headed. In all her years of marriage, Lawrence had not once looked at her like that.

She remembered her wedding night and the fear she'd felt at the lack of compatibility, seeking blame within herself—believing for a long time that she lacked something fundamental.

Now she knew that to be false, for Salvador's hands roaming over her naked skin set her entire being on fire—each nerve ending begging to skip ahead to the end, where she knew the culmination of many years of suppressed sexual desire lay, ready to burst apart at his touch.

Even with the temporary nature of their agreement, he took his time to make her feel at ease, giving her compliments she'd not heard in many years, and it hurt her to admit how much his hunger for her surprised her—to the point where she could hardly believe it, thinking it some farce that was a part of modern courtship.

Her dress fell to the floor with a hushed rustle, pooling into a heap behind her. The soft breeze coming from the open window caressed her skin with its warm touch, highlighting her state of undress. When was the last time she had stood in front of a man wearing nothing but her underwear?

He gathered her up in his arms with a reverent softness, his fingers moving over her skin, exploring every rise and dip of her body. When he unhooked her bra, he stepped back to let it fall on the floor. The look of excitement in his eyes made her laugh and roll her eyes at the same time.

'You've seen breasts before, Salvador,' she said, when he kept staring.

'But I've never seen *yours* before. They're like a work of art.' He stepped closer, his hands moving up her torso to palm her breasts, each thumb brushing over the peak of a dark brown nipple, sending an exquisite trickle down her spine and into her core.

She gasped at the gentle touch, her mind wiped clean of any second thoughts or doubts she had found there just a few seconds ago. All her senses were trained on Salvador and where their bodies connected. Her hands started to move on their own, finally freed of the restraints her overthinking had placed on them. They found the hem of his T-shirt, slipping beneath it to feel the warmth of his skin against her palm. His back was broad and strong under her fingers, and she pushed the fabric further up until he leaned back so she could pull the shirt over his head.

A smile like the one she'd seen on his lips just moments ago appeared on hers when she beheld Salvador's naked upper body. She had seen him like this before, but the memories of those occasions were nothing like the reality—probably because her desire for this man was at an all-new high. Salvador had been incredibly attractive as a young adult, and the years that had passed since she'd last seen him had only refined what handsomeness had already been there.

Yara bit her lip as her gaze wandered further down, her hand moving along his firm chest in unison with her eyes, drawing small circles in his chest hair before moving lower. She swept over this happy trail, following it to the point where it disappeared beneath his waistband.

'That won't do,' she mumbled, more to herself than to Salvador, flicking open the button of his trousers and pulling the zip down.

Salvador groaned when his trousers slipped down his legs, the only restraints on his erection now the fabric of his underpants. Yara brushed over the bulge with her hand and bit her lip when he flexed his hips in response, leaning into her touch with an enthusiasm that was foreign to her. Had anyone ever craved her touch this badly? Had she ever wanted to burn the way she was willing to in this moment?

The last remains of her hesitation fell away at the sound of deep and undiluted pleasure coming from Salvador when she touched him, daring to move the last barrier of clothing out of the way so she could wrap her hand around him.

'*Deus… Yara.*' Hearing her name from his lips turn into a moan set her blood ablaze, emboldening her in her actions.

She wrapped her hand around him, moving up and down in slow pumps, savouring each one as Salvador twitched under her touch. His breath left his nose in strained huffs, all his muscles tense as Yara placed her mouth on his collarbone, tracing kisses over the planes of his chest and down his abdomen to his navel.

When she sank to her knees, his strong hands wrapped around her shoulders as if bracing for what was to happen next. Her tongue darted over his tip, hesitant at first but then growing in boldness as Salvador's body moved under her touch, his throaty groans accompanying her moves as she drew all of him in.

His fingers dug into her flesh as she went on, her name clinging to his lips in a desperate plea for release that sent a shiver down her spine. Knowing the pleasure rippling through him was her doing, that she was the one shooting lighting through his body, easing and contracting his abdominal muscles with each sweep of her tongue over his tip—it almost undid her on the spot.

Yara let her eyes drift closed, relishing the feel of him against her, but the quiet moment lasted only a second before his hands tightened around her shoulders and a moment later she was pulled onto her feet, pulled out of the delicious stupor her ministrations had put her in.

The glazed look in his eyes as he crushed her against him brought another wave of heat to cascade through her body. His lips found hers, drawing her into a hurried kiss, tongues and teeth clashing, conveying the intensity of the fire she'd stoked in him with her mouth alone.

'I need to have you right now,' he growled in between kisses.

His hands found the seam of her panties, and one flick of his wrists dropped them to the floor. He pulled her into another long and indulgent kiss, his chest heaving against hers, then he grabbed her by the hips and lifted her up. Yara gasped when her feet lifted off the ground, and she wrapped her legs around him for stability as he carried her towards a large couch on the other side of the open-plan living space.

'On the couch?' she asked when she realised where he was carrying her.

'We'll spend enough time in the bedroom after this one,' he replied, a feral expression curling his lips upward.

Yara writhed against him as he walked her over, feeling his length press against her slickness, ready for him. But instead of pouncing on her when he dropped her on the spacious couch, he knelt on the carpet and grabbed her calves. She gasped in surprise when he threw her legs over his shoulders and seized her hips again to draw her closer to his mouth.

'What…?' The rest of her words died on her lips, turning into a drawn-out moan when his tongue nestled into her folds, Salvador taking her like a man lost in the desert, finally finding an oasis to quench his thirst on.

'You thought I would let you have all the fun?' he said between licks, bringing her closer to the edge than she had been in years—and she was ready to go there with Salvador. Her muscles started to tense, the surrounding room drifting out of focus as stars began to dance in front of her eyes.

'Wait,' she huffed, pawing at his head until he appeared in front of her face. 'I want us to…together.'

Yara's senses came back to her as she examined her own awkward phrasing. Sex had not been part of her life in recent years, and when it had been it was with selfish lovers, who hadn't taken the time to give as much pleasure as they took. Already Salvador was so different from that, she didn't know how to react—had forgotten how to ask for a simple thing like that.

But Salvador, sweet and thoughtful, understood without her having to use many words. He scooped her into his arms, quickly lifting her again. As he held on to her he reached for the drawer of the side table, pulling it open and grabbing a condom that he pulled over his erection. He smiled when he was done and pulled Yara back on top of him. She had her legs on each side of his body, his impressive length strained against her, nudging in the right place and making her writhe with anticipation.

'Are you comfortable like this?' he asked as his hand came up to touch her cheek with a gentle brush.

Instead of replying, Yara angled her head down, drawing his lips onto hers and letting a passionate kiss do her talking. That he even bothered to ask showed her the man he'd always been and how big a mistake she had made when she let her parents convince her that there was someone more worthy out there.

He groaned against her lips when she released the tension in her legs, easing herself onto him. They looked at each other for a second as she settled down, an unspoken bond forging between them. All the words they'd been unable to say, all the dreams and plans of the future they had never got to have—these and more pictures floated in the tiny space between their bodies, hitching up her heartbeat until she could feel it in her throat.

So much lost that could never be recovered. But at least they would have this moment—this weekend—to live as if they had the rest of their lives together.

Pleasure mingled with the tiny needles of regret burying themselves inside her soul as they moved their hips together, their lips clashing and their breaths increasing, each thrust bringing them closer to the togetherness Yara had been craving the moment they'd started talking like friends again.

She gasped when Salvador picked up the speed, whispering her name into her ear as his hand slipped between them to stroke her as they both neared their climax together. Her hands dug into his shoulders, her head lolling backwards as her surroundings drifted away once more, making way for the moon and the stars twirling around in front of her blurred vision.

And when her climax arrived with an unexpected ferocity, interrupting the dance of stars with a powerful thunder blinding her to everything but the exquisite pleasure electrifying her body until she was nothing more than a bundle of frayed nerves—she screamed as Salvador had promised she would, both from the delicious torture raking through her body, and from how much her heart ached for him.

Yara realised, as he convulsed beneath her hands with the same kind of intense pleasure, that her insecurities around who she was had robbed her of the potential for something amazing—Salvador, who had found a way past her defences and was showing her a glimpse of what life could have been like.

What a cruel joke that she should get one weekend to pretend her affection for him could be more than just a fleeting moment. It couldn't, not with their lives being in such different stages. Not after she'd hurt him so much by abandoning him. A lifetime would not be enough to make it up to him.

But Yara decided she would give in, even if it was just for one weekend. Two days were better than none, and if she couldn't have the rest of their lives, she'd settle for forty-eight hours.

Anything to be with him.

If Salvador had thought that this would be enough to reset things between them, he realised late into the night how sorely mistaken he was. They'd made their way towards the bedroom eventually, getting drunk on their passion for each other until exhaustion had demanded its tribute and they'd passed out in each other's arms. As if they'd been meant to sleep like that all their lives and they just hadn't known.

Those thoughts darted around in his brain as he watched her sleep. He knew he'd gone too far when he pulled her tight against his chest, her perfect form fitting flush against his as if they were made for each other. With his chin resting on top of her head, he breathed in her scent, relishing the smell that brought youthful memories back into his mind.

Long-forgotten need stirred further in his chest—the exact opposite of what he had wanted to achieve with this weekend away. Finally sleeping with each other should have closed the circle, but instead it had just extended into a completely different shape, leaving him with a quaking heart and worry pulling at the corners of his lips.

No matter how fierce the yearning in his chest grew, they could only ever have this weekend. It was what they had agreed on, and he wouldn't let some wayward emotions lead him astray. Not when he was so alien to her world.

Though his feelings for her were changing—coalescing into something so real and tangible—he didn't dare to look at them for fear that his acknowledgment would be the missing piece that would break his resolve.

Their relationship had always been volatile, and Salvador needed calm and focus. Keeping Felix safe while dealing with the ongoing issues of his family was his number-one priority that he couldn't get distracted from. And Yara… She had her own life to live, outside of Brazil.

He would cherish this time they had together, but after

that they'd have to go their separate ways again. If not…
Salvador didn't know what he would do for her if he was
brave enough to try—or foolish enough to let himself.

CHAPTER NINE

DESPITE HIS PLAN for a walk around the lake, they didn't make it out of the house that day. Both of them tried, each attempting to untangle their limbs from one another, only for the other to stop them with hunger in their eyes.

When Salvador had finally managed to tear himself away—from both the gloomy thoughts of the future and Yara's delectably soft and supple flesh—he made it as far as the en-suite shower before she found him, sinking back onto the floor and finishing the promise of pleasure he'd glimpsed in her when they first arrived at his place.

They ate their breakfast in comfortable silence, sitting close enough to each other that they could lean into the occasional caress. Nothing could disrupt their harmony—as long as they kept away from the fragility of their temporary arrangement.

'Still up to seeing Lagoa Bonita?' Salvador asked when they had finished, pouring coffee into two travel mugs.

'Of course,' she said with a laugh so bright and full of joy that his knees grew weak for a moment. He wanted to hear that laugh for the rest of his life.

Only that laugh was not meant for him to keep, but rather borrow for the small amount of time they had left together, and he needed to remember that.

Despite the ongoing turmoil in his stomach, he reached out his arm and relished the feel of her dark skin against his when she draped her hand around his arm and let him lead her outside.

His house was close to the small lake, something he'd intentionally kept an eye on when he'd shopped around for a property. Though Lagoa Bonita was steeped in the memory of Yara and their relationship that had ended too soon, he'd still been able to enjoy the lake by himself on the rare days that he'd managed to go there—long before his nephew became his ward and he'd had some time on his own.

'Do you miss having time to yourself here?' Yara asked, as if reading his thoughts.

He looked around, taking in the neighbourhood of colourful houses as they crossed the street until the grass turned to sand. 'Yes, I do—though I have no regrets about moving back to Brasília for the sake of my nephew. With Felipe being in and out of prison, along with the rest of his extended family, Felix needed stability more than I needed time to myself. Or a relationship, for that matter.'

The word *relationship* hung between them, highlighting the fragility of their arrangement and how much it pained him to think about it.

If Yara had noticed his hesitation around the word, she didn't let on as she said, 'I would have never thought that man trouble would be something we'd have in common.'

Her hand slipped down his arms until their palms lay against each other. She threaded her fingers through his, folding them over and gently tugging at his hand as they continued their walk.

'I think I'm considered a bit of a late bloomer.' Like a lot of people in his community, Salvador had struggled at first, trying on a lot of different labels before he found the one that expressed himself the best. Most of his youthful exploration had been so tied up with Yara and their developing relationship that he had never considered who or what else he might like until she was gone. Though her leaving was wrapped up in a lot of pain and regret, it had opened up a whole new world for him. One where he had found his tribe.

'How come?' she asked, genuine curiosity in her eyes. How was he supposed to explain that to her without sounding like a lovesick man who had sworn off women because of the one who'd got away?

That wasn't true, but Salvador would have to drag up a lot of exes to prove this point.

'I wasn't really interested in dating anyone after...' His voice trailed off. He'd started the sentence without thinking of how to finish it.

'After I left,' she finished for him, letting him off the hook with a small smile.

Despite their long conversation about moving on from what had happened, he still struggled to see completely past it when it had been such a painful time in his life.

'My father got into some more legal trouble when I was at med school, splitting my focus between studying and worrying about what madness Mum and Dad had got themselves into. So I didn't really get to think about my attraction to anyone until my first year as a trainee doctor in a hospital. And you know how much time we had to think about dating.'

Yara laughed, a sound like music drifting through the air. 'I was already married by then, but I slept in enough on-call rooms to know *everything*.'

'I saw male colleagues in secret first, unsure if I was straight, gay or just in the mood for something different. At that time my brother was the only person I had in my life with my parents in and out of prison, and he wasn't really the person to support his older brother through his sexual awakening.'

He paused, unsure if he had shared too much with her, if she even wanted to hear so much of his past that wouldn't have happened with her in the picture. But a curious spark lit up her eyes as she parted her lips and said, 'Did someone help you in the end?'

Salvador nodded, recalling his own struggles. 'I was always okay with the idea of being bisexual, but I became a lot more outspoken about it when Felix was born. I wanted him to have an uncle that was unashamed of who he was and whom he loved.'

'What about Felix's mother? You haven't really mentioned her.' Her tone was gentle, as if she wasn't sure if she wanted to ask the question.

Salvador shook his head. 'She's not around any more. Felipe says they knew someone was investigating them, so she took off. No one knows where she is, and she hasn't tried coming back for her son.'

'That's so sad for him...' she said with a frown.

He only nodded, and they remained quiet as they walked through the warm sand, the morning sun already bright in the light blue sky. They were in for a lovely day, Salvador thought, and that wasn't just because of the weather. He paused when Yara gasped. They had come over a sand dune and were now looking down at Lagoa Bonita. The water was of a deep blue in the middle and grew lighter the further out it went, the shallow edges of the lake mixing with the surrounding sand, shifting the hue of the water to a light green.

A few towels were spread around the sands, with different sized groups of people clustering around each other, enjoying the final warm days before the approaching winter would bring a chilly wind to the lake. Salvador actually preferred the chill to the sunny days, simply because when there was no one around this place felt like his own private oasis, where he could withdraw and think.

Not that he got to do much of that since he'd received custody of Felix.

He held on to Yara's hand as they sauntered down the dune, placing the large picnic blanket they'd taken with them near the shore so they could look at the water while they sat. Salvador let out a deep sigh of contentment when she sat down next to him, snuggling closer and laying her head on his shoulder as his arm came around her side to draw her in closer. This—sitting with her in this moment and enjoying the morning sun over Lagoa Bonita—had no business of feeling so right, so…meant to be, when he knew this was no more than an illusion, just waiting for the tiniest interruption to cause the glass to shatter.

But even now he knew all of this, he couldn't help but enjoy the moment as if it could last for ever. For the first time in years, Salvador saw the world around him with clarity, as if he had needed her to lift whatever fog his family's trouble had enveloped him in. In one short week, she had become the missing piece, slotting into his life as if he'd just been waiting for her.

How was that even possible? Why now, when he was so wholly unavailable?

'What's on your mind?' Yara's question drew his attention away from his contemplations. His hand grazed up and down her arm, leaving tiny goose pimples in their wake.

'I…' He hesitated, looking for the right words to deflect that question. There was no way he could tell her about those thoughts. They had both agreed that this was nothing more than a weekend to 'get it out of their system'.

'How is Bianca doing?' He steered the conversation in this direction because that was what he wanted—to talk less about him and more about her.

The tension in her shoulders each time she mentioned her family was visible to anyone who knew how to read her, and apparently Salvador still very much knew how.

'She's Bianca, doing Bianca things... Though she's been looking after our mother ever since Dad passed away. After they sold the house, Mum moved into a gated community, and Bianca got a place near by so she could help her.' Yara stopped for a moment, smiling up at him. 'She's still working as a primary-school teacher, and also still trying to make it as an artist.'

This time Yara laughed, rocking into his body in a way that set his skin on fire again. After the rather sleepless night they'd had, he thought he might have been completely spent in the morning, but the river of desire for this woman was nowhere near stemmed, flowing through his body with each beat of his heart. If they weren't in such a public place, he might have climbed on top of her right at this moment.

'I'm glad she's always been happy with life in Brasília. It gave me the opportunity to leave and pursue what I was passionate about—to an extent, at least. My parents both had some rather strong ideas about what I should do with my medical degree.'

Salvador rested his hand on her stomach, drawing lazy circles with his fingertips. He remembered her parents having a firm grip on Yara and the decisions she made in life. When he'd met Mr and Mrs Lopes in their home so many years ago when he and Yara were just friends, he'd sensed their disapproving looks. They hadn't wanted their daughter to be associating with a 'street rat'.

It sounded as though her match with Lawrence Silvia had come from them, and that they had exerted quite a bit of influence over their daughter to get her to agree.

He was fairly new to the parenting game, but even so he could hardly imagine telling Felix who he should and shouldn't be with based on what *looked good* for the family name.

'So they wanted you to become a travelling diagnostician, or was that your idea?'

Yara stopped to think for a while. Not because his question deserved due deliberation, but rather because she had asked herself that question and come up short. She knew *she* had wanted to become a doctor, a plan her parents had been in full support of, and her interest in diagnostics had developed during med school when they were learning the different steps that led to a definitive diagnosis. The pieces fitted together like a puzzle, each new piece of information either confirming or ruling out a possible disease to the point where all answers had been assigned. Yara, who had perfect recall of every single thing she'd ever read in any textbook, excelled at solving those puzzles like no one else.

'I wanted to go into diagnostics, especially with how obscure the field still is. There is no formal training for it, and any physician who has a well-rounded background and is good at solving problems can become a diagnostician. My fellow practitioners and I are kind of self-styled in that sense.' She paused to chuckle, leaning into the warmth coming from Salvador's body. His hand on her stomach caused butterflies to stir inside it, making her shiver with every other circle he drew on her skin.

'I focused on general medicine, hoping to eventually find a way to focus on the diagnostic work of a hospital,' she continued, retelling a sequence of events only a few people around her knew. 'By the time I was done with my trainee years in practice, I was already married. My parents had arranged this blind date with the son of a business partner of theirs. He was a bio-medical engineer working for an up-and-coming start-up in the United States. We met a couple of times, with each subsequent date gaining more enthusiasm from both of our parents, and so…we ended up getting married after a short period of dating.'

So much of her self-worth as a woman had been tied up in her failing marriage that it had taken her years to realise how she had trapped herself in this loveless arrangement, and even longer to see how her parents had pushed her in this direction. Their approval had meant so much to her that she'd confused the infatuation with Lawrence for love and accepted his proposal, believing that her parents had her best interests in mind—not theirs, as it had turned out.

'I worked as a consultant for his company for a while, advising them on their market strategy for medical devices, which kept me in boardrooms and offices rather than in practices and hospitals. When they sold that company, Lawrence found a new position, but they already had their consulting staff on board, so I was left without a position.'

'He just left you out to dry when he found a new job?' His low voice was barely more than an incensed growl seeping through her pores and causing a shiver to trickle down her spine. The way he felt protective on her behalf, as if what she had been through was as outrageous as she perceived it from the inside, squeezed her heart so tightly she was sure it was going to burst. How could she have ever let anyone convince her that this man was not worthy of her? This decision would go down as one of the worst she'd ever made in her life.

'Turns out that kind of selfishness helped me establish my own career. I was able to use the connections I made during that time to get a few consulting gigs at actual hospitals, and when the opportunity to travel to different places to see patients came up, I jumped at it. Lawrence and I, we...' Her voice trailed off, and she noticed that Salvador's hand had stopped dead on her stomach as well. She sensed the ripple of tension going through his muscles, as if he was readying himself to come to her defence once more.

This was the painful part of her past, the details no one got to hear—not Bianca, not their mother, no one. Because even though she'd seen Lawrence for who he was ages ago—a self-centred opportunist more interested in her parents' money than being a real husband—she had stayed, because she was too ashamed to admit that she had made a mistake. That she had made many mistakes because she had a blind belief in the people who had raised her, not seeing that they were far more concerned with their family legacy and what people from the outside would see when they peered at it.

It was the reason why they had opposed her girlhood relationship with Salvador—there was no way of softening his family history and the trouble they had been through. It didn't matter to them that he was nothing like that. All they had cared about were the optics—just the same with her marriage. Her feelings for him had been irrelevant from the very start.

'We weren't happy for very long. I got married to him because I thought that was what my parents expected from me, and he proposed because he saw me as some sort of golden goose who would bring my parents' money with me into his start-up.' Admitting to her own blindness like that stung all over, and Yara squeezed her eyes shut to will the mounting humiliation away. 'I was so stupid to put so much trust into my parents, believing they were looking out for me.'

The tension she sensed building next to her snapped, and a moment later his other arm snaked around her, crushing her into his chest in an intimate hug. The surrounding noise faded away until it was just the two of them sitting on that plaid blanket in their own personal oasis of stillness and quiet.

His hands found her face, pulling it upward and towards him so he could plant a gentle kiss on her mouth, that tacit touch conveying so much more than words ever could.

'You're not dumb, unless you think I was dumb for thinking my parents would eventually change and see the error of their ways,' Salvador said when their lips finally came apart, peering deep into her eyes.

'What? No, of course not. How could you not believe that things would get better?'

'See? Of course, you would believe the best of the people who are meant to love you.' His words were gentle, caressing her in a deep part of her battered soul that yearned for just a bit of acknowledgement and care—things Salvador had been giving her over the last few days with such generosity and abundance that a part of her was afraid to leave. What would happen if she reached out and grabbed him tight enough so he couldn't slip away from her and do to her what she had done to him? The thought wormed itself into her brain, nestling into her until Salvador became all she could think about. But she

knew she would be selfish to try. Yara had been the one
to insist that whatever happened this weekend would only
be for the duration of those two days. She had a life to get
back to, and he had his nephew to take care of.

But weren't those things that they could do together?
There was only one way to find out, and even though she
now knew they were not only compatible as friends but
also as lovers, her heart quaked at the thought of rejection, fearing the damage it would do to her already broken
self. After all, it was her, once again, changing the rules
and deciding that their relationship needed to change.

'Thank you, Salvador,' she whispered, her face nestled
into the crook of his neck so he couldn't see the pain in
her expression. 'I've carried this weight with me for a
long time, not knowing how to deal with it.'

His throaty chuckle drifted down to her ears. 'The
Yara I know would seek to blame herself before seeking
it in others. You're too kind to think anyone might have
impure motives, and even though you might get hurt
some more, I hope you won't let anyone change that about
you. It's a good thing to have as a person.'

His right hand rubbed up and down her back while the
left one came up to her face. Nimble fingers traced the
line of her jaw until they reached her chin, lifting it up
once more to meet his eyes. The dark intensity she had
got to know over the last few days was gone, replaced by
a warmth and deep affection that took all the air out of
her lungs, forcing her to swallow the gasp growing in her
throat. It was how he had used to look at her as a teenager. The lines around his mouth and eyes were new, so
was the occasional grey streaking over his temples, but
the glow was the same—and in that moment Yara fell
over that cliff for him, diving into the depth of feelings
she hadn't dared to thirty years ago.

Maybe there was a chance for them, if she was brave enough to reach out and grab it.

'Salvador…' The words caught in her throat, and loud laughter interrupted her thoughts as a group of people walked by them, each person seemingly talking over the others.

Maybe he'd sensed what she was about to confess, or maybe Yara was reading too much into the situation, wanting to ascribe meaning to something that was no more than a whim. But before she could find the courage to pick up her thoughts again, Salvador shifted underneath her and brought some space between them.

'Let's have a walk around the lake. If you remember this angle well, just wait until you see the other side,' he said as he got to his feet.

Despite the daze her thoughts were in, Yara snorted. 'The other side? Salvador, I can see it from here. Lagoa Bonita is a tiny little bead of water. I can use my imagination to see the other angle.'

Salvador pulled her up from the blanket and hauled her into his arms, wrapping his arms around her for a heartbeat, each one enjoying the closeness of the other— and the knowledge passing through them that they had to enjoy it while it lasted.

They spent the way back to Brasília in comfortable silence, neither of them feeling the urge to fill the space between them with unnecessary words. Despite their time together having been brief, Yara was buzzing with energy and feeling alive for the first time in many years. It was as if she'd been living her life in a daze, just wandering from one escape to the next, always on the lookout for that missing piece she sensed in her soul without ever understanding what it was.

Until this weekend, when she finally understood that it was Salvador.

A thought that brought a nervous flutter to her stomach. She had sunk way too deep into their old relationship again, to the point where she didn't know how she was going to extract herself from it. They had made a deal when he invited her away for this weekend—no strings attached.

Now she had gone and changed the rules. Or at the very least, she had changed her mind. Despite the obstacles and warnings she had put between her and him, Yara had fallen in love with Salvador. Though their teenage romance ended too soon, she now had the opportunity to fix it. There was no more parental influence, no one to stand in the way of what she wanted except for her.

'You went to see Bianca. Did you see your mother as well?' Salvador asked, hitting eerily close to the thoughts she had been chasing around in her mind.

'Ah…no. Though I will probably see her next weekend. Bianca is throwing a party for our cousin's engagement, and, as the Lopes matriarch, my mother needs to be there to be seen.' Magda Lopes was just over eighty at this point, but she still made it to every single social event involving her family.

Salvador tilted his head at her. 'You think it'll take you another week to diagnose Mr Orlay?'

'No, I believe the diagnosis will be finalised at the start of the week. There are three potential diseases, so now it's a matter of going over all the symptoms again and ruling them out until the last one remains.'

'But you'll stay until the weekend?' There was something about his tone that sent a spark flying across her skin, settling in the pit of her stomach.

Was it hope softening his voice? A longing for her

to stay longer? Or was that her lonely mind clinging to something that wasn't actually there just because she had realised the extent of her feelings for Salvador?

'Yes, Bianca twisted my arm. Said she would haunt me wherever I went next if I don't spend some time with her before I leave. Plus, I haven't really had time to dig into my emails and see what cases have come my way, so I don't know where I'll be going next.'

A part of her had avoided looking for her next job, though she wasn't sure why. She was far into Mr Orlay's diagnosis, confident that when she saw him tomorrow she would be able to rule out two of the three potential diseases and confirm the diagnosis. Then she would have the rest of the week to make some calls and arrangements for her next trip—a part she usually looked forward to when finishing a case. Only this time the thought came with a bitter aftertaste. It meant leaving. Again. When they had just reconnected on such a deep level.

'I thought maybe you were avoiding Magda because of your divorce and I…' He stopped himself from continuing his sentence, earning him an inquisitive look from Yara.

He pulled the car to the side of the road, and she realised that they had arrived back in Brasília. To her right, the high-rise building her hotel was in grew into the sky, its glass front glistening in the setting sun.

'You what?' She tilted her head, looking at him, eyes fixed on his face as he kept staring straight ahead.

'I was going to offer you my support if you did want to speak to her. Not that having me with you would make any conversation with her easier, but maybe it would help you.'

Yara's lips fell open as she looked at Salvador and processed his words. Was there a faint flush covering his cheeks or was the dimming light of the sunset playing tricks on her eyes? Either way, the gesture was just as kind and thoughtful as he had shown himself to be over the last week—and beyond that during their time together as teens.

She was not ready to let him go.

'I have somewhat of an indecent proposal for you, Dr Martins,' she said after a moment of consideration. The weekend couldn't end here, not when she had so much more to tell him.

He turned his head to face her, his eyebrows arching up. 'And what would that be?' His voice dropped low when he said those words, leaving no doubt in her mind that he knew exactly what kind of proposal she was thinking of. One fuelled by passionate nights tangled in each other's arms.

'I'm staying here until the end of the week. So…if you had a mind to extending our one-weekend-only arrangement for the week…' She left the rest of the sentence unsaid and watched as Salvador's jaw tightened, his eyes dipping below her face and gliding over her body.

Then he opened the car door abruptly, getting out and circling around the car to open her door for her. Yara took his outstretched hand to get out herself, and a moment later Salvador's body was covering hers as he pressed her against the side of the car, the cool metal on her back a stark contrast to the heat seeping into her body at the places where he met her skin.

His eyes narrowed on her, hunger shining in them as he bent down to kiss her on the lips.

'I have to stay at my place tonight, but I'll see you tomorrow at the hospital,' he said, his voice barely concealing his need for her after no more than a brief kiss. 'And we can take it from there.'

He let go of her, standing up straight and reaching for the back door to retrieve her bag from the seat.

'Do you want to go to the party with me?' she asked on a whim, thinking about the offer he'd made when it came to speaking to her mother.

Facing the Lopes matriarch with the news of her divorce gave her more anxiety than she wanted to admit. What other forty-seven-year-old woman was fretful about seeing her own mother? Having Salvador beside her would set quite a few tongues wagging, but Yara found that after this weekend she didn't care any more. Salvador, who had every right to still be furious with her, had accepted her back in his life with a gentleness that was far beyond her expectations. While he needed time to get to know her again, he'd been open to her words and reasoning. Not like her parents, who had only ever judged her by their own standards rather than seeing her as herself. But Salvador had acknowledged her as her own person, even at her very worst, and even though she had hurt him so much he was standing in front of her now, offering his support when it came to facing her mother again.

If he could accept her the way she was, why was it such a monumental request for her mother? Shouldn't she be the one to stand by her daughter, no matter what?

Salvador may have touched on the feelings she kept locked away for many years, but in doing so he did more than just spark a flame inside her heart. He showed her how much time and effort she wasted trying to live up to unattainable standards.

Yara was done living her life the way other people thought appropriate.

Salvador paused, and she wondered what was going through his head. He'd be walking into the den of the people who had rejected him just because of who his parents were. Then he leaned in again, brushing a soft kiss against her temple. 'As long as I don't have to look at anyone's rashes or ingrown toenails.'

'What kind of parties does your extended family throw that this is something you're worried about?' Yara laughed.

'One where they make sure to take advantage of their physician cousin,' he replied with a wry smile that turned into a genuine one when she put a hand on his cheek.

'Thank you, Salvador. For this weekend, and for coming with me to wrangle my family.'

'I'll see you tomorrow at work, *fofinha*.' He kissed her again, a lot more softly and deliberately this time, as if she was precious cargo that couldn't withstand too much force. Then he waved at her with a knowing grin, circling the car again to his seat and driving off.

Yara touched her lips where the ghost of his kiss still lingered, her knees weak from the impact this man had on her.

One week. That was the length of time she had to find the courage to tell him how she felt about him again— or to decide to walk out of his life again, with no turning back.

Yara had one week to decide whether to risk it all for Salvador, or to leave again without ever fulfilling the promise of their blooming relationship.

CHAPTER TEN

'MR ORLAY HAS Guillain-Barré Syndrome.' The room went quiet as Yara announced Henrique Orlay's diagnosis with a finality that only a diagnostician of her calibre could voice. Guillain-Barré was an exceedingly rare autoimmune disease that affected so few people each year. Salvador himself had only heard about it when they had spoken about the results of the tests during a short coffee break.

Now she had the entire team of doctors working on the case assembled in a conference room to discuss the diagnosis and the next steps for the patient.

Chief Sakamoto was the first to speak. 'Guillain-Barré Syndrome... I don't think we've ever seen this disease in the hospital during my time as the Chief of Medicine,' he said, and the surrounding room rumbled in agreement. 'How did you get to the final diagnosis?'

Salvador let his gaze wander around the room, looking at the assembled doctors and nurses to see slight scepticism in some of their faces while others showed relief at finally having an answer to what ailed the patient all of them had worked so closely with.

'Mostly through the process of elimination,' Yara said with a generous smile that hit him right in the gut, sending showers of warmth flying through his body.

The warm sensation mingled with the dread her impending departure caused to stir in him. Against his better judgement and all his rational thought warning him against letting them get too close, he'd grown attached to her over the last ten days in ways he had never anticipated—or he would have never participated in a weekend of carnal desire away from the rest of society.

Now that he put it in a different light, he couldn't believe that he had for even a second thought this was a good idea. Some other part of his body had taken over the thinking duties when that decision had been made.

'We first believed his symptoms—bilateral arm weakness—to be a result of his valve replacement. A connection anyone would have made, though the typical side-effect is usually isolated in the left arm.' She paused, looking around the room as some people murmured again. 'There were no tumours on Mr Orlay's scans, nothing to show any disruption where information from the brain might not be reaching the rest of his body.'

This time, her sparkling brown eyes met his as she gave him a short nod with just the hint of a smile. Enough for Salvador's stomach to drop at how much he *wanted* her—not just in his bed, but also in his professional life, diagnosing patients in his hospital. Their connection had transcended something as simple as sex, showing them how well they worked together—both when it came to diagnosing patients and in emergency situations.

Salvador didn't know what to make of the myriad conflicting emotions blossoming in his chest, making it hard to see and think. They had an agreement, after all, and he was not free to give more—not with how many problems he brought with his family.

Felix needed stability and continuity in his life to break out of the criminal cycle his father had modelled for him. It was up to Salvador to provide that environment, and it was always going to be at a cost. Though when he thought of the sacrifices he made for his family, he thought of both time and money.

Now Salvador had to make another, but he was unprepared for how much this one already stung. He wasn't sure if they even needed to have a conversation, was hoping deep down inside that he could avoid it. If he stood face to face with Yara and spoke about the kernel of love growing in his chest, he wasn't sure if he'd be able to walk away.

But she wasn't rooted to one place while he was—an obstacle that could only be overcome with another sacrifice. One he couldn't make. And he could never ask her to give up anything either.

How could he ask her to come into his world, knowing he would never fit into hers?

'So, with Dr Martins' help, we performed a nerve-conduction velocity test so we could map out exactly where the signal was getting lost.' He perked up when he heard his name from her lips, looking over at her with a veiled expression. The look of pure and light affection that she gave him hitched his pulse up a few paces. How was he supposed to find the strength in him to go back to his life as if she'd never returned?

Yara pointed at the TV in the conference room, now showing the test results of the NCV they had performed. 'The F waves on the first test were in the abnormal range. We ran the test again today and the F waves are absent.'

One of the doctors raised her hand. 'Is a NCV test how you distinguished this from something like transverse myelitis? Because in the previous scans, there seemed to be an inflammation in the spinal cord.'

'Yes, that's right. One of the first things we did is perform a spinal tap to get a look at the spinal fluid, and from that alone Guillain-Barré can be misinterpreted as transverse myelitis or polio.' She paused to nod at the doctor, thanking her for her question. 'Polio, of course, hasn't been seen in Brazil since the eighties, and, since the patient doesn't travel, this was an easy one to rule out.'

The room gave their congenial acknowledgment and Salvador nodded his encouragement with a gentle smile tugging on the corner of his lips.

'With the nerve-conduction velocity test and the spinal tap pointing towards an autoimmune disease, the final days have been a matter of observing the patient to see if the weakness in his arms and legs remained consistent on both sides.' She paused, looking around the silent room. 'And that is how we ended up with Guillain-Barré Syndrome.'

The room broke out in hushed whispers as the involved physicians discussed the diagnosis, and the general sentiment among them was quite clear—they were impressed. Hell, Salvador was probably more impressed than any of them for reasons that went much further than he could explain to any of them.

Not only was she the *hottest* woman he'd ever known, but she was also generous, kind and so incredibly smart that she kept the staff of an entire hospital on their toes as she figured out what ailed their patient when none of them could. And she remained humble while doing so, taking the time to gather the entire team to share her thought process and to give them some closure as they wrapped up the case.

Yara was in a league of her own, and for a painful moment the old wound she'd inflicted on him popped back open, leaving him stunned. Of course, she had run away from him so many years ago. She was a once-in-a-life-time genius, meant for such tremendous greatness that Salvador couldn't even comprehend where it might take her. There was no way she was ever going to waste her time with him, who'd had to raise himself because his parents were either in jail or off losing what little money they had on the next big scheme.

How could he ever be enough to such a woman when his life was so complicated and hard? How could he even *ask*?

'As for the next steps…' This was the part Yara hated. She'd spent a lot of time unravelling the diagnosis just for her to end it on a sad note. 'You all know there are no known cures for autoimmune diseases at this point in time. What we can do is medicate for the current symptoms and adjust the treatment plan as his disease progresses, and as new medications are approved. It's not all bad news, though. Mr Orlay may have to learn to live with this as best he can, but at least we were able to tell him what's wrong. In my experience that counts for a lot.'

The room stayed silent this time, and Yara knew that sentiment well. They were all highly competitive individuals and none of them liked to think they lost against an unbeatable foe—even though that was a reality she faced more than others with the work she had chosen.

Chief Sakamoto stood up from his chair. 'And that brings Dr Silvia's time here to an end. We appreciate your expertise and all you were able to teach us. Dr Xander will take over further treatments of Mr Orlay, so if you have any questions, please go and talk to him. Thank you for your time, everyone.'

The gathered physicians shuffled to their feet, threads of different conversations reaching her ears as she searched the faces for the familiar one she'd seen just a few moments ago. Her eyes lit up with instantaneous affection when she spotted him. With his shoulder leaning against the wall and his corded arms crossed in front of his chest, Salvador looked like a delicious piece of masculinity, and she had to fight the urge to walk over there and throw her arms around him in some kind of primal territorial move.

Because he wasn't *hers*. Not really. Not until she found the courage in her to tell him that she wanted to be with him. *If* he wanted to be with her...

The additional week she'd given herself had gone by much quicker than she had anticipated, with only three more nights left. Salvador had come to her hotel room every night, always leaving after a couple of hours to get back to his home and to Felix.

Tomorrow was her cousin Flávia's engagement party, and the last night they had together. She had extended an invitation to Felix as well. There'd be lots of children his age to hang out with, so he wouldn't feel lonely among a bunch of adults. But Salvador had declined the invitation, not specifying why he didn't want to bring his nephew along—and it was that small part that had bothered Yara ever since.

Did he not want her to meet his nephew? Was that why he wasn't bringing him? The rational side of her brain could come up with a handful of other reasons why he wouldn't want to bring Felix along, but the emotional side, the one reacting to Salvador so fiercely, went into a blind panic at that specific thought. Because that meant he kept his heart out of their entire affair—unlike her, who had fallen again so hard that she didn't know what her life was supposed to look like without him.

Her heart dropped into her stomach when he shifted

his gaze onto her, sending her one of his rare smiles as he pushed himself off the wall and made to come over, only to be interrupted by Chief Sakamoto.

'Dr Silvia, if you have a moment, I'd like to discuss something in my office.'

She hesitated a moment, her eyes still on Salvador, who in turn looked at the chief and finally shrugged.

'Of course, lead the way,' she said, and followed the man down the corridor and into an office that was a lot smaller and down-to-earth than she'd expected. It was smaller than any other senior-staff office she'd seen during her travels, which spoke volumes about Dr Sakamoto's priorities for his hospital.

'Great work on Mr Orlay. We were fortunate that you came in when you did. While we do have resources, Centro Médico Juliana Amala is still growing, and our neurology department is only beginning to form.' He pointed at the seat across his desk, and Yara sat down, accepting his praise.

This was another part of her assignments she didn't like—the debrief with the Chief of Medicine. One of two things was about to happen. He would feel the need to justify *why* his doctors weren't able to diagnose the patient. Something Yara really didn't care about. She didn't consult on those cases to be right. She did it because she had a gift, and she needed to use it to help people. But her intervention sometimes left teams feeling inferior, as if somehow they should have been able to do it on their own.

If that wasn't the reason Chief Sakamoto had asked her into the office, then he was about to make her an offer to be a permanent member of staff. An offer Yara always immediately batted away, no matter how much money or prestige or influence they offered her.

Because once upon a time she'd needed the freedom her career offered her. The less time she spent at home, the better—though that behaviour had led to her avoiding taking responsibility for her unhappiness in her relationship. Though Salvador was different, he was sweet and freeing, never forgetting what *she* wanted. Would staying in one place be such a bad thing when he was who she was staying for?

'Now, I'm sure you get this everywhere you go, but I have to ask just on the off-chance that you might say yes. I think your talent and methods are incredible, Dr Silvia. What would it take to convince you to join my hospital?' Dr Sakamoto paused, his gaze fixed on her, and Yara hoped he couldn't see her pulse flutter at the base of her throat. 'With you at the helm we could become Brazil's number-one diagnostic centre, where people come with the most difficult cases.'

Yara leaned back in her chair, the usual immediate rejection clinging to her lips, not quite ready to pass the threshold.

The chief seemed to sense her hesitation as well, pouncing on the opportunity he saw open up in front of him. 'Name whatever you want, and we'll make it happen. I want to make this a good deal for you because you coming to work in my hospital will increase our influence across the country.'

There was nothing Chief Sakamoto could dangle in front of her—at least nothing that was his to give.

She wanted Salvador.

'Thank you for the offer, Dr Sakamoto. Let me think about this.'

When she walked back past the conference room, no one was in there any more. Yara frowned at the disappointment pooling in her stomach.

It wasn't as if she had anything to discuss with him—other than her life-altering feelings for him. That wasn't something she planned on discussing here. She needed some privacy for that—as well as courage to push through with actually speaking the words pounding against the walls of her chest.

I love you.

What was so hard about that?

CHAPTER ELEVEN

'*Minha irmã*...you need to sit down and have a drink,' Bianca said, placing a firm hand on her sister's arm and pulling her down onto one of the chairs placed on the pavement.

The council had agreed to close several local streets for the afternoon in return for a small donation and if the entire neighbourhood was allowed to attend—an offer her cousin Flávia happily accepted. As someone who enjoyed being the centre of attention, she couldn't have enough people at her engagement party.

There were many groups of people clustering together, and each time whispers went through them Yara craned her neck to see if Salvador's arrival was setting any tongues wagging.

She wished for a moment that they had established some ground rules for this party—even though they had a terrible track record of following those. Were they supposed to keep their distance? Or live as they did when it was just the two of them? It wasn't as if either of them had acted in a particularly secretive way around people. At work they kept their distance simply because that was the professional thing to do.

'What are you so worried about?' Bianca offered her a glass of caipirinha, which she took without registering, taking a small sip. The crushed lime perked up her senses as it slid down her throat, making her cough at the sudden acidity.

'I wasn't really planning on a great reunion between Salvador and Mum. Now that I'm putting these words out there, I actually think this is a truly terrible idea, and I don't know what came over me.'

Bianca frowned at her. 'It's been thirty years... I'm sure everyone has moved on from things.'

'Do we have the same mother?' The words came out with more bite than Yara anticipated, and she regretted her tone the second she heard her words.

How differently their parents had treated the sisters had been a topic of long discussions between tears and spilled wine. Because Bianca had come as a surprise to her parents almost ten years after their first daughter was born, she hadn't felt the weight of the Lopes legacy on her shoulders and had received a lot more leeway from their parents when it came to both her career and the fact that she chose to love herself first and foremost.

Yara was glad her sister was spared the scrutiny of both their parents, being able to develop her life in the way she wanted to.

'I'm sorry... I'm just nervous. You know she doesn't know about the...divorce.' The word still felt weird on her lips. From the very crib, Yara had been raised as an overachiever. Divorce sounded so much like giving up, even though she couldn't be happier to finally be free of that loveless relationship.

Now she only needed to somehow broach the topic with her mother.

'It's so silly how much this is making me sweat. I'm forty-seven! An accomplished doctor, well respected in her field.'

'Oh, are we bragging about our titles now?' Both Yara and Bianca whipped their heads around when that deep voice cut through the crowd. The low bass seeped through Yara's pores, nestling itself into the area behind her navel, where it promptly lit a roaring fire to pump heat through her entire body.

'Salvador, you made it.' Yara jumped to her feet, taking the three steps that separated him from where the sisters were sitting. 'I was looking around for you.'

'Rosalinda and her son saw me, so I stopped to catch up with them. Do you remember her house?' He looked around, pointing at a building a couple of streets down with a sky-blue fence around the garden.

Yara laughed when she followed his pointing finger. 'Didn't she have mango trees in her garden?'

'Yep, and she knew exactly who was responsible for her missing fruit. She just demanded ten real from me.'

'Ten? Her mangoes were nice, but that is daylight robbery. You didn't give it to her, did you?'

Salvador shrugged, a smile playing on his lips. 'I had to. She had her cane with her, and I'm still scared of her.'

Yara laughed, picturing him being chased by old Rosalinda and her cane. Though Salvador had been from a completely different background to her, her neighbours and relatives had soon come to know the boy hanging out at the Lopes' house. Some had been warm and welcoming like Rosalinda, who had never cared where he came from, only how he treated Yara. Others, though, had leaned more in the direction of her own mother, condemning his character before they could get to know him just because of his parents.

The whispers they heard today were much quieter from the latter people.

Nevertheless, a smile stayed on her lips as she looked

at him, affection running so deep in her veins that she wanted to throw her arms around him. But was that the kind of relationship they were having in public? They hadn't even mentioned it when she invited him to the engagement party. His role was supposed to be around emotional support as Yara faced her mother for the first time in many years. Would he want to do that from the back row, or right by her side while holding her hand?

Holding hands in public didn't seem very no-strings-attached, but then again, nothing about their affair so far spelled anything remotely casual.

The air around them grew tense. Yara's smile froze in place as she kept staring at him, unsure how to react or how she should move on from the conversation. How was she supposed to act around him? That question sent her brain into a tailspin, unable to decide.

That was when Salvador stepped forward, dragging his knuckles over her cheek in an affectionate gesture, and lowered his lips to hers, brushing over them in the hint of a kiss before he straightened up again. His gaze was fixed on someone behind her, and when Yara whirled around to look at her sister he slid his hand into hers, their fingers intertwined.

Her heart leapt into her mouth when their skin touched. Her mind was falling from one spiral to the next, now solely focused on where his hand was touching hers and what that meant for them. Was this a grand declaration in front of her old friends and neighbours? Or was this just part of that *thing* they had agreed on—and it didn't mean as much as she would like it to mean?

Or…was it possible that he felt the same way? Today was the day of her deadline. Either she told him, or she would for ever lose the chance at a future with Salvador.

'Bianca, good to see you again.' Salvador stepped towards the chair where her sister sat.

'Likewise. I'm surprised how many people still know your face around here when you lived on the other side of town.'

Salvador barked a gruff laugh. 'We spent a lot of time roaming outside to avoid the glares and verbal jabs from your parents. They were bound to notice that strange boy hanging around the Lopes offspring.'

'Oh, I remember other things…' Bianca wiggled her eyebrows up and down, giving Yara the signal that she'd spent enough time around her sister with the man she was hopelessly in love with. If she stayed here any longer, those caipirinhas might make her reveal more than was appropriate.

'Do you want to do the rounds and say hi to people? Flávia is somewhere over there, getting counsel from the neighbourhood elders on how to create a successful marriage.' She waved her hand to the other end of street, where a large crowd had gathered around some tables that had been brought outside from various houses.

'That sounds like interesting advice.'

'It does?' Yara raised a sceptical eyebrow at him.

Salvador pulled her a few steps forward, nodding at people as they recognised them. 'You don't want to learn how people built their lasting marriages?'

A cynical snort left her nose, the bitterness she felt still so raw that its intensity surprised her. 'The way to have a lasting marriage is not getting married in the first place. I learned my lesson with that.'

They stopped on the pavement, Salvador's gaze gliding over the people surrounding them before he looked at her. The friendly spark she'd seen in his eyes as he had approached her was gone, replaced by a thick veil that wouldn't let her read what lay beyond it. His expression became closed off.

'You don't want to get married again?' His voice sounded strangely distant and in an instant Yara saw all her plans slip through her fingers. Was that what he wanted from her? Marriage? When he knew how broken the last one had left her?

To give someone that kind of sway and control over her again would take so much out of her. She wasn't sure she was free to give this piece of her to anyone any more. Not even to Salvador, the man who had bypassed all the barriers she'd put up around her heart, as if he'd always been in there, just waiting for her to be ready.

But a second marriage? The concept struck unprecedented fear in her heart, making her recoil from the thought of ever signing a marriage certificate again.

'I've been through this before, and it didn't work out. When I needed to get out for my own sanity, it made things so much harder to unravel when I just needed to be gone.' Lawrence had not made things easy on her, holding her to promises she had made out of obligation to her family, thinking that her infatuation for this man was true love.

'What about—?'

'*Minha filha*—it's really you!'

The blood froze in her veins when the voice of her mother drifted towards her, rendering her immobile and unable to act for a few seconds. Salvador's arm came around her hip as he sensed her tense up, enveloping her with his warmth to lend her whatever strength she needed.

'*Mãe... Oi...*' she said as she turned around to face the encounter she'd been dreading the moment she set foot in Brasília.

'*Filhota*, I'm so glad to see you...' Magda Lopes' voice trailed off as she stepped closer, her milky eyes scanning the man whose arm was draped around her daughter's waist, holding her close to his body. 'That's not—'

'Mama, I'm sure you remember Salvador? He used to hang out at our house a lot when we were at school together.' Yara had to admit that although she was a meticulous planner, she had not at all thought about what would happen if her mother saw her snuggled in Salvador's arms.

The perplexed look on her mother's face gave her a strange sense of vindication that she didn't want to examine too closely.

'Of course. How could I forget?' Her note was teetering between friendly and disapproving, these two polarities tightly wrapped into a pinched smile that lacked any warmth. 'I guess, then, I shouldn't ask about your husband. I mean, you've already shown all the neighbours—'

'Ex-husband, Mãe. After many years of not even living on the same continent any more, I thought it was time to finally rectify the mistake I made when I agreed to marry him. A mistake that you and Dad pushed me into for your own selfish reasons.' A dam deep down within her broke when she said those words, the beginning of catharsis, and she finally came clean about the things she'd carried on her shoulders so long.

'I'm sorry? You cannot be serious. Your father and I always had your best interests in mind.' Her mother grabbed at the thin silken shawl wrapped around her neck, an indignant look on her face.

'Please spare me the lecture. You want to tell me you had my best interests in mind when you threatened to withhold my tuition if I didn't stop talking to Salvador? You saw Salvador and me getting closer, and you were worried what Dad's friends at the yacht club would say about the questionable upbringing of my boyfriend. If you had never interfered, if my happiness had not come second to your desire to keep the family name in pristine condition, maybe I would have ended up marrying this man that I was supposed to be with, saving me years of unhappiness that I've only now started to claw back.'

The words flowed over her lips without restraint as the final walls around her hurt soul came down, and she had once again Salvador to thank for it. He showed her that she was good enough with his acceptance of her, despite all of the mistakes she'd made. The burden of her own guilt lifted, making her feel lighter than she had in years. So light that she hadn't noticed Salvador tense up beside her as she spoke.

Under any other circumstances, Salvador would have excused himself a couple of sentences ago to let Yara and her mother deal with their tension in their own time. But he knew how much Yara had worried about that moment—and none of that concern was wasted from where he was looking at it.

He was also in the unique position where the argument involved him as well. Though he knew her parents had interfered in their relationship, he hadn't realised how far they had gone to stop them from being together. They had truly gone to the lengths of withholding her tuition money, threatening her placement at med school? He couldn't even be angry at her any more, knowing the truth. This was an impossible decision to make.

But the ringing in his ears didn't come from the piercing look Magda Lopes hurled his way. No, the rushing sensation was due to the words Yara had said, that snippet replaying in his head over and over again, until the words lost all meaning.

I would have ended up marrying this man that I was supposed to be with. Him.

Yara believed they would still be together without her parents' undue influence over her.

Confusion stirred its cold fingers in the pit of his stomach, mingling with the heat her blurted confession summoned to his body, bringing forth a storm that roiled through his insides. Her stalwart resolve that they would still be together touched him in an unexpected way. How would their relationship have changed once he started to notice his same-sex attraction? Or was he overthinking this, finding problems where there were none?

When he'd brought up marriage, he hadn't thought much of it. Nor when he'd decided to kiss her in front of her old neighbourhood. It had just felt right, as though being with this woman was what he was supposed to do with his life.

They weren't supposed to talk as if these things were for *them*. It didn't matter that Yara was too hurt from her previous marriage because he wasn't about to propose. They weren't a couple, no matter how easy it felt to hold her hand and walk among neighbours as if they were. But she didn't want to commit to a relationship like that, while Salvador couldn't do without it.

Except now Yara was standing next to him proclaiming to her mother that they were meant to be—and still would be if her parents hadn't interfered.

The two concepts warred in his chest, pulling him in different directions as he struggled to reconcile her feelings for him with her fear of giving someone so much of her. How could both be real?

'Yara, if you could come over and we can talk just between us,' Magda said with a pointed glare at him. The conversation had moved on without him when the turmoil within him had broken loose at her words.

'I'm done having conversations with you.' Yara's hand tightened around his, squeezing it with the trepidation that must have been rising within her. His protective instincts kicked in and his arm looped tighter around her waist, drawing her closer, even though the proximity was tearing at his heart.

'This is Flávia's engagement party, and we're not having this discussion here when we should be celebrating. If you want to talk I'm open to it, but only if you accept my decisions.'

Magda's complexion lost all colour as she stared at her daughter with a surprised expression. 'Is that how it is? Don't think I will stand here and watch you make terrible life choices.'

'Good thing you won't be invited to my engagement party when it happens,' Yara retorted.

All the insecurity and fragility about this moment floated to the surface, and he wanted nothing more than to pull her into his arms, to kiss the tension away. But Salvador was frozen himself, unable to put his own turmoil aside. Uncertainty was something he didn't deal with very well, leaving his nerves frayed.

'Let's go,' Yara mumbled, drawing him away until they were surrounded by people.

They stayed silent as they wove through the crowd, their only connection their clasped hands. Every now and then someone stopped them to talk to either Yara or Salvador, some of them smiling with genuine joy that the two had finally got together, showing them a version of the future they couldn't have.

This moment was only one of many sacrifices he had

to make to keep Felix safe—though none had hurt as much as his heart compressing in his chest right now. Walking around the neighbourhood, chatting to people and slowly pulling Yara out of her gloomy mood, had shown him a window into a life he couldn't have, even though every fibre in his body yearned for it.

How had he fallen in love with Yara again?

'I didn't realise how much they had manipulated you,' he said, when they moved on from a group of people asking them about their work in the hospital.

Yara had gone into details about her travels and some of the rarer conditions she helped diagnose in different countries. Her face lit up when she spoke about it, twisting the long and thin knife deeper through his ribs, stealing the remaining air in his lungs. He'd fallen in love with this woman when their lives couldn't be more different.

'I didn't want to talk about it, though now I'm not sure why. I guess I felt insecure about it. Like, what would you think of me if you knew how weak I had been, choosing my tuition over you?' she said, with a thin laugh.

'They forced you to choose your future over some boy you liked. I can understand your choice. Hell, if you had told me about it back then, *I* would have made that choice for you.' Salvador pulled her closer, a need to protect her surging as the other half of his brain told him that he needed to stop right this moment. He *couldn't* be her protector, not when he already had someone else to look out for.

But her words were stuck in his brain, playing on repeat as he struggled to reconcile what she had said with what they were doing.

I would have ended up marrying this man that I was supposed to be with.

'Yara…' He stopped in his tracks to face her and the

deep breath she took when their eyes met told him everything he needed to know—that this hadn't just been a throwaway comment, and she knew he was going to ask about it now.

The buzzing of his phone interrupted them, and he slipped it out of his pocket. 'Oh, it's the babysitter. I have to get that.'

He pressed the green answer button, holding the phone to his ear. 'Hey, Ciara, what's up?'

For the second time today, everything around him went quiet as the blood rushed to his ears. 'What happened?'

Yara looked at the chest X-rays, a deep line between her brows, before turning back to Salvador, who was nervously pacing up and down the empty examination room they had retreated into when Felix's films had arrived. She still wasn't clear on what exactly had happened, only that she was looking at a broken rib and a potential pneumothorax.

Salvador had huffed at the diagnosis of the on-duty physician, pushing a tablet with Felix's medical history and the report from the paramedics into her hands. She had thrown an apologetic look towards the doctor, who didn't seem to mind as much as she would have.

'I'll take one more doctor, I don't care about the consequences,' he'd said, and left them with the care of Felix.

She put a hand on Salvador's arm to stop him from pacing. 'It's okay. Nothing too bad has happened. Once I know what the lung sounds like, I'll page someone from Paediatrics to place the chest tube. A few days of rest and he'll be as good as new.'

His features darkened, worry mingling with something much more menacing as he drew a sharp breath.

'Nothing too bad happened. Ciara told me the police came by my apartment to inform her that Felix had sneaked out of his room to meet up with some friends. They were found on someone else's property trying to *break in*.'

Her eyes widened at the unveiled terror now surfacing in Salvador's features. She wasn't quite scared, but the distress etched into his gaze made her feel off kilter. 'I think we need to focus on his health—'

'And you know where I was while he was off hanging out with the wrong crowd? I was at that party, playing pretend marriage with someone who will never commit to me in this way. I let myself be distracted when I really needed to be paying attention to Felix.'

He moved his arm away from her hand—now hovering aimlessly in the air—and turned his back towards her. Tension rippled through his muscles, his hands flexing by his sides as he stepped away while taking deep breaths.

Yara blinked as she stared at an invisible point between his shoulder blades. Hurt bloomed in her chest, driving the air out of her lungs and leaving her empty, struggling. *Playing pretend marriage?* Was that how he felt about their time together? As if the deep affection filling the place between them was nothing more than a game they had indulged in for far too long?

A distraction? The room around Yara turned wobbly and strange, her legs not really knowing where they could stand without losing equilibrium. His words drove a searing spear into her chest, cracking her open with a wound so great, her vision blurred as tears pricked her eyes.

She wiped them away with the sleeve of her lab coat, squeezing them shut and forcing herself to remember how to breathe. Salvador was scared and cornered. Something terrible had just happened to his nephew, the boy who had become like his son. Hurt people lashed out, striking at the first thing they could control—whether deserved or not didn't matter. Right now, he wasn't a doctor working in this hospital, but the visitor of a loved one who needed her full attention.

Gathering the paper-thin resolve she had clawed together from the distant corners of her mind, she straightened her posture. 'Parents are not allowed in the emergency department, Salvador. Go and wait in the paediatric wing. I'll have them page you once he's ready to be transferred.'

She didn't wait for his reply before stepping out of the room and into the patient room where Felix was lying in a bed, his expression one of pain, but otherwise alert.

'Hi, Felix. I'm Yara, and I work here with your uncle,' she said, putting on her best patient-care smile as she shoved the encounter with Salvador far down behind her mental shields. 'How are you feeling?'

'Bad...'

She had to chuckle at the straightforward answer. Salvador and his nephew were alike in that regard. When she noticed that he was craning his neck to look at her, she fetched a stool from the far end of the room and sat down at his bedside.

'Can you tell me what happened? The paramedics told me they think you slipped and fell.' She didn't mean to pry any details out of him, but rather cover all angles of his diagnosis, since she didn't know the circumstances that had led to his fall. Had they been having a fight? Had he hit his head, maybe?

Felix stared at her with apprehension, his dark eyes the same shade as Salvador's. A stray strand of anxiety broke free from the tight cage she had put on anything relating to him and she squashed it down with more effort than expected.

'Are you…the woman Tio has been seeing this week?' he asked after a moment of consideration.

Yara's eyebrows rose, almost vanishing into her hairline. How could he have possibly guessed that? She shot a quick glance over her shoulder to check her surroundings. Had he been able to see them arguing just a few moments ago? But though there was a window in the patient room, the blinds were drawn, so he couldn't have seen them.

What was she supposed to say to that? She furrowed her brow, then quickly decided on the truth. The boy was astute and observant enough to notice what his uncle had been up to the last two weeks, so he deserved at least some parts of the truth.

'Yes, that's me. I've known your *tio* since we went to school together.' His expression became closed off, and Yara reached out her hand as if to stop it from happening. 'But don't worry about how I know him. I'm your doctor, so I'm not allowed to share anything with your uncle unless you give me permission to do so.'

'Really?'

Yara nodded. 'Yep. It's called doctor-patient confidentiality. I might share important information with your guardian only to the extent that is necessary to inform your treatment. But your *tio* won't be involved in any procedure since he is your legal guardian.'

A pained expression fluttered over Felix's face at the mention of the guardianship, too quick for her to read it. Guilt? Or was it just the discomfort of his injuries?

'My…friends wanted to go to this fancy house. There was a big party near by, so they figured it would be empty. They boosted me over the wall since I'm the strongest and I could lift them over, but then I lost my footing and fell down the wall.'

Yara nodded, her expression schooled into professional detachment. 'How did you land? On your head? On your side?'

'On my stomach,' he replied, now looking down at his hands.

'I see. Well, that's mostly good news, then. You have a cracked rib and a part of your lung collapsed—which is not even half as scary as it sounds. It just means there is a bit of free air in your chest cavity that we need to remove. But we'll call a specialist from Paediatrics for that.'

His breath left his nose in short bursts. Yara reached out when she saw tears form in his eyes. 'I'm really sorry. I know this was stupid. I didn't know that this was why the boys had invited me to come along with them until we were there.' Felix's chest started to heave as he gulped down air, the weight of his own conscience becoming too much for him to bear. 'Tio is going to be so mad.'

'It's okay, Felix. That's not something we need to worry about right now.' She got off the chair and sat on the bed instead, taking his hand in hers and squeezing it with a reassuring smile. 'First, we want to get you back on your feet, and I promise you, the only thing your *tio* is worried about right now is your wellbeing.'

The boy calmed down, nodding at her with a small sob that wrenched at her heart. She could see Salvador's influence in the way Felix spoke, worried about disappointing his uncle by doing something forbidden.

'So, here's what we're going to do. I'm going to find someone to transport you to your room, where a doctor will explain the next steps in your treatment to you. You'll definitely need to stay here overnight for observation, but that's something we'll all discuss together with you and your *tio*.'

Felix nodded, swiping at the tears forming in his eyes and biting his lip anxiously.

'Anything else you want to ask me before I go?'

Some of the tension in his face faded and his mouth opened, a question on the tip of his tongue. 'Are you Tio's girlfriend?'

Yara blinked several times at the question. That was not what she had expected when she asked him if he wanted to know anything else. 'Um… No, I'm not.'

The hot blade that had slowly been forcing its way up between her ribs plunged deeper at her words, and she bit the inside of her cheek so as not to wince.

'Maybe you should be. Uncle Salvador has been a lot happier in the last two weeks, and you're the only thing that changed for him.'

Her heart slammed against her chest, wiggling at the blade still stuck in her ribs, and rippling a profound and tremendous pain through her body that almost made her gasp out loud. She quickly got up from the bed, turning around and dabbing at her eyes again, struggling to keep her composure.

When she had finally put her face on again, she turned around to smile at Salvador's nephew. 'That'll be nothing compared to how happy he'll be to see you once you're all patched up,' she said, the smile not quite reaching her eyes as she reached out and patted the boy's hand one last time before leaving the room.

His words echoed in her head. He'd given her a piece of information she had been missing. One that stood in direct contrast with what Salvador had barked at her just a few moments ago. But he was in distress, worried sick about his nephew. She would be foolish to let his words carry too much weight.

Salvador being happier than his nephew had ever seen him meant he might feel the same way about her, after all. But she needed to tell him—now.

While Yara went to check on Felix, Salvador did as she had asked him to and went up to the paediatric department, where he sat down in the waiting area for only a few minutes before the nervous energy took over and he started pacing the corridors, only curtly nodding at the colleagues that recognised him from Radiology.

After the paediatrician had placed the chest tube, Salvador had finally been able to step into the room, hugging his nephew as tightly as he could with a broken rib. By the time his doctor had gone over the next steps, Salvador could see the pain medication kicking in, for Felix could barely keep his eyes open.

There were two tracks playing in his mind concurrently—what Ciara had heard about Felix's accident, and the conversation he'd had with Yara not even an hour ago.

His heart was sick with grief and worry for his nephew, thinking he'd somehow failed him and that Felix was already walking a dangerous path where Salvador couldn't reach him. He'd given everything he had—*everything*—to keep Felix from tumbling, building safety nets and securities along the way to catch him whenever he strayed. He had even given up on dating, believing that all his attention should be on his nephew and raising him to be a good person.

Then Yara had dropped back into his life, upending it without even meaning to. She had arrived and suddenly the world was in colour again when it had been sepia for so damn long. He'd fallen the moment he spoke to her again, realising that the hole in his chest was left there when she had disappeared from his life—and only she could fix it.

Yara. The one who'd got away.

He'd been so eager to lose himself in that tantalising ancient love that he'd become complacent in other parts of his life. He'd stopped paying so much attention to Felix, choosing to spend his evenings with Yara rather than at home, watching over the boy. It was *his* fault that this had happened today—and, though Salvador's heart was breaking, he had to make sure he was never so careless again.

Yara hadn't come up with them after she handed the case over to the paediatric consultant. Was she still in the hospital? He fished his phone out of his pocket to check his messages, but she hadn't contacted him. Maybe his unkind outburst had been enough to drive her away.

Salvador shivered as he remembered, the truth of his hesitation to commit laid bare. The pain and anger he carried within him had festered into something tainted inside, that ugly insecurity rearing its head the second he was pressed into a corner. In his mind he knew the difficult situation Yara had been in. Her parents had threatened her future, and with that, her entire life.

But the knowledge of that didn't change the fact that the wound in his heart still bled, ripped open by her sudden presence in his life. Salvador had spent years on his own as the quiet voice in his head whispered words of caution and betrayal. A result of the deep hurt that had never healed. How could he trust her to be in his life—to be in Felix's life—when the faintest amount of pressure made him close off and retreat?

Feeling the weight of this day bear down on his shoulders, Salvador sighed and let himself drop into one of the chairs in the waiting area, burying his face in his hand.

The soft crinkle of plastic pulled him out of his contemplations. Yara sat next to him and held out her hand.

'Crisps?'

'We didn't eat when we were at the engagement party. I know I can't convince you to go home and sleep, so you have to eat whatever the vending machine has to offer.' She shook the bag of crisps at him until he grabbed it from her, turning the package around in his hands as the tension rippled through the air between them.

'Thanks for looking after him,' he said when he couldn't stand the silence any more.

'Of course, least I could do…' She hesitated, her open hand hovering in the air between them before she closed it into a fist. 'He's going to be fine. The chest tube is already out. Some sleep and night-time observation to ensure he doesn't have concussion, then he can go straight back home.'

'That's not what I'm worried about,' Salvador mumbled, his head falling back into his open palm, rubbing the weariness out of his eyes.

'I don't know how much my opinion matters to you at this point, but I think he just made a mistake—like you did when you were twelve.' The way she paused in between her words, selecting them with care and intention—it was so unlike the way Yara spoke to him that he looked up. His brow knotted as he scrutinised her.

Of course, his earlier outburst had affected her. He would have been a fool to believe otherwise. Maybe this was his chance to let her go, end it once and for all. They weren't going to work out, not with so many obstacles already in their way.

'He wouldn't be in this hospital right now if I had paid

better attention to him,' he said, the fear-fuelled fire in his stomach roaring back to life.

'Maybe. Or maybe he would have. He sneaked out of the house. If the babysitter didn't know, you wouldn't have, either.'

'But I would have known who the boys are. I would have known who he's hanging out with. If I hadn't been distracted…' He stopped himself before he could finish the sentence, but the damage was already done.

Yara leaned back, and the mist in her eyes made him hate himself. Why had he let it go so far? Why had he agreed to this in the first place, when she was the one person who knew how to get under his skin? From the very beginning, they'd trodden a perilous path and were now surprised that they had broken each other.

'Please…finish that sentence.' Her voice was thick, and she blinked several times, wiping the gloss from her eyes.

'Yara, I'm sorry. I think we…maybe we let ourselves be carried away by this little affair.' Salvador dared to reach out but withdrew his hand when she flinched away from him.

'This little…? That's how you think about what's happened between us? And here I thought…' She got off her chair, turning her back to him and tilting her head up to look at the ceiling. Her shoulders rose and fell with every big breath, and he felt each breath in his own chest—each one getting harder to get down as the air between them thickened.

This was it. Their final moment.

'I thought you loved me too. Because that's what I came here to say. That I love you, and I didn't care about what you said earlier,' she finally said, and even though the words had lived in his head since he'd pulled her to him the first time they'd slept together at his house in Planaltina, they thundered through him, searing his very soul.

The words burned on his lips, the urge to say them back to her tearing through him. There she was, the woman he'd desired for so many years, telling him she loved him—with such pain in her expression that he almost caved in on himself.

'Yara, I…' The rest of the sentence refused to pass his lips. Because where would that leave them? She was going tomorrow, and he had his nephew to take care of, the worry for him so strong that he had lashed out at her the moment the pressure became too much.

He had, once again, shown himself to be unworthy of her—unable to ever bridge the gap between them.

'I will not stand here and let you tell me that I was only a *distraction*—that this meant nothing to you, when I know what I sensed between us.' A fire had entered her eyes, burning with an indomitable spirit that he had nothing but admiration for. In a different life, he would have been the fuel for that fire.

'We both agreed what this would be. The rules—'

Yara didn't let him finish his sentence. 'Screw the rules! Just for one moment, humour me and do not hide behind technicalities, Salvador. I know I messed up thirty years ago. I know it now. Hell, I even knew it back then. Now I'm scarred and hurt, but I want to try. For you. For us.'

'Enough that you would marry me?' The words flew out of his mouth before he could stop himself, hitting at the heart of his insecurities with Yara—that he wouldn't survive if she left him again.

'Are you…? I… Is this a…proposal?' She whispered

the last word, her eyes so wide he could see the sliver of white surrounding them.

'Would you accept?' He stood now, too deep into this to back out. He never wanted to ask her to give up anything in her life, but she spoke about *us* when they were at such different points in their lives.

'I… Salvador, I can't.' Her chest fluttered with every breath.

'Me neither.' He shook his head, his heart cracking. They were so close to figuring it all out, but the more he looked at it, the further they drifted away. 'I have Felix to look out for now. I just can't be involved with someone who won't stick around when it counts.'

Shock widened her eyes when he said those words, and he noticed her slight recoil. Her mouth opened and closed several times before she finally cleared her throat, once again blinking rapidly.

'So, it comes back to this. You don't trust me because I left.' Bitterness laced her words. 'I made a mistake, Salvador. And even though you now know the truth of how my decision came about, I still own it.'

The sight of her pain was almost too much to bear. Each breath closed his chest tighter until his heart burst into tiny fragments.

'You had to do right by your family back then. I have to do the same now. Felix has had enough turmoil to last a lifetime. I don't mean to add more to it.' The finality in his tone settled in between them, bearing down on the silence spreading in the room that only their breaths interrupted.

Yara took a step towards him, the spark in her eyes gone and the deep hurt etched into her features, summoning his protectiveness forward—but how could he protect her from himself?

'I should go… I still haven't congratulated Flávia on her engagement.' It was a flimsy excuse to leave, probably the first thing that had entered her mind when she searched for an elegant exit, but Salvador nodded.

'It's only been a few hours. I'm sure they'll be going all night.'

'I… Yes, okay… I'd better leave then. *Tchau*, Salvador.'

Their eyes met for what he knew to be the last time, and he looked deep into them, creating a mental image of the small constellation in her eyes for him to keep. He wanted to remember her—if they couldn't be together, at least he'd have that.

'Tchau, fofa.'

Yara took a step back, then another, until she finally turned on her heel and walked around the counter and out of sight. When he couldn't hear her footsteps any more, Salvador broke apart, falling back on the chair he'd been sitting on. Pain shot through his body as if he'd been sliced open from one side to the other, exposing everything weak and vulnerable for whoever looked close enough.

Somehow, it hurt even worse than it had thirty years ago, leaving him empty and hollow. The space inside his chest, the one she had occupied with such confidence and space, lay bare again, its edges burning with an acute awareness of what was missing.

The ultimate sacrifice—to keep his focus trained on Felix. No matter what the personal cost.

CHAPTER TWELVE

AFTER THE FIRST night Felix showed some signs of a traumatic head injury, so the paediatric specialist treating him decided it would be best to keep him in the hospital for a few more days, just to be on the safe side—something Salvador was a lot happier about than his nephew. Having him stay at the hospital meant he'd be able to work while also keeping an eye on him.

And work was the only thing keeping his mind off his wretched experience ever since Yara had left—again. Though this time it was because he couldn't let her back into his life. Pushing her away had taken every shred of strength in his body, and even now, days later, he was wracked by guilt and doubt, one foot always ready to run back to her.

Though she was gone, probably already in a new country working on a case no one else could solve.

His phone buzzed, and he looked down from his screen, where he'd been deconstructing a complex full-body scan to understand what they were looking at. The charge nurse from the paediatric department was paging him, prompting him to furrow his brow.

When he'd gone there to check on Felix that morning, they'd told him he would be discharged in the evening so

Salvador could take him home. Had they pulled the discharge forward because they needed the bed?

'I'll be right back,' he said to his colleague, sitting next to him at a different computer, and headed to the nurses' desk in Paediatrics.

The nurse guided him towards Felix's room, and only her nonchalant and unhurried demeanour kept the panic for his nephew's safety at bay. If something had happened, he would sense it in the way they treated him, wouldn't he?

When he stepped into the room, Chief Sakamoto was sitting on a chair next to Felix's bed, playing a game of cards with the boy. Both looked up when Salvador entered.

'Ah, Dr Martins. Come over here and sit down.' The man waved at a chair next to him, and a different alert went off in the back of Salvador's mind. Why was the Chief of Medicine playing cards with his nephew? He and Salvador were not close enough for this to be normal.

'What's going on here?' He paused, looking at each of them with narrowed eyes. 'Is this some kind of intervention?'

He almost snorted at the thought but was glad he didn't when the room remained quiet.

'I came by the other day just to check on your nephew and make sure he had everything he needed—and he told me he's a bit worried about you, Salvador.'

Salvador? The use of his first name transported him back to his childhood days, when he'd known he was in trouble if his mother used his full name on him. His eyes darted to Felix, who was suddenly very interested in seeing what pattern was printed on the back of the playing cards.

'I thought you were a bit distracted myself when I last

saw you after transferring Henrique Orlay to a long-term care team.' The mention of the patient drove a sharp pain in between his ribs, and he hid a wince.

It happened a lot as he walked around the hospital, passing places he and Yara had spent time together or talking to people who had been on the case and hearing their admiration of her. Yara had been at this hospital for only two weeks but somehow the corridors were imbued with her memory, everything evoking a sense of familiarity and home in his chest—followed by mind-numbing pain that surpassed what he'd gone through the first time she left by several orders of magnitude.

Last time Salvador believed something significant in him had broken. Now he knew that it couldn't be repaired. He would be less than whole for ever, because that one piece of him belonged to her—no matter if they were together or not.

'I spoke to your colleagues as well, and they expressed similar observations ever since...' Chief Sakamoto didn't finish his sentence, instead looking at Felix, who finally stopped shuffling the cards around in his hands to face his uncle.

'Tio, you miss Yara, don't you?' Felix asked.

Salvador's mouth fell open—at the sheer bluntness of the boy and how much he had observed about him. Had he somehow picked up on the depth of his feelings for Yara? How was that even possible? Before his accident, they had never even met.

'I...don't see how that's at all relevant,' he replied, and didn't like the way his voice wavered—or how Felix and the Chief exchanged a knowing look. 'And I don't see how this is any of your concern. I've been doing my job, haven't I?'

'Martins, you've been as exemplary as ever—and yet

your nephew wasn't the only one who noticed something off about you. It was questions from your colleagues that prompted me to seek out Felix. They said you were so heartbroken that I feared something awful had happened here.'

'Something awful *did* happen here.' The words flew out of his mouth, and rapid breaths expanded his chest as he probed for the deep and hidden place the words had come from. 'She's gone again.'

Chief Sakamoto exchanged another loaded look with Felix, a sensitivity beyond the boy's years shining in his eyes as he nodded, a voiceless message passing between them.

'Seems we just got to the bottom of this. Felix said it had most likely to do with Dr Silvia.'

Salvador turned his head towards his nephew, his mouth pressed into a thin line. 'How could you know about her?'

The boy hesitated, his hands scrunching up the blanket on his legs. 'I don't want to get into trouble…'

'You're already in trouble, no matter what you say. Might as well speak your mind, *filho.*'

Son. A word that had been dancing on the tip of his tongue for several months, waiting for the moment when it felt *right* to say. Because he might be Felix's uncle, a title he cherished more than anything, but in this moment their connection ran a lot deeper. Hell, he'd been so worried about Salvador that he'd got the Chief involved. If he was going to tell him something, it would be now.

'You were much more relaxed in the last two weeks, much…happier. I thought Tio always seemed a bit sad, maybe because of Dad or because you had to take me in. But then suddenly you were happy again…' A pink flush appeared on Felix's cheeks, something Salvador would normally have found adorable if he hadn't been so stunned by what his nephew had shared with him.

'I'm sorry, Felix. You had so much to deal with, and it sounds like I made my unhappiness part of your burden.'

Felix had put up with his unhappiness, seeing it as clear as day when he had thought he was hiding it so well. The small kernel of regret inside him exploded, uncoiling its roots and digging deep into his flesh.

He thought he needed to sacrifice everything to keep Felix safe, and by doing so he had put all his misery on those young shoulders. It dawned on him that he needed to live his own life and weave it through the threads of Felix's, rather than stop existing just so he could watch over his nephew.

'I don't know how to make it right, but I will try. Yara, though… I think I drove her away for good. By now, she's probably halfway across the world.' Salvador's chest tightened more, making each breath a hard-fought battle. He'd made a mistake, and he didn't know what to do.

The Chief cleared his throat, drawing Salvador's attention to him. 'Well… I did offer her the chance to stay here and run her own department.'

'You did what?' Salvador stared at Chief Sakamoto with wide eyes, the implication of his words just sinking in.

'She hasn't accepted it, but she hasn't refused it either. I asked her two days ago if she had an answer, and she asked for more time to think. So…she hasn't said no.'

She hadn't declined the Chief's offer? His pulse took a tumble, and when it found its rhythm again it increased in speed so much that Salvador could hear the blood rushing through his ears. She hadn't said no. Yara would have said no if she was hell-bent on leaving. She didn't play hard to get—in fact, he had been the one causing the problems between them.

'You think she's still here?' Was it possible that he could fix his mistake—or at least try? Take the words back before it was too late?

'Go and find her. Felix isn't going to be discharged until you're back. I'll make sure of that,' Chief Sakamoto said with a congenial smile. 'And when you do find her, tell her that I need an answer.'

Salvador hesitated a moment, looking at his nephew, who encouraged him with a nod as well. He took another deep breath and left, fumbling for his keys in his pocket. If Yara was still in Brasília, there was only one place she'd feel safe enough to let her guard down.

The scent of chamomile drifted into the living room, and Yara scrunched up her nose at it. The last few days had been a blur of tears, sleep and chamomile tea that her sister forced into her hand at every opportunity—to the point where she didn't want to see a single cup of that stuff for several more months.

There was no doubt about the healing properties of the plant, but there wasn't a cure for what Yara was experiencing—complete and utter heartbreak, to the point where it was hard to breathe.

It had taken several nights of take-aways and soothing nature sounds to work through what had happened between her and Salvador, something that still left her raw on the inside. She had found the courage to tell him she loved him, and, though there had always been a part of her that knew he might not say it back, she was still crestfallen when her worst-case scenario became a reality right in front of her.

'He doesn't love me back…' Yara mumbled, making her sister look up from her crocheted blanket.

'We've been over this before, but I'll say it again—you *must* know that's not true. I saw you at Flávia's engagement party. Everyone did. He was practically worshipping you.' They had this exact conversation several times a day whenever Yara fell deeper into the hole of her own misery.

It just didn't make sense. If he loved her, why was she here right now, hiding in her sister's guest room until she could think about the future again? Because without even planning, her perception of her life had changed, and she had created space for Salvador and whatever family they were going to become.

'My neighbours are already collecting money to get another permit for a party because they are certain you and Salvador are going to be next,' Bianca continued, and Yara snorted at that suggestion.

'I'm never getting married again. It hasn't ended well for me,' she grumbled.

'Don't you think that might be the problem and why Salvador ultimately said he couldn't be with you?'

'What? Because I don't want to marry him?' She glared at her sister, ignoring the indignant look on her face.

'No, that you say marriage didn't end well for you when that's not true. Marrying *Lawrence* didn't end well for you. It has nothing to do with marriage itself. But you cling to that thought and wield it like a shield around you. Maybe Salvador really wanted to be with you, but you were too worried about protecting yourself from the perceived threats of marriage.'

Yara recoiled at the intensity of her sister's words, her lips parting in an instant rebuttal that died in her before she could voice it. A sharp pinch in her chest stopped her from saying anything, and a cold sense of dread pooled at the bottom of her stomach. The truth of Bianca's words hit her like a wall of bricks, crashing down on her until they were too heavy for her to breathe.

'I…thought he loved me too. When our parents were so happy about my relationship, I thought I had everything I needed to move on—that we would learn to truly love each other with time.' She had carried those words inside her for so long, her shoulders sagged with relief as the weight lifted off. 'I turned my back on Salvador because I thought Mum and Dad knew best, that they would never push me in a direction that wasn't the right one for *me*.'

Bianca put her blanket aside and moved to the spot on the couch next to her, putting an arm around her shoulder. 'I'm sorry you suffered so much, but the only person telling you who you should be with now is you.'

'No wonder Salvador couldn't say it back. He's only ever known me as a person easy to influence. I've never shown him that I'm ready to do anything to make this happen—that I no longer run.' She looked at her sister with wide eyes as the realisation hit her. She had done exactly the same thing she'd done thirty years ago—she'd walked out on him without putting up a fight.

'What do you want to do?' Bianca asked.

'I can't just expect him to say it,' Yara said, shaking her head. 'I have to fight for it.'

A grin spread over her sister's face. 'That sounds a lot more like my big sister.'

Yara got up and looked around, her mind kicking into action mode the way it did when she was doing her initial diagnosis. 'I have to go to him.'

'Yes!' Bianca jumped up with her and walked into

the kitchen before returning with her car keys, throwing them at her sister. 'Take my car. It's faster than waiting for a taxi.'

Yara gripped the keys, holding them to her heaving chest, and nodded at Bianca. She forced herself to take each step of the staircase with deliberation when everything inside her urged her to take them two at a time. Salvador was not going to go anywhere. He might even stick to his previous conviction, but she wouldn't let it stand without a fight. He was worth a thousand battles, if that was what it took to show her sincerity and love.

She flung the door open—and stood face to face with Salvador, his hand raised in an imminent knock.

His gaze bored into hers, an undeniable spark in his eyes that brought an unexpected weakness to her knees. 'What are you doing here?' she whispered.

'I was coming to see you.'

'Weird. I was doing the same thing.'

'That *is* weird.' Salvador chuckled, and the sound vibrated through her, finding its way into her core and lighting a gentle fire there.

'Salvador, I—' She didn't get much further before he pulled her into his arms, crushing her against his chest in an embrace that conveyed everything words couldn't. He kissed the crown of her head, his hands clutching at her as if she was his lifeline, saving him from treacherous waves.

'Let me go first, because I need to say something I should have said ages ago. I love you, Yara. All of you, without compromise. I don't care about anything else but being with you.'

The words she'd been yearning to hear rang in her ears, threatening to rob her of any remaining composure. She tilted her head back and shuddered when he obliged her silent plea, brushing his lips over hers. Her knees turned to rubber under the kiss she'd been longing for since their conversation in the hospital.

The piece that went missing thirty years ago slotted back into place, a warm wholeness radiating through her entire body as she leaned against his chest. When he finally let go of her lips, she looked up at him and saw that same wholeness reflected at her.

'How is Felix?' she asked, and the smile on his lips further weakened her already unsteady legs.

'I love that you're asking about him first.' His hand came up to her face, brushing over her cheekbone. 'He's fine. Actually, he was the one who made me realise what a huge mistake I'd made.'

Yara remembered what Felix had said to her as well— that Salvador finally seemed happy again. 'What a smart boy you have.'

'Yeah, we do.' He paused, only a slight hesitation in his words, as if he was afraid what her reaction would be. 'I wasn't being considerate of your experience, thinking that we can only be a family in one specific way—when that couldn't be further from the truth.'

Yara shook her head. 'I shouldn't have left again. Not without putting up more of a fight. That's why I was rushing out of the house to come and talk to you. What happened to me with my marriage scared me so much, it blinded me to what else could be waiting out there.'

His arms tightened around her as she pressed her cheek against his chest. His lips moved over the crown of her head again, each spoken word becoming a gentle kiss. 'I don't need anything more from you than this right here, Yara. Everything else we can figure out.'

'Even if I don't want to get married?' She swallowed the lump in her throat.

'I don't care about any of that, *amor*. If we get married or not, if you want to keep travelling around the world—you and I are what matter here.'

'Salvador…' Her eyes burned with tears she blinked away. Here he was standing in front of her, telling her with a steadfast belief that they could be together no matter what—something she wished she had believed thirty years ago. She would not waste this second chance she'd received.

'I'm staying,' she said, and sensed the tremble in his body. 'Dr Sakamoto offered me my own department. He wants his hospital to become *the* diagnostic centre in Brazil.'

'I could never ask you to stay here if you don't…'

Yara shook her head, raising her face towards his once more. 'This is what I want. I want you and Felix together here in our home.'

CHAPTER THIRTEEN

'THIS IS ONLY a mild case of encephalitis. Who sent me this file? Neurology should be able to diagnose this by themselves.'

Yara looked up from her screen and saw Salvador standing in her doorway, arms crossed in front of his chest—an amused smile curling his lips. He smiled a lot more these days, something she had noticed ever since they'd moved in together to his house in Planaltina. After speaking to Felix about what had happened on the night he ended up in the hospital, as well as what was going on between Yara and Salvador, they decided a fresh start all round would be the best way forward.

Felix's new school was within walking distance from their house, and small enough so they knew everyone in his class.

Months had passed since then, with Yara working tire-lessly to grow her diagnostic department to the size she needed to run it on a larger scale. Sometimes she missed her solo practice and her adventures travelling around the world—until she saw Salvador standing in front of her like that and everything faded into the background.

'I thought it made for an interesting scan for your trainees, so I sent it up. Excuse me for causing offence, Dr Lopes.' His tone didn't match his words, a playful lilt accompanying everything.

Yara got off her chair, looking at Salvador first, before her eyes drifted to the name on her door: *Dr Yara Lopes, Head of Diagnostics*.

Another step she had to thank him for. For the longest time she'd believed her married name to be intrinsically linked to her professional success, fearing that people would stop recognising her work or her abilities if she took that final step to absolve herself from her failed marriage.

'Is it already time?' she asked, buried so deeply in different cases that time had passed her by unnoticed.

'It's okay. I'm sure no one will notice if we are late to our own party,' he quipped, earning him a playful slap on the shoulder.

He caught her left hand, taking it in his own and looking at it with a reverence that caused a shiver to trickle through her body. Their eyes locked for a heartbeat, then he lowered his lips to her fingers and kissed the delicate white-gold ring on her ring finger.

'Let's go,' she said, wrapping her hand around his and pulling him out of her office.

As it turned out, her old neighbourhood had been right to collect money to pay for the next party permit—and that it was Yara and Salvador who would be celebrating.

'Did you hear anything from your mother?' he asked as they stepped out, and Yara shook her head.

'Yes, she'll be there. I hope once things quieten down we can have some time to talk things through,' Yara said, shrugging when Salvador's concerned gaze met hers.

'I'm fine, *amor*. Besides, Bianca will be there to help her understand.' She leaned in and whispered near his ear, her lips grazing over his skin as she spoke. 'You don't have anything to worry about. I have you, don't I?'

* * * * *

THE SINGLE MUM
HE CAN'T RESIST

JANICE LYNN

MILLS & BOON

To Reesee.
Love you and am so proud of you.

CHAPTER ONE

"YOU'RE LOOKING AT him again."

While her best friend plopped down in a chair at the nurses' station, Nurse Jenny Robertson jerked her eyes away from where six feet of male physical perfection had gone into an Intensive Care Unit room at Chattanooga General Hospital.

"Don't be ridiculous." She tried not to sound too defensive at Laura's observation. Tristan Scott's dark, slightly wavy hair, sky-blue eyes and infectious smile did catch her eyes too often, but she wasn't acknowledging that to her bestie. "You just happened to look my way as I just happened to look up and he just happened to be there. That's all."

Roger Pennington's hazel eyes crinkled with amusement. "That's a lot of 'just happeneds.'"

"A whole lot." Laura's gaze shifted to where Tristan could be seen caring for his patient through the ICU's glass wall facing where they sat. A respiratory therapist, another nurse, and a tech were helping get his new admit settled. "But you and every other single woman who works here thinks our newest travel nurse is hot. Rightly so. If I hadn't felt the immediate sparks between you two, I'd be all over that scrumptiousness."

Roger snickered. Jenny rolled her eyes.

"If you think he's all that, go for it." Why had her stomach just twisted into a tight wad? Irked at herself, she lifted her chin. "You have my blessing to be 'all over that scrumptiousness.'"

"Your blessing?" Roger leaned against the rounded station desk that separated their workspace from their patients' rooms. "What is this, like 'olden days' girl code or something?"

Jenny pointed her finger at him. "You stay out of this."

Grinning, he held up his hands in mock defense. "Yes, ma'am."

"We've been friends since kindergarten," Laura reminded. "I know you better than anyone. Deny it all you want, but you like Tristan."

"If you know me so well, then you should know that, even if I did find him attractive and was willing to become involved, which I don't and I'm not," she quickly added, "I'd never choose someone I work with."

"Otherwise, she wouldn't have been able to resist dating me."

Jenny and Laura snorted. Roger, who had dated the same woman since high school and was still completely infatuated with the ultrasonographer.

"You'd be a lonely man, Roger, if women got to choose who they were attracted to," Laura teased then turned her attention back to Jenny. "Admit it. Tristan gets you twitterpated."

"He's not my type." No one was her type. As in literally "no one." She didn't want a type or another man in her life. Some mistakes shouldn't be repeated. With few exceptions, she considered herself an intelligent person. Romantic involvements made up the bulk of her big life goofs.

Roger's face scrunched with exaggerated mortification. "Hot isn't your type? That seals the deal. You and I would never work."

Sighing, Jenny pushed away her tablet then swiveled her chair to face them.

"The man is a travel nurse," she pointed out, her tone clearly equating the label to the Bubonic plague. "He's here today, gone tomorrow. The last thing any of us needs is to get involved with someone who we know isn't staying."

"He'll be here three months."

Jenny gave Laura a "So what?" look.

"Three months is time for a whole lot of fun." Laura waggled her brows.

"Oh, yeah." Smirking, Roger gave her a high five.

Jenny shook her head at their antics. "I don't need that kind of fun."

"Girl, you need that kind of fun more than anyone I know," Laura insisted. "How long has it been? A year? Two? Three?"

Jenny's cheeks caught fire, or sure felt as if there were flames consuming them. Blazing infernos.

"It's not been nearly long enough that I've forgotten all the heartache that follows falling in love." She grabbed her tablet and tapped the screen a couple of times. Maybe if she looked busy, they'd leave her alone.

Roger's tone turned serious. "Please tell me you're not still hung up on he whose name we don't say? He never deserved you."

Did he mean Geoffrey or Carlos? Probably Geoffrey. He'd been her biggest heartbreak. Carlos had just been a brief reminder of why she was better off single.

"No, he didn't deserve me, but he taught me a valuable lesson that there are more important things in life than sex."

Like human decency and keeping promises you made to love and be true forever. People still did that, right?

"I wouldn't be opposed to a relationship with someone who believed in forever, someone who would always be there, but I've yet to meet someone with staying power. Besides, I don't miss sex," she continued. Who had time for sex? She sure didn't. Her life was full. "I'm abstinent by choice and content with that decision."

"Content is the wrong word choice when you're discussing your lack of a sex life." Laura's nose curled. "Girl, you need to have sex."

"I'm not sure what I missed, but I definitely missed something."

Flames engulfed Jenny's face, again. She'd missed Tristan coming out of his patient's room.

"Jenny was trying to convince me that sex isn't important." Laura filled him in, her dark eyes twinkling with merriment that he'd joined the conversation.

"Not if you aren't having sex with someone special," Jenny clarified, not sure why she felt the need to defend her stance.

Tristan's baby blues that had all the Intensive Care Unit agog studied Jenny. "Is there currently someone special in your life?"

Was he asking if she was having sex? It had been years. It was likely to be years before she had sex again, too. Or maybe she never would. She didn't mind. She'd liked sex okay, but it wasn't the be-all and end-all.

The way Tristan looked at her had her wondering if one night within those muscled arms would have her begging for more rather than feeling content to sleep alone night after night. Was that why he'd occupied so much of her thoughts since his arrival? Because her body instinctually recognized his in some Neanderthalian species-must-go-on way?

The timer she'd set on her phone beeped.

"There are a lot of special someones in my life," she assured with the smile she usually wore when her friends weren't harassing her about her love life—or lack thereof. "Currently, the special someone in Room Three needs my attention." With that, she rose to check on John Rossberg. John was a sixty-two-year-old who'd been admitted with acute respiratory failure secondary to viral pneumonia. Putting on her personal protective equipment, she entered his room and exhaled with relief to have escaped the conversation.

Stepping up to his bedside, she silenced the beeping alarm.

"Good evening, Mr. Rossberg. This is Jenny. You're stuck with me again tonight," she told the unconscious man who had been her patient the evening before, as well. "As I told you when I came in after shift change, I was glad to hear you had a good day. Your white blood cell count has started coming down and your renal function is some better. Those are really good signs."

She liked talking to her patients, even the unconscious ones. Many of them were aware of at least bits and pieces of the world around them. She wanted to be a light in that dark world and often thought how lonely and scary it must be for a comatose patient to be aware of what was going on around them but unable to communicate.

"Your wife was here when I arrived tonight. She's a lovely woman and sure does love you. She's gone home for the night, but said she'd be back first thing in the morning. Have I told you that you have excellent taste? She's such a sweetheart. She showed me photos of your grandchildren earlier this week. I told you about that, remember?"

She continued to chat while she changed out the empty intravenous fluid bag to a new one. "They are so cute and close in age to my four-year-old son, Sawyer. I know your family is anxious for you to get well so you can take your grandkids fishing. Your wife told me that was something special you do with them. Sawyer hasn't ever been fishing, but he adores the water and fish. We visited the aquarium and he absolutely loved it. I'm hoping to get him into swim lessons this summer. He's on a wait list at a facility near our home."

Once she had the bag updated, she rechecked his equipment. When finished, she lingered. Yes, she was avoiding going back to the nurses' station. Yes, if they were still there, her friends could see her and knew what she was doing. No, she wasn't ashamed to admit it. Not to herself.

"You don't mind my staying in here a bit longer, anyway, right?" she asked her patient, patting his hand. "You're much better company than my coworkers."

Especially her temporary coworker.

Tristan was bothersome. He had thrown her off-kilter the first night they'd met and every work night since. He was friendly, funny, helpful, and his smile reached his eyes. Jenny might not be interested, but she wasn't blind. Laura hadn't been wrong in calling him hot. He fit right in with their tight-knit ICU crew.

When she'd triple-checked Mr. Rossberg's vitals and told him all about the late spring Tennessee weather, she left the room, stripped off her protective gear and properly disposed of it, then sanitized. There wasn't anyone at the nurses' station when she got back there, but her reprieve didn't last long.

Tristan came out of the new admission's room and leaned against the edge of the desk.

"Everything okay with your patient?" he asked, giving her one of those smiles that reached his eyes, dug dimples into his cheeks, and had butterflies performing acrobatics in her belly.

Giving a polite-but-nothing-more smile, she nodded. "No new issues. I just needed to change his IV bag over and check his drips."

"Glad to hear it." He sounded sincere. Perhaps he was. He seemed to genuinely care about the patients. They'd had some excellent travel nurses on her unit, but the uncaring ones' lax attitude and frequent disappearing acts always irked. Their patients were people with loved ones. Their lives mattered and nothing with their care should be taken for granted.

Nodding, she went back to charting her encounter with Mr. Rossberg and hoped she didn't accidently insert the words *Tristan*, *scrumptious* or *great smile* anywhere into the record.

Tristan sat in the chair next to hers. "I'm sorry if I made you uncomfortable earlier."

"It wasn't your fault you walked up on Laura being Laura," she said without looking up.

"Still, I had no right to insert myself into a personal conversation. I'm sorry."

Ugh. Why did he have to be so nice? And so *hot*?

"No problem," she fibbed. Everything about him was problematic. His good manners, his dark, wavy hair that she longed to touch to see if it was as soft as it looked, his blue eyes that reminded her of the sky on the clearest of days, his frequent smile that reached those eyes and put an extra sparkle there, his... Ugh, yes, he was problematic. Monumentally so.

"Not that there's anything wrong with your choice,

but I can't help but think that it's a shame you aren't interested in a relationship."

Jenny's breath caught. Was he making a general observation or implying personal disappointment?

"My choices aren't any of your business."

He gave a sheepish grin. "You're right, and I need to apologize yet again for letting my curiosity get the better of me. Sorry."

"Curiosity killed the cat," she recited, keeping her tone flat so he wouldn't mistake it for flirting.

He chuckled. "I'm no cat."

Possibly not, but he was a man and probably tomcatted with the best of them. No matter how fluttery he made her insides, she needed to remember that.

She gave a tight smile, then focused her eyes on her tablet. But her mind was on the man watching her from where he hadn't budged. Trying to ignore him, she tapped on her screen in the hope of finishing her charting.

"Have I done something to make you not like me, Jenny? If so, I'd like to make that right." He cleared his throat, causing her eyes to open and her gaze to collide with his. "Actually, what I'd like is for us to be friends. Maybe after our shift ends, we could start over by my taking you to breakfast."

He wanted to take her to breakfast? To be friends? Jenny fought the urge to rub her temples. What was it about this night and people putting her on the spot?

There was something fragile in Jenny's big brown eyes; something that twisted Tristan's insides. From the moment they'd met, he'd wanted to know more about her and to erase the wariness that shone when their gazes met.

"There's a great place in the converted old warehouse

building where the apartment I've rented is. It's not too far from the hospital."

"I figured you must live close as I've seen you bicycling to work."

"Cycling is great exercise and the complex really isn't that far away."

"Many of the older buildings that had sat empty for decades have found new life over the past few years. I'm glad."

Pleased that she hadn't immediately shut him down as he'd expected, Tristan nodded. "There are photos of the revitalization process hanging along the main floor's hallway. That floor is filled with shops, a workout facility, and a few restaurants. The upper floors are apartments. Mine's a small, furnished penthouse studio. The atmosphere is great. The food is even better."

She hesitated only a moment before doing as he'd expected.

"It sounds nice, but no thank you. As for the other—" fatigue etched itself onto her lovely face "—you've not done anything."

"Then you just don't like me?"

There was something off in the way she related to him compared with the other nurses, one of whom was also a travel nurse who had only started a week prior to Tristan. He'd seen her laughing with the guy on several occasions and had had to tamp down the jealous flash that had hit him at how easily she'd talked with him.

"I don't know you," she said defensively, sounding more flustered and shifting in her chair.

"And don't want to?" Part of him warned he should let it drop, but he might never get another opportunity to set the record straight. If there was something he could say, could do, that would put her at ease, that could have her smiling and laughing with him, then he'd jump through whatever hoops he needed to, to make that happen.

"You won't be here long," she observed, not meeting his eyes. "Whether or not we get to know each other is irrelevant."

Jenny didn't want a short-term relationship. He got that. He wasn't looking for a relationship, short or long, but from the moment he'd met her, he'd been intrigued.

"I'll be here for three months. That's long enough to make friends."

"That's long enough to make an acquaintance," she corrected. "Friendships take years."

She was wrong on that, too. He'd made many good friends during his life adventures. People he could call up and chat with or go months, years even, in between seeing without awkward feelings when they reconnected.

"You don't believe two people can meet and instantly know if they connect as friends?"

She harrumphed. "Friends at first sight?"

"Yes."

Her expression was doubtful. "And you thought this about me when we met? That we would be friends at first sight?"

"I'd hoped we would be friends. That's what I thought when we first met, that you were someone I wanted to be friends with. I still want that."

He couldn't recall having ever met someone he'd so instantly wanted to know. Jenny had been smiling at something someone had said and Tristan had been instantly hooked, wanting to see her smile again, only with him being the cause of her happiness. When she'd turned and her big brown eyes had collided with his, visions of kissing her full lips had hit him so hard he'd mentally doused cold water over his thoughts to prevent what could have been an embarrassing situation.

How he'd reacted had caught him off guard. Her stand-offish reaction even more so because he'd swear that he'd seen mutual attraction in that initial moment. Whatever he'd seen, she'd masked her emotions, smiled her way through introductions, and high-tailed it into a patient's room, avoiding him the rest of the night.

"Other than Laura, I don't fraternize with my coworkers outside the hospital, and Laura doesn't count since we've been best friends since elementary school." Jenny's expression became thoughtful. "I don't spend a lot of time with Laura away from work these days, either." She shot a tight smile. "You'll understand why based upon the conversation you walked in on."

Leaning back in the chair, he crossed his arms. "How long have you worked at Chattanooga General?"

Frowning at his question, she hesitated then said, "Four years."

"That makes you what? About twenty-six or twenty-seven?"

"Twenty-five," she corrected.

"This was your first job after graduation?"

Eyes narrowed, she nodded.

"Did you do a clinical rotation at this hospital?"

"No, I did clinicals at Erlanger, which was a wonderful experience, and then my last rotation was in Ringgold." Her face pinched, making him wonder if that experience hadn't been so wonderful. "Laura convinced me to apply here as it's where she'd done her clinical rotations and she loved it. She knew I had no plans to apply in Ringgold." Perhaps realizing she'd revealed too much, her expression darkened. "I'm glad I did, as we both landed in the ICU."

Tristan suspected knowing what had happened in

Ringgold would reveal a lot about Jenny and why she had so many walls. Probably a man she'd met there, but who knew? He'd bite his tongue rather than ask when he knew it would shut down their current conversation.

"Are you originally from Chattanooga?"

She nodded. "Not far from here."

"Did you always want to be a nurse?" he rushed on, wanting to get her beyond where her thoughts had gone, in the hope she wouldn't take off on some pretend nursing mission when all was currently calm on the unit.

"My mom is a nurse. I've always admired how she took care of people." Jenny's tone softened. "She's the best, so kind and gentle with those in her care. It makes sense that I want to be as much like her as I can."

The love and admiration she felt laced her words and Tristan felt a twist of envy. How great it must be to be so proud of your parents?

"Well, she raised you right, or maybe it's just good caregiver genetics, because you're a great nurse, Jenny."

Her cheeks pinkened. "I— Thank you, but you've only been here a couple of weeks, so you might want to save that observation for a few months from now."

"I knew you were a wonderful nurse after the first night I worked with you."

Filled with curiosity, her eyes met his. "How can you be so sure?"

"You're efficient. Constantly on task to make sure your patients get great care. Smart. Compassionate. And your coworkers love you, as do your patients. How much they do says a lot."

"Most of my patients are unconscious, so there's that."

He laughed. "True, but they love you when they wake up and see the kindness on your face that matches the kindness in your voice when you're talking to them even when you're not sure they hear you."

"How do you know I talk to my patients?"

"There are glass walls separating the rooms from the hallway," he pointed out, grinning as he told her the obvious. "I've seen you talking to your patients. You're constantly chatting away, even to the unconscious ones. Your face gets so animated at times that I wonder what you could possibly be saying to them with such enthusiasm."

"You've met my best friend. It's quite possible that I chat with unconscious people as a reaction to her." Jenny's lips twitched. "Besides, for all you know, I could be telling them to get off their tushes so I can give their bed to someone else or so I could have an easy go for the rest of my shift."

"I'm going with my gut on this one. You're a good nurse. The compassionate kind I hope I'd get if I were ever in an intensive care unit."

Her cheeks pinkened again. They did that a lot, the splash of color contrasting with her fair skin. Dark hair, dark eyes, porcelain skin that brightened at the lightest comment.

"Let's hope you never are." She bit into her lower lip. "Is there something you're wanting, Tristan? Because a game of Twenty Questions and flattery will not win points with me."

Was that what she thought he was trying to do? Flatter her? For that matter, what was he trying to do? He liked his life uncomplicated. Jenny was complicated. He might not know a lot about her, but he was positive she made Riemann's hypothesis seem as nothing more than simple mathematics.

"I want to be your friend." *More than that*, an inner voice whispered. He had never dated coworkers during his short stints, not even ones who knew the score and were as footloose and fancy-free as he was. Jenny wanted someone who was going to stick around. And yet, he admitted that if she crooked her finger, that rule would be tossed to the wind.

"You'll have to settle for being my temporary co-worker," she said without a smile or finger crook. "I'm not in the market for new friends."

CHAPTER TWO

THE FOLLOWING NIGHT, Jenny managed to avoid being alone with Tristan. Knowing her friends were watching, she'd even managed to act seminormal around him while under their eagle eyes. The night had been uneventful to where just past midnight they'd finished their charts, had recently assessed their patients, and were sitting at the nurses' station. The group had been giving recommendations on local spots for Tristan to visit.

"Have you checked out the Ocoee or the Nantahala?" Roger asked when Tristan mentioned he'd worked a couple of summers as a white-water rafting guide. "They're great for kayaking or rafting, although probably not as challenging as what you did in Colorado."

"I've not, but a rafting trip is on my Chattanooga to-do list. I've been curious about the Ocoee. I'd seen it's only about an hour. I've not looked into the Nantahala as it's further away. Which river do you recommend?"

Roger smiled. "Lucia and I have done each one a few times. The Ocoee has higher-graded rapids and is closer, but the Nantahala is great, too."

"I've done trips down both, too," Crystal, the charge nurse, said. "Roger's right. They're so much fun. I've not been in years."

"I've been once, but it was years ago, too, with a church youth group," Laura said, glancing toward Jenny. "Do you remember that? Your mom had gallbladder surgery and you didn't get to go."

Jenny nodded. At the time, she'd been sad, but she hadn't been able to leave her mother at home alone. She'd always choose family over fun.

"We should put a trip together," Laura suggested, her eyes bright with excitement. "We can go up on a weekend we have off, camp, raft, and have a great time. Doesn't that sound like fun, Jenny? You'd finally get to go down the river."

"I don't feel as if I've missed out, Laura. Sixteen-year-old me may have wanted to go, but adult Jenny has better things to do. White-water rafting isn't my thing."

"What is your thing?"

All eyes went to Tristan, including Jenny's. "Not much. Work, sleep, eat, spend time with family. I'm completely boring."

"I find that difficult to believe."

Her coworkers' gazes bounced back and forth between her and Tristan. Jenny fought a sigh. Why were they looking at them as if they were the evening's entertainment?

"Regardless of what you believe, it's true." She didn't see boring as a problem given it meant nothing unexpected ever happened. Boring was good.

"Don't listen to her." Laura spoke up. "She's cautious not boring."

Jenny glared at her friend.

"I work at a hospital. I see what happens when people aren't cautious. There's no reason to take unnecessary chances." As Sawyer's mother, she had to be cautious. How could she not be when he depended upon her?

Tristan's brow arched. "You never take unnecessary chances?"

"Life has taught me that being cautious is in my own best self-interest. I get hurt when I'm not cautious."

Jenny had revealed far too much. But since Tristan had asked and the others were all waiting for her response, so be it.

"Caution isn't always a good thing, Jenny," Tristan countered earnestly. "The world would quit advancing if no one took chances. Just think of the medical field alone if no one had ever tried something different."

The conversation was cut short by two patient alarms sounding almost simultaneously, one of which was Mr. Rossberg's and the other was a patient of Roger's. They jumped up simultaneously.

"Sorry, not sorry, I've got to go." Grateful to leave the conversation, Jenny stopped only long enough to put on protective gear before entering the ICU room.

Even with his volume-controlled ventilator system and supplemental oxygen, John Rossberg's blood oxygen saturation level was dipping into the low- to mid-eighties. His baseline oxygen had been running in the upper eighties to low nineties since his admission. The PIP— peak inspiratory pressure—had elevated to just above thirty, meaning it was taking more work by the machine to achieve a set ebb-and-flow inhalation pressure. Thus, the triggered alarm. The PIP level wasn't so high, however, that Jenny immediately thought pneumothorax, but she couldn't rule out that he didn't have a collapsed lung or even pulmonary edema.

Quickly, she did a visual assessment, noting the symmetric rise and fall of his chest while she checked his pulse oximeter, making sure it had a good connection. Convinced it did, she checked his endotracheal tube, making sure his bite block was doing its job to prevent him from biting into the tube and that his lip line location was still good. Both were perfectly in place.

Listening to his chest, she detected air movement throughout his lung fields in sync with the ventilator breathing for her patient. She also heard crackles that shouldn't be there.

"Okay, Mr. Rossberg, what's going on here?" she asked, checking his extremities for swelling that might indicate fluid overload. His compression hoses were working, there were no noticeable changes in the size of his legs or arms. He was being fed via a nasogastric tube and the markings on the NG tube were still where they should be, so he likely hadn't aspirated from a feeding. But it wasn't impossible.

"You aren't trying to build up fluid in your lungs, are you? You know that doesn't make this nurse happy, right? No worries, though. I'm going to contact your doctor to let him know what's going on, get a portable X-ray ordered, along with anything else he wants done, and then I'll suction the mucus to hopefully help you get rid of whatever is causing those extra lung sounds and increased peak inspiratory pressures. We'll have your lungs clear soon."

Or at least clear out as much of the sputum as she could to where it wasn't interfering so much with his oxygen saturation and lung pressure. With the respiratory failure that had sent him into multi-organ breakdown, he was so fragile and at risk for complications.

"I can't have you getting pneumonia." She continued talking to him despite nothing on his monitors changing in response to her doing so. He probably didn't know she was there. Maybe, under the circumstances, that was better, because she didn't want him sensing how concerned she was at the changes in his vitals readings.

"Need help?" Tristan asked, coming into the room. With the mask covering the lower half of his face, the blue of his eyes popped even more. "I knew from the last time we were in here that it was about time to turn him, so I thought I'd see if you needed help with that or anything else."

As much as she'd rather it be someone other than Tristan, she'd take what help she could get. Turning Mr. Rossberg with all his lines was a two-plus person job. "His oxygen saturation has decreased, his PIP is above thirty, and he has crackles in his lower lobes bilat. If you'll get suction started, I'll call Dr. Willis. He'll want to get a portable chest X-ray ordered and repeat labs at the minimal."

"Sure thing." He set about inserting a suction tip into Mr. Rossberg's endotracheal tube as Jenny called the intensivist.

"Dr. Willis said to order the X-ray and bloodwork," she said when she'd hung up her phone. "I'll put the orders in so Radiology and the lab can get someone up here."

Entering the orders into the electronic medical system, Jenny glanced to where Tristan was suctioning her patient, noting the rusty-colored sputum he was removing from Mr. Rossberg's lungs.

Perhaps having sensed that she was looking his way, Tristan asked, "Pneumococcal pneumonia?"

"Maybe. His original PCR test showed viral with no bacterial. As much as I hate to think he's picked up a nosocomial bacterial infection while here, it's possible." She sighed, her mask causing the warm air to fan the portions of her face beneath the material. "His white blood cell counts were normal earlier today and were decreased at time of his admission."

"Which is consistent with viral." Glancing at the rusty sputum again, Tristan's gaze then met hers. "You think he's bleeding?"

In Mr. Rossberg's condition, with the endotracheal tube, it was possible that he'd suffered an injury in placement or that the tube had irritated already fragile tissue.

"I doubt it. His sputum isn't bright red, so, if it's blood, it's old and mixed with mucus." She shrugged. "If a bleed, we'll know soon enough." She hoped that wasn't it. She wasn't sure Mr. Rossberg could survive surgical repair of a bleed if it came to needing that. "We'll get a culture and a new PCR test sent off."

"Right," Tristan agreed as Jenny finished adding the orders for another polymerase chain reaction test.

"Given his current status, it isn't the priority, but I'll need to turn him to a Semi-Fowler position after his chest imaging." While the staff rotated his on-side positions every couple of hours to help prevent bedsores, she knew that given his current condition, the on-his-back bed angle would better facilitate his lung expansion and ventilation. "We'll need at least one other person in here to help make sure his lines stay in place."

"Laura is helping Roger with one of his patients. That's why you got stuck with my help, but they may be finished by the time the radiology technologist gets the bedside chest view pictures."

Jenny nodded. "If so, we can call for Crystal, or if she's busy then one of the respiratory therapists can assist. I've entered another consult at Dr. Willis's request. You want me to take over the suctioning or to draw his labs?"

"Get the labs and I'll finish up this."

In silence they worked together, taking a short step-back break as the X-ray technician took her shots.

"Looks like fluid build-up bilateral, worse on the right," the tech said. "I'll get these off to the radiologist for an official reading and have him message Dr. Willis."

Once Mr. Rossberg's pressures and sats were some-what improved, although not back to his baseline, Jenny, Tristan, Crystal and a male respiratory therapist pains-takingly repositioned him.

Jenny and Tristan worked on one side. Crystal and Blake worked on the other, taking extreme care as, inch by inch they moved him onto his back. Twice during the move, Jenny brushed against Tristan. Twice she had a blink of awareness of how close he was, how easy to work with, and how very virile.

The man gave off so many pheromones that even in this crazy moment her body couldn't not react. Stupid primal instincts. Mother Nature had a wicked sense of humor.

When they finished, Crystal and Blake left the room. Wanting to stay close until she was assured Mr. Ross-berg's vitals were going to remain stable, Jenny remained near her patient's bed, as did Tristan.

"Even if only minimally improved, he seems stable at the moment, so I'm off to check on my patient," Tristan told her, standing next to where she watched the rise and fall of Mr. Rossberg's chest. "Anything I can help with before I go?"

Grateful no monitors displayed how her heart rhythm sped up at his nearness, Jenny shook her head. "I appreci-ate your help. Thank you. I'll be in here awhile as I want to be close in case anything changes, but if you need help repositioning your patient, buzz me."

Although his mask blocked the lower half of his face, his eyes crinkled, letting her know he was smiling. "No problem. I was glad to help. I enjoy working with you, Jenny."

She felt the same. Unfortunately.

Later that night, Jenny leaned against the breakroom counter, eyes closed, waiting for the toaster oven to finish heating her early a.m. "lunch." John Rossberg had remained stable, with no evidence of active bleeding, a pneumothorax, or a pulmonary embolism. Though his white blood cell count had significantly spiked, his differentials indicated that he had developed a secondary infection. Dr. Willis had prescribed a strong antibiotic as a precaution while they awaited his test results.

"You okay?"

Jenny sighed. Like a bad penny, Tristan kept showing up. Did he purposely seek her out? *Why ask what you already know?* He did. Part of her was flattered and another frustrated as not being near him would be easier.

"It's after four in the morning, so I'm a little tired, but otherwise, I'm fine."

"Yep. Tonight's flown by."

She was glad he thought so. For the most part, she felt as if it had dragged.

"You sure you're okay? You're rubbing your neck," he pointed out.

Jenny's hand fell. She hadn't noticed.

"I was concerned that you might have injured yourself when we turned Mr. Rossberg—he's a good two hundred pounds—or perhaps when you were helping with Mattie."

She shook her head. "Like I said, I'm fine. Just a little tired. How is Mattie?"

His new admit from the night before had come to the

floor in multiple organ failure after the young woman had overdosed on a benzodiazepine prescription.

"Alive, still. Barely." He exhaled a long breath. "I always find taking care of overdose patients difficult."

"Really?" The toaster oven beeped. Jenny pulled her food from it, testing to make sure it was warm throughout, then breathed in the delicious aroma of her mother's chicken casserole. Geneva loved cooking and, by and large, Jenny let her reign in their kitchen. "That surprises me, because we see some icky stuff."

"It's more that most of our patients are battling something they didn't have much direct control over. With an overdose patient—" he shrugged "—I can't help but think that they should be out living life and not fighting for every breath in an ICU."

"There are those who would argue that an addict doesn't have much direct control over their choices, either," Jenny observed, her tone soft as part of her understood, agreed even, with what he was saying.

"You're right," he admitted. "I should keep that in mind. It just seems such a waste of a precious life."

He wasn't wrong.

"I doubt any of our overdose patients woke up one day and thought 'I want to be an addict.'"

"Most don't mean to overdose, either," he agreed. "But far too many end up with something laced with bad stuff or they accidentally take too much."

Jenny nodded. "I struggle the most with the ones who intentionally take too much or self-harm. Did you bring something to eat? I have way too much chicken casserole and am willing to share."

Now why had she just offered to give him some of her food? That was something a friend would do and she'd already pointed out that they weren't going to be friends.

"That smells wonderful and it is tempting." He opened the fridge and pulled out a drink bottle. "But I typically just drink a protein shake while at work."

She wrinkled her nose. "For your entire twelve-plus-hours shift? How do you survive?"

Although grabbing a bite was almost impossible some nights, Jenny never willingly skipped her meal break.

He grinned. "No need to worry. I'm not wasting away."

Jenny couldn't prevent her glance from roaming over his broad shoulders and thick chest that tapered at his waist. She swallowed the lump in her throat. Yeah, he definitely wasn't wasting away.

"I eat a big meal before coming to work," he continued. "While working, I find I do best if I don't eat a lot, just drink plenty of water and protein."

"That seems to be working well for you." Duh! Why had she said such a stupid thing?

His eyes sparkled. "I'm glad you think so."

Yeah, she'd stepped right into that one. Rather than respond, she took a bite of her casserole. A small bite as she sure didn't want to risk choking and him thinking she'd purposely set up his having to save her.

"Laura tells me that you two went to school together your entire lives, including nursing school."

Jenny was grateful for the subject change. "Yes, we attended University of Tennessee together after graduating high school."

"In Knoxville?"

"Chattanooga," she corrected. "University of Tennessee has five campuses, including Knoxville and Memphis."

"That's right. Was Roger in your class, too?"

"I didn't meet him until I came to work here after..." Jenny paused. She did not want to discuss Geoffrey with

Tristan. "After nursing school graduation," she finished, hoping he bought her cover.

Tristan's eyes darkened just enough that she knew he'd picked up that she hadn't said what she'd almost originally intended to. Rather than prompt her for more information, he said, "Laura's a good one."

"You won't hear any arguments from me." Well, except when it came to Tristan himself and Laura's teasing about his extremely warm temperature. Being around Tristan really was like being in a torrent heat wave. *Hot. Hot. Hot.* Resisting the urge to fan her face, she said, "She's my best friend."

Tristan's patient pager went off. "Hmm, none of Mattie's lines should need changing. I checked them right before coming in here to grab my drink."

Popping the top back onto her meal prep container and shoving it into the fridge, she offered, "I'll go with you in case you need an extra set of hands."

Already heading toward the door, he smiled. "Thanks."

"No problem. Good patient care is always my top priority."

That was the only reason she'd offered to help.

"Good morning," Jenny greeted the four-year-old sitting at the kitchen bar and munching on his cereal a few exhausting hours later. She kissed the top of his tawny head, loving the fresh smell of his shampoo, then walked over to the woman stirring a teaspoon of sugar into a "Volunteer" coffee mug. "Morning, Mom. Did you have a good night?"

"Every night spent with my grandson is a good night," her mom assured her, handing over the coffee. "Just as every night with you was a good night when you were growing up. Still is, actually."

"Love you, too." Jenny took a sip, savoring the hot decaffeinated liquid hitting her throat. She preferred caffeinated, but never indulged when she had to be asleep in less than an hour. Her rest schedule was on a tight timeline. She didn't do anything that might throw it off kilter. "Mmm…that's good. Thank you." Her gaze met her mother's. "For everything."

Gratitude was mild for what she felt. She'd have found a way when she'd gotten pregnant during nursing school, but having the support of the best woman she'd ever known and having her to stay with Sawyer on the nights Jenny couldn't be home had made finishing school and going to work so much easier. When Jenny worked weeknights, the day shift replacement charge nurse came in a few minutes early for the report so Jenny could skedaddle as quickly after shift change as possible. It wasn't much time but being there as a part of her son's mornings…well, she hoped someday he'd realize how important it was to her, how much she wanted to be there for him, and to be a part of his life.

"You're welcome, honey." Geneva smiled. "I put the lunch you had prepacked into his school bag and started a load of towels in the washer that you'll want to change over when you get back from dropping him off at school."

Her mother had offered to drop him off on her way to the assisted living where she worked an eight-to-five shift, but Jenny had always refused. She prized the precious time spent with Sawyer each morning and seeing his smile when, after she'd walked him into his preschool, he'd turn and wave.

"Mom, did you know that Grandma likes frogs?" Sawyer asked seemingly out of the blue in between bites of his breakfast.

"She does?" Suppressing a smile, Jenny's eyes went to her mother's.

Sawyer's soft, curl-covered head bobbed up and down. "We watched a show about frogs last night, and she helped me look them up online so we could learn more." His eyes lit with excitement. "Grandma liked that."

Jenny's mother smiled indulgently. "What can I say? He's broadening my horizons one amphibian at a time. We searched for the frog species you kiss to transform into a Prince Charming, but never came across that breed."

"You want to kiss a frog? I thought you liked Giles."

"I do like Giles. The frog was for you."

Jenny groaned. "The only frog I'm kissing is sitting in this chair. Let's see if he turns into a prince." She placed a noisy kiss on Sawyer's cheek then pulled back to stare at him. "Nope, not a prince yet. Maybe it takes a bunch of kisses."

She began kissing his cheeks over and over, triggering giggling protests.

"Stop. Stop. I'm not a frog."

Jenny paused in her sloppy cheek kisses to inspect him. "You sure about that?"

He nodded his head. "Grandma wants to find a big frog for you so you can be a princess like in the fairy tales."

Jenny snorted, glancing toward her mother. "She does, does she? You'll have to remind her that amphibians can be royal pains and I'm quite content with my life as it is."

Content. There was that word again. Because she was content, that's why it had popped up again. Why did others not seem to believe that?

By the time Jenny got back home after her preschool run, changed the washed towels over to the dryer, showered and climbed into bed, she'd get about six hours of sleep before going to pick Sawyer up from school. It wasn't a lot, but it would suffice.

Yawning, she set her alarm then rolled over, expecting to go to sleep as she usually passed out when her head hit the pillow. Instead, Tristan's face popped into her head. His handsome, smiling face.

"Ribbit."

Oh, no, he hadn't just said that! Tristan was not a frog who would magically morph into Prince Charming from a kiss. He was a travel nurse who would kiss today and be gone tomorrow.

She squeezed her eyes tightly shut as if that would somehow make him disappear from her mind.

"Ribbit. Ribbit. Ribbit."

Seriously, if the man wanted to be her friend then he'd best just shut the croak up and stay out of her head. She didn't need his interfering with her sleep.

Only, for the longest time, she couldn't stop the thoughts of him, of his smile, of his easygoing nature, of his "hotness." When she finally slept, she dreamt he really was a frog, complete with a lopsided crown sitting on his handsome head.

CHAPTER THREE

"NEED HELP?"

Jenny did, but she'd been looking for Roger, not this man, smiling so big she feared she might fall right into his dimples. She was more than a little irritated with him, through no real fault of his own. But short of lifting Mr. Rossberg by herself, yes, she needed his help.

Because of him, she'd barely slept and when she had, he had played a lead role in her dreams.

Dreams? Ha, more like an X-rated movie that had started out with a frog-morphing-into-a-prince kiss. She'd awakened breathless and achy.

Her eyes dropped to his mouth. His very talented, kissable mouth that had done amazing things to her.

No! His mouth wasn't talented and had never been anywhere near her lips, her neck, or anywhere else. Of course, he'd been phenomenal because it hadn't been real. He probably had bad breath or a saliva disorder or some other warty ailment that would turn her off. No one was as perfect as he seemed. Not even in fairy tales.

"Yes, your help would be great." Not really, but her patient came first. At home…well, at home, he wasn't welcome. Hopefully, today was a one-off because of Laura and Roger's crazy conversation, those innocent brushings against each other when they'd been repositioning

Mr. Rossberg last night, and the odd kissing-a-frog conversation with Sawyer and her mother.

"You look tired. Did you not get much sleep today?" Tristan eyed her as he slipped his arms through his protective gown.

She frowned, trying to determine if he was concerned or if he somehow knew that it was his fault she'd not gotten her usual six hours of shut-eye between dropping off and picking up Sawyer.

"Is that your way of saying I look bad?" she asked, trying to focus on the negative where he was concerned rather than on how her heart was tapping a funny rhythm at his closeness. Not a normal *lub-dub, lub-dub* beat, but a wacky *rib-bit, rib-bit*. What was wrong with her?

"I didn't say you looked bad. I said you looked tired. There's a difference." His eyes were full of appreciation. "I doubt you ever look bad."

She harrumphed. "I've already pointed out that flattery will go nowhere with me."

"I'm not trying to flatter you, Jenny." He sounded sincere. "Just pointing out the truth."

"Yeah, well, you've never seen me fresh out of bed." Her words spilled forth naturally, without thought. The second they did, she cringed at how he could interpret them. At how she interpreted them, possibly because in her dreams he had seen her fresh out of bed just a few hours ago.

"You don't wear much makeup, so it's hard to imagine that you'd look that different, but you know best, so if you say so…" Then he surprised her by grinning. "For whatever it's worth, I even understand. It takes me hours to achieve all this."

Biting into her lower lip, she tried to determine if he was teasing. The twinkle in his eyes said he was, and he'd never come across as vain, more unaware of how truly attractive he was, if anything.

"I'd hate to see you not trying if that—" snarling her nose, she gave him an up-and-down look "—takes hours."

Had that been her teasing back? No. No. No. She needed to keep her guard up, remain professional, not playful.

"You're right. You shouldn't see that." He smiled then gestured to her patient's room. "Any sign of regaining consciousness?"

Jenny shook her head. "I keep hoping I'll get to work and hear that he woke up, but nothing so far. His pneumonia doesn't seem to be clearing."

"It's never easy when our patients don't get well, is it?"

Jenny paused in donning her protective equipment to stare at him. She wasn't sure why, but she hadn't expected the deep compassion in his voice.

"No, but Mr. Rossberg is going to get better. I refuse to let him not."

Tristan's eyes smiled above his mask. "I stand by my initial assessment."

"What's that?" she asked, stepping into Mr. Rossberg's room.

"That you're a great nurse. Your mother must be so proud to know you followed in her footsteps and take such good care of your patients."

Warmth spread through her at his compliment.

"I— Thank you."

"Better be careful, Jenny, because if I didn't know better, I'd think my flattery just worked a little with you." His tone was soft, teasing, as they made their way over to Mr. Rossberg's hospital bed.

"You keep thinking that if you like, but I'll know better, Kermit."

His forehead furrowed. "Who?"

Fighting a smile, and a bit of horror at what she'd called him, Jenny shook her head then touched her patient's arm. "Mr. Rossberg, it's Jenny. I'm here with another nurse, Tristan. He's helped with your care before, remember? He's going to assist while I suction some of the secretions built up in your lungs, so you get better air exchange, isn't that great? We're going to have you breathing easier soon so you can go fishing with that adorable grandson of yours."

"We're having a team-building event next weekend," Roger announced, dropping into the chair next to Jenny's at the nurses' station. "Your presence is required."

First tapping Save, Jenny glanced up from her charting. "What kind of event?"

"White-water rafting." Roger's voice filled with excitement. "After our conversation about it, we decided to put together a trip with Tristan."

Jenny's stomach twisted.

"Perhaps you'll also recall from that conversation, that I'm not interested in white-water rafting."

Or in spending time with Tristan outside of work.

"Come on, Jenny. At least hear me out," Roger insisted. "Like what Laura suggested, we're driving to the Ocoee, camping on Friday night, rafting on Saturday, camping again that night, then driving back on Sunday, sleeping all day, then working all Sunday night."

He made it sound so simple, but Jenny shook her head.

"You forget that I'm not free to just take off for a weekend camping trip on the spur of the moment." Nor did she want to. She cherished her weekends with Sawyer when she was not scheduled to work. There was always lots to be done around the house, but she let him pick an activity for them to do together. She never knew if he was going to want to make cookies or go to the park or play board games. Sawyer's pick was as spur-of-the-moment as she got these days.

"Couldn't your mom watch Sawyer so that you could go with us?" Laura asked as she joined them. That her friend immediately knew what they'd been discussing said they'd been talking about it just prior to Roger returning to the nurses' station. "Not that I don't love hanging with Sawyer," Laura continued, "but it would be so good to spend time together away from work. It's been forever since you and I did that."

Guilt hit that they only spent time together at work or when Laura joined her and Sawyer. Did that make her a bad friend?

"I hate to ask when she already does so much." Not that her mother wouldn't jump all over sending Jenny if she thought there might be a few frogs around. That had her dream popping back into her head. Yeah, the last thing she needed was a camping trip with Tristan around. "Y'all go. Have fun. White-water rafting really isn't my thing."

"How do you know?" Roger asked.

Jenny blinked. "What do you mean how do I know? I just do."

"Have you ever been white-water rafting?"

She shook her head. "You know I haven't because Laura mentioned the missed church trip."

"You might enjoy rafting," he offered.

"I might not and then I'd be stuck in a flimsy raft floating down a raging river."

"Not that raging," Roger corrected.

"Says the guy who plans to jump out of an airplane to celebrate his thirtieth birthday this fall," Jenny quipped.

"You should do that with me." At her horrified look, Roger grinned. "Fine. No sky-diving for our Jenny, but at least say you'll think about going on the rafting trip."

"Besides the obvious reasons for my not going on y'all's impromptu trip, I don't own the first piece of camping equipment."

"You don't need anything," Laura declared. "I've got an extra sleeping bag and you can stay in my tent with me. I'll pack double, right down to bringing extra water shoes, so no excuses. It'll be like a sleepover. All you need to do is say yes."

The yearning in Laura's voice got to Jenny, but she wasn't asking her mother to keep Sawyer, not when doing so put herself in danger. She didn't mean the rafting part, either. Being around Tristan threatened her far more than taking on the river.

"I appreciate the invite, but I'm a mom first. My weekend off work is my time with Sawyer. As much as I adore y'all, I'm not giving that up to go rafting."

"Giles's grandson will be visiting with him this weekend."

Propping her cell phone between her shoulder and her ear, Jenny watched the timer count down on the toaster oven warming her work "lunch." She'd been running nonstop since arriving earlier that evening and was glad things had settled down early enough for her to make a call to tell Sawyer good-night and to chat with her mother afterward. That her mother's voice rang with happiness had Jenny smiling. Her mother had been dating the widower who worked at the assisted-living home with her for about a year and they'd been hinting about marriage. Jenny liked Giles, but even more, she liked how her mother lit up when she talked about him.

"He's bringing Eli to the aquarium in Gatlinburg on Friday night. There's a sleepover event with church," her mother continued, her voice breathy. "Giles invited Sawyer and me to go with them. Please say yes."

Her mother wanted Sawyer to do a church sleepover on the same weekend as the rafting trip? Had Laura called her mother and arranged this?

"I'm sure he'd have a great time." They'd visited the Chattanooga aquarium but had never been to the one in east Tennessee, much less slept over. No doubt Sawyer would love an overnight excursion. "When a group books an event, they sleep under the shark tank there, don't they? He'd be so excited that he might not sleep a wink."

"That's what Giles said—that we would be sleeping under the sharks. I'm not sure how I feel about that," her mother said with a low laugh, "but I know Sawyer would love it. We thought we'd spend the weekend in Gatlinburg and do some things with the boys, maybe minigolf or go to Parrot Mountain."

Jenny's stomach twisted. Other than when she was at work, her son had never spent a night away from her. "You want Sawyer to spend the whole weekend with you and Giles in Gatlinburg?"

"We'd watch him closely," her mother promised, blasting Jenny with guilt. Her mother loved Sawyer and wanted to have this fun trip with him.

"Oh, Mom, you know I trust you completely with Sawyer. It's not that, it's just…you already do so much, and for the whole weekend? Are you sure you want to take that on, too?"

"Absolutely. This would be such a fun weekend for us. I really do love spending time with him."

"Sawyer or Giles?" she teased, taking her dish from the toaster oven and testing the temperature.

Her mother's laugh said it all. "Giles is a good man, Jenny. I really think he might be the one."

The knot in her belly tightened. Not that she didn't want her mother happy, but mostly, she didn't want her hurt.

"I'm happy for you, Mom." She really was. Jenny's father had left before she'd been born. She only recalled a few men in her mother's life. A very few, and none of them had stuck around for long. Based on the one breakup conversation she'd accidentally overheard, she was to blame for that. Her split with Carlos had pretty much been an echo of that. Some men didn't want to be seriously involved with a woman who was a package deal.

"Now, how about you spend this weekend finding that Prince Charming frog to make you happy?"

Jenny snorted. She should have known their conversation would eventually turn to her finding a man. Everyone seemed to think she needed one.

"I am happy, Mom. No frog, or Prince Charming, required." She spoke the truth. She was happy. She had a good job, a home, her mom and Sawyer. Plus, her mother's homemade lasagna, she thought, taking a bite of the spicy pasta. Mmm… Life was good.

"That's not really what I meant. Of course, you're happy. But wouldn't it be wonderful to have someone to share that happiness with? You're a beautiful young woman, Jenny. I don't want you going through life alone the way I did."

"I think you're biased, Mom, but I appreciate how you see and love me." Jenny took a deep breath. "I'm also glad you've met someone who has given you so much happiness. I like Giles a lot. But that doesn't mean I want that, too. I have you and Sawyer. I'm content."

Content. Why did that word keep popping up and seem to be a negative? Content was good, right?

"I worry about you, Jenny. I can't bear the thought of you sitting at home alone. Come with us."

For a moment, Jenny considered doing just that but then thought better of it. Her mother would be throwing every single male on the trip her way. No thank you.

"Promise me that you won't volunteer to work at the hospital."

"Volunteering at the hospital is a good thing. The extra money would come in handy to do some things around the house I've been wanting to update. Plus, I want to get that playground for Sawyer's birthday. Volunteering to work is exactly what I should do."

"You're going to work all weekend, aren't you? If he was here, you'd take the time to play rather than work." Her mother sighed, sounding as if she was considering canceling her own plans.

Jenny didn't want that. As much as the time away from her son was going to have her missing him, Sawyer would enjoy it.

"Actually, I got invited on a camping trip to the Ocoee with Laura and some of our work friends. I hadn't thought to go, but since Sawyer will be with you, I think I might."

What was she saying?

"Seriously?" Her mother's tone brightened. "That's wonderful. It's been ages since you've done anything fun. You'd have a marvelous time."

Jenny wasn't so sure about that, but she could practically hear her mother's smile, so wasn't going to do anything to dissipate that. They finished talking then she hung up her phone.

Alone. For the whole weekend. Maybe she should volunteer to work.

Or she really could go rafting with her friends and pretend for one weekend that she was a carefree mid-twenties woman who was embracing life.

CHAPTER FOUR

TRISTAN HAD NEVER seen Jenny in anything other than her nursing uniforms. He'd not expected her to be wearing scrubs when she and Laura came out of Jenny's house, but he'd not been prepared for seeing her in casual clothes, either. A brightly colored T-shirt, loose shorts, exposing long, toned legs, a long braid, and a worried expression completed her look. The worried aura, he recognized. It was one she wore around him much too often.

Other than the worried look, he liked Jenny out of her work attire.

He liked her house, too. In a tree-lined neighborhood not too far from the hospital, the houses were older, but overall appeared well kept. Jenny's yard boasted a few massive oak trees and some shade-loving plants bordering her driveway. A couple of brightly colored flower baskets hung from her front porch railing and two navy rocking chairs that perfectly matched the window shutters added to the homey feel. A checkered pillow that said "Home Sweet Home" was angled in one of the chairs. A wooden fence blocked the backyard, providing privacy from whatever she had hidden back there. Was Jenny a hot-tub-on-the-deck person or perhaps an avidly extreme gardener?

Their gazes met and he smiled, hoping she'd do the same. She didn't.

He might be looking forward to this time to get to know her better outside of work, but she didn't feel the same. At some point over the weekend, he'd let her know that she had nothing to worry about. He was great with just being her friend. Usually, that was what he preferred anyway. He didn't get involved with coworkers, but there was something about Jenny to the point where, had she been interested, he'd make an exception to his rule. Regardless, he didn't want anything serious. Between his parents' crazy marriage and subsequent divorce, and there being too much world to experience to get stuck in one place, he'd never wanted that. Just the thought of being tied down too long made his chest tighten around his lungs.

"Is that it?" He gestured to her single bag then glanced toward her for confirmation.

"Laura assures me that this is all I need to bring." She didn't look convinced. "It's all she had on the list she texted me."

"I've got you covered on everything else," Laura reiterated. "If there's something I've missed, someone at camp will have extra, so quit worrying."

"Do I look worried?" Jenny made a face at her friend and Laura stuck out her tongue then laughed. Something about their camaraderie tugged deep inside Tristan. They'd been friends for years. What did that feel like? To have someone in your life that long? He had friends, he reminded himself. Not friendships like theirs, though. Just people he'd connected to during his short time with them and that he'd maintained a loose relationship with over the years. What would it be like to have someone who knew everything about you and loved you all the same?

Shaking the thought, he reached for Jenny's tightly clutched bag.

"She's right. Other than personal items, everything should be good. Plus, according to the GPS map I was looking at last night, our campsite isn't far from a convenience store. We can always pick up anything needed."

"Good to know." Her fingers slowly releasing her bag, she gave it to him and he packed it into the back of his SUV, along with his gear and the supplies he'd brought.

"I've never camped," she admitted. "Hopefully, I won't be a deadweight."

"You won't be." He'd been looking forward to this time with her since hearing that she was going on the trip.

First giving him an odd look, Jenny went to climb into the back of the SUV.

Laura shook her head. "Let me ride in the back. You know when I'm not driving, I sometimes get motion sickness and that, for whatever reason, I do better in the backseat with headphones on than upfront where I can see out the window."

Wincing at the prospect of riding in the front with him, Jenny hesitated at the door while Laura settled in. Was she going to climb into the back, too, and have him chauffeur them around?

"I'll have my audiobook going, so y'all just ignore me," Laura advised as she motioned for Jenny to climb in then slipped on her headset. "I only have a few hours left and have been dying to get back to this story."

"Be my copilot?" Tristan asked, hoping to put Jenny at ease. "You can keep me on task on these backroads so that I don't make Laura's motion sickness worse. If it gets too bad, we can let her drive and I'll get in the back and let you ladies have the front."

"I— Okay." She climbed into the passenger seat and snapped her seat belt. "Just tell me what you need me to do as the copilot and I'll help however I can."

"Relax," he suggested. It's what he wanted her to do more than anything. To relax and enjoy herself and not get so tense around him.

"That's going to help you drive better?"

"Possibly. I don't want you stressed. This trip is supposed to be fun, so you shouldn't look as if you're headed to the dentist to have your wisdom teeth cut out."

To her credit, she smiled.

"That's better," he encouraged. "Now, if I can just keep you smiling. Want me to tell you corny nursing jokes?"

"Just get us there safe and I promise I'll smile the moment we arrive."

Because then she'd escape being in a vehicle with him? From his peripheral vision he saw her fold her hands in her lap and turn to look out the window. He suspected she wished she had headphones and an audiobook, as well, so she had an excuse to shut him out.

"Find us a radio station?" he suggested, thinking music might be a good icebreaker. Music was always good.

"Sure. What type do you like?"

"Anything is fine, but my favorite is classic rock," he admitted, pulling out of the parking spot.

"As in Led Zeppelin, Aerosmith, the Rolling Stones, the Doors, and that type of classic rock?" She sounded surprised.

Glancing her way, Tristan grinned. Who knew she'd be a classic rock fan, too? "Who's your favorite?"

"I grew up listening to a lot of Eagles and Fleetwood Mac with my mom and now I find myself smiling a little on the inside any time I hear something by either group."

His love of music had developed opposite from hers, more of an escape from reality than something to ground him to it. Music had been a constant in his life, his familiar friend when starting over somewhere new.

"Does your mother live close?" he asked for a distraction from his thoughts as much as curiosity about Jenny's life.

"Very." Amusement laced her tone. "We live in the same house."

Interesting and not something that he could imagine willingly doing at her age. Or at any age that he was old enough to have done otherwise.

"That is close."

"Honestly, I don't know what I'd do without her." Genuine love and appreciation oozed from her words. "She's a nurse at a local assisted-living home."

"Does living together make dating difficult?"

"Not at all. She dates regularly."

Tristan chuckled. "I was referring to you."

"I've already told you that I don't date."

"But your mother does?"

"Yes. She has a boyfriend. I suspect they'll marry at some point, and I'm great with that. She deserves every good thing, and he makes her happy. He works with her at the assisted-living facility, but he's in the office." She tapped her fingers against her thighs in rhythm with the radio's beat. "How did we get on this topic?"

"What do you want to talk about?"

"With you?" Her question revealed too much for his liking, but finally she shrugged. "Tell me about being a travel nurse. Where's the coolest place you've worked?"

"Maine," he answered without hesitation. "I'd put in for a rotation in Alaska, but that didn't pan out. At the time, I didn't have as much experience as the hospital there wanted. If something opens up, I may try again. I'd like to spend time around Juneau."

She twisted a little in her seat to more fully look at him. "Apparently, we have poor communication skills as I'd actually used the term 'cool' to mean awesome rather than temperature. But tell me about Maine."

"Cool is too mild a description for my time in Maine. I worked inland, fairly close to the Canadian border, in a small-town hospital. My rotation was from fall until late spring. It was cold, sometimes we'd get twelve inches of snow at a time, and it never warmed up enough for it to melt away, so it just kept building upon itself until spring."

"I don't think I'd like that."

"It was great by me since I knew I wasn't staying long term. I went to experience the snow, skiing, and to just take in the frozen beauty of the area. It's a gorgeous place."

"If you say so. I'm not a fan of being cold." She rubbed her arms to emphasize her point. "Is there somewhere you intend to eventually take a permanent hospital position?"

Just the thought of being trapped in one location made his throat tighten.

"No. I don't see myself staying anywhere more than a year maximum. I like the three- to six-month rotations I'm on. It's a great timeframe for checking out the area and finding hidden treasures away from the usual tourist spots."

In a couple of months, his Chattanooga contract would be up, and he'd be moving on to his next location. Chicago had made a nice offer, as had Wisconsin, but he'd not yet decided. Maybe for three months at one or the other, though, and then he could take a spot somewhere Deep South for the winter months rather than heading further north.

"I can't imagine moving around so much."

Tristan couldn't imagine not. What would it be like to come home to the same place night after night, week after week, month after month, year after year? He liked his studio apartment, but it was just a place to sleep. Clearing his throat, he said, "I like seeing the world."

"That's what the internet and television are for," she countered.

Something in the way she said it had him asking, "You're kidding, right?"

She didn't say anything.

"You don't like traveling? Seeing the world first-person rather than through someone else's perspective?"

"I'm happy in Chattanooga," Jenny attested. "I have a good life here."

Then the truth, as much as it boggled his mind, hit him. "Have you ever been out of Chattanooga, Jenny?"

"Of course, I've been out of Chattanooga. To Atlanta a few times and Nashville."

Claustrophobia clawed at him at how confined she'd been. "Is that it? What about vacations?"

"Those were vacations," she said, her tone defensive.

"We need to get you out of Chattanooga and let you see the world," Tristan mused.

Jenny shook her head. "My world is in Chattanooga."

"Yeah, but—"

"Seriously, this isn't an argument you can win. You do you and have no roots. I like my roots and that they run deep. Chattanooga is my home. My family is here. I'm happy here."

Awe that she had meant what she'd said, that she really was happy within her small geographical bubble, shook him. Jenny truly didn't care if she traveled beyond her immediate circle. Her roots bound her as surely as if they encased her within their treacherous tentacles.

Or maybe they grounded her so the strongest wind couldn't topple her resolve.

"I didn't mean to offend you," he said and meant it.

"You didn't. You... Okay, so maybe I was defensive. Sorry."

"It's good that you feel so passionate about your home."

"This coming from the guy who just said he wasn't ever settling down anywhere."

"That doesn't mean I can't appreciate that you're passionate about where you live. Besides, I've always heard that home is where the heart is."

"And your heart is only home for three to six months at a time?"

Had his heart ever been in any of the places he'd lived?

"Don't knock it until you try it," he advised, not liking how their conversation kept making him question himself, when it was she who should be questioning her life choices. Who stayed within a hundred miles of where they were born their entire lives? "There's something liberating about seeing the world."

"There's something comforting about the familiar, too," she countered. "A few years back, our landlord decided to sell the house my mom had rented most of my life. The one where you picked me up this morning. With the help of the bank, I bought it. I love the way walking through its doors makes me feel."

Why did listening to her make him feel as if he'd been the one deprived, rather than her?

Taking a deep breath, he swallowed the knot in his throat. "How's that?"

"Proud. At peace. Safe." Her voice became almost nostalgic. "Loved."

Jenny didn't see her house as just a place to sleep, but more of an extension of who she was. Roots. Hers were deeply embedded and gave her strength. Unease settled in his stomach. Unease that what she'd described was as foreign to him as living out of a suitcase was to her.

"Are you a Braves fan?"

Twisting in her seat to look at him again, she hesitated, making him wonder if she'd picked up on how uncomfortable their conversation had made him.

Rather than pry, she nodded. "Is there any other team?"

Breathing a little easier, he laughed. "Maybe we could catch a game."

Was he asking her on a date or suggesting going with their work crew on another group trip? As foolish as he considered the conversation they'd just had, and knowing she was more apt to agree to a group activity, if pressed, he'd have to admit he wanted it to be just the two of them.

"Have you been to a Braves' game before?" she asked rather than comment on his invitation.

"I've seen them play but not in the Atlanta stadium. I caught them in Boston."

He and a neighborhood kid had snuck in to watch the game. Rollo hadn't been the best influence, so it was just as well they hadn't stayed in that apartment long. Thinking back, he tried to summon the warm fuzzies Jenny got over her home and couldn't. Instead, he barely recalled which apartment they'd even lived in at the time.

"Did you do a rotation in Boston, then?"

He shook his head. "I lived there during my early teen years."

"Is that where you're from? Massachusetts?"

"I'm not from anywhere. We moved a lot." They'd moved so often, he'd sometimes felt as if his real home was the backseat of his father's beat-up king cab truck or whatever junker his mother had sweet-talked off a boyfriend.

"Your parents liked to travel, too?" Jenny asked, pulling him from the past.

"You could say that." His parents hadn't traveled to see the world, though. His mother's moves had had more to do with escaping creditors and ex-boyfriends. A tradition she'd continued until the day she'd died during his last year in nursing school. His father had worked construction, still did; wherever the next job took him was where Travis Scott resided.

"My dad left before I was born," Jenny surprised him by saying. She safeguarded everything personal so much that the insight to who she was felt like a precious gift. "Mom didn't have money for travel, but I never did without anything and was rich in love. She's my rock."

Rich in love? There went that weird feeling in his stomach again.

Tristan stared ahead at the winding road that snaked along the river. He tapped his fingers on the steering wheel to the music's beat. The melody failed to calm him. Not once had he thought of his mother or father as his rock, nor had he ever felt rich in love. Most of his childhood, he'd felt more like a millstone around their necks, dragging them down with his presence.

Maybe if he'd had Jenny's idyllic-sounding childhood, he'd feel at home somewhere and want to stay. But nowhere had ever felt like home. He doubted it ever would, which was just as well since he preferred being footloose and fancy-free. The world was a big place and he wanted to see it all.

"I can't just stand here doing nothing," Jenny insisted after they'd checked in at their campsite. They, along with Roger and his girlfriend, who'd fallen in behind their car on the drive, were the first from their group to arrive, but the others were close. "I need to help."

"Roger, Lucia and I have our tent," Laura assured her, spreading out the nylon material. Then, with a grin, suggested, "See if Tristan needs help."

Of course, her friend wanted her to help Tristan.

She glanced toward where he was setting up his tent. Roger and Lucia's tent was to the left of Jenny and Laura's. Tristan's was quite a ways back from the others. Jenny bit into her lower lip.

She didn't want to be thrown together with him all weekend, but apparently that was what was going to happen. She should have gone to the aquarium with her mother and Sawyer.

Or maybe she just needed to relax and quit worrying so much. It didn't matter how much she was thrown together with Tristan. Nothing was going to happen. Nothing like what her friend was hoping, at any rate.

Chatting with Tristan on the ride had been…well, not horrible. He was interesting and, once they'd gotten beyond the topic of travel and his one awkward period where he'd changed the subject and she'd kept wondering what he was thinking of, he'd made her laugh. Mostly with corny nurse jokes. But laughing with him had felt… good.

Taking a deep breath, she walked the thirty yards or so to where his tent was set up on the opposite side of the fire pit, near the outskirts of the campsite. Had he purposely chosen to be further away? Or maybe he thought that when the others arrived they'd fill the gaps?

"Laura sent me to help," she said, not wanting him to read her being there wrong. Friendly, but not too friendly. That's what she was going for.

"Thanks." He half smiled, digging a dimple into his cheek. "You want to gather some kindling? I brought a few bigger pieces, but we'll need smaller sticks to get our fire started for later tonight."

It wasn't chilly but the temp would drop once the sun set. A fire would feel good. Plus, what was camping without a campfire? She should learn all she could so that she could take Sawyer without being totally lost. She had to start looking at this trip the right way. It was research. "If you'll show me an example of what we need, I'll help."

He found a handful of small sticks and pine needles. "Anything like this would be great. We'll get enough for tonight and tomorrow night."

Jenny gathered sticks, stacking a small pile next to the block-edged area where they'd build their fire. Several others had arrived and were unloading their wares, setting up their tents and laughing. She greeted her co-workers, met their significant others for the ones who'd brought a plus-one, then went off to gather more fire-starting wood, searching through the nearby trees for various-sized pieces.

"Finding much?" Tristan asked.

Jenny held up her sticks. "I've got a pretty good pile going next to the fire pit. I wasn't sure how much we'd need, so thought I'd get a bit more, just in case."

"Sounds like a good plan. Allergic to poison ivy?" he asked, motioning to her wares.

"Not that I know of." Her palms instantly starting

to itch, she glanced down at the wood. She had a general idea of what the plant looked like, was well aware of what the rash looked like from her nursing school days of working in the emergency room, but she was far from an expert on poisonous vegetation. "Is that what I'm holding?"

"No, but it is what's growing on that tree next to you. I wasn't sure if you'd noticed and didn't want you rubbing against it in hope of a reason to get out of the trip tomorrow."

"Oh. Right. Sorry." She backed away from the tree. "I've never had a reaction, but I've never gone tromping through the woods, either. Although getting out of the rafting trip tomorrow sounds tempting, I'm not a fan of itchy rashes."

"I hear you." Picking up a medium-sized branch that had fallen from a tree, he placed his foot on the limb for stabilization and snapped it into more manageable pieces. "It's hard to imagine living here and not spending a lot of time outdoors."

"I didn't say that I didn't spend a lot of time outdoors, just that I haven't gone tromping through the woods," she clarified, bending to pick up another stick.

From spring to fall, she mowed their lawn weekly then tended to their flower beds. Seeing the brightly colored blooms adding splashes of color made her happy. Her mother, too. Other than the garden box that she'd let Sawyer plant vegetable seeds in and their small aboveground bed she'd bought at a local home supply store, Sawyer didn't seem to care one way or the other about their landscaping efforts. However, he did love their trips to a nearby playground on her days off and when the weather permitted.

"Watch for snakes," Tristan warned.

Jenny froze. "Snakes? No one mentioned snakes."

Sleeping in a tent took on a new, unpleasant twist. If she slept at all.

"They won't bother you unless you bother them," Tristan continued, "but keep an eye out on where you're stepping and picking up sticks. I don't want you accidentally startling one and getting bit."

She didn't move. "I'm nervous enough already and now you mention snakes. Someone should have warned me. All this time, I thought the river was the biggest danger."

"Don't be nervous, Jenny. I just wanted you to be careful but didn't mean to make you worried." He touched her shoulder and shockwaves shot through her. Just a simple touch, with her cotton T-shirt separating their skin, and yet every nerve ending within her focused on what he'd meant to be a comforting gesture. Her head spinning, she stepped back to steady herself.

"We probably won't see any," he noted, "but I promise I'll fend off any snake we encounter."

Although he was teasing, she had no doubt that he would. That truth shone in his eyes and did funny things to her belly. She'd never had a man in her life who'd promised to protect her. From a crawling reptile or anything else. That she believed Tristan would, at least for the weekend, had her clearing her throat and taking another step back. She didn't need some wannabe white knight messing with her world.

"You're the only thing I'm worried about fending off," she admitted, trying to stop the softening in her chest. She absolutely could not fall for him. To do so was nothing short of emotional suicide. He was leaving in less than three months. Here today, gone tomorrow.

Face pinching, he shook his head. "There you go with

that stellar impression of me again. Someday you're going to realize I'm not that bad."

Guilt hit. She hadn't meant to offend him. Or maybe she had, to put some emotional distance between them. During the drive, once they'd quit talking about personal things and had just been chatting, relaxing had been much too easy. She needed to keep up her guard. Not only that, to stay on the offensive to actively fight to protect her heart.

With that in mind, she straightened her shoulders. "Don't count on it."

Curiosity shone in his eyes. "Because?"

Because the way you make me feel terrifies me. Because the way my heart pounds when you're near leaves me near breathless. Because the way my insides dance when our eyes meet throws me off kilter. Because the way I can't stop thinking about you rattles my logic.

"Because I suspect you're not that good, either."

Too bad she didn't believe her own claim. There were things she suspected he would be very good at. Her eyes dropped to his mouth, flashbacks of her dream—*dreams!*—hitting her.

He's a terrible kisser, she told herself. *Horrible. The worst.*

"You might be right on the 'not being that good,'" he chuckled, "but I like to think I'm a decent guy."

Visions of him kissing her, asking her how that one was, had her swallowing hard. None of it was real.

Knowing he had no clue where her crazy thoughts had just gone, she shook her head. "You'll be gone long before you'll have time to convince me of that."

Thank goodness, because maybe then she'd quit thinking about him, quit wondering about his lips and how bad or good they were.

But when her gaze met his and her stomach fluttered with the intensity of a riled hornet's nest, she wondered if it was already too late for him to not fill her mind and dreams.

CHAPTER FIVE

LAURA HAD BROUGHT an extra fold-up chair and blanket for Jenny, and along with most of the group, they sat around the campfire, basking in its glow and listening to Tristan.

Jenny hadn't known he played the guitar. She also hadn't known he sang. Then again, why would she?

Perhaps it was the influence of how her hormones reacted to him, but his smooth tone lent itself well to the Eagles' "One of These Nights."

Several chimed in during the chorus, but Jenny remained silent. Had he purposely chosen the number due to their conversation during their drive? Or due to the lyrics?

The warm flicker of the fire was plenty to ward off the mild night's chill, but Jenny liked the feel of the fuzzy blanket. Perhaps because having it wrapped loosely around her body made her feel shielded from what was happening to her every time Tristan glanced her way.

"You ready to admit he's hot?" Laura whispered.

Jenny snorted, glancing to where her bestie sat next to her. "I thought I already had. Besides, was his hotness ever really in question?"

Laura laughed. "Y'all seemed to be getting along during the drive."

"We were discussing the weather."

"Yeah, right. I wasn't so into my audiobook that I didn't notice you laughing. Since when has Tennessee weather been humorous?"

He had made her laugh. "Can I help it if he kept telling dumb jokes? Eventually, he wore me down and I started laughing in hopes he'd stop."

"Right." Laura's look shifted to Tristan. "So, you admit he's hot and he makes you laugh." She flashed her eyebrows. "I think you should go for it this weekend."

Wrapping the blanket tighter around her, Jenny gulped before hesitantly asking, "Go for what?"

"Him," Laura said without hesitation. "He seems a great guy. And before you start in with your arguments, so what if he's not going to be here long? You're a single mom who never does anything for herself. This weekend is all about you, not Sawyer or work or anything except *you*. Why not have some fun for a change?"

"You say that as if I'm miserable. I'm not. And, even if I was, I certainly don't need a man to have fun. That's what the entire weekend is supposed to be about. Me having fun." Jenny bared her teeth in a cheesy smile. "This is me having fun."

"The life of the party," Laura teased. "I've watched you keep your nose to the grind for years now, Jen. I know you love being a mom, that Sawyer makes you happy, and that you like your job. But the reality is that spending your time with Tristan is another type of fun."

"Yeah, the kind of fun that led to me being a single mom while still in college," she reminded her. "No thank you. I wouldn't trade Sawyer for anything in the world, but I don't need more of that particular fun in my life."

Laura shrugged. "There are ways of preventing pregnancy."

"Which sometimes don't work. You know it's not the

single-mom part that's the problem. It's the headache of a man in my life and all the drama that involves." And the heartache because she had been crushed at the depth of Geoffrey's deception. Engaged to another woman, one he'd gone on to marry just as planned. How could Jenny have been so blind? How had his fiancée so easily accepted his infidelity and married him anyway? And then Carlos, who'd realized he didn't want to be involved with a single mom. Or maybe he'd known all along and had just used her while he'd had the chance. Either way, he'd left. "No thanks."

"What drama? It's been eons since you've dated."

"I don't have to have been on a date to have witnessed the drama. You go through it every time you have a new boyfriend." At Laura's look of disbelief, Jenny elaborated. "There's the elation phase, where you're walking in the clouds because you're so infatuated. Then there's the reality part, where you settle into the relationship. Then there's the breakup, where the world becomes gloom and doom. After that, you repeat the cycle." She shook her head. "That's not for me. Not again. Not when I know how much it hurts. Not when I have Sawyer to think about."

Wincing, Laura stared. "Girl, when did you become so cynical?"

They both knew.

"You call it cynical." Jenny shrugged. "I call it being realistic."

"There are people who find true love," Laura insisted.

"Yeah, well, none of the people I know have, at least, not the romantic kind." But she did know true love. She never doubted that her mother and her son loved her with all their hearts. She gave her friend a pointed look. "I'm including you and me in that lack of romantic true love."

"It's not from lack of trying on my part," Laura refuted. "Someday I will find a man who appreciates all this." She waved her hand up and down her curvy body. "But I disagree with you that we don't know someone truly in love. Look at Roger and Lucia. They're happy."

Jenny glanced at the couple roasting marshmallows over the fire. Every so often, they'd share a special look and, yeah, that was love in their regard for one another. Or, more likely, lust. "They're still in the honeymoon phase. Give them time."

"They've been together for years and are perfect together," Laura pointed out. "How did I not realize how deeply this cynicism went?"

"After Carlos, I decided it was best to avoid the dating cesspool. No need to dive in with the first pretty face that comes along." A pretty face attached to a fit body that held a good work ethic, a kind heart and a humorous personality, but who was keeping tabs?

"Say what you will, but Tristan Scott's a cesspool I don't mind bathing in."

At her friend's suggestive eyebrow waggle, Jenny snorted. "I personally prefer the shower houses we passed on our way in."

Laura nudged her. "Take my advice, and you won't need a cold shower."

The following morning, despite her awareness of the man sitting to her left on the wooden bench, Jenny focused on everything the instructor was reviewing on whitewater rafting safety.

"You okay?"

She cut her eyes to Tristan but didn't answer. She didn't want to risk missing some key information that might save her if she came out of the raft.

Lord, please don't let me fall out of the raft.

Keep her hand over the end of her paddle at all times so that she didn't allow it to hit another rafter or lose it. Never put her feet down if she fell out of the raft because she could get trapped in the rocks and the current would then push her under. Keep her life jacket on at all times—no worries on that one. Listen to what her guide said at all times. Yep, that one wouldn't be a problem, either. She'd be hanging on to the instructor's every word.

Only, apparently, their raft wouldn't have a guide from the outdoor center.

"What do you mean we qualify to go down without a guide?" she asked a few minutes later when Roger made the announcement. She didn't share his excitement.

"Tristan was an instructor in Colorado," Laura told her. "Same difference."

"No, it's not. We aren't in Colorado," Jenny countered, anxiety rising. "We need someone familiar with this river. Not one halfway across the country."

"Relax, Jenny. Lucia and I are experienced rafters," Roger promised. "Of our group, you're the only one who has never been down the river. Most have been several times. The river's water level is average today. We've got this."

Jenny bit into her lower lip, her eyes going back and forth between her friends and settling on where Tristan tightened his life jacket strap. He'd remained quiet during her protests. When his gaze lifted to hers, she wondered if she'd see annoyance at her protests, or perhaps humor at her worries. Instead, concern shone in his blue depths. Not concern over the trip, but that same protective gleam that had shone when he'd promised to keep her safe from any snakes they might encounter.

"It'll be okay, Jenny," Lucia assured her, giving her

a quick hug and drawing her attention from Tristan. "I was just as nervous when Roger brought me for the first time a few years back. We've made several trips now and always have a great time."

Heart still pounding at the look she'd shared with Tristan, she focused on Roger's girlfriend. "But you had a guide all those times, right?"

"We have a guide this time, too," Laura, Lucia and Roger said at the same time and then laughed.

The others just smiled and went about making sure their life jackets were on and appropriately snug. They were her friends. She trusted that they wouldn't put her in undue danger. And yet…

"Here, let me check your life jacket," Tristan offered, coming over to her.

"Please do. I've never had a reason to wear one and may have gotten it wrong," Jenny said.

"Life jackets are pretty basic. You're a quick learner and did a great job," he confirmed even as he gave her strap a tight tug. "Relax and have fun, Jenny. I'm not going to let anything happen to you."

There he went making promises to protect her again.

Sucking as deep a breath as the snug life jacket would allow, she nodded. As crazy as it was, she believed that he'd truly do his best to keep anything from happening to her.

Unfortunately, there were some things beyond his control.

"I know you'll do your best to keep me safe," she admitted, staring up at him, wishing he'd step back considering how close he was from where he'd adjusted her strap. When he didn't, she stepped back, but stumbled.

On cue, Tristan's hand grasped her arm, steadying her. "You okay?"

No, her mind screamed. Even through the rubbery raincoat the outfitter had supplied to go under her life jacket, the heat of his touch burned her, threatened to have her stumbling around with the shockwaves of it.

"Fine." She pulled her arm free. "Thank you."

"Anytime." His smile was electric, lighting up his eyes with amusement. "For the record, you look cute in your helmet."

Tugging on her chin strap, she rolled her eyes. "Has no one ever told you that women don't want to be called cute?"

"Not that I recall," he admitted, looking amused. "Would you be okay with me telling you that you're beautiful?"

Heat singed her cheeks. She doubted that even the most iconic beauties could look great while wearing her current gear, but she forced a smile. "Thank you. For the compliment, for checking my vest, and for keeping me upright. Make sure to tell me if I'm not doing something right today. I don't want to put us in danger with my inexperience."

Reaching out, he cupped her face, his thumb brushing over her chin strap and sending shivers all up and down her spine. "You're going to do fine, Jenny, and by the end of the day you're going to be a pro."

Finally, Jenny seemed to be relaxing. Tristan had caught her laughing a couple of times at something Laura said, but mostly she kept glaring and rolling her eyes at her friend. Their raft had the five of them. Roger and Lucia were at the front. Jenny and Laura took the middle, so they wouldn't get hammered by the waves quite as much, and he was at the back. Roger and Lucia had done a great job following his called-out instructions, so they'd hit the rapids at just the right spots to avoid the many rocks that jutted up or were semi hidden beneath the surface.

"Keep your hand around the T-grip." Tristan spoke loud enough over the rapids for Jenny to hear as their raft made a few up and downs over a fast, bumpy section. He didn't want the end of her oar smacking him or anyone else in the face.

"Got it," Jenny responded, wrapping her hand back around the tip she'd momentarily let go of. She'd been holding on to it so tightly earlier that he was surprised she'd let go.

"Everyone, paddle hard right," he called, guiding them through a rocky section.

"Woohoo!" Roger cheered, holding up his oar when they exited the rapid to a calm section. "That was awesome."

From his position behind them, Tristan saw Jenny nod, heard her laughter, and relief filled him. He wanted her to enjoy today. Whether or not she did mattered more than it should. He loved the sport and wanted... What did it matter what she thought? He was only here a short time.

"From what I learned when studying the river last night, we have a short stretch of calm before we hit the next rapids. Anyone ready to pull over to shore for a snack and rest break?"

"Sounds great," a few called out.

He directed them to a flat pebbly shoreline. When close enough, Roger jumped out into the midcalf-deep water and guided the raft up onto the rocks enough that the others could disembark without stepping directly into the water. Once they were out, Tristan got out, too, pulling the raft even further up on the pebble bed so they didn't have to worry about the boat taking off without them.

"Here's sanitizer," Laura said, passing around a small spray bottle.

Smiling, looking a little cold from the icy water, Jenny had sat on a downed tree trunk along the edge of the bank and had her face lifted toward the sun.

"Having a good time?"

Keeping her face raised and eyed closed, she said, "Much better than I was expecting when we pushed off this morning."

"That's not saying a lot," he quipped, knowing the answer to his question by how the earlier stiffness of her movements was gone and she looked at peace with the sunlight brightening her face. Angelic, he thought. And so beautiful with the tiny curling-from-dampness hairs that had escaped her ponytail framing her face and her full lips slightly parted.

Longing to touch them sucker-punched him, threatened to drag him over to her, so he could taste their lushness for himself. Wincing, he mentally plunged himself into the icy river.

"True. My expectations were pretty low," she admitted. "I didn't think I'd like going over the rapids, but it's exhilarating."

The excitement shining in her eyes was exhilarating and had him wondering if he was going to have to take a real dunk into the water.

"I enjoy the rapids the most, but only because there's balance," he confessed. "It's like life. There are times of peace and calm, and times of fighting to keep from being swept away. It takes both to fully appreciate each moment."

"You're giving me a philosophy lesson based upon white-water rafting?" She looked at him with laughter in her eyes.

The amusement in her honey-brown eyes triggered an excitement within him that far surpassed any the rapids had produced. "Maybe, but it's true. One only appreciates the calm points because of the times of adversity." Knowing he needed to break eye contact before he started spouting poetry to go along with his philosophy, he turned from her and opened a waterproof bag where he'd packed snacks and drinks. Laura hadn't seemed to mind when he'd asked for details on what Jenny liked and he'd told her that he had Jenny's rafting trip covered.

"We have lunch packed for a later stop, but we'll all be grateful for our meal tonight. We're grilling burgers." He handed her a water bottle that he'd had clipped to the raft. "This is yours. I should have told you that earlier."

Seeming surprised that he'd brought her one, she smiled. "Thank you."

"You're welcome."

Taking the bottle, she twisted the top off. Tristan's eyes were mesmerized by the working of her throat as she took a long sip then glanced his way. "How did you end up as a rafting guide?"

"It was during the summer of my freshman and sophomore year of college."

"Is that where you attended college? In Colorado?"

He shook his head. "I started university in Virginia but ended up finishing my nursing program in California."

"California? After spending at least part of your teens in Boston? Good grief, you really have lived all over. So, while you were living in Virginia for college, you spent your summers working in Colorado? How did that happen?"

"My dorm mate was from there and was working as a guide on the Colorado River. It didn't take much for him to convince me I should get trained and work with him."

Staying in the same place for his nursing school had been the longest time he'd lived in one location. Spending the summers elsewhere had helped his itchy feet. "It was a great experience."

"The Colorado River sounds intense."

"After some of the rapids we crossed today, I'm surprised that you're saying that, but the truth is that even a calm-appearing river can be dangerous if not respected. You never know what's lurking beneath the surface."

"Did anyone ever get hurt on your watch?"

"Just once when a guy let go of his T-grip and busted up his friend's mouth."

Jenny winced. "Poor guy."

"That's one of the most important things to remember when in the boat."

"And keeping my toes up is one of the most important things to remember if I fall out of the boat?"

"It is *the* most important thing to remember if you're out of the boat," he corrected, not liking the thought of Jenny falling out. "Let's keep you in the raft and not have to worry about where your toes are."

"I'm great with that plan."

"Me, too."

He handed her a trail mix packet then grabbed one for himself. "Here. You need sustenance. You've got a lot of paddling to do before the day is done."

Jenny turned up the bag, pouring a generous helping of the mix into her mouth. "Mmm…" She licked salt from her lips. "That's good."

"That's hunger talking." Hunger was talking to him, too. Loud and demanding and with an urgency that had him thinking he should go dunk his head in the chilly river to abate his thoughts, pronto.

"Maybe," she agreed then glanced at where he sat

next to her. "Thank you for taking care of me today. I haven't exactly been a bundle of friendliness, so I particularly appreciate you making sure I stay safe, and for my water and snack."

Pleasure filled him. Not that he wanted her ingratiated to him, but he liked that she was looking at him with a smile in her eyes and on her mouth.

His glance dropped to her lips. Her full lips that she must have thought had another bit of salt on them because she licked them again.

Fighting the urge to groan, Tristan took a sip of his water. The cool liquid went down wrong and triggered a coughing spell as he tried to swallow.

"You okay over there?" Roger called from where he, Lucia and Laura were having their snack.

"Fine," he assured him between coughs. "Water went down the wrong way."

"Don't get choked up or Jenny will have to resuscitate you," Roger teased.

Jenny giving him mouth-to-mouth would be worth getting choked up.

When he turned back, she was studying the water as if it was extremely interesting, but overall, she seemed relaxed. He'd count that as an improvement.

Had he not already known, the way his new coworkers purposely kept pushing him and Jenny together, leaving them semi alone, would have clued him in to their approval of something happening between them.

Too bad Jenny didn't agree, because the more Tristan got to know her, the more he wanted something to happen, too.

Jenny followed Tristan's instructions, keeping her hand tightly over the T-grip as he told the group to paddle hard right or left.

Adrenaline filled her as they surged through the river, as they battled one rapid after another and came out the other side. Yeah, she could see how people enjoyed taking on the elements and feeling as if they'd conquered something with every bend of the river successfully navigated.

Not that she'd want to go back, but she'd be lying if she said she was as miserable as she'd thought she'd be when she'd let her friends convince her to go.

You wanted to go. Admit it, a voice inside her prompted. *You wanted to see the man behind you away from the hospital. To see what he was like away from the constraints of work.*

That meant what? she wondered while paddling in whatever direction he instructed.

He was an excellent guide, always calm, always precise and loud enough with his orders to be heard without being overbearing or outright yelling except when the sound of the water was deafening around them. He was like that at work, too. Was that how he was in all aspects of life? Calm, focused, able to guide those around them to keep them safe?

"Roger, do you see what I see?" Tristan called out, referring to a group ahead. Their raft, along with a couple of rafters in the water, floated far down the river without the remainder.

Her feet lodged as far beneath the seat in front of her as she could get them tucked, Jenny's stomach sank as they got closer and closer to a man propped against a boulder, stretched out toward a person who wasn't moving. Just beyond, two rafters had somehow made it to shore and were motioning to the ones in the water with the rapids bubbling fast around them.

"Hard right," Tristan ordered, pointing their raft in the direction of the shore and the people. The water rushed, but it wasn't the fastest or bumpiest area they'd traversed, and they managed to maneuver near to where the rafters were in the water and shot straight on top of a boulder, causing their raft to get stuck about fifteen feet from where the closest rafter stood.

"Oh, God," she prayed, helplessness washing over her as she realized the closest rafter was a teen girl and she appeared stuck. Her fingers gripped some type of greenery growing in the water and Jenny suspected that desperate hold was the only thing keeping her from being pushed beneath the water.

Grabbing a bag Jenny hadn't previously paid any attention to, Tristan moved to the front of their stuck raft, swapping places with Roger's girlfriend, who quickly moved to the back of the raft.

"Everyone okay?" he called. They didn't look okay to Jenny, but she supposed asking was protocol just as asking was the first thing one did with CPR.

"A man went overboard and, in my efforts to get him, our raft got stuck and capsized. Kira's foot is trapped. I'm not stuck, but not able to get to her. Every time I move forward, the water slams me back into this boulder," the man in the water answered. He was positioned to use one of the large rocks for leverage to stay put. One arm held on to the rock and the other was stretched to the girl, but she was beyond his reach. "I almost got swept down the river the last time I tried."

Turning his attention to the teen, Tristan asked, "Kira, are you hurt?"

The quivering girl didn't answer, just stared at them with panic in her eyes. Panic and yet distance shone in her gaze, too. Hypothermia or shock or both?

"Kira, we're going to get you loose," Tristan promised. "You're too far away to reach my oar for me to pull you into our raft, so I'm going to toss a rope to you. I'll throw it upriver. The water will bring it to you. I need you to grab hold."

Seeming to come out of her haze, the girl nodded. "I'm so cold."

The splashes of water were frigid, and Jenny could only imagine how cold the teen was, being submerged up to just beneath her breasts.

He tossed the rope, but the girl watched the end go by without letting go of the greenery she clung to. Tristan pulled the rope back up.

"Kira, I know it's scary to let go, but I need you to grab hold of the rope so I can get you in our raft. Are you ready?"

The girl hesitated but finally nodded. Tristan tossed the rope, and with a held breath, Jenny watched the end float past the petrified girl again.

"I—I can't do it."

"You can," Tristan reassured her, his voice so confident that he almost convinced Jenny of the girl's ability.

"I'm so cold that my arms won't work," Kira said.

Tristan looked to Roger. They seemed to share some secret guy code and the next thing Jenny knew, Tristan had gone into the water, him holding one end of the rope and Roger having the other, securing it.

"No!" Jenny couldn't contain her cry as Tristan battled the water to close the short distance to the girl.

Fear seized her. This. This was what she'd been afraid of, and they'd all made light of her concerns. She'd let loose, let herself enjoy the ride, and now Tristan was in the water and the young girl was ghostly white and looking as if she were about to lose consciousness.

"Be careful," she whispered, her breath catching as

Tristan made it to the series of rocks jutting up from the water. He used a rock to propel himself toward the teenager.

"Yes!" Laura cheered when he got stopped a few feet from where the girl was taking a beating from the water around her.

Jenny's throat was too constricted to say anything. Watching him bob around in the bubbly water had her nerves a wreck.

Rope secure, Tristan made his way to the teen. When he reached her, everyone let loose with whoops and hollers. Everyone but Jenny because reaching the trapped girl wasn't enough. They were both still in the water, along with the other raft's guide. The water hadn't magically stopped to let them leisurely get the girl loose. They were still in danger.

She'd cheer when they were safely out of the water.

CHAPTER SIX

"YOUR NAME IS KIRA?" Tristan asked the trapped teen as he assessed the situation to see how to free her while keeping himself safe in the process. The water shot around him, threatening to pull him along with its powerful force.

"Yes," she said, her teeth chattering. Panic and fatigue shone in her eyes from her battling to stay upright.

The current was strong, whipping at Tristan, and creating a struggle to close the small gap between him and the girl. One slipup and he could end up with his own foot trapped. He wouldn't let the consequences of that happening into his mind. He needed to focus.

"Hi, Kira. My name is Tristan. I'm going to get you out of the water." Somehow, he would. "Talk to me about what's going on beneath the surface. Are both feet trapped or just one?"

"Just my right one."

Good. Maybe she'd be able to help push herself free when they made their move. "Tell me what you feel."

"I can't feel anything except cold."

She probably hadn't been in the water long prior to their coming upon the group since they'd been able to see the raft and the two who had floated down the river. But the water was cold and, if it hadn't already, it wouldn't take long for hypothermia to set in.

"I'm going to free your foot, Kira, but you're going to have to help me so that I don't injure you further when I'm pulling you free. Can you do that?"

She nodded.

Water swirled around them. The current tugged at him as he tried to maintain a secure footing of his own in an attempt to get an idea of where Kira was trapped and how best to free her. He had no visual of how she was wedged. If he pulled wrong, he could break her ankle, if it wasn't already, or he could cause the rocks to cut her, or any number of other injuries. When it came down to it, he might not have a choice, but if there was a way that he could free her without further injury, he'd do his best. Maybe he'd get lucky, and he'd be able to move the rock trapping her enough so that she could wiggle her foot free.

The water roared deafeningly around him, blocking out all other sound as he maneuvered on the rocks. Almost, he was close enough. Just another step—

Surprising him, Kira lost her grip on the greenery. Knowing he only had a tiny window for success before she'd be forced beneath the water, he grabbed at her life jacket, barely catching hold of the strap and lifting her up.

Sobbing, Kira stared at him with wide, scared eyes.

Fighting to keep his footing, he lashed the end of the rope through her life jacket. "Once I have your foot loose, my friend Roger will pull you to our raft."

Tristan got the rope secured around her, to where, if it took him a while to free her, at least Roger could keep enough tension in the rope to keep her upright. The water around them was too deep for him to free her foot with his hands without his going under water, which would mean him battling the current and his life jacket. Even if he could, the water was too murky and aeriated for visibility. He had to use his energy wisely.

Using his foot as a guide, he realized she was trapped beneath a jagged edge of the large boulder. He wouldn't be moving the rock, but maybe he could help her wiggle her foot free without causing further damage than whatever she'd already sustained.

"At my signal, and with as much strength as you can, I want you to force your foot in the direction you think it needs to go to be free."

Shivering, Kira nodded, and Tristan called to Roger, "At my signal, pull the rope with all your might."

At Roger's thumbs-up, Tristan took one last deep breath then went for it, knowing that if he didn't free Kira, it might be impossible for him to regain a decent footing for a second attempt, leaving them no choice but to forcibly dislodge her regardless of the cost to her foot.

"Now!" he yelled as with all his strength he pushed them in the opposite direction from the water flow and upward into the tug of the rope, praying it worked.

By some miracle it did.

Exhausted, Kira lost consciousness in his arms, but Tristan kept a tight hold on her as Roger and the women pulled them toward the raft. Once there, Roger grabbed the teen's life jacket and pulled her onto their raft, still wedged on a boulder, by falling into a sitting position.

The girl safely in the raft, Roger was back on his knees and held out his oar, the T-grip end toward Tristan. His arms like jelly, Tristan grabbed hold and let his coworker pull him.

"We've got to get the guide," Tristan said as he toppled into the raft. Adrenaline driving him, he got to his knees and undid the rope from the girl.

"Maybe he can float down the river to a calm spot, like the others," Roger suggested.

"Let's try to get him in." Tristan signaled to the guide that he planned to toss the rope to him. At the man's nod, he found the strength to throw it.

Laura and Jenny were attending to the teen while Roger and Tristan pulled the guide to their raft. Lucia stayed at the helm, oar in hand in case they got dislodged from the boulder.

They quickly had the guide on the raft.

"Name's Steve and, man, was I glad to see you," the guide said. "Great job. Our whole raft capsized and two got stuck. I got one free and to shore, but couldn't make it to Kira—ended up losing my oar in the process of trying, and wasn't able to do much until help arrived. Thank God, you weren't far behind us."

Tristan nodded then turned to where Jenny and Laura were bent over the unconscious girl. "How is she?"

"Hypothermia and her ankle's broken," Jenny said, not looking up from where she tended to the teen. "Abrasions and one spot that needs a few stitches. The cold water kept the bleeding slowed."

Jenny lifted the towel she'd pressed to the area to reveal the wound.

"She probably got the cut when we were freeing her," Tristan admitted, hating that there hadn't been another way.

"It could have been so much worse," the guide pointed out.

What the man said was true. Assessing how their raft perched on the boulder with the water sluicing around them, Tristan calculated the best way to free them so they could get Kira further medical care.

His eyes met Jenny's and what he saw there stole his

breath as surely as if he'd plunged back into the water. Her dark eyes swirled with concern. For him.

Just a natural response given the situation, he reminded himself. What he saw meant nothing. Still, her look had him wanting to high-five the sun.

Later, he thought. Later, they'd talk. Now, they had to get moving.

"Jenny, I want you in the center to keep a hold on Kira. We only have a short section to get through before we'll be in calm waters, but we don't want to lose her out of the raft. Lucia will take your spot and Steve will move up front with Roger." He gave a reassuring smile then glanced around at the rest of the crew. "Let's get this raft to shore and call for help."

Sitting in the middle as Tristan had said, Kira positioned between her legs, Jenny kept her arms around the girl to provide as much warmth as she could as the raft bumped its way through the river to reach where they could paddle to shore. Roger and Steve jumped out and pulled the boat onto the pebbly embankment.

Once there, everyone but Jenny, Tristan and the girl got out of the raft. Steve called for help while Tristan and Jenny tended to Kira.

"Not awake yet?"

Rubbing her palms over the girl's arms to increase circulation, Jenny shook her head. "No, but her pulse is strong and she's breathing okay."

"Good. Keep her wrapped. I'm going to check her ankle."

He knelt next to where Jenny held the girl.

"You were very brave." Jenny watched him pull a small first-aid kit from his life vest.

"It's not a big deal, just what I used to do," he said, setting about cleaning the open wounds with disinfectant.

"You could have been hurt. I was scared for you," she admitted, continuing to rub the girl's arms. Surely, Kira would wake up soon?

Tristan glanced at her and grinned. "Does that mean I'm growing on you?"

His smile held that flirtatiousness that set off warning bells. Heaven save her from gorgeous men with dimples and cleft chins.

"I hope not."

He laughed. "Well, if it would help make that happen, I'll volunteer for more water rescues."

At the thought of him back in the raging river, Jenny's stomach clenched. "Don't you dare. Lord forbid that there's need of any more water rescues."

"You're right, but it's the thought that counts." He pushed the deepest gash together and strategically placed a Steri-Strip across it, pulling the cold skin closed and then taping a piece of gauze over the area. "Do I get credit for being willing to volunteer to impress you?"

"You don't have to volunteer to impress me, Tristan. I've been impressed since the moment we met, and you know it." She sighed. "Everyone knows it."

If she'd thought his grin appealing before, this one was positively wicked.

His mouth opened and Jenny could only imagine what he'd been going to say, but he was stopped by Kira rousing and mumbling something incoherent.

"Hey, Kira. Glad to see those eyes again." Tristan smiled at the girl, but in a way that, although just as appealing, was gentle and reassuring rather than flirtatious as his smile had been with Jenny.

That she was out of the water hit, and Kira burst into tears.

"Shh. It's okay," Jenny soothed, hugging the girl.

"Your ankle is broken, and you've got a cut that'll need sutures, but help is on the way and you're going to be okay."

Seeing that the girl was awake, Steve came over. "We're not that far off the main road, so help should be here soon."

"That's good news, isn't it, Kira?" Jenny said to the girl, holding her close.

"Everyone from our raft is accounted for and fine," Steve noted. "As a matter of fact, here come two of them now. That's your parents making their way down the bank."

Sure enough, the two who had made it to shore were now just a few yards away where they'd taken off on land in the direction the raft had been floating.

From that moment, everything happened fast. A rescue unit arrived and took over. Steve profusely thanked their group for their heroics, as did the others from the overturned raft. A few snapped photos of Tristan. He shook off their claims of heroism, seeming embarrassed by the attention, and saying it had been a team effort.

As they were no longer needed, and with a lot of dread on Jenny's part, they set back off in their raft.

"What happened with Steve's raft is a one-off. Just remember, if you go out, toes up at all times," Tristan reiterated.

Jenny pushed her toes as far as she could beneath the seat in front of her, wedging them into the rubbery crevice. Having been reminded of the dangers lurking beneath the water's surface, her initial fear was back rather than the happy adrenaline she'd felt earlier as they'd rid-den wave after wave. The last thing she wanted was to go overboard.

They paddled for an hour prior to stopping at where they'd have lunch.

"You're tight as a drum," Tristan pointed out once they exited the boat. Laura had snuck off for a bathroom break and Roger and Lucia had moved to a grassy area up on the embankment for a semiprivate picnic.

Lingering next to where he pulled items from the raft, Jenny shrugged. "I keep thinking about Kira."

"She'll be okay. It'll take her a while, but she's young and should fully recover."

Jenny trembled. "You saved her. I was so scared for her, and you knew just what to do."

"If we hadn't come along, someone else would have," he said, his voice calm, soothing. "All the guides are trained for rescue. Any of them would have done what I did. Probably better than I did."

Jenny wasn't having his modesty. She'd witnessed what he'd done, how fearlessly he'd jumped to action with little thought to his own safety. "I thought you were wonderful."

"There you go making me want to look for volunteer opportunities." He grinned. "Seriously, as much as I appreciate your praise, it wasn't a big deal."

"It was to Kira and her family. To Steve, too. He felt terrible about what happened although, from the sounds of things, he couldn't have prevented it."

"No guide wants someone to get hurt during their watch."

"The Colorado River lost a great guide when you started nursing school."

At her praise, Tristan's gaze shot to hers, as blue as the sky above them.

"But I'm glad it did," she continued, "because you're a wonderful nurse and our patients are lucky to have you caring for them." She paused, took a deep breath. "As difficult as I find admitting it, knowing you makes me lucky, too."

Standing, he stared down at her, his eyes searching hers. Although, for what, she wasn't sure, just knowing that whatever it was, she didn't think she was strong enough to deny him anything he wished.

"Jenny, I—"

"Phew, I feel lots better," Laura announced, joining them and then spraying her hands with the sanitizer. "And will feel even better after we have a bite to eat. Anything water-related makes me so hungry."

Wanting to grasp hold of his arm to stay him from turning away, wondering what he'd been going to say, Jenny held her breath, hoping he'd continue, but knew the moment had been lost.

After one last look, Tristan pulled out the waterproof bag that held their lunch. He tossed a granola bar and sandwich to Laura, then handed Jenny hers.

"Eat up. We've still got a few hours on the river."

Jenny grabbed her water bottle then found a place along the bank to sit to watch the water while she ate. Hard to believe the sunshine-dappled river that appeared so peaceful had not so long ago loomed dark and dangerous.

"It really is beautiful here," Laura said, sitting beside her. "I'm sorry your first trip had drama. I've never seen a rescue, much less participated in one. Most of the time folks fall out of the boat and just float to the next slow spot, then get pulled back up into the raft. No big deal."

Jenny wasn't sure about that.

"Steve seemed like a nice guy," Laura continued, taking a bite of her sandwich.

Jenny's eyes widened. "Is that why you were all smiles with him while we were waiting on the ambulance? Because he was a 'nice guy'?"

Laura grinned. "Something like that. I got his phone number."

Jenny shook her head. "I can't believe you picked up a guy."

"Hey, nice guys are difficult to find."

"So difficult that you met one while floating down the river."

Laura gave a so-sue-me shrug. "If you have half a brain, you'll quit fighting the attraction between you and Tristan and pick him up, too."

"I already have his number and it's not one I should call."

Laura rolled her eyes. "The man saved a girl's life. The least he deserves is a hero's kiss."

She wanted to kiss him. When they'd been standing there, she'd wanted him to take her into his arms and kiss her. What had he been going to say?

But she wasn't ready to share that with Laura.

"Your new guide friend might not appreciate you doing that."

Unfazed, Laura shrugged. "Then I guess it'll have to be you who gives Tristan a kiss for being so brave."

A shower had never felt so good. Jenny let the lukewarm water rush over her body. The spray wasn't particularly strong but washing away the river in the tiny stall of the campground's shower house was heavenly. She lathered her hair, rinsed and conditioned. Oh, yeah, this was heavenly.

The remainder of their rafting trip had been uneventful.

If you could call being more and more drawn to Tristan uneventful.

What was it about him that appealed so much? Yes, he was gorgeous, but she'd met more traditionally handsome men. Yet none appealed the way he did. Not even Geoffrey or Carlos. *It's his eyes*, she thought. How when he smiled, his eyes smiled, too. Or maybe it was just the smile in general. He had a great smile and he wielded it often. Where most of the men she knew wielded arrogance as a second skin, Tristan didn't seem that way at all. When Roger had been telling the others from their group what had happened, Tristan had yet again downplayed his role, citing that the rescue couldn't have happened without a team effort.

Jenny rinsed then towel dried her body, knowing her muscles should feel achy from the strenuous river trek, but instead feeling revitalized.

Feeling alive and good and…feminine.

The river water had obviously gone to her head and clouded her mind. Maybe some type of parasite had invaded her and was making her have the thoughts she'd been having all afternoon. Thoughts no doubt triggered by her bestie's crazy suggestions. Kiss Tristan. Was Laura insane?

Dressed in black leggings and a Rock City T-shirt, hair still wet but combed through, Jenny made her way back to their campsite.

The first person she saw was Tristan. Like her, his hair was damp from his recent shower. Wearing shorts, a T-shirt and comfy-appearing sandals, he looked completely relaxed as he took a sip of his drink then laughed at something someone said. He turned, their glances met, and her lips curved upward of their own accord. That had to be it, because her brain knew better than to smile at him just because he'd grinned at seeing her.

Heart pounding, she closed the distance to where he stood with her friends.

"Better?" he asked when she joined him, Laura, Roger and Lucia where they chatted near Tristan's 4Runner.

"Much," she admitted, still smiling and trying not to berate her silly mouth for its traitorous actions. "I'm also starved. Something smells amazing."

"Burgers are on the grill. There are drinks in the cooler. Help yourself."

Jenny lifted the lid, bypassed the alcoholic options, and grabbed a water. Her friends had pulled chairs over, but Tristan sat on the back of his open hatch.

"Have a seat," he offered, patting to the spot next to him.

She'd been in the raft with him all day, but for some reason, sitting next to him on the SUV seemed intimate, as if she were pairing off with him. And despite the tumultuous thoughts playing through her mind, she wasn't ready to publicly do that. "I should help with dinner."

"We all tried," Laura proclaimed, Roger and Lucia nodding their agreement.

"Blake and his wife refuse to let anyone near the grill, saying cooking dinner is their treat. Based on the way it smells, they've got things under control." Tristan's attention still connected to her, he took another sip. "Plus, there's only so much room by the grill. Stay."

"I… Okay. I'll put my bag in the tent and be right back." She tossed her toiletries into the tent she shared with Laura then, needing a moment, climbed in and ran her fingers through her damp hair again and started plaiting it into a single long braid. Sitting with her friends before a meal was no big deal.

But when she returned to where Tristan still sat on the open hatch of his 4Runner, he was alone.

"Where are the others?"

"Laura got a call. Roger and Lucia said something about going for a walk." He shrugged. "Looks as if it's just you and me until they get back."

It wouldn't surprise her if they didn't return but had purposely left her with Tristan. She sat across from him in Laura's vacated chair.

Not seeming surprised that she'd not chosen to sit beside him, Tristan lifted his drink in a salute.

Why had she sat at all? Jenny wondered moments later when they were still sitting in silence just looking at one another. She couldn't say it was a completely awkward silence, but it wasn't comfortable, either.

It was…disturbingly exhilarating.

"Barring what happened to Kira, I enjoyed today." She was chatting, not to fill the silence between her and Tristan, but to block her own thoughts.

"Once you relaxed and gave it a chance," he pointed out. "I love the thrill of riding down the river."

"It showed. Thank you for keeping us all safe."

"You keep giving me credit where credit isn't due, but I'll take it."

"I figured you would," she teased. Then, watching the sway of his feet where they hung off the end of his SUV, she asked, "So now what do we do?"

He shrugged. "Sit, eat, drink, be merry while enjoying each other's company and being out in nature."

"And not being at work," she added.

"There's that, but I love being a nurse."

"It shows. I meant what I said earlier. Your patients are lucky to have you. You're a great nurse, Tristan. One of the best travel nurses we've ever had."

His eyes twinkled. "You keep complimenting me and I'm going to get a big head."

She doubted it but smiled. "Fine. You're terrible. I hate it when I'm assigned to work with you. I…" She paused because she had hated it, hadn't she?

Only, not really. She'd just wanted to hate it.

Instead, as much as she'd denied it, she'd been drawn to him as surely as a moth to a flame, moving purely on instinct when what should have been happening was that instinct telling her to get out of Dodge before she got burned.

"Laura's phone call was from Steve. She'd invited him to hang with us tonight. From the sound of it, he was on his way and needed directions to our campsite."

"To hang out with her, you mean?" Jenny asked, grateful he'd changed the subject. "She mentioned that she'd gotten his phone number. If he called, then he must have gotten hers, too."

"Either that or she texted him, letting him know she was serious with her invitation and giving him the chance to decide if he was interested."

Jenny nodded. "That's probably what she did."

"He asked me about her after we were all ashore—if she was single. I mentioned it to her. I guess she's keen on him because, within minutes, she had his number and was inviting him for burgers tonight."

"That's great. I hope they hit it off." Mostly, she did, although she worried about her friend getting hurt when it didn't work out. After all, how could it when they didn't live or work anywhere near each other?

"Me, too," Tristan admitted then added, "I'll admit that when he pulled me aside, I was grateful he wasn't interested in you."

Eyes wide, Jenny's gaze shot to his.

"I owe you an apology because I told him you were taken before he even got a chance to say who he liked. I didn't want to risk it."

She let what he was admitting digest.

"Does it upset you that I told him you weren't available?"

She shook her head. "No. I'm not interested in Steve."

"But you are interested in someone?"

Jenny took a deep breath. She was. Him. Out in the woods, real life seemed far away and, letting herself fantasize that she could look him in the eyes and tell him that she liked him, that she'd wanted to throw her arms around him and kiss him at several points during the day, didn't seem nearly so farfetched. And yet, still she hesitated.

"Jenny?" he prompted. "Are you interested in someone? In me?"

A movement beyond his vehicle caught her attention and she leapt to her feet. "Oh, there's Laura now. I should ask her about the phone call with Steve."

Behind her, Tristan laughed. "Running away, Jenny?"

"As fast as I can," she called over her shoulder as she made her way to Laura.

But she suspected her feet couldn't move nearly quick enough to keep her from being caught.

CHAPTER SEVEN

"MARSHMALLOW?" TRISTAN WAVED the bag in front of Jenny. Their eyes had been playing games all evening. Hers making contact, sometimes looking away, sometimes studying him for long moments, as if trying to figure him out.

"Sure." She smiled up at him. "Why not have a big fluff of sticky sugar?"

"Especially when it's melted and sandwiched between chocolate and graham crackers." He waggled his brows and extended his arm to help her from her chair.

"Exactly." Jenny eyed his hand and he thought she'd stand without taking it, but with a sharp intake of breath, she placed hers in his and let him help her to her feet.

Within his, her hand was warm, small, almost fragile. Yet he knew exactly how capable it was; that she worked hard and used those hands to care for her patients shift after shift.

Her eyes dropped to their hands then glanced up at him with questions in her gaze. Before he could say anything, she pulled free. "Thanks."

Moving to a vacant chair close to the fire, she speared her marshmallow prior to extending it above the fire so the confection could melt.

"Slow and steady," Tristan observed from where he watched her hold the white puff above the flames.

"Pardon?"

"You roast your marshmallow with a great deal of patience, letting it slowly melt rather than burn to an impatient crisp."

"I like the gooey inside but not the black outside, like Roger and Lucia were making theirs last night. Not that I've had the chance to do this often. Just once at a church gathering," she admitted, smiling at him. "But I recall that I didn't like it burned."

"Then you may want to move that," he suggested, gesturing to her marshmallow that had caught fire.

"Oh!" She jerked back on the roasting stick. Unfortunately, the flaming marshmallow had softened so, when she yanked, a hot glob flung straight toward her.

Tristan flipped the bag he held in front of her and the marshmallow smacked against it. Dropping the bag, he put out the fire with his shoe, kicking the remainder of the debris-covered confection into the fire pit.

"I'm so sorry," Jenny moaned. "Your shoe is going to be a mess."

Probably, but it would clean.

"I'm just glad it didn't hit you." His body had seemed to move in slow motion when he'd realized what was happening. He'd never have forgiven himself if he'd let her hurt herself doing something he'd suggested.

"Thanks to you, I'm fine," she noted, but her eyes dropped to his hand. "But some did splatter onto you." She winced. "If I'd been thinking, I'd have known better than to do something so stupid. Sometimes I'm such a klutz."

The burn registered about the time she pointed out where the tiny white glob stuck to the back of his hand.

He'd been so worried the marshmallow was going to hit her that he hadn't noticed.

"You're not a klutz. It's not a big deal. I have burn cream in my first-aid kit," he assured, carefully removing the sticky glob from his sensitized skin. The area stung but was less than a centimeter in diameter. "I'll be fine."

Going with him to his SUV, she popped open the cooler next to his truck and scooped out a piece of ice. The sloshing of the ice against the side of the cup she used seemed to match the throb of his burn as he dug out the first-aid kit.

Once he'd settled onto the back of the SUV, Jenny took his hand and placed the ice on the burned spot. "It's my fault you got burned. I feel terrible."

Having her touch him was worth enduring much worse than the minor burn. For that matter, where she held his hand to steady it so she could press the ice to the injured skin burned much more than the marshmallow had.

"Obviously, we now know that I can't be trusted with a flaming marshmallow," she mumbled as she kept the melting ice to his wound.

"The nursing care that follows more than makes up for your lack of marshmallow skills, but in the future, I'll roast them for you."

Her gaze lifted to his. Swallowing, she loosened her grip on his hand, but kept the ice in place over his burn.

Her fingers shook. "What exactly is it you want from me, Tristan?"

Great question. And one he didn't know the complete answer to. For the moment, looking into her big eyes, the reflection of the moonlight dancing in their depths, he knew exactly what he wanted. He wanted to kiss her, to taste the fullness of her parted lips, to feel her against him.

But he suspected if he said those things out loud, she'd retreat into her tent, possibly not to make an appearance until it was time to leave. Still, he wouldn't lie to her.

"I've not made it a secret that I'm attracted to you and would like to know you better while I'm in Chattanooga."

Taking a deep breath, she glanced down to where she pressed the ice. "You seem to be a great guy, Tristan, but you and I would never work. You have to know that."

"Because I'm only here for a few months?"

"That, but mostly because of Sawyer."

Tristan's stomach twisted. When he'd asked Laura if Jenny was dating anyone, her friend had laughed, shaken her head, and told him to go for it. Had she been setting him up for failure or trying to interfere with a bad relationship she didn't approve of?

"Who's Sawyer?" Why was his heart racing so at his question?

Although obviously emotionally torn, she smiled, and there was no doubt it was a real one. Whoever Sawyer was, Jenny was hooked.

"My four-year-old son. He's my whole world."

Tristan's jaw dropped. Jenny had a kid?

"I didn't know you were a mom." Some of the things that had been said at the hospital clicked into place. Had everyone just assumed he'd known and so had never felt the need to say anything?

Jenny gave him an odd look. "I'm not sure how you didn't. I talk about him a lot at the hospital."

"You've not exactly been the mecca of conversation with me since I arrived," he reminded her, still trying to process that she was a mother. "Quite the opposite."

"True, but I didn't purposely try to keep you from knowing about Sawyer. He's the best part of my life."

Tristan mused on that. Jenny had a son.

"But I was trying my best to keep away from you. You scare me."

"Me?" he asked, shocked that she'd made such a revealing admission. "I've never seen myself as scary. More like the goofy guy next door who is friends with everyone."

"You've obviously never seen yourself through a woman who doesn't want to get hurt's eyes. Believe me, you're scary."

Her admission gutted him, made him want to go all white knight to whomever had hurt her and made her so cautious.

"Sometimes facing our fears is the best way to get over them. Just look at how you overcame your fear of the river today and ended up having a good time, despite a few ups and downs."

What was he saying? Better yet, why was he saying it? He didn't typically date coworkers or women with kids. Jenny was both. He should steer well clear. Instead, he clung to the fact that she still held his hand and that her touch singed his flesh much more than the gooey marshmallow.

She also held his interest. More so than any woman in recent history. Maybe ever, as he sure couldn't think of anyone who'd affected him the way she did.

"You may be right about that. And, if it was just me that I had to look out for, maybe I would be brave enough to do just that, but it's not just me. I have Sawyer to consider." She took a deep breath then stared directly into his eyes. "No matter how much I'm attracted to you, and it's no secret that I am, I'm not interested in bringing a man into my and Sawyer's lives who won't be here more than a few months. Letting Sawyer get close to someone who isn't going to stick around wouldn't be fair."

What she said made perfect sense.

"I get that, and on some level, even agree," he admitted. "I don't want to hurt you or your son. Maybe we can be friends."

She half laughed. "Do you really believe that's possible?" Her tone said she didn't.

"I'm not sure, but I do know that the most exciting part of this weekend is that you're here, and that the moment you touched my hand, the only burn I felt was where our skin touched. Maybe you're right and that means just being friends won't be easy when I want more, but I'm willing to try if you are."

Although she kept the ice in place, she immediately released her hold of his hand. "I—I'm not sure what to say."

He shrugged. "There's no rule that says you have to say anything."

"Yet I feel as if I'm supposed to say something. Not doing so just feels awkward."

"My intention isn't to make you feel awkward, but I get the impression that you do feel uncomfortable around me."

"Of course, I do. You're scary, remember?"

"We really need to work on that. Tell me, Jenny, what is it you find the scariest about me?"

Her forehead creased.

"Don't worry about the big picture of my scariness. Just tell me what scares you right now in this moment?"

She swallowed, closed her eyes and asked, "The scariest thing about you at this very moment?"

He nodded.

"That once upon a time I'd have jumped at the chance of spending time with you, having sex with you." She took a deep breath. "Even knowing you'd leave me. Now...well, I've learned from past mistakes and have to make better choices. You aren't a good choice. I won't have Sawyer hurt."

She said her son's name, but her own pain shone on her face. Who had hurt her? Someone had. Her defensive posture triggered a swirl of emotions within him. Most of which didn't make sense. Protectiveness. That one he got. He liked taking care of people, wanted to help them heal. It was a trait he believed made him a better nurse. But it was more than just protectiveness. There was this strong urge to prove her wrong, to convince her that he was a good choice, that getting to know him would be the best decision she could ever make.

A smart man would ignore what he saw in her eyes, what he felt every time they were near each other, and just take her at her word. A smart man wouldn't point out the vulnerability in her eyes demanded he do something to heal the gaping wounds another lover had caused.

He was no knight in shining armor. It wasn't his place or desire to do anything beyond being friendly with his coworkers. And yet he couldn't walk away.

"This isn't as complicated as you're making it. We're each intrigued by the other, but we are in agreement that a romantic relationship is out of the question. Why can't we just enjoy each other's company, at least for the rest of the weekend, no sex necessary?"

Yeah right, on the "no sex necessary." Jenny wasn't buying it. Men had been saying that to women since the beginning of time so they'd lower their guard and their pants. Why else would Tristan want to spend time "getting to know" her when he'd soon leave if not because of physical chemistry? That, they had in spades. Gigantic bunches. Explosive chemistry that made her want to rip off his clothes and kiss him from head to toe.

She wished it wasn't so, but just making eye contact with him put her off kilter in ways no man ever had. Tristan had some major pheromones going and they were making her insides dance to a crazy tune.

"Come on, Jenny. Letting go to enjoy the rest of the weekend together shouldn't be such a difficult decision to make. It's not as if I'm asking you to marry me."

Jenny flinched. Ouch. His comment shouldn't have stung, but it did. Tristan wanting to marry her hadn't crossed her mind. And yet, foolishly, she did feel hurt, as if he were somehow implying she wasn't good enough to marry.

Or perhaps Geoffrey's taunts had come back to haunt her? Not that Geoffrey had been free to marry her since he'd already been engaged, but at the time Jenny hadn't known that. She'd just known that an amazingly handsome and charismatic doctor had swept her off her still-in-nursing-school feet, promised her his undying love and, like the naïve twenty-year-old she'd been, she'd believed him.

For all she knew, Tristan had a fiancée or even a wife and kids somewhere.

Why did the thought cause a fresh wave of pain? Swallowing the sob that wanted to escape, she took a deep breath instead and gestured to Tristan's burn. "Is the ice helping?"

He let out a frustrated noise. "I guess that means you're finished talking about us?"

"There is no 'us.'" Her words sounded more confident than she felt, which strengthened her to continue on the offensive. "You're a great-looking man, Tristan, not to mention smart and funny, and a genuinely nice guy. I imagine lots of women are attracted to you. You'd be much better off spending your time pursuing one of them.

I'm not worth the trouble. I have a kid." Hadn't Carlos implied that made her unworthy of his love?

"You're worth the trouble, Jenny. Give me this weekend to show you."

Frustrated, she pushed against his chest. "I'm not sleeping with you, Tristan."

"That's not what I'm asking you to do. I'll be here for less than three months and, if you ever have a relationship again, you need it to be more than a short-term one. Fine. Let's just enjoy being together with no pressure for anything more instead of throwing walls up between the attraction we feel for each other."

"Walls aren't a bad thing."

"In certain scenarios, I'm sure you're right, but in this case they're not good. You don't need walls around me, Jenny. I'm not going to hurt you."

"You can't guarantee that you won't hurt me."

He hesitated. "No, I guess not. But we both know where the other one stands. That I'm leaving soon and there wouldn't be anything permanent between us. Let me be the opportunity for you to be reminded of how much fun life is."

Life was fun. She had fun when she read Sawyer a story, when they went to the park and she pushed him as high as he'd go on the swings with him begging her to go even higher, when they played games and he'd giggle incessantly when he beat her. When... She paused. All the fun moments flooding her were tied to Sawyer. Not a single one was something revolving around her own life other than as his mother.

Part of her didn't mind. She loved being Sawyer's mother. But another part, the part that screamed to her that she was only twenty-five years old, was young, and healthy, and that it wasn't wrong to be attracted to a beautiful man…well, that part minded.

What Tristan said was as hopeless as it was tempting.

"How do I magically make the way I feel disappear? How do I lower those walls when it's easier to leave them up and not worry about getting hurt or having Sawyer hurt?"

The glow from the moonlight flickered in his eyes, dancing with a mesmerizing rhythm that lured her further under his spell. "Promise you won't be mad and I'll tell you."

She sighed. "Please don't say that my sleeping with you would make the awkwardness go away, because we both know that would only make things worse."

"I don't know that, but that wasn't what I was going to say. Close, though."

"What?"

"Not sex, but we need to kiss."

Jenny rolled her eyes. "Of course, you think that."

"Hear me out. What if there's all this sexual tension between us and one kiss would dissipate it? If one kiss could put you at ease to where you could treat me no different from any other travel nurse doing a rotation at the hospital? If what you say is true, that you don't want a relationship with me during the time I'm here, getting rid of the attraction would be the perfect solution."

Jenny considered what he was saying. As much as she thought he was just wanting to make out, maybe he was onto something. If he was a bad kisser, then she'd be grossed out and whatever it was that lit up inside her when he was near would stop and he'd be just another guy, like Roger, and maybe this tension inside her would subside and they could be friends. Or at least coworkers, rather than her feeling all fluttery inside.

Or maybe she was just tired of fighting what she felt, what she saw in his eyes. Maybe, despite all her protests and reasons why she shouldn't, she really did want to throw caution to the wind and cling to any reason to kiss him.

Maybe she wanted to kiss her completely-wrong-for-her frog despite knowing he'd never morph into her Prince Charming.

Aware that no one could see them where his SUV was parked, Jenny acted purely on gut instinct, stood on her tippy toes and pressed her mouth to Tristan's.

Jenny's mouth was warm, soft, *fragile*. Like a delicate butterfly's wing brushing against Tristan's lips. He suspected if he applied the slightest pressure she'd fly away. Even though he longed to deepen their kiss, he stood still, keeping his hands to his sides and ordering himself to be content with her lips touching his.

In the moonlight, he could see her closed eyes, could see the uncertainty on her face, could feel her body quiver. Or was that his body? He wasn't sure. He just knew that kissing Jenny wasn't going to make the ache inside him go away, but rather intensify his reaction every time she was near.

He hadn't thought it would. Not really. But it had been worth a shot when she'd been so adamant that they couldn't be together. He should be the one being adamant. Instead, he was shaking like a teenaged boy receiving his first kiss.

His gaze never leaving her, he watched the play of emotions the moonlight lit across her face. He'd never expected Jenny to take his suggestion seriously. That she had had blown him away. That her mouth pressed against his blew him away.

It took all his willpower to let her pull back, knowing that she might never allow him this close again, that he might never breathe her breath or feel the warmth of her body again, but he managed, somehow. If only there was more light so he could read everything her now-open eyes revealed as she stared at him. Awe, wonder, curiosity, regret? He couldn't be sure, he just knew emotions were high.

Afraid he'd say the wrong thing if he opened his mouth, he waited so he could take his cue from her. But she didn't say anything, just seemed to be registering what she'd done.

Please don't regret this, he mentally ordered. *Please give us a chance.*

A chance for what? he wondered. He didn't allow that curiosity to take hold, just lived in the moment, prepared for Jenny to push him away when what he wanted was to hold her tight. Just when he thought she was going to retreat, she pressed her lips to his again, this time with more pressure, more exploration, and as much as he didn't want to crush her fragility, he kissed her back.

Still, the kiss was more sweet than passionate. More tasting, exploring, than consuming, but it wouldn't take much for him to fully ignite and go up in flames. Her touch was that powerful, he was that receptive to what was happening.

A bit breathy, she pulled back and stared up at him, her eyes full of wonder and concern. "That just brought things to a whole new level of awkward."

"Bad?" he asked, willing her to admit that it hadn't been, that she'd felt the magic of their complicated touch.

She shook her head.

Hope blossomed. "Good?"

After a moment's hesitation, she sighed. "You already

know you're a great kisser. To even suggest that our kissing would make this…whatever this is between us…go away was ludicrous. You tricked me and now I need to think about this."

"I wasn't trying to trick you. It could have worked." He touched her face, brushing his thumb across the softness of her cheek. "Don't overthink what happened, Jenny. You'll drive yourself crazy and it accomplishes nothing."

"All the same, I do need to think about what just happened." She took a few steps back. "Everyone will be heading to their tents since we have to be up early."

He could feel the walls going up. Frustration hit at how much he wanted to claw them down into such rubble that she couldn't ever hide behind them again.

"Jenny?"

She paused.

"In case you were wondering, had you asked me about our kiss, my answer would be good. Very, very good."

CHAPTER EIGHT

"You left this in my vehicle."

Wiping the sleep from her eyes, Jenny stared at the man standing on her front porch. Was she dreaming? She'd gone from seeing him with her eyes closed to waking from her doorbell ringing and finding him freshly showered, wearing jeans and a navy T-shirt, standing on her front porch.

"Tristan? What are you doing here?" That he held her hat in his hands registered. "You didn't need to bring that to me. I mean, you could have brought it to work this evening. That would have been fine."

"Bringing it by wasn't a big deal and this way you don't have to worry about keeping track of it at work."

"Thank you." She took the hat from him, saw her mother's car pulling into the drive, and felt a moment of panic. Could she just make Tristan disappear so that her mother and Sawyer didn't see him?

But even as she thought it, Tristan turned to see who she was looking at, and Jenny faced the inevitable. Sawyer and her mother were about to meet Tristan. The man she'd kissed and wanted to do so much more with. She hadn't, though. She'd kissed him and walked away because he was no frog prince.

Sighing, Jenny brushed past him to help her mother.

"Hi, Mom," she said as her mother's car door opened. "How was your weekend?"

"I was just about to ask you the same." Her mother motioned to where Tristan stood on the porch. "From the look of things, I'm guessing things went well."

Was she implying that Tristan had stayed the night? Jenny gawked at her mother's knowing look.

"I left my hat in Tristan's vehicle this morning when he dropped me off." There, she'd let her mother know that he hadn't stayed the night. "He found it and was just dropping it by. He just got here."

"Tristan. I've not heard you mention him. He's who you went camping with?" her mother asked, obviously intrigued.

"I went with a whole group from work. Tristan just happened to be who Laura and I rode with to the Ocoee." Her friend should have been with her on the way back home, but had bailed, choosing to ride with Roger and Lucia. "It's not a big deal." Hoping her mother didn't see right through her and somehow know Jenny had kissed him, she opened Sawyer's door. "Hey, you. Did you have a great weekend with Grammy in Gatlinburg?"

Grinning, Sawyer nodded as she undid his safety seat. "Eli and I slept under the shark tanks. You have to go do that, Mom. They were huge. You'd love it."

Jenny smiled at her world. "Sounds as if you loved it. I sure missed you."

His blond head bobbed up and down as he climbed out of the car. The moment his feet were on the ground, Jenny wrapped him in a hug.

"I see you have a new friend with you. Did Grammy get you that?"

"Grammy let me pick any stuffed animal I wanted. I started to get a shark. That's what Eli got. But then I saw him." He held up a stuffed sea turtle, but his attention moved beyond her. "Who's that man?"

"A friend from work," she answered, her cheeks flushing as she realized Tristan was walking toward them rather than waiting on the porch. Not that waiting would have helped since her mom and Sawyer would have to walk right past. *Say goodbye and leave*, she willed, but of course that wasn't what he did.

Tristan gave one of those eye-sparkling smiles. "I'm Tristan. I'm a nurse at the hospital with your mom. You must be Sawyer."

"I am." His good manners kicking in, Sawyer stuck out his hand in the most adorable way. "Nice to meet you."

Jenny's heart melted. How could he look so big and so tiny all at the same time? And why was her heart thudding so hard at his meeting Tristan?

Tristan's glimpse shot to Jenny and he grinned before returning his attention to Sawyer. "Did I hear you say something about sleeping under a shark tank?"

Sawyer nodded. "There were sharks everywhere."

Tristan's eyes widened with overexaggeration. "Was that at the aquarium? It sounds really cool."

Excitement filling his eyes, Sawyer nodded. "I went with Grammy and Giles and Eli to Gatlinburg. Sharks were swimming around us all night."

"Weren't you scared?"

"No." Sawyer giggled. "They were in a tank."

"That's good." Tristan bent to Sawyer's level. "Who's your friend?"

"This is my sea turtle. I named him Freddie, but that's not what the sea turtle at the Chattanooga aquarium's name is. There are two sea turtles there." Sawyer talked a mile a minute, showing Tristan his stuffed turtle. "I like sea turtles."

"The kid likes anything that's in the water," Jenny's mom interjected with what Jenny could only describe as a delighted giggle. "I'm Geneva, by the way. So, you and Jenny work together?"

Oh, Mom, please don't.

"For a short while. I'm a travel nurse and only here for a few months."

"Travel nursing? That sounds adventurous." Her mother popped the car trunk. "Sawyer, be a dear and grab your things."

"Can I help carry something?" Tristan offered, earning major brownie points from Jenny's mother.

Her eyes lit up. "Would you mind? That would be wonderful."

And that was how Tristan ended up inside their house and invited to stay for a late lunch.

"If I'd known we were going to have company, I'd have had something ready, but we're sure glad you came by today anyway," Geneva told him while pouring Tristan a glass of sweet tea.

"He's not here to socialize, Mom, just to drop off my hat."

"That doesn't mean we shouldn't feed him. He might be hungry."

Her mother had no idea.

Jenny wavered between wanting to smack her own head with her palm and being amused at how her mother carried on. You'd have thought Jenny had never brought a man home. Then again, there hadn't been many. A few in high school and her early university days, then Geoffrey after she'd started nursing school, and Carlos a few years ago.

"No problem, ma'am," Tristan assured her. "But Jenny's right. I just stopped by to bring her hat. She left it when I dropped her off this morning."

"That's what she said earlier." Had her mother not believed her? "So, y'all had a great trip?"

"I did," Tristan confirmed. "I'm not sure we'll convince Jenny to go rafting again, though."

"Oh?"

"Tristan had to rescue a girl who was stuck in the river."

"Under the water?"

"Just her foot was wedged under a rock."

Sawyer swam his turtle through the air. "If Freddie had been there, he could have freed her."

"Freddie would have come in handy," Tristan quipped.

"That reminds me," Jenny mused. "I need to check to see if you got into the next session for swimming lessons."

The timing of the previous session hadn't worked for her work schedule, but after this weekend, now more than ever, she wanted Sawyer to know how to swim.

His big eyes met hers. "Can Freddie go, too?"

"You think Freddie can offer some tips?" Jenny asked, reaching for her cellular phone. "If so, then I'm all for it. Excuse me while I pull up my email. Sawyer has been on a wait list for the next session, and I'll need to confirm quickly as I don't want to miss getting him in."

Unfortunately, the email said that the remainder of the summer sessions were full but they'd notify her if there were any cancellations.

"Everything okay?"

Jenny shrugged. "Just frustrated that Sawyer's still on a wait list. I'd hoped he'd learn to swim this summer, but short of finding someone to give private lessons, that may not happen."

"I can teach him."

Jenny blinked. "You?"

"Sure. I'm a trained lifeguard and there's a pool at the apartment complex where I'm staying. With Freddie's help, teaching Sawyer would be a breeze."

Sawyer's eyes were huge, pleading. "Can I, Mom?"

How could she say no? If she let her attraction to Tristan get in the way of Sawyer learning to swim and something happened, she'd never forgive herself.

"Oh, that's wonderful, Tristan," Jenny's mother praised, clasping her hands together and eyeing him as if he were the greatest thing ever. "Sawyer needs to know how to swim and what better way than being taught by a friend?"

Jenny could think of several dozen, but she had to do what was best for Sawyer. What was best for her son was making sure he learned to swim.

"I… Mom's right. That would be great. Thank you."

"Yay! Did you hear that, Freddie? I'm going to learn to swim!" Sawyer jumped around, the turtle snug in his arms. "Can we start today?"

Tristan shrugged. "I don't have to be anywhere until work tonight."

"Don't you have something you need to be doing? Sleeping, maybe?" Because Jenny needed time to assimilate that Tristan would be teaching Sawyer to swim.

He shook his head. "With sleeping last night, I'll take a short nap before going into work, but otherwise, I'm free."

Sawyer continued to bounce with excitement. "Can we please, Mama? Freddie likes swimming."

"Freddie, eh?" She sighed, not seeing a way around saying yes. "Fine. If Mr. Scott is okay with giving you a swimming lesson, then we can go for a quick one today."

"Yay!" Sawyer danced around the room. "Freddie and I are going swimming."

Jenny's mom beamed at Tristan. "You saved a life this weekend and now you may save another."

"Mom!"

"Well, it's true," her mother insisted. "One never knows when knowing how to swim will be needed. Sawyer might save a life one day that will have been made possible by Tristan's generosity. Kudos to him for being so generous with his time."

What her mother said was an echo of her earlier thoughts, so she knew she was fighting a losing battle to say anything else in protest. Instead, she met Tristan's gaze. "I really do hope we aren't keeping you from something."

Taking a drink of the sweet tea her mother had insisted he have, Tristan smiled. "My laundry and I appreciate that more than you know."

"Understood." Why was Jenny smiling back as if her mother wasn't watching?

"Will you jump into the water?" Tristan asked the boy. He wasn't sure if offering to teach Jenny's son to swim was overall a good idea or not, but he'd taken training years ago, upped his lifeguard certification when he'd worked in Colorado, and helping a kid learn to swim was the right thing to do.

"Is it over my head?" Sawyer asked, looking and sounding nervous despite his earlier enthusiasm.

Tristan shook his head. "I'm standing, not swimming, so it's not over your head. Jump and I'll catch you."

Sawyer's eyes widened. "You can catch me? You're sure?"

"I'm sure I can."

"Sawyer, why don't I hold Freddie while you take your swimming lesson," Jenny suggested from where she sat on the edge of the pool, her long legs dangling in the water. He spied blue straps tied around her neck, but she wore a baggy T-shirt and shorts over them. Just as well. Her toned legs were enough of a distraction. Everything about the woman distracted him.

Sawyer gripped his turtle tighter. "Freddie likes the water."

"He does," Jenny agreed. "But I sure would like him to keep me company while you and Mr. Scott are doing your lesson."

"Tristan," he corrected. "Call me Tristan."

"Mr. Tristan," she countered, her attention staying on Sawyer.

"Better than Mr. Scott," he conceded then turned back to the boy. "Freddie would be great company for your mom while we're in the water. Moms sometimes get nervous during swim lessons."

Hesitantly, Sawyer handed over the stuffed turtle. "I guess Freddie could stay with her. He is great company."

Jenny watched Tristan try to convince Sawyer to jump into the water. The kid was usually gung-ho on everything, so to see him hesitant made her heart hurt. Did he sense her fear? Her nervousness for him?

Not that she thought Tristan would let anything happen to him, but accidents happened. Just like the girl who'd had to be rescued the day before. Not that there were any rocks or rapids in the apartment complex's pool, but still, Jenny's belly was all quivery.

"Okay, kiddo, today we are just going to do the basics, get you used to the water, and have a little fun. You ready?"

Standing on the side of the pool next to her, Sawyer nodded.

"We can hold off on you jumping into the water for later," he wisely suggested, earning a look of relief from Sawyer. "For now, let's get you in the water for your first superhero lesson."

Sawyer's eyes widened. "Superhero lesson?"

"Yep. First, there are some superhero rules that you should know."

From where he stood at the edge of the pool, Sawyer hung on to Tristan's every word.

"Rule number one. At no point will a superhero be forced to do anything he or she doesn't want to do."

Sawyer nodded.

"Second rule—" Tristan held up two fingers "—is that superheroes have to trust their teacher completely and have faith in the knowledge that their methods will develop the superhero's own superpowers. A superhero must listen closely and do exactly as their teacher instructs. Self-doubt is a supervillain's weapon and superheroes can't give in to their evil powers."

Sawyer looked hesitant on that one but, realizing what he was doing, quickly lifted his little shoulders.

Jenny fought smiling.

"And the third rule is the most important one of all."

Jenny waited with more interest than Sawyer.

"Superheroes must smile lots because smiles boost one's powers and ward off villains."

Sawyer blinked. "Smiles?"

Tristan nodded. "Absolutely. The more you smile, the better superswimmer you're going to be."

"So, if I smile enough, I'll be a better swimmer than Freddie?"

Tristan glanced at the stuffed turtle Jenny held. "I've

never seen Freddie that he wasn't smiling, so you've got your work cut out for you on that one, kid."

Sawyer bared his teeth in a smile so big the corners of his mouth squished his cheeks.

Happiness spread through Jenny and she covered her mouth to cover her own smile.

Tristan laughed. "That's a really great start. I think I felt your superpowers growing."

Sawyer's smile morphed into a more real one.

"Let me check to be sure." Tristan reached out and took Sawyer's hands. Jenny's breath caught at the sight of her son's tiny hands in Tristan's strong, capable ones. Hands that had held hers the night before, that had cupped her face while they'd kissed. "Yep," he continued, moving to a shallower area, "your powers are growing. Now, the first thing we are going to do is that, while holding my hands, you're going to come into the water. I've got you, so remember not to let any villains douse you with self-doubt."

Sawyer took a deep breath then slid off the side of the pool and into the water. Tristan held on to his hands. "Great job," he praised, easing Sawyer into the water to stand on his own feet. "That was perfect."

"I'm not scared of the water," Sawyer declared, but stayed close to Tristan. "Mom has brought me to the pool before and I played in the water, but it was only up to my knees."

"That's a great head start on today's lesson. So, this next step is a super easy one and I'm going to do it first." Tristan got on his knees and managed to dunk his head completely under the water.

Water droplets ran down his face, his throat, his muscled chest. Resisting the urge to fan herself, Jenny swallowed.

Brushing his hair back from his face, he grinned at Sawyer. "Now, let me see you do that."

With only a moment's hesitation, Sawyer did exactly as Tristan had done.

Jenny clapped, to which Sawyer bowed.

"Perfect, except your mom didn't clap for me."

"You need affirmation?"

His eyes twinkled. "From you? Absolutely."

"What's af-for-mation?" Sawyer asked, tugging on Tristan's arm.

"A reinforcement and acknowledgment of doing something well."

"Mom, clap for Mr. Tristan, too," Sawyer insisted. "He needs af-for-mation."

"I'll keep that in mind the next time he does something well," Jenny promised.

Tristan's grin had her breath catching and she half expected him to say something flirty. Instead, his focus returned to Sawyer, who was clinging to his every word. "Now, let's walk to the other side of the pool. You want to hold my hand, or you got this?"

As an answer, Sawyer took off for the other side of the pool, Tristan quickly falling into step beside him. Together, they tapped the side of the pool, high-fived each other, then turned to head back toward Jenny.

"Woohoo! Good job, guys! Y'all rock," she said with exaggerated enthusiasm and fist pumps.

"Good job, Mommy."

Lips twisting, Tristan nodded. "Right. Good affirmation, Jenny."

Tristan led Sawyer through a few water games, allowing Sawyer to become more and more relaxed in the water and mesmerizing Jenny with how great he was with her son.

"Okay, next up is your flying lesson."

Sawyer's eyes widened again. "I'm going to learn to fly?"

Tristan tousled his hair. "With a little help. Ready?"

His hand around Sawyer's waist, Sawyer's arms stretched out in front of him as Tristan guided him over the water's surface as if he were flying across it.

"Look, Mom, I'm flying," Sawyer called, his giggles melting Jenny's heart.

"I see that." She also saw the complete adoration in Sawyer's eyes when he glanced up at Tristan.

She wasn't so sure that the same didn't shine in her own eyes.

"Remember we just got back from camping," Tristan said as he unlocked his apartment door so Jenny could take Sawyer to the bathroom. He'd come in that morning, brought in his gear and unpacked clothes, but most of his equipment sat right where he'd put it next to the front door.

"No worries," Jenny said. "I'm not going to white-glove test the baseboards."

His scrutiny automatically dropped to the baseboards. The clean baseboards, fortunately.

"The bathroom is this way." He pointed them toward the bathroom. "Help yourself."

When Jenny started to follow Sawyer into the room, he frowned. "Mom. I can do it. I'm not a baby."

"Right. I knew that." She smiled at him. "Okay. Don't bother anything."

He gave Tristan that "Moms!" look then went into the bathroom. Tristan wasn't surprised at the resounding click of the lock.

"I… Sometimes I forget how grown up he's getting."

"Nothing wrong with wanting to take care of your kid."

She smiled. "Thank you for that, but I'm positive that, in this case, he wouldn't agree with you. I think I embarrassed him."

"No harm done."

She smiled again then wandered around the open apartment, pausing to look out the window before turning back to him. "You're sure you actually live here?"

He furrowed his brow in question.

"Other than your gear by the front door, this could be anyone's home."

"This isn't a home, Jenny. It's just a place to sleep while I'm in Chattanooga."

"Is there a home somewhere?"

Clammy heat burned his skin. "What do you mean?"

"You've mentioned several places where you've lived during your childhood and as an adult, but is there somewhere you go to be 'at home'?"

"My life isn't like yours, Jenny. There is no building I walk into and get warm fuzzies. To me, houses, apartments, tents—it's all the same. Just a place to sleep."

"And in these places where you just sleep, you never try to make them feel…homey?"

"Why would I do that? I don't plan to stay."

"Do you have any family, Tristan?"

"My father works construction. I'm a lot like him, living in an area until the job is done then moving on."

"And your mother?"

Nausea twisted his stomach. "She passed a few years ago."

Sorrow darkened Jenny's eyes. "I'm sorry."

Tristan was spared having to say that it hadn't mattered by Sawyer's opening the door.

"I'm all done," he announced, rubbing his hands together.

So was Tristan, because he didn't like Jenny making him look around his bare-bones apartment and comparing its emptiness to the warmth of her house.

Not her house, her *home*.

CHAPTER NINE

"YOUR NOSE IS PINK."

Jenny glanced across the hospital bed at Laura. "I got a little too much sun this weekend."

"I didn't notice it this morning before we left the campsite," Laura pointed out as she tucked in a fresh sheet.

"Yeah, about that, what's up with you bailing on me and my having to ride back with Tristan alone?"

Laura smiled. "You should be thanking me for being such a good friend."

"I was thinking of trading you in for a more loyal model," Jenny countered.

Laura and Jenny maneuvered their heavily sedated patient back onto the bed. "Go ahead, if you can find one, but a more loyal friend doesn't exist. I'm the best there is. You're so lucky."

"So you've been telling me since kindergarten."

Laura laughed. "You'd think you'd believe me by now."

Jenny's stare met her friend's, knowing that she did believe her. Not that there had ever been any doubt. Still. "I need you to stop throwing Tristan and me together."

"Because you've realized he's a great guy?"

"He is a great guy." An amazingly great guy who had the body of an Adonis and a heart of gold. "That was never in question. However, I'm not looking for a guy, much less one who will be gone in a few months."

"Don't you think he'd be a good one to cut your teeth on, though?"

"What?" Jenny gasped at her friend's suggestion.

"You know, dip your toes back into the dating scene. The fact that he's only going to be here for a few months is a plus. That way, if you're so rusty that you screw up royally, no big deal. He'll be gone and no one will be the wiser."

"Or I could just not and save myself a lot of hassle."

"But there's no fun in that. Admit it. You had a great time with him this weekend."

She had. Even more so that afternoon with Sawyer. How had Tristan convinced her to eat with him prior to Sawyer and her leaving his place? They'd only been going inside for Sawyer to use the bathroom and dry off, not to stay for grilled cheese sandwiches, which was the only thing he'd offered that Sawyer had said yes to.

"Your entire face got too much sun," Laura teased as they checked to make sure all the patient's lines were still in place. "Pink looks good on you. So, tell me what happened."

"He came back to the house around lunchtime." Making the admission felt liberating, as if confessing that Tristan had been at her house made it a little less taboo. Not that it was taboo. Just…

Laura's jaw dropped. "You invited him over? You sly girl."

Jenny shook her head. "That's not what I said. I left my hat in his 4Runner and he brought it by."

Why was it so much more difficult to tell Laura about Tristan than any of the other secrets she'd shared with her bestie over the years? Even with Geoffrey and Carlos, she'd not held back in telling Laura all the humiliating details.

Laura gave a thumbs-up. "Nice. Women have been using the 'leave something behind' trick for years. I'm proud of you, Jenny!"

"I didn't purposely leave my hat." Had she been a fool to confess so much? Probably, and she wasn't done yet. "He offered to give Sawyer swim lessons."

Laura clasped her hands together. "Oh, Jenny, that's wonderful in so many ways. This shows he isn't like Carlos, and I know how upset you've been that the classes were full. When does he start?"

"Whether or not he's like Carlos is irrelevant. Although, ultimately, he'll leave just as Carlos did. As far as the lessons, today."

"What?" Laura's hands clasped together. "I knew it. Your nose isn't pink from this weekend. You were out in the sun with Tristan. Did you have a great time?"

Yes. She had.

"Sawyer did. I sat poolside while he and Tristan were in the water."

"I don't blame you. That man has a beautiful body, all rippling muscles and brawn."

Jenny rolled her eyes, but Laura continued. "How was it?"

"The water? Cool, but not bad compared to the river."

"Not the water." Laura snorted. "Sawyer and Tristan meeting. I know what a big deal that is to you."

"He's all Sawyer talked about during our drive home from his lesson and then he had to tell Mom everything, too." She sighed. "He's pretty infatuated."

"And Sawyer's mom? Is she infatuated, too?"

Jenny sucked in a deep breath and shrugged. "She's

trying to keep her wits about her, but he doesn't make it easy."

Laura gave a low squeal. "I knew it. From the moment I saw you two together, I knew it."

"We aren't together."

"Not from lack of wanting to be on his part. The man is crazy about you."

Nervous energy zapped through her. "How can you be sure?"

"Have you seen how he looks at you? Jenny, when you're anywhere near, he can't take his eyes off you. And, for the record, you suffer from the same affliction. It's why I don't feel even a smidge of guilt for throwing you together with him."

Jenny didn't deny it. She was certainly suffering from some type of affliction.

"Also, for the record, in all the years I've known you, I've never seen you so taken with someone. Not even he whose name I won't say because he doesn't deserve to have his name said, or the jerk who came after him."

Jenny wanted to deny what Laura said but couldn't. Seeing Tristan with Sawyer, watching how wonderful he was with her son, had toppled any doubts. She was taken with Tristan.

"I'm not sure what I should do," Jenny admitted, hating how vulnerable her feelings toward Tristan left her.

"How about you quit worrying about what you should do, and just enjoy the next couple of months?"

"That's pretty much what he said Saturday night when—" She gave a tight smile. "I wish it was that easy, that I could just turn off the voices in my head."

"Oh, you mean when you two snuck off from the campfire?" Laura waggled her brows.

"I helped him put burn ointment on where I burned

him with that flaming marshmallow," Jenny noted. "Although, I'll admit, I didn't realize you'd even noticed as you seemed quite cozy with Steve. Forget Tristan. Tell me what's up with you and rafting boy."

As they pulled off their PPE, Laura laughed. "Me and 'rafting boy' are good. I'm seeing him tomorrow."

"Tomorrow?"

"He's busiest on the weekends," Laura told her as they headed to the nurses' station.

"I guess that would be the case. Just be careful, Laura. He's not exactly stick-around-forever material, either."

Laura's brow arched. "Because he's younger than me or because he works for a rafting company?"

"He probably meets lots of women that way."

Laura snorted. "Sure, he does. That doesn't mean he drives almost two hours to see them."

"Probably not, but you seem to be diving in. I don't want you hurt when he probably goes through a lot of women each summer."

"You're wrong," Laura insisted then shrugged. "But if so, then I'll count myself lucky that I was one of them. He lives in Georgia but has worked for the rafting company the past three summers. He'll be starting an internship next summer with a law firm in Atlanta and says he's enjoying every moment of this last summer of freedom."

"And you plan to help him do that?"

Laura nodded. "Every chance I get. He's a great guy."

"You just met him."

"Sometimes, you just know these things, you know?"

"No, I don't know."

"Sure you do. You knew it when you met Tristan, but you're too far stuck behind those walls you built after Geoffrey to realize it. Quit hiding and get back to living, Jenny."

"What are you two lovelies talking about?" Roger asked as he and Tristan joined them at the desk. Roger had just had a new admit that they'd gotten settled.

Jenny and Laura exchanged looks then Laura turned toward Roger. "About how you're turning thirty in a couple of months and we're planning to come out to support your big face-plant."

"Let's hope that's not what it is." Roger laughed. "Just a couple of months left in my twenties. That's not that long."

"And yet a lifetime's worth of memories can be made in much less time," Tristan said, his blue gaze meeting Jenny's. They'd been busy since shift change and she'd only caught glimpses of him up to this point. Looking into his eyes, she saw the answers to the questions that had plagued her since arriving. Tristan planned to take her lead on how they acted around each other. The ball was in her court to do with as she pleased.

"Jenny tells me you're giving Sawyer swim lessons," Laura blurted out, forcing the issue. "She also mentioned how great you were with him and how cute you were in your birthday suit. I mean—" she giggled "—your swimsuit."

Jenny guffawed at her friend's claim. "Oh, yeah, I'm trading you in. Y'all have fun. I'm going to chat with Mr. Rossberg."

Later that night Tristan ended up in Mr. Rossberg's room with Jenny. He'd been stable for over twenty-four hours but showed no signs of regaining consciousness despite decreased sedation.

"Tell me more about what you said to Laura about my birthday suit."

"We both know that I didn't say anything about your birthday suit to Laura."

He laughed. "Just wishful thinking on my part then."

Jenny stared at him. "You'd have been happy if I'd discussed you with Laura?"

Helping her to roll Mr. Rossberg so he could be washed, he pointed out, "She's your best friend. If you're discussing anything about me with her, that's a good sign."

"A good sign of what?"

"That you aren't immune to my charms."

"We established my lack of immunity on Saturday night."

Keeping a firm hold on Mr. Rossberg, his lips twitched. "I need a reminder."

"You won't be getting one."

"That's disappointing to hear. You know how I need your affirmation." Her eyes lifted to his and, grinning, he added, "Plus, I've been looking forward to our next kiss."

Jenny sucked in air. "You're impossible."

"Where you're concerned, I'm possible," he assured her. She bit into her lower lip and longing hit him. "As a matter of fact, the only thing that seems impossible is my not kissing you again."

"Is that why you volunteered to teach Sawyer to swim?"

He shook his head. "I did that because he needs to know how to swim."

She stared at him a moment, shock registering in her eyes. "You're telling the truth."

One brow lifted. "Did you think I wasn't?"

"I thought…well, you know."

"You thought it was because I want to spend time with you? You're not wrong, Jenny," he admitted, wanting to be completely transparent with her. "I do want to spend time with you, but my teaching Sawyer to swim is about Sawyer and keeping him safe. He's a great little guy."

Pride brightened her face. "Thank you. He is wonderful. I'll feel so much better knowing that he can swim."

"Sure thing. I do have one request, though."

"What's that?" she asked, finishing washing Mr. Rossberg then putting a fresh hospital gown on him.

"I want you to get in the water with us."

"Me?" She paused in straightening the gown. "Wouldn't my being there just be a distraction?"

"You're a distraction no matter where you are, Jenny. You distract me." Night. Day. Swimming. Working. Sleeping. Dreaming. She seemed to never leave his mind.

"I… I'm sorry. Or maybe I'm not, because you're a distraction to me, too, so it would be unfair for this distraction to be one-sided."

Pleasure at her admission filled him. Even more so that she was smiling as she said it. Her walls were still there, but she'd opened the gates, letting him in, at least temporarily.

"You'll bring Sawyer over tomorrow afternoon?"

She nodded. "We'll be there, but I'm making no promises about getting into the pool with you. Just message me when you wake up and I'll bring him by after I pick him up from preschool."

Good. He looked forward to seeing Sawyer. And Jenny. The swim lessons were a win-win as he found giving them gave him great satisfaction, as if he was making a difference in the kid's life during their short time together.

He wouldn't think about that yet, when he'd leave and not be a part of Jenny and her son's lives. Then again, he usually didn't stress about leaving at all.

There was nothing usual about Chattanooga, though.

"You won't be asleep?" he asked, not liking where his thoughts had gone. He wasn't even close to leaving, so he sure shouldn't be stressing about it already.

"I'll go to sleep after I drop him off at preschool in the morning. If you wake up early, then I'll still be asleep."

From across the hospital bed, he eyed her a moment. "How about you message me when you wake up? I'm sure I get more rest than you do, so I don't want to wake you if you're still asleep."

She amazed him with all she managed to do, between work, mother, daughter, and her house.

"My alarm will go off at three."

"That's not a lot of sleep." She really should get more rest.

Jenny shrugged. "It's enough, and spending time with Sawyer before going into work is important. Way more important that getting that extra sleep."

"You're a good mom, Jenny."

Cheeks flushing pink, she gave a nervous laugh then smoothed out the white blanket covering Mr. Rossberg. "You could tell that from meeting Sawyer once?"

"I could tell that from seeing you with him, listening to you talk about him this weekend. I wish I'd…" He stopped, knowing what he'd been about to say but halting that train of thought. "He's a lucky kid to have you for a mom."

"I don't know about lucky, but he's loved."

"That's why he's lucky." Battling memories of his childhood that were trying to surface, Tristan took a deep breath. "You think Mr. Rossberg is enjoying our conversation?"

Jenny smiled. "Normally, when I'm in here, I hope

he hears every word, but maybe not so much when I'm with you."

"You hear that, Mr. Rossberg? I think it's time for you to wake up so you can have a real conversation with your nurse."

"I sure hope you wake up soon," Jenny told the man, touching his arm. "Your family would be thrilled, especially your lovely wife. She's ready to take you home just as soon as you're able."

Watching her with her patient, something moved inside Tristan's chest. Physiologically, he supposed that was impossible unless it was a gas bubble, but he'd swear something monumental shifted at the gentleness with which Jenny cared for her patients, her son, even with the way she was with her mother.

Jenny cared for those around her.

When she glanced up and their eyes met, he had to tamp down the urge to wrap his arms around her and hold on for as long as she'd let him.

Yeah, Chattanooga was different, and all because of the woman smiling at him.

Sawyer shook his head, slinging water in a three-hundred-and-sixty-degree direction.

Jenny held up her hands, shielding herself with the fluffy beach towel she held. "You're like a wet puppy."

"I want a wet puppy." Sawyer wiggled as Jenny wrapped him in the towel.

"Puppies are big responsibilities," she commented, patting him dry.

Wide eyes the same color as her own met hers. "I have responsi-billies."

Jenny grinned, resisting the urge to hug him to her. "No promises, but I'll think on it, Sawyer."

Sawyer turned to where Tristan had joined them. "Do you have a dog?"

Water droplets falling onto his broad shoulders, Tristan shook his head. "I travel a lot."

Jenny's eyes were traveling a lot, following the path of those drops as they rolled downward. She visually traced one down his chest and abs until it disappeared at his waistband, then gulped as heat spread through her.

"Couldn't you bring a dog with you when you travel?" Sawyer asked.

Seemingly oblivious to the effect he was having on her internal temperature, Tristan considered Sawyer's question. "I guess I could. I never had a dog while growing up, but I remember wanting one, too. My dad always said it wouldn't be fair to an animal to move around as much as we did, and I took him at his word and have never really given getting one much thought as an adult."

Jenny studied Tristan, noting the way he averted his glance from her as if he didn't want her to see his eyes. He wrapped a towel around his shoulders and made a play at drying off from where he'd been in the pool. Maybe he hadn't been quite as oblivious as she'd thought.

Or maybe his mind was somewhere else completely. That was where hers should be. Somewhere other than how attractive she found his body, because seriously? Was she really looking at his hairy legs and wondering how they'd feel brushing against her smooth ones?

"As long as you love him and take care of him, it would be okay to get a dog, wouldn't it, Mommy?"

Nothing like Sawyer putting her on the spot, but at least his question had her dragging her eyes from Tristan. "It would depend upon your job, Sawyer. Tristan works long hours. What would his puppy do all day while he was at work?"

"Play," Sawyer said as if it were a no-brainer. "When I grow up, I'll have a dog." His face squinched up with thought then brightened. "I'm going to have a dozen dogs!"

"A dozen?" Jenny and Tristan asked simultaneously. Sawyer nodded.

"What will you do with a dozen dogs?" Jenny asked.

"Love them and play with them," Sawyer replied, dancing around in his towel.

"Good answer, kid," Tristan told him, earning a grin.

Jenny laughed. "Don't encourage him."

"It could be worse."

Jenny arched her brow in question.

"He could be asking for a pet s-n-a-k-e."

Jenny gave an exaggerated flinch. "Nope, not happening."

Sawyer glanced back and forth between them. "What did he spell?"

"Tristan thought you might prefer a reptile to a furry puppy," Jenny explained.

"I want a frog and a puppy," Sawyer clarified then turned to Tristan. "My grammy likes frogs, but Mama says I can't have one to keep in the house."

"Frogs like being outside. It's where their food and friends are."

"But if she'd let me keep one in the house, I'd be his friend and give him food," Sawyer explained, his expression genuine.

"There's that." Mouth curving upward, Tristan glanced toward Jenny. "What say you, Mom?"

"That puppy is looking better and better."

Tristan kept his hands around Sawyer's waist, helping glide the boy over the water as he paddled around, arm floaties in place. His support wasn't needed, but until Sawyer said he could let go, then Tristan would keep his hands on him.

"Look at me, Mama," Sawyer called, splashing around. "I'm swimming."

"You're doing great, Sawyer," Jenny praised from where she sat at the side of the pool. Some days she sat on the edge with her feet dangling in the water and some days she sat beneath a sun umbrella to keep out of the sun. Always, she slathered up her fair skin with sunscreen. Sawyer's, too.

Tristan had offered to help with her sunscreen a few times, but she'd just smile and tell him she had it. She had it, all right. She had him in a jumbled mess of hyperawareness of every move she made.

Even with his focus on Sawyer, his body zoned in on where she sat poolside with her feet dangling in the water.

Both he and Sawyer repeatedly tried to convince her to get in the water with them, but she'd not done so. Had it not been for the rafting trip, he'd have questioned whether she could swim.

"He's a natural." Tristan praised Sawyer's efforts. "I think he may be part fish."

Sawyer giggled. "I am. Swish, swish, swish." He stroked his arms back and forth as Tristan had shown him. Pride filled him. The kid really was picking things up fast.

Jenny laughed. Her face was lighter, brighter, than Tristan had ever seen her.

Jenny loved her son. No wonder. The kid was awesome. Probably because he was Jenny's. He'd not heard Sawyer mention his father, nor had Jenny, but more and more Tristan grew curious about where the man fit into their lives.

"I'm a hungry fish," Sawyer announced, making chomping sounds as he moved through the water.

"A shark?" Tristan asked, laughing as he launched into some *da-dum, da-dum, da-dum* sound effects.

"Yes!" Sawyer didn't get his reference, just nodded and continued to bite at the water as Tristan "swam" him from one side of the pool over to near where Jenny's feet dangled in the water.

"We'd better feed this fish before he gobbles us up."

Uncertainty settled into Jenny's eyes. "We're taking up so much of your spare time. I don't expect you to go with us to eat. We don't want to be a bother."

"You're no bother," Tristan assured. "I love seeing how quickly our little shark is progressing. Before long, he'll be doing cannonballs off the diving board."

Sawyer splashed his hands in the water. "What's a cannonball?"

Tristan told him, and Sawyer twisted to stare up at him, floating on the water with Tristan's hand beneath his waist. His floats wouldn't let him sink, but Sawyer wasn't confident enough yet to venture away from Tristan's assistance.

Sawyer's eyes were wide. "Can you do a cannonball?"

"It's been a while, but yeah, I can cannonball."

"Show me," Sawyer requested. "I want to see."

Tristan's gaze met Jenny's and she shrugged.

"Okay, hotshot shark," he told the boy in his arms. "But if I've gotten too old for this, your mom will have to dive in to save me."

Sawyer's expression filled with concern.

"I'm kidding," he quickly assured him then lifted the boy to sit beside Jenny on the pool ledge. "The cannonball is pretty basic. You stay here next to your mom while I jump, okay?"

Sawyer nodded.

"Don't you make me have to come in to save you, Tristan Scott," Jenny warned, pulling her hat brim lower to shade her face.

His challenge met hers. "Would you save me, Jenny?"

"You shouldn't risk it," she warned, a smile playing on her lips. "I might not be strong enough to pull you out."

But he had no doubt that if he were in trouble, she would do her best to save him.

"Guess I won't attempt my double backflip then." He placed his hands to each side of Sawyer. "What your mom is saying is that even when you've been swimming for a long time, it's still always smart to use your brain and not take unnecessary risks. And never swim alone. You shouldn't be afraid of the water, but you should respect it. Always."

Sawyer nodded. "I like swimming with you."

"Ditto, kid. Ditto."

It was true. Tristan did like swimming with Sawyer and was so proud of how the kid no longer seemed afraid of the water. Soon, he'd be all over the pool with just his arm floaties and then Tristan would wean him away from using them.

Tristan swam to the ladder and climbed out of the pool to walk to the diving board. "Watch closely," he called to Sawyer. "Because, before summer is over, I bet you will be doing cannonballs, too."

Tristan stood on the tip of the diving board then bounced into the air, tucked his legs up beneath him and wrapped his arms around them. "Cannonball," he yelled just before he hit the water, making a big splash.

"Yay!" Sawyer cheered.

He swam over to where he could see Sawyer's and

Jenny's submerged feet, then came up right in front of them, slicking his hair back from his face.

"That was great," Sawyer exclaimed.

"You want to do one?"

Sawyer's eyes were wide.

"He can't get on the diving board yet," Jenny noted, sounding a little mother-hennish.

"He doesn't have to get on the diving board. I was going to let him jump in and I'll catch him."

"With him doing a cannonball?" Jenny looked dubious.

"Well, it might be better if he does a shark instead."

"What's that?"

"It's where you put your hands out in front of you then jump."

"Isn't that just a regular dive?"

Tristan shook his head. "Nope. It's the shark. Now, stand up and put your hands up." He demonstrated what he meant.

"Like this?" Sawyer perfectly mimicked Tristan's every move.

"Exactly like that. Now, when you're ready, I want you to jump in to me."

Without hesitation, Sawyer did just that, jumping in. Despite the boy's floats, Jenny's breath sucked in so hard Tristan heard it over the pounding of his heart in the seconds before his hands closed around Sawyer's waist and he lifted him up through the water and into the air.

"You did great, kid!"

Sawyer shook his head, squinting at Tristan as water ran down his face. "Again!" he cried. "Again. Again. Again."

Tristan laughed.

"You've started something now."

"Who needs the gym when they have a boy in the pool?" Tristan teased. He caught Sawyer a dozen or so more times before Sawyer remembered he was hungry.

Wrapping his little arms around Tristan's neck, he looked him in the eyes. "Since I did good, can we have pizza for lunch?"

"Kid, you did so good you can have filet mignon for lunch if that's what you want."

"Pizza," Sawyer repeated then leaned over and play bit his shoulder. "I'm a hungry shark."

"Sawyer! Tell Tristan you're sorry."

"He was just having fun." Tristan hadn't been prepared for the playful nip. It hadn't hurt but had caught him off guard.

"Biting is not okay," Jenny insisted, frowning at Sawyer.

"But I'm a shark. Sharks bite."

"Well, Mr. Shark, you're in time-out because Tristan isn't shark food."

Sawyer's facial expression fell.

"Really, it's okay, Jenny. He barely nipped me, and it didn't hurt. It didn't even leave a mark." He glanced at his shoulder. "Much," he amended, giving her a wry grin. How did she ever discipline the kid? One tiny pout and he was ready to give him whatever he wanted. "I guess we should have fed this little shark when he first told us he was hungry."

Tristan and Sawyer got out of the pool. Sawyer stayed close to his side, avoiding going to his mother as long as he could. Tristan understood. Jenny had not looked happy about the bite.

But when Sawyer made it next to her, she didn't yell or scream, as Tristan's own parents would have done had he done anything they'd disapproved of. Instead, she looked Sawyer in the eyes and talked to him in a low voice.

Sighing, Sawyer nodded then turned to Tristan. "Sorry I bit you."

"No worries, kid." He hated that the boy had gotten into trouble, but he had to admit that watching Jenny parent Sawyer was fascinating. Not that everything about her didn't fascinate him. It did. From the light freckles that the sun had kissed the tip of her nose with to the love that shone in her eyes for her son.

"Go grab our bag from the table, okay?" she asked him. "Walk, don't run."

Sawyer nodded and took off fast-skipping.

Jenny's attention immediately went to the slight red mark on Tristan's shoulder. "I'm mortified he did that. I can't believe he bit you."

"He's a kid. Kids do silly things. I hate that you had to scold him on my account. You didn't have to."

"I didn't want him to think that was okay. I can't have him biting another student at preschool or when he starts kindergarten this fall."

Made sense, and he felt a little less guilty. "You're a good mom, Jenny."

She gave him an odd look. "Because I don't want my kid biting other kids? I'd say that's pretty basic parenting."

She might be surprised at how little basic parenting some moms and dads did. How little his own had done. He'd generally been an afterthought.

"I meant in how you handle him altogether," he clarified.

"Most of the time it's more of a figure-it-out-as-I-go kind of thing." She gave a nervous laugh. "I worry that I'm going to do something that messes him up, you know? That as an adult he'll be in therapy and they'll tell him it's all my fault for being a terrible mom."

"If he has to go to therapy, it won't be because you're a terrible mom, Jenny. You're a great mom."

Her cheeks pinked. "Thank you."

"He's doing really well."

"I couldn't believe he jumped in like that. It's a little scary, honestly."

"He's got this. I'm going to work with him tomorrow without his floaties."

"You think he's ready?"

He nodded. "I know he is. Like his mom, he's a natural."

"You've not seen me in the water to know whether I'm a natural or not," she reminded him.

"About that…" he teased, waggling his brows as he moved toward her.

"You wouldn't." But as she said it, she started scooting away from him.

Laughing, Tristan scooped her up. Her body was warm from the sun and his was growing hotter by the second from having her in his arms. Skin against skin, to where every fiber of his being was aware of hers.

"Put me down, Tristan," she insisted. Even as she wrapped her arms around his neck, she squirmed to get free. "I should remind you that the last person you held bit your shoulder."

He mentally groaned as an image of Jenny love nipping his shoulder hit.

"You're not going to do the same, are you?" And, if she didn't quit squirming, he was going to embarrass them both.

Her gaze locking with his, her arms still around his neck, she stilled except for where her fingers had threaded into the hair at his nape. "You know I'm not. Just as you're not going to throw me in the pool."

Goose bumps covered his body at her fingers entwined in his hair. He wanted her. From the moment he'd met her, he'd wanted Jenny. "You think not?"

"You don't have a death wish, do you?"

He laughed. "You don't scare me, Jenny."

Although, truth be told, the way her fingers toying at his nape had his body responding as if he were a puppet on a string, the way she felt in his arms, the way he felt looking into her eyes, the way he felt when he was with her and Sawyer, terrified him.

So much so that without another thought, Tristan shifted his weight and dropped into the pool with his arms still holding Jenny close.

Maybe the dunk would do something to cool off his libido and ease his crazy thoughts.

"I can't believe you did that," she sputtered as she came up from the water, clinging tightly to him.

Holding her close, as he wasn't sure how strong her swimming skills were, Tristan stared down into her beautiful face, her beautiful wet face. "Oops. I must have lost my footing."

Jenny scoffed. "Right. That's exactly what happened."

"I knew eventually you'd come into the water to play," he teased, thinking the cold water hadn't eased his reaction to her in the slightest. If anything, her wet body wrapped around his only served to heighten his awareness.

"I should have known it would be because you tossed me in," she accused.

"I never let go of you, Jenny, nor will I." Realizing what he'd said and how powerfully those words shook him to his very being, he cleared his throat and added, "In the water, I mean."

CHAPTER TEN

WHY HAD TRISTAN'S voice broken? Jenny wondered, clinging to him.

Had he felt he needed to clarify what he'd meant?

They both knew he would let her go. When his time
in Chattanooga was up, he'd leave, and she and Sawyer
would be left behind.

The thought of him gone broke her heart because it
was difficult to imagine returning to life without him.
Her son was crazy about him. She was…she was pressed
against him, their bodies wet, his arms holding her waist,
her arms around his neck, and their faces were so close
that his breath teased her lips.

If she wanted to kiss him, all she had to do was lean
in just a little and their mouths would touch.

"Jenny," Tristan said, his voice almost a growl. Hunger filled his eyes. He must have realized how mere cen-
timeters separated their mouths, how her wet body was
wrapped around his as they bobbed in the pool water.

Her gaze dropped to his mouth. She knew how talented that mouth was, how precious his lips, and how his
kisses made her crave things she'd thought forever gone.

"Kiss me," she whispered, needing to feel more than
his breath on her lips.

"Now?" Tristan's voice held surprise. Surprise Jenny

understood because he'd put her under a spell that she couldn't seem to break. "Yes. Now. Later. Tonight. Kiss me."

Tristan's breath sucked in. "You drive me crazy, you know that?"

"No more so than you drive me," she countered, staring into his eyes and cupping his handsome face. "I want you to kiss me."

"Jenny," he moaned, leaning his head toward hers.

"Hey!" Sawyer shouted from the side of the pool, holding their swim bag. "I didn't know you were getting in the pool."

"Neither did I," Jenny called, her gaze not leaving Tristan's. His whole body had tensed at Sawyer's interruption. Or maybe that had been hers. She couldn't believe she'd forgotten Sawyer was there, that she'd become so entranced with the gorgeous man holding her that she'd abandoned herself to his charms.

"I convinced your mom to go for a swim," he said, looking toward Sawyer.

With his attention on Sawyer, Jenny seized her moment. With all her might, she jumped upward then came down with as much force as she could, pulling Tristan under the water with her. When they came up, she wiggled to free herself and made a beeline out of the pool.

"Run, Mama. He's after you!" Sawyer warned, jumping up and down at the edge of the pool and giggling with glee.

Jenny was swimming as fast as she could, but she was no match for Tristan.

"Argh!" she squealed as his hand clasped around her, turning her to him.

"You know I have to make you pay for that, right?"

"You started it," she returned, her chest heaving from her escape efforts.

"Did I?" His eyes sparkled more brilliantly than sunshine bouncing off water. "Make no mistake, Jenny, we've barely begun."

"He caught you, Mama!"

Tristan had caught her. In more ways than one.

His time in Chattanooga was rapidly ticking away. He could say they were barely started, but their time together was already over half gone, and making the most of every precious second left seemed more and more imperative.

"You're going to love the jellyfish," Sawyer told Tristan as he gave them a personal tour through the Tennessee Aquarium as if he was on their payroll. "And in the next section there's penguins."

"Penguins?" Tristan looked impressed. "Real ones?"

Sawyer nodded. "When I grow up, I want to work here and take care of the fish and birds who live here."

"That sounds like an interesting job," Tristan admitted, his look meeting Jenny's as he gave her hand a quick squeeze. Jenny couldn't help but smile and squeeze back.

Look at her, acting like a giddy teen, holding hands and making googly eyes, she thought. No wonder. Every moment away from work was spent with Tristan one way or another. Swimming lessons, eating, taking Sawyer to the park, and even during household chores, he was by her side. Deep down, she knew she was making his leaving that much worse by letting him consume her every moment. She also knew that she wasn't strong enough to push him away. Soon enough, he'd be gone.

Until then she'd...she'd what? She didn't know exactly how to label what was happening between them, but whatever it was put joy deep in her belly, and Sawyer's, too.

"Mama likes penguins, too," Sawyer continued, pulling against where he held Tristan's other hand, "but she likes people best because she wants to take care of them. I want to take care of animals."

"You prefer the two-legged kind of animals, eh?" Tristan asked, his eyes twinkling as he winked at Jenny.

"The two-legs kind?" Sawyer asked, his face contorting with lack of understanding.

"He means people," Jenny clarified for her son. "And, yes, I do. I can at least see them coming." She gave an exaggerated shiver. "Snakes don't have legs."

Tristan grinned then shared a look with Sawyer. "Maybe we'll see more snakes before we finish our tour."

Sawyer nodded. "We will. Big ones and little ones."

A commotion up ahead caught Jenny's attention. A seventyish woman lay on the floor and a gray-haired man knelt beside her.

"Bess?" He shook the woman, but she didn't respond.

Jenny glanced toward Tristan, but he was already rushing that way. To his credit, he hadn't let go of Sawyer's hand, and her son was skipping along beside him to keep up.

Jenny took off after them.

"Sawyer, stay right here," Tristan ordered as he knelt next to the couple. "Hi. My name is Tristan. I'm a nurse, and this is Jenny. She's a nurse, too. What's going on and can we help?"

"We were walking around, looking at the fish, and my wife collapsed to the floor," the man told him, relief showing on his face at their appearance. "Please help."

"Have you called 9-1-1?" Jenny asked. The man shook his head and Jenny pulled out her phone to make the call.

"Is it okay if I check her?" Tristan asked as he leaned in to see if the woman was breathing. "Soft, but steady breaths. Pulse is regular but bradycardic."

"What does that mean?" the man asked, fear in his voice. "Is she going to be okay?"

"Her heart rate is a little slower than normal," Tristan explained, lifting the woman's feet. "Here, I want you to hold her legs up like this. Sawyer, you okay, bud?"

"Huh?" the man asked, but did as Tristan said.

Sawyer nodded. "I can hold a foot."

"Just stay close because we may need you to help do that," Jenny said, proud of how calm he was and for his offering to help. Still on the line with the emergency operator who'd just promised to dispatch an ambulance, Jenny turned back to the man, "Does your wife have any health problems?"

Clasping the woman's feet, the man nodded. "Not recently. She had a heart attack last year but has been doing good. Her cardiologist cleared her to go on this trip. She's diabetic and—"

"She's diabetic? What was her blood sugar this morning? Do you have her meter with you?" Tristan asked from where he had his ear pressed close to the woman's chest, attempting to listen to her heart sounds.

"I'm not sure if she checked it this morning. We woke up late and were running behind. She does have a meter. It's in the car, I think. We're parked in a lot nearby. Do you want me to get it?"

They were in the middle of the aquarium. Jenny hoped they had the woman revived or further assistance there long before the man would have time to go to his car and get back to them.

A growing crowd had gathered around them and Jenny asked, "Does anyone have a glucometer? How about a glucose tablet or something sweet? Maybe a piece of candy?"

Someone produced a meter kit and handed it to Jenny. Another woman gave a chocolate bar.

"Can someone get us a soda or juice in case her sugar has dropped and we need it?" Jenny asked as she knelt next to Tristan. "I'll prop up her upper half if you want to try giving her some of this."

He nodded, broke off a small piece of the chocolate bar and placed it in the woman's mouth. Once it was there, he unzipped the glucometer kit, turned the machine on, cleaned one of the woman's fingertips with alcohol then popped her with a lancet. It wasn't ideal since he didn't have gloves, but he carefully got a drop of blood into the test strip.

Within seconds, the machine's display read thirty-eight.

"She has hypoglycemia, meaning her sugar is too low. That's why she's unconscious. We need to get her sugar up." He checked the woman's mouth then placed another tiny piece of chocolate beneath her tongue. "Does anyone have anything else sweet? A packet of sugar, even?"

Jenny supposed it was possible someone might have such an oddity in their purse, but no one spoke up.

"Sir, you can gently put her feet down. Tristan had you holding them up in case she wasn't getting good circulation to her heart, but that doesn't seem to be the problem."

Fortunately, the guy who'd taken off to find a pop machine was back with a bottled soda and handed it to Tristan.

"Let's get some of this in her, stat," Tristan said, twisting off the cap.

Phone cradled between her ear and her shoulder as the dispatcher continued to talk, Jenny held the still-unconscious woman's head up to where Tristan could carefully pour some of the soda into her mouth.

Sweat drenched the woman's skin and dampened her hair. Jenny knelt to use her thighs to leverage the woman so holding her in an elevated position was easier.

Sawyer moved next to Jenny, putting his hand on her shoulder. "Is she going to be okay, Mommy?"

Hating that he was witnessing the hypoglycemic event, but so proud of how brave he was being, Jenny nodded. "I think so, honey. Her body doesn't use sugar properly and hers is too low, so her body is trying to protect her by letting her sleep until we can get her sugar up. Once we do that, she should wake up and she'll start feeling better."

His little hand patted her. "I hope so."

Jenny hoped so, too.

"Bess?" the woman's husband said, bending over her. "Can you hear me, Bess? Your sugar is low, but these people are helping you. Wake up, Bess."

"What's your name, sir?" Jenny asked, hoping to get him to move from over the woman's face.

"Felix."

"Felix, can I get you to step back a little?" Tristan asked. "It would be great if you would hold Bess's hand and keep talking to her so that when she wakes up she isn't as frightened. Tell her she's okay."

The man did as Tristan asked.

Tristan kept putting small amounts of soda in the woman's mouth, making sure she reflexively swallowed before adding more.

Soon, Bess's eyes popped open and she began to come around.

"Mama! She's awake," Sawyer exclaimed, jumping up and down. "It worked!"

"Ma'am, I'm Tristan and this is Jenny. We're nurses.

Your blood glucose dropped too low, and you lost consciousness. We've been working to get sugar in you. Can you take a drink for us?"

Staring blankly at him at first, her eyes shifted to her husband then back to Tristan. "You're doctors?"

"Nurses," Tristan repeated, checking the woman's pulse, again.

"Okay," the woman said, scooting as if to sit up.

"Take it slow," Jenny encouraged, helping her into a sitting position and continuing to support her in case she got light-headed or passed out again. "We don't want you going out on us."

"Drink, Bess. It'll make you feel better," Felix urged, giving his wife's hand a squeeze. "You sure scared me."

By the time the ambulance arrived and the paramedics got to them, Bess was sitting up and sipping on the soda. She was still pale and clammy, but should be fine once the aftereffects of her hypoglycemic episode wore off.

"Thank you for your help," Felix told them, shaking their hands.

"No problem," Jenny replied, hoping that it really wasn't, and that Sawyer wouldn't be bothered by what he'd witnessed. She glanced around, looking for where her son had gone and didn't initially spot him.

Hunkered by an octopus display, he watched them.

Going over to him, Jenny squatted next to him. "Hey, big guy. You sure were brave."

"I didn't feel very brave."

Jenny wanted to wrap him in a big hug. "Are you kidding me? Those superhero lessons have been paying off. You were amazing."

His expression brightened. "Do you think Tristan thinks so?"

Because Tristan was his superhero. No wonder, with

the way he doted on her son. Watching him interact with Sawyer the past few weeks had her doing a bit of hero worship, too. He wavered from responsible adult role model to playful kid at heart. With her, he was steadfast, smiling, attentive, willing to keep things on the lowdown at the hospital, not that she didn't think her coworkers knew something had changed since the rafting trip. Everything had changed and yet, really, nothing had. When the time came, Tristan would leave, and she doubted she would ever be quite the same.

"I'm sure Tristan thinks you were brave. How could he not when you were such a great help?" She gave Sawyer that hug as much for herself as him, kissed the top of his head, then straightened. "Now, how about we go find those horseshoe crabs you were telling me that we could touch?"

After Jenny closed Sawyer's bedroom door, Tristan followed her back into the living room. Her mom must have gone to bed while they were in Sawyer's room because Geneva was no longer watching television.

Rather than sit or ask him to sit, Jenny hesitated just inside the vacated room, nervously fiddling with her shirt hem. "Thanks for helping me get him to bed. He loved that you sat with him while I read his stories."

"It was my pleasure. He's a great kid," Tristan told Jenny and meant it. He'd never spent much time around kids, but Sawyer was the best. And when he smiled, Tristan's insides did a funny flip-flop because of the genuineness. "I was so proud of him today at the aquarium. I've seen grown adults not handle situations as well as he did."

Leaning against the back of the sofa, Jenny smiled. "I was proud of him, too. I was worried that it might have bothered him more than he let on, but he seemed okay, didn't he?"

Tristan nodded. "After dinner, he heard me call Felix to check on Bess and heard me say she was doing great, that they checked her out in the emergency room, decided it was truly just a hypoglycemic episode, and they discharged her. Other than telling his grammy how his mommy was a hero, he's not mentioned it. I think he'll be fine."

"Ha. It wasn't me he kept referring to as a hero. It was his favorite swim instructor."

Tristan smiled. "His only swim instructor."

"There is that. Thank you for teaching him, for taking us to the aquarium, and for burgers and ice cream afterward. And for...well, everything. He adores you."

Her words warmed his insides. "I promised I'd take him if he swam from one side of the pool to the other, and he did."

"While wearing his arm floats."

"That counts. Besides, he'll be able to do it without his floats soon enough, too. For now, it's important he knows I keep my promises."

Jenny's gaze lifted and Tristan's stomach clenched at the emotions swirling in those honey depths. What was she thinking? Because, if he didn't know better, he'd think she was wondering if he planned to keep his promises to her. The only promise he recalled making was that he wouldn't hurt her, at least not intentionally.

He'd do his best to keep that promise. The last thing he wanted was to cause Jenny pain. He wanted her to smile when she thought of him.

"We're still on for swim lessons in the morning?"

She nodded. "As long as you don't mind. I worry that we're taking up so much of your free time. You've mentioned all the things you'd planned to do while living in Chattanooga and instead you've spent most of your time with us."

"Plans change." For the better, because no hike or tourist attraction could possibly have been as fulfilling as spending time with Jenny and Sawyer. He regarded her for long moments as she picked at a loose string along her shirt hem. "Are you ready for me to leave?"

She hesitated. "Do you want to stay for a while, Tristan? We could watch a movie or play a game or something."

"What kind of game?" he asked, curious and wondering if they weren't already playing a game that could be dangerous to both their emotional well-being.

"Most of what we have are kids' games."

"Candyland and Hungry, Hungry Hippos?"

Her lips twitched. "We have those."

"I imagine Sawyer would be upset if he discovered we'd been playing those without him."

"You're right. He would," she conceded then glanced around her living room as if searching for something to entertain him with. Didn't she know he'd be content to just sit and hold her hand? "You want to see what's on television then?"

He wasn't ready to leave, so he nodded. "Is there anything in particular you want to watch?"

"I'm not sure what's on. I don't watch much television, so whatever you want to watch is fine."

Tristan sat on the sofa, but rather than pick up the remote, he turned to Jenny and stared at her.

"What?" she asked, her cheeks pinkening in the soft glow of the lamplight.

"You told me I could watch whatever I wanted."

She eyed him curiously. "And you're looking at me?"

"There's nothing else I'd rather be looking at."

The soft glow of the lamp illuminated her flushed cheeks. "You're so smooth with the words."

Was that what she thought? That he was feeding her lines?

"I'm stating the obvious."

"That you want to look at me?" she asked, tucking her hands beneath her thighs as she continued to lean into the sofa.

"Surely you know that by now? I can't not look at you whenever you're near. Not touching you at work is a lesson in discipline and patience, but I agree with you that it's best for you that we carry on as close to as we were before as possible."

"I don't want people feeling sorry for me after you leave. I think they're going to, anyway, but the less they know, the better." Her glance cut toward the hallway leading to her son's bedroom. "I... Would you want to sit outside? Sometimes I sit in the porch swing at night and just think."

"About?" he asked, following her to her back patio.

Outside, a warm breeze carried the sweet smell of the honeysuckle vine growing along her fence.

Picking up a pillow, Jenny took a seat on the two-person swing. "Lately? You're what I think about."

CHAPTER ELEVEN

HIS CHEST EXPANDING at her admission, Tristan sat next to her and laced his hand with hers. "I'll take that as a compliment."

Twisting toward him, she tucked one leg beneath her. Rather than look at him, she stared at their interlocked fingers, visible in the light filtering out from the house. "You should. I never dreamed I'd let another man get close to me again."

Her raw admission had him lifting her hand to his lips and pressing a kiss there. "I'm glad you did, Jenny. The past few weeks have been wonderful."

Rather than verbally answer, she squeezed his hand.

"Sawyer's dad hurt you?"

Her flinch revealed as much as her words. "He did, but only because I let him. I should have known better."

How any man could have had Jenny and Sawyer and let them go was beyond Tristan. The man had been an idiot.

"Tell me about him."

Sighing, she straightened and gave the swing a little push so they began to sway back and forth, the creak of the chains creating a soothing rhythm. "Geoffrey was a gorgeous, successful doctor, and I was a naïve nursing student doing a clinical rotation at the hospital where he worked." She paused and he wondered if she'd said all she was going to say, but then she continued. "He was older than me. Eighteen years older, but at the time, thirty-eight to my twenty didn't seem like a big deal. All that mattered was that he showered me with attention, and I fell head over heels for him without remembering that if something seemed too good to be real, it was."

"He was married?" Tristan guessed.

"Close. Engaged."

"Engaged yet dating you?"

She nodded. "He was wonderful, sending flowers and doing lots of little things that made me feel special." She made a humph sound. "I thought he loved me, and we'd be together forever, so I quit saying no. After that, our relationship was just about sex on his part, right up until I got pregnant. He wanted me to get an abortion."

Pain shot across Tristan's chest at the thought of Sawyer having never existed. "You obviously didn't do that."

"No. My mom was a single mom. She could have chosen not to have me but didn't. Instead, she raised me with love, and I had a great childhood. I never considered doing anything other than the same when I realized I was pregnant."

"Does this doctor help you with Sawyer?"

Jenny sighed. "He paid child support until I finished nursing school. After that, I offered to let him sign over all rights to me in exchange for a small lump sum to be put into a college fund for Sawyer. He jumped at it and never batted an eyelash at signing away all his parental rights." She pulled her hand free and rubbed her palms over her bare arms. "He just kept saying he couldn't believe how little I asked for when he'd have paid more to be rid of me and my 'brat.'"

Her voice wobbled and so did Tristan's emotions. "He's a fool."

"I think so, but his loss is my gain. Prior to that, I'd worried that he'd show up for his visitation and eventually might want to take Sawyer from me." She glanced his way and met his contemplation with sad eyes. "I guess that sounds really bad. I wouldn't have kept Sawyer from his father, but when I knew he didn't want him, didn't love him, it would have been devastating to watch him drive away with our baby."

Tristan couldn't imagine the agony of having that happen. "I'm glad you never had to."

"Me, too, mostly. Having seen Sawyer with you this summer made me realize that he needs more male influences in his life, though."

"Not his father, surely?"

She took a deep breath then exhaled slowly. "I wouldn't stop Geoffrey from seeing Sawyer if he wanted to, but I don't think he ever will. He and Sonya are married and have two kids now."

"Poor woman."

Jenny shrugged. "She knew what she was getting and didn't care. She knew about me, confronted me to let me know I wasn't the first and wouldn't be the last, that she knew Geoffrey was a beautiful man and that women found him attractive. I… I was shocked at how little she was fazed that he'd been cheating on her for months and that I was pregnant. I'd have been devastated." A strangled noise sounded from deep in her throat. "I was devastated."

Her pain ricocheted through him and he pulled Jenny to him, wrapping his arm around her to hold her close. "Of course, you were. Any sane person would have been. Sounds as if they deserved each other."

"I guess so. I haven't talked to them in years, not since he gave Sawyer to me. With them living in Ringgold and him being a physician, I hear his name from time to time, but that's it."

"I'm surprised you continued to live here."

"This is my home, Sawyer's home, and where I want to raise him. My mother is here. I have no plans to ever leave Chattanooga, especially not because of a man."

Tristan had no plans to stay.

"You're sneaky—you know that?" Not that Jenny minded Tristan surprising her with a day trip to Atlanta.

"Some would call it romantic," he pointed out, grinning at her as he held out his hand to help her down from the 4Runner.

Taking his hand, Jenny stepped onto the concrete floor of the crowded parking garage. "Is that why Sawyer's not with us?"

Guilt played across his face. "I considered bringing him, but your mom suggested that he stay with her."

Jenny sighed. "She's matchmaking."

"That doesn't bother me."

"It should, because she's planning on you sticking around awhile." Forever was more like it. With the slightest encouragement, her mother would be booking a wedding venue.

More guilt flashed. "We both know I won't, Jenny."

"It's not me you have to remind," she quipped. "I'm well aware that this time next month, you'll be gone."

He started to say something, but Jenny held up her hand. "Let's not have this conversation today." Or ever. "It's been a long time since someone has surprised me with something 'romantic' and I just want to enjoy the day without overanalyzing."

Hesitating a moment, he nodded. "Then let's hope your team wins."

"They will," Jenny assured him, waiting as he opened the back hatch. "What's that?" she asked when he handed a bag to her.

"Another surprise."

Feeling a little giddy, Jenny looked into the plastic and laughed when she saw its contents.

"I didn't know how else to have you dressed for the part without giving away what we were doing."

Pulling the jersey out of the bag, she realized there were two.

"One's for me. I figured you'd suspect if I had it on when I picked you up this morning." He took the larger shirt from her then pulled his T-shirt over his head.

Hello, biceps and abs. Had the temperature just gone up several degrees or what? She slid her fingers into her pockets in an effort to keep them from exploring the indention that ran down his chest and disappeared into his shorts. The man had a beautiful body.

"If you pull out a giant foam Brave's finger, I'm going to think I died and went to heaven," she said to distract herself from the view.

"If a foam finger makes you happy, we can buy one on our way into the stadium." He gestured at the jersey she held. "Your turn."

Jenny laughed. "Yeah, right. Nice try, but I'm not changing in the parking lot."

"Have it your way," he teased, tossing the shirt he'd removed into the back and picking up a clear heavy-duty plastic bag that contained hats and sunscreen. He clasped her hand. "Come on. You can change into your shirt while I'm grabbing some drinks and dogs."

"Oh, baby, this really is a romantic surprise."

"You'd rather have candlelight and caviar?"

"No way." She wrinkled her nose and began singing "Take Me Out to the Ball Game."

"Yes!" Jenny yelled, jumping up from her seat as the Braves' third baseman caught a pop fly, finishing the inning.

"Having fun?" Tristan asked, grinning at the jig she was dancing and wondering at how even her goofy movements stirred his insides in ways no woman had.

"Are we winning?" she countered.

He gestured to the scoreboard. "We are. Seven to four."

"Which is why I'm smiling and having fun."

He laughed. "You wouldn't be if we were losing?"

Glancing at him, she gave him a big, teeth-showing smile. "Does that answer your question?"

He laughed again. "You're welcome."

Settling back into her stadium seat, she lifted her gaze to his. "I really do appreciate you bringing me today."

"I know. I was teasing you."

"I just didn't want you to think I was ungrateful."

"I didn't. I've seen the pure joy on your face as you've bopped around with excitement."

"It's an exciting game." The fans began chanting and she joined in. "Mom brought me a couple of times when I was younger, but this is the first time I've been to a game since Carlos and I—"

"Who's Carlos?"

She wrinkled her nose at him. "Seriously? You want to discuss my ex-boyfriend today? You don't see me plying you for all the nitty-gritty details of your past relationships."

"No, I don't want to discuss an ex-boyfriend today."

Or ever. "And, there's not much to tell you about my past relationships."

Her eyes narrowed. "Don't try to convince me there are no girlfriends past, because I won't believe you."

"There are girlfriends past, but none that really mattered."

"Because you've never stayed in one place long enough to fall for someone?"

"Apparently falling for someone doesn't require staying in one place for very long."

Realizing what he meant, she gave him a cheesy smile. "Are you saying you've fallen for me, Tristan Scott?"

"You know I have."

"You are a sweet-talker."

He knew she was trying to make light of what he was saying, but making sure she knew she was special felt imperative. Maybe because he knew her past relationships hadn't gone well.

"There's never been anyone like you, Jenny. You're a fantastic person. Smart, funny, an amazing mom and a great kisser."

"Speaking of kissing—look!" she gestured toward the stadium. Glancing that way, he saw they were up on the JumboTron. "I think we're supposed to kiss now."

Tristan didn't need to be told twice. Leaning toward her, he grinned then pressed his mouth to hers for a kiss. Probably because they were being watched, she made a wide-eyed, gob-smacked, happy expression when they pulled apart.

"Did I mention that you're a great kisser?" he asked, reaching for her hand.

Eyes shining brightly, her lips curved. "The way you're looking at me makes me believe that."

The way she was looking at him made him want to believe in a lot of things. That was pure craziness.

"The truth must be on my face, then," he told her, leaning in and stealing another quick kiss.

"Thank you, Tristan," she whispered when they parted. "For everything. I've had a great time."

"The day's not over yet." Excitement filled him at what else he had in store.

She arched a brow at him. "There's more after the game?"

He nodded and she glanced down at her shorts and Braves' jersey. "Whatever it is, I hope it's casual."

The Braves won their game, but Jenny was convinced she was the real winner. How had Tristan pulled off passes to meet some of the team? She'd gotten a ball autographed by two of her favorite players and another she didn't know much about as he was a rookie but was sure she'd grow to love.

"Just wait until Roger and Laura hear about what we did today," she mused from the passenger seat as they traveled north up I-75. "They're going to be so jealous."

"You plan to tell them you spent the day with me?"

Although he was looking at the road, Jenny rolled her eyes. "You think Laura doesn't grill me at the beginning of every shift, wanting to know if I saw you and, if so, what happened and how did that make me feel and what did you say and blah, blah, blah?"

Tristan took a quick side look. "What do you tell her?"

"That you are giving Sawyer swim lessons and..." She paused, trying to decode her emotional ramblings to her best friend. She liked him, but she was going to get hurt. He was a phenomenal kisser, but that was as far as they'd gone physically. Her pulse launched into orbit when he was near, but her brain kept saying to proceed with caution.

"And?" he prompted when she remained silent.

"And I like you." There, she'd admitted what all her ramblings were about. She liked him. Jenny liked Tristan. A lot.

"What does Laura say to that?"

"That she's happy for me and that I should throw caution to the wind and have as much fun as I can for as long as I can."

"Sounds like Laura."

Jenny nodded. "I'm sure Roger knows, but he doesn't say much, just smiles and occasionally gives a nod of approval when he catches me watching you." Heat flooded her face. "I, um, not that I watch you a lot, but…well, you know."

"Watch all you want, Jenny. I'm flattered you'd want to look my way." Appearing thoughtful, he tapped his fingers against the steering wheel. "There's probably no way for our coworkers not to know when they see us together."

"You think we're that obvious?"

"That I want you is stamped over every fiber of my being. I imagine they see that, that you see that, when our eyes meet."

Jenny's breath sucked in. Yeah, she saw, but hearing him say the words aloud added depth to the intense sexual chemistry that was always present no matter how much she questioned or tried to squash it.

"You think they assume we're having sex?"

He shook his head. "I'd guess the opposite. There's a certain familiarity that comes with having sex."

Trying to decipher what he meant, she asked, "You mean that we wouldn't want each other as much?"

"I didn't say that," he quickly corrected. "That first kiss proved that everything we share is just going to make me want you that much more. I'm talking about the way a couple touch and look at each other when they intimately know every nuance of the other."

Jenny's heart pounded. Her eyes closed. What would it be like to know every nuance of Tristan's body? Of his lovemaking?

He'd never pushed for more than a kiss, probably because she'd claimed abstinence and he was respecting that. She liked that he honored her wishes and didn't push the issue, only…well, more and more she longed to turn her dreams into reality.

"Do you have to go?"

Tristan's heart broke at the sadness in Sawyer's eyes. Eyes that were so like Jenny's. He'd seen that sadness there the past few days as their time together dwindled. Saying goodbye to Sawyer was almost as difficult as saying goodbye to Jenny was going to be. He'd never wanted kids, couldn't imagine possibly putting a child through what his parents had put him through, and yet Sawyer made him think he was missing out on something wonderful.

When he left Chattanooga, he *was* going to be missing out on something wonderful. The boy in front of him and his mother.

But that didn't mean he could, or should, stay.

"I do have to leave, bud. My job is finished."

From where he sat at Jenny's kitchen table, Sawyer asked, "Couldn't you find a new job?"

Tristan's heart ached. "I already have a new job. In Chicago."

Sawyer sighed. "Is that far away?"

"Pretty far." Too far. Forever far.

Sawyer glanced over to where Jenny leaned against the kitchen counter. "Will your car drive there, Mama?"

She flinched, her face pale, telling Tristan everything he needed to know about her thoughts on his leaving. She didn't want him to go, either. Maybe he could arrange his schedule so he could fly to Chattanooga once a month to see them. It wouldn't be nearly enough, but at least it would be something.

Jenny knelt beside her son. "Sawyer, Tristan will be busy when he moves. Even if I could get off work, he isn't going to have time for us to visit. He'll be working and having to unpack his stuff and having new adventures."

Jenny's explanation had Tristan pausing. He'd been about to offer to fly them to him or to fly back to Tennessee. Despite her earlier reaction to Sawyer's question, there was something in her voice that warned him he should remain silent and let her explain this to Sawyer.

As far as new adventures, life beyond this room loomed unenticing.

"We could help him," Sawyer insisted. "He likes my help."

"I have work, he has work, and you'll be starting kindergarten soon," Jenny said with resignation. "Grammy would miss us."

"Grammy could go, too." The kid had a comeback for everything Jenny said. "She likes Tristan. She says he's good for our family."

Jenny sent Tristan a pleading look. One that said *Don't make me the bad guy here.*

He took a deep breath then looked Sawyer directly in the eyes. "I'm going to miss you, too, kid, but I have to go, and you have to stay here. That's the way life works sometimes."

"I don't want you to go." Sawyer's lower lip trembled, and Tristan would have sworn the floor shook. He felt that off kilter, that jolted.

"I know, Sawyer. You make me not want to go."

That was the truth. He'd never had trouble leaving a job. Leaving was what he did. What he'd always done. His whole life. It's what his dad had done. What his mom had done. It was all Tristan had ever done. All he'd ever known and thought he wanted. Yet…

"Maybe I can come back to visit someday."

Aware that Jenny was frowning at him, Tristan hugged Sawyer, breathing in the scent of kids' shampoo, savoring the feel of Sawyer's tiny arms wrapped tightly around his neck.

"I hope so," Sawyer told him, hugging a little tighter. "I don't want you to forget me."

"Never going to happen," he promised, kissing the top of Sawyer's head. The affection had been instinctive, impulsive. "I'll always remember you and how proud I was of you for jumping off that diving board and swimming to me. You're unforgettable, Sawyer. Never doubt that."

Yeah, he'd not wanted this, but Sawyer and Jenny made him wish he did, because imagining not having them in his life boggled his mind.

Or was that his heart?

Jenny wasn't sure how much more she could take of the lovefest going on. She was having a hard enough time at the thought of Tristan leaving, of how her insides were shattering, of how she didn't know how she was going to go back to the contentment she'd known before him when she'd experienced such happiness with him. But hearing the pain in Sawyer's voice, seeing how distraught he was,

was pure torture, riddling her with guilt that overshadowed her own pain.

She'd known better than to let Tristan into their lives. She'd known he was leaving, had known that letting her son get close to him would only lead to heartache. She hadn't known how hungry Sawyer was for a man in his life, hadn't been prepared for Sawyer to latch onto Tristan and fall so in love with having a male influence.

"That's right. That dive was unforgettable. Superhero worthy." She gulped back the tears forming in her eyes, willed herself to be strong, and pasted a smile to her face. "I was proud and nervous for you."

Sawyer tossed Tristan a "Moms!" look.

"I never doubted you, but I'll admit I was nervous, too," Tristan said, ruffling Sawyer's hair. "You did great. Keep practicing and you might make it to the Olympics someday."

"What's the Olympics?"

Jenny rested against the kitchen counter, watching while Tristan explained what the Olympics were in a way a four-year-old could understand.

The rest of the evening, Sawyer stayed close to Tristan, taking the quickest bath in history, and insisting that Tristan help tuck him into bed.

"Will you read my bedtime story?" Sawyer's wide eyes pleaded with Tristan. Jenny reminded herself not to be hurt, that Tristan would be gone the following day, and this was Sawyer's way of holding on until the last second to the man who'd become such an integral part of their family.

"I… Okay. If that's what you want. You pick one."

Sawyer went to his bookshelf, glanced over his options, then pulled out two books. He glanced her way. "I thought you would want to read one, too, Mama."

Smiling, Jenny nodded. "You know I do."

"I see what you did there, kid," Tristan said, laughing low. "Smart move, getting two bedtime stories."

Feigning innocence, Sawyer held up his books. "Which one do you want to read?"

Tristan glanced at the books then chose the one with a big red dog on the cover. Climbing into his bed, Sawyer scooted over and patted his mattress.

"You have to sit beside me when you read, that way I can see the pictures."

Tristan nodded and complied.

When Jenny continued to stand, Sawyer frowned. "Mama, you can't see the pictures."

She was too busy staring at Tristan and Sawyer cuddled together reading the story to look at the book anyway. Never would she have imagined how much the image choked her up, made her knees weak, her head spin.

That, she thought. *That's what I want.*

What she couldn't have.

"I'm fine," she managed to say despite her tight throat.

But Sawyer wasn't having it and Jenny sat on the opposite side of him. Not that it helped her to see the pictures. Her eyes blurred with tears.

Still, she held herself together, laughed at the appropriate times, and relished the warm little body next to hers who was her whole world and whom she wanted to protect from every ache and pain the world might throw his way.

Sawyer giggled. He asked questions. He looked up at Tristan with pure adoration and hero-worship, and Jenny found herself doing the same. Why couldn't he have wanted to stay in Chattanooga? Why did he have to leave when she and Sawyer cared so deeply for him? When they didn't want him to go?

When it was her turn, Jenny took the second book and focused on the words.

"Mama, you're not reading it right," Sawyer insisted, frowning. "You didn't make the caterpillar be me."

Jenny tended to edit stories to feature Sawyer as she read them to him, making him the main character of each adventure, making things happen to him, and he loved it. She'd just been reading the words without any animation or Sawyer ad-libs. No wonder he was speaking up.

Telling herself to get her act together, she threw herself into the story, making it as animated as she could, pausing to have her fingers form a mouth to munch on his belly a few times. Sawyer giggled, turned to Tristan several times to make sure he was paying attention, and looked at him with complete adoration.

"One more?" Sawyer asked when she finished, yawning even as he did so.

Jenny shook her head. "You've had a big day and it's already quite a bit past your bedtime."

"But I'm not tired." Another yawn escaped.

"Good night, Sawyer." She kissed his forehead. "I love you to the moon and back."

"And across the oceans and all the lands," he said, completing their ritual.

Jenny's heart squeezed.

"Night, buddy." Tristan touched his arm. "Sleep tight."

Sawyer's eyelids appeared heavy, but he wasn't so tired as to have forgotten what was happening. "You'll be gone when I wake up?"

Tristan nodded.

A mixture of a yawn and a sigh escaped from Sawyer. "You can stay here if you change your mind because we love you."

A strangled sound roared in Jenny's ears. She wasn't quite sure if it had originated from her or Tristan, just that she could barely breathe at her son's innocent declaration.

No, they did not love Tristan.

They didn't.

Sawyer might, but she didn't.

She wanted him to stay, but she didn't love him. She couldn't.

Only, whether she wanted him to be or not, Sawyer was right.

She loved Tristan.

CHAPTER TWELVE

"He doesn't make leaving easy, does he?" Tristan asked when he and Jenny went to the living room. Sawyer had been sound asleep almost before they'd closed his bedroom door.

"He's never had anyone he's felt close to that's left, so it's hard for him to comprehend that you're going to be gone."

Tristan sat on the sofa, ran his fingers through his hair. "His childhood is so different from mine."

Jenny sank onto the opposite side, tucked her leg beneath her, and turned toward him. "In what ways?"

"All I knew was leaving," he admitted, surprised at how much he was about to tell Jenny when he'd never talked to anyone about his childhood, and yet he didn't hold back. Telling her made what he would be doing the following day easier. Knowing would help her understand why he couldn't stay.

"After my parents split, I was back and forth between them, but I mostly stayed with my dad. He worked construction and was constantly on the move, rarely waiting for a job to finish before moving to another. Changing schools two or three times during a year was nothing."

"Goodness," Jenny breathed.

"Mom stayed in the South, but only lived in a spot

long enough to run up bills she couldn't and wouldn't pay prior to taking off," he continued, not liking the pity in Jenny's eyes, but knowing he was unable to stop the train wreck he'd started. "I was shuffled back and forth between them just enough to give the other a break to mess up their lives a little bit more."

"That must have been hard on you."

He hadn't liked it. The going back and forth, the never having anything more than he could carry with him because he never knew what, if anything, of his things would still be there when he returned. Or where he'd be returning to. It had been much better to never get attached to things or people because they were interchangeable in his parents' world. Nothing had been sacred.

"It's all I ever knew, so I'm not sure I'd say it was hard." He'd just accepted it as the way things were, never questioning the constant moves too much to begin with. It had been all he'd known. He couldn't recall exactly the point that he'd realized his way of life was so different from his classmates'. Maybe it hadn't mattered because by that point leaving was as much a part of who he was as it was his parents'. He expected to leave, had formed every friendship with the knowledge that it would eventually end. "It was just different from Sawyer's."

Jenny nodded. "And mine. I've lived here, in this same house, most of my life, and have barely left the state." Her glance met his. "I can't fathom the life you lived as a child."

"It wasn't all bad."

"It must not have been, or you'd have settled down in one place rather than continuing to move around as an adult now that you have control over your fate."

"I doubt I'll ever 'settle down in one place', Jenny."

How was that for honesty? "The need to be on the move is in my genes."

"But you could stay if you wanted to," she suggested, her voice barely audible.

Why did guilt prick him? And had that been accusation in her tone?

"You've known from the beginning I wouldn't stay," he reminded.

She nodded as if she understood. He wanted her to understand. But it was obvious she didn't.

"Do you ever miss any of the places you've lived? Or the people you've met?"

"I'm going to miss you and Sawyer, Jenny. What I told Sawyer was the truth. I won't forget him." He met her big honey-colored eyes. "Or you, if that's what you're wondering."

Her eyes shone, biting him with more guilt before she glanced down at her hands. "Yes, I guess I was wondering that. Sawyer sure is going to miss you. He's grown so attached to you."

Sawyer. Yet, in her eyes, he saw the truth. Jenny would miss him, too. How could she not? They'd spent every spare moment together the past few weeks.

"The feeling is mutual." Regarding Jenny and her son. "I've never spent much time around kids, but he's great." The thought of not seeing Sawyer again; of not knowing if he'd continue practicing his swimming… If he'd get that puppy he wanted so badly… If he'd grow up to be a marine biologist or if he'd change his mind on what he wanted to be a dozen times before reaching adulthood… If his hair would stay a pale blond or if it would darken as he aged… If— "I really am going to miss him. And you."

Jenny's throat worked. "I want to say something, feel

as if I'm supposed to say something, yet I don't know what to say."

Her voice broke. He could see how much she struggled to appear as if all of this was no big deal, as if his leaving was no big deal. It never had been in the past.

Leaving Chattanooga was a huge deal.

"You don't have to say anything, Jenny." Maybe it was better if they didn't say anything. "Will you move over here and let me hold you one last time before I go?"

She hesitated and he sensed her defenses were already popping into place. He even understood. He didn't want to hurt her and knew she felt pain that he was leaving, knew Sawyer hurt that he was going. But he couldn't stay. He never stayed. He had obligations elsewhere.

If he wanted to stay, he'd eventually leave. It was in his blood. And then what? He'd hurt them even more. Better that he left now than to give a false sense that he'd stick around.

But as Jenny snuggled against him, he wondered what she'd say if he was the type of person who could stay by her side forever. Because as he wrapped his arms around her, he really wished he was that type of man.

"Thank you," he whispered, kissing the top of her head. "I want to put this moment to memory."

Jenny wiped at her eyes.

He nuzzled his face into the softness of her loose hair. "Don't cry, Jenny. Not over me."

He wasn't worth her tears.

"Who says I am?"

Sweat popped out on his skin as her words hit then logic erased his own self-doubts. Of course, she was. Her brave defiance had him smiling despite the ache that he was hurting her.

"Guess that was my own wishful thinking getting in

the way of rational thought," he mused, wondering what she'd say if he admitted how much having met her meant to him, wondering what she'd say if he admitted it would be easy to give in to his own sorrow. "Since it's not me causing your eyes to leak, tell me what is."

She sniffed then said, "I realized I'm going to have to find someone else to help me with my yardwork."

Tristan laughed. But just as quickly as the humor hit, it faded. Jenny would find someone to replace him, not just to do yardwork with her, but to spend time with her and Sawyer. She'd smile at someone else, laugh with someone else, hold hands with someone else. Kiss someone else.

The thought gutted him, but the thought of her and Sawyer being alone forever gutted him even more.

"Promise me that you'll let someone help you after I'm gone."

She pulled back enough to stare into his eyes. "I was joking about the yardwork, Tristan. I've always done my own and never expected you to help with that. You insisted, remember? I never asked you to do that."

"I know you didn't expect me to, and I never felt as if you did. I wanted to help you, Jenny. I wanted to make your life easier and to see the joy in your eyes when your projects came together. You need someone in your life." Someone who wasn't him. "I don't want you shutting yourself off from the opposite sex again. Date, enjoy life."

Her gaze narrowed. "How can you sit there and tell me to date and enjoy life after…after…" She took a deep breath. "You and I are different, Tristan. I can't just randomly bring men in and out of Sawyer's life. You were different." She sucked in a deep breath. "You are different."

Tristan's pulse pounded so hard he could barely breathe.

"I didn't want to do this, if you remember. I didn't

want to get involved with you because you scared me from the beginning. I... I could barely think straight when you were near. Not just because you're gorgeous, but because there's something about you that I'm instinctually drawn to in ways I can't put into words.

"Even now, I can't look at you and not want to touch you." Her eyes dropped to his lips. "Not want to kiss you." Her gaze lifted. "I can't believe that after tonight, I'll never see you again, Tristan. That I'll never kiss you again." She placed her hands against his cheeks. "Or touch you. How am I supposed to just forget you and 'date someone else and enjoy life' when you're who I want?"

Jenny wanted him. His chest soared at her admission, but warning bells went off just as loudly.

"I'm flattered, Jenny, but you'll forget me."

How many promises had he heard over the years that someone would never forget him? He'd moved around enough to know that people forgot, they moved on. Jenny would, too.

She shook her head. "You're wrong. That's not who I am."

Tristan gulped back the lump in his throat. "What are you saying, Jenny?"

"Stay with me," she whispered, her hands trembling against where they cupped his face.

That he'd stay forever tempted the tip of his tongue. Sweat drops popped out on his forehead. He needed to leave before he made promises he couldn't keep.

"Tomorrow we'll say goodbye, but give me now, Tristan," she urged, "to abate the rest of my lonely nights. Give me you."

Jenny couldn't believe she was saying the things she was saying.

Panic darkened Tristan's eyes and had heat pouring off

his body. Fine. There was panic in her, too. Panic that to-night was the last time he'd be hers and what a fool she'd been not to embrace every moment, every experience, with him to the fullest.

As vulnerable as she felt, she wouldn't back down. Why should she? Either way, he'd be gone tomorrow.

"You don't know what you're saying, Jenny."

She snorted. "Seriously? I'm a grown woman. I know exactly what I'm saying, and so do you. I'd ask if don't you want me, but I know you do."

Along with that panic, it was in his eyes. She'd seen desire in his eyes many times over the past few months. Tristan wanted her. He looked at her and saw an attractive woman. When he could have had his choice of women, she was whom he had chosen to spend his time with even though she'd refused to have sex with him.

That knowledge emboldened her, fed her desire. Taking his hand into hers, she stood and pulled him to his feet.

His fingers laced with hers. "What are you doing, Jenny?"

But rather than say anything, she led him to her bedroom. When they were inside, she shut the door and locked it, just in case. If Sawyer awakened, she didn't want him coming to her room and surprising them.

She walked over and flipped on her bedside lamp, turned and looked to where Tristan stood by the door. He didn't move, didn't smile, just stared at her as if he was frozen in place. Maybe he was.

Maybe she was dreaming. It felt surreal, as if she floated to him and reached around him to turn off the overhead light. Eyes locked with his, she grabbed the hem of her shirt and pulled it over her head.

Eyes locked, almost as if he were afraid to let himself look at what she'd uncovered, Tristan sucked in air. "Jenny!"

"Shh…" she breathed, putting her finger over his lips. "You have a beautiful mouth, Tristan. I want to feel it against me."

"We can't do this, Jenny. Not now. Not when I'm leaving tomorrow." But even as he said it, he kissed her fingertip. Once. Twice.

"If not now, then never," she whispered, tracing her finger over his bottom lip. "Never doesn't work for me, Tristan. Kiss me."

"Never doesn't work for me, either." Still, he hesitated, cupping her face. "Are you sure, Jenny? This won't change that I'm leaving tomorrow. I don't want to hurt you further."

"I'm sure." To prove it, she slid her hands beneath his T-shirt and lifted it over his head, revealing his broad shoulders and muscled abs. "Mmm… I've wanted to do this for so long," she admitted, brushing her fingers over his stomach, reveling in how her touch had him sucking in a deep breath.

"As I've watched you with Sawyer in the pool, do you have any idea how unbelievably much I've wanted to touch you here?" She bent and kissed his chest, his muscles tight beneath her lips. "And here." She pressed another kiss to his tight stomach. "And here and here and here."

Goose bumps stood at attention over his skin, and he groaned. "If you don't stop that, tonight is going to be a very quick, disappointing experience for you."

She shook her head. "You're not going to disappoint me, Tristan."

He put his hands around her waist, lifted her to where she looked directly into his eyes.

"You're right. I'm not going to disappoint you, Jenny. Not tonight," he promised. "Tonight, I'm going to give you more pleasure than you've ever known and then I'm going to give you more."

Leaning forward, Jenny pressed her mouth to his, kissing him with all the passion surging through her, kissing him without holding anything back on how she felt. She wanted him.

She loved him.

Tomorrow, he'd be gone, and she'd deal with that then. For now, he was hers and she planned to seize every moment.

Streaks of light began eating away the darkness. It was past time for Tristan to have left. He should have gone hours ago. Instead, he'd lain in Jenny's bed with her warm body snuggled against his.

She'd been asleep since minutes after the last time they'd made love. But other than a quick power nap that had ended when she'd shifted in her sleep, he'd slept very little. The feel of her naked body moving against his had awakened him, and ultimately her, as he'd had to have her again and had roused her with his mouth until she was as hungry for him as he'd been for her.

That had been a couple of hours ago.

He'd ordered himself to leave, but he'd kept delaying, soaking up the feel of her cradled in his arms and unable to bring himself to get out of her bed.

But he was running out of time. To stay longer was to risk Sawyer waking and finding them. Having to explain why he'd stayed the night would be bad enough, but having to say another goodbye to the child, to Jenny, he wasn't sure he could do it.

Carefully, he disentangled his body from hers.

Jenny sighed in her sleep but didn't waken.

Dressed, he hesitated by the door. Leaving had never been this hard, but that didn't stop him from doing so.

CHAPTER THIRTEEN

"He was just gone when you woke up?"

Keeping a close eye on where Sawyer ran around the park playground with several other kids, Jenny nodded at Laura's question. Leaning back against the wrought-iron bench they sat on, she sighed. "Maybe it was better that way. For him to just go without tearful goodbyes."

But if that was true, then why did she ache so unbelievably much? When the sunlight streaming in through her bedroom window had warmed her face, causing her eyes to open, she'd felt such happiness until she'd seen the empty spot next to her and known he was gone. That he'd snuck away without telling her goodbye had hit her hard.

"I can't believe he just left like that."

"He and Sawyer had already said their goodbyes." Memories of the night before rushed through her mind, and she swallowed. "I guess we'd said ours, too, just without words."

She'd made love with Tristan. She refused to call it anything else, because what they'd done, what they'd shared, had been so much more than sex.

Glancing at Laura, she gave a tight smile. "I shouldn't be telling you this."

"Hello. Best friend." Laura tapped her chest. "You're supposed to tell me everything."

Jenny nodded. "There is that. Thank you for always being there for me through thick and thin."

"Girl, you do the same for me when I need you."

"Maybe, but it sure seems like I'm always the one who makes a mess of her life."

"Is that how you feel, Jenny? Because when I look at you, I see someone who has her stuff together."

"What do you mean?"

Laura gestured toward where Sawyer was playing. "Look at him. You are doing such a great job raising him."

"Ha. It doesn't feel that way."

"Well, you are. He is happy, and healthy, and has a mama who loves him with all her heart."

"He is a great kid." Echoes of Tristan having said the same thing the night before rang through her mind. How long would everything remind her of something he'd done or said?

"You not only made it through nursing school, but you did so with honors."

"I don't know if I could have done it without you, especially after I got pregnant. You were a lifesaver."

"You could have, and you would have. It's who you are," Laura assured her. "Our whole lives, you've always known what you wanted. You work hard and never halfway do things. Most of the time you achieve the goals you set out for yourself, Jenny, including buying your mom's house. I've always been so proud of you, my friend."

Jenny sniffed. "No fair making me cry. I've already done that too much today."

"Don't cry. Be happy. You had an amazing three months with one of the hottest guys we've ever met."

"He's so much more than just hot. He's smart, funny, patient, kind—"

"You're in love with him, aren't you?" Laura interrupted.

Jenny took a deep breath. "It would be better if I wasn't."

"Girl, you weren't supposed to fall in love with him, not when you knew he wouldn't stay."

Jenny shrugged. "Like you said, I never do things halfway."

Sawyer came running over to her, his small hands going palms down against her thighs. "Mama, are you crying because Tristan is gone?"

Jenny's heart squeezed that Sawyer immediately thought her tears were due to Tristan. She didn't want him to worry about her or to make his own sorrow worse, so she shook her head. "No, baby. Aunt Laura told me something sad, but I'm just fine."

She would be, too. Laura was right. When Jenny set her mind to something, she could achieve anything. Maybe she took the long, hard route to getting there, but eventually she did arrive.

She'd get there on getting over Tristan to where eventually he would be a fond memory of the man who'd shown her what love could be.

Two weeks had gone by since he had left Tennessee. Two long and lonely weeks.

He missed Jenny. He missed Sawyer. And he was barely into his three-month contract in Chicago. Prior to his Tennessee stint, he'd have enjoyed the breeze off Lake Michigan cooling him as he pounded the pavement during his run. Prior to Tennessee, he'd have taken up the pretty waitress's offer to come watch the theater show she was part of in her wannabe-a-big-star-someday efforts. Prior to Tennessee, he wouldn't have had to exhaust himself to the verge of collapsing just to grab a few hours' sleep. He'd not had problems sleeping since he was a kid.

Now, when he closed his eyes, all he saw was Jenny. Her smile. Her eyes. Her hands as they'd clasped his, tightening and releasing over and over. Her body beneath his. Her soft cries of pleasure haunted his dreams.

Had either of his parents ever struggled to leave someone? Some place? If they had, they'd never let on. He wasn't sure they'd struggled to leave him when they'd dropped him off to whichever one he hadn't just been living with. To the contrary, they'd felt relieved to be free of their parenting burden.

Jenny had struggled with his leaving. Sawyer had struggled. They'd wanted him to stay. Had anyone ever wanted him to stick around the way they had?

Had anyone ever wanted to stick around the way he had wanted to?

Yet, he'd left. Why? Why hadn't he been able to let himself consider staying in Chattanooga to see what happened between him Jenny? Why hadn't he told her all the emotions that had overwhelmed him when she'd come apart in his arms? That he'd never before known what they'd shared in or outside the bedroom?

Pausing to lean forward, hands on his knees, Tristan gasped for air.

He couldn't do this. Not a moment longer.

Before he could remind himself of all the reasons he shouldn't, he pulled out his phone and dialed her number. She didn't answer. Not surprising. It was midday. If she'd worked the night before, she'd be sleeping. Knowing she'd know it was him who had called anyway since she'd have a missed call from his number, he waited to leave a message, trying to think of what to say in the few seconds before the beep prompted him to speak.

How could he convey how crazy he felt without her? How much he missed her and Sawyer? That he ached to be back in Tennessee? That when he looked around his new apartment all he saw was emptiness?

"Jenny, it's me. I was checking to see how you and Sawyer are doing. Chicago is great. The hospital admin cares about their patients. Not like there, you know, but they're better than most." He hesitated then added, "You should come up here and I can show you around. Then again, I guess Sawyer has started school and you can't. Or maybe your mom can watch him for a few days, and you could come up. Sorry. I'm probably not making sense." Not even to himself. "But I was jogging, and I thought I'd see how you were doing and let you know I was good."

Before he went into a complete idiotic babble, he hung up the phone.

Not his smoothest call, but Jenny had a way of knowing what he was saying even when the right words didn't come out. She'd know he'd called because he missed her.

She'd know he was an idiot for leaving her and Sawyer.

He knew he was an idiot for leaving.

Wasn't that why he'd lain in bed watching her sleep for so long before he'd gotten out and driven back to his rental? He'd not bothered trying to sleep anymore but had packed the remainder of his meager possessions into his 4Runner and headed north. Once, while sitting in heavy traffic on I-24, he'd considered going back, but he wasn't someone who stuck around. Much better to have left the way he had to where, hopefully, her thoughts of him were good.

If she thought of him at all.

She'd said she would, that he had her heart. If that were true, if she really had given herself to him, would it have changed anything?

She had given herself, he scolded himself. She'd never have given her body if he hadn't had her heart.

He really was an idiot.

Jenny clasped her phone long after it had quit ringing. Oh, how her heart had leapt at the number on the screen. And, oh, how she'd struggled not to answer it and beg him to come back to Chattanooga.

Perhaps the thought that she might do just that had been what had given her the strength not to answer.

"Who was on the phone, honey?"

Jenny tucked her phone back into her pocket. "No one, Mom. Now, are you sure you don't want to take more of the dishes with you?"

Her mother shook her head. "Giles already has a houseful. I shouldn't take anything you and Sawyer might need."

"Sawyer and I are just fine. Sawyer is already talking about moving into your room and us turning his old room into a play area."

Jenny's mom gave a watery smile. "This is a lot more difficult that I thought it would be. I should just stay here."

"Mom, you're getting married. Of course you're going to go live with Giles."

"But you might need me. Sawyer might need me. Giles and I can wait on getting married."

"Oh, no. There is no way I'd let you put off your wedding because of Sawyer and me. Giles makes you happy, happier than I've ever seen you. Mom, I can't imagine not having had you here with me during Sawyer's first few years, but the reality is that I'd have been okay, you know?"

Her mother smiled. "I know, but that doesn't mean I have to leave now."

"Actually, it does," Jenny corrected. At her mother's wide-eyed shock, she clarified. "Not that you can't come back if Giles isn't good to you, but Mom, I know he's going to be great. He wants to love you and take care of you. Sawyer and I will always be here, but you need to go and do you."

Her mother swept her up into a big hug.

"Knock, knock," Giles said, coming into the living room then, seeing them hugged up, stopped. "Am I interrupting? I can come back later if I need to."

"No," Jenny answered, giving her mother one last squeeze. "You're not. You're a part of this family, too, about to be, anyway, and are always welcome."

Giles smiled and wrapped them both in a bear hug. "Same goes for you and Sawyer at our place, right?"

Still teary-eyed, Jenny's mom nodded.

Sawyer poked his head out of his room and frowned. "Y'all are all mushy."

"Get over here so you can be mushy, too," Jenny told him, laughing.

He hesitated then, giggling, ran over to them and wrapped his arms around her and his grammy's legs.

Yeah, maybe life wasn't what it could have been had things been different with Tristan, but life was good.

She'd keep making it better. For Sawyer and for herself.

That would be a lot easier if she cut the strings completely where Tristan was concerned. Taking his calls, even going to see him or allowing him to visit, would only keep the scab ripped off a deeply wounded heart.

A deeply wounded heart that her son had also experienced but seemed to be doing a little better with. He'd only mentioned Tristan twice today so far, compared to the dozens per day he averaged.

As much as she missed Tristan, they'd said their goodbyes.

For the rest of the day she told herself that, even did a decent job convincing herself. But late that night, knowing she was right to keep her break from Tristan clean didn't keep the tears at bay.

Children were much more resilient than brokenhearted women.

"I'm so glad you agreed to go with us to celebrate Roger's birthday."

"Once I mentioned it to Sawyer, he's spoken of little else," Jenny told her friend as she opened the back door to help Sawyer out of his car seat. She'd driven separately from her friends as they'd had to be there much earlier to be ready for their jump. That Roger had recruited several of their friends to make the plunge with him didn't surprise Jenny. If she'd not had Sawyer to think of, she might have done so, too.

"I mean who doesn't want to hang out at a private airstrip and watch your crazy friends jump out of a plane, right?"

Sawyer grinned as he jumped down from the car to the hot pavement. "I wish I was big enough."

Jenny's breaths quickened. "Yeah, well, I'm glad you're not as I'm not quite ready for you to jump out of planes."

Sawyer grinned. "Someday I will be big, though."

"I know," Jenny told him, ruffling his hair. "You're going to be a wonderful young man and I'll be a very proud mother. I am a proud mother."

He beamed up at her.

"And Sawyer could be a proud son as there's still time if you want to jump," Laura teased.

"Not happening. Sawyer and I are here for the show, not to fling ourselves out of a perfectly good plane, but you have fun with that."

Sawyer tugged on her arm. "Mama, can I stand by the fence and watch the plane?"

Jenny glanced over at the metal fence separating the parking area from the airstrip. There were a couple of picnic style tables close by.

"Sure. Go ahead. I'll be there in just a bit." She'd packed a cooler bag with drinks and snacks for while they waited. Plus, she wanted to have sunscreen handy to reapply to herself and Sawyer.

She grabbed her bag from the back, but as the trunk lid was closing, her gaze caught Laura's. The hair on her arms prickled.

"What is it?"

"I need to tell you something. Maybe I should have told you before, but to be fair I only knew for sure last night and I didn't want you to miss out on today if he wasn't really going to be here."

Jenny's breath gushed out of her as surely as if she had dropped from a plane and was plummeting in a free fall.

"If who wasn't really going to be here?" Not that she didn't know. No doubt he was here to jump with Roger as part of the birthday celebration.

"Tristan!"

Jenny closed her eyes, took a deep breath, then glanced to where her son excitedly bounced at the fence, calling to a group that had come out of the hanger.

"Tristan! Tristan," Sawyer called, waving his arms back and forth.

"Someone is glad to see him," Laura pointed out and

then gave Jenny a hug. "I've got to go. Forgive me for not telling you, okay? It was for your own good."

Jenny watched her friend jog across the parking area and disappear inside the hanger, then glanced back to where Tristan had come through the fence gate and knelt next to Sawyer.

"I've missed you, too," she heard Tristan telling him as she walked up. Why did each step seem in slow motion? Why did her heart beat so crazily hard? He'd left her without saying goodbye. She could argue that he'd been saying goodbye the entire night, but she couldn't cut him any slack. Not if she wanted to get through the day. She had to hold strong.

"Mama, Tristan is back and is jumping out of the plane, too," Sawyer told her the moment he realized she was close.

"I'm only back for the weekend, bud," Tristan clarified, straightening to his full height prior to meeting Jenny's stare. "I fly back to Chicago on Monday."

Those blue eyes probed hers, left her weak-kneed, left her wanting to throw her arms around him as Sawyer had done. Instead, she kept her cool and gave him a tight smile. "You came in for Roger's birthday?"

Studying her, he nodded. "I'd promised I would do this with him."

"With you living in another state, he'd have understood if you hadn't," she pointed out.

"I wouldn't have understood. I keep my promises."

Her gaze dropped to his lips, saw them moving as he spoke, but in her mind all she could think was that the last time she'd seen him had been in her bed. With that thought came a whole influx of memories better not recalled.

"Tristan, they're ready for us," Steve called from where the group still stood.

He nodded then turned back to Jenny. "I'm glad you two are here. I wasn't sure if you would be."

"We didn't know you'd be here," she said tightly.

"But we're glad you are here, aren't we, Mama?" Sawyer piped up, reminding Jenny that everything they said, did, was being observed by her son, and likely their friends, as well.

"The more, the merrier," Jenny said for lack of knowing how else to answer.

Jenny wasn't happy he was there. Tristan ran his fingers through his hair and sighed. What had he expected? That she'd throw her arms around him in an embrace the way Sawyer had?

He'd known better.

She'd not answered any of his texts or calls since he'd left, including the one he'd made from Roger's the night before.

"I'll see you when I'm back on the ground."

"Wave at me from the sky," Sawyer requested.

"Sure thing." He glanced toward Jenny. "Do you want me to wave at you?"

She hesitated then shook her head. "I'm good, but thanks."

She was good. The best.

Nodding his understanding, he fist-bumped Sawyer and then turned, planning to join his group.

He'd only taken a few steps when Jenny stopped him, her hand grasping his arm.

"Be careful," she said, her voice strained.

His glance met hers. So much swirled in those big eyes of hers that he felt as if he were already free-falling.

"I always am." Except when it had come to protecting himself from becoming too entangled with Chattanooga. Throwing caution to the wind, he leaned forward and pressed his lips to her cheek.

Her eyes not wavering from his, Jenny sucked in a breath.

"We'll talk later," he promised, "after I'm back on the ground. For now, wish me luck."

"I wish you luck."

He took a few steps then turned. She was still standing in the same spot. Her finger was pressed to her cheek where he'd kissed her.

Crazy joy filled him. Crazy because seeing her filled him with such happiness, but how could she ever forgive him for all the mistakes he'd made and was sure to continue to make? How could a woman as wonderful as Jenny ever love a man whose feet never stayed in one place long enough to make roots when hers ran so deep?

Just beyond her, Sawyer waved with the exuberance the kid showed for most things in life. Tristan waved back and entered the open hanger to join the others who were already being strapped up.

"She's missed you," Laura said from where she stood on the mat, her arms outstretched and her tandem jumper adjusting her straps.

"Maybe," he admitted, shaking hands with the man he'd met earlier and whom he'd be jumping with. "Tell me what to do."

Soon their group was taxing down the runway with lots of whoops and hollers for the cameramen who were recording their jumps.

Jenny, Sawyer and a few others were sitting by the fence, watching as they took off. Sawyer was still waving, and Jenny did the same as the plane rolled past them.

Why did the conversation he planned to have with Jenny knot his stomach so much more than the fact he was about to jump out of a plane at fourteen thousand feet?

CHAPTER FOURTEEN

JENNY READ SAWYER his bedtime story then tucked him in. Between watching the skydivers and then eating lunch at the mountaintop restaurant overlooking the Sequatchie Valley, he'd had such a big day that he'd not made it to the end of the book before he'd been sound asleep.

She paused in his bedroom doorway a few moments, watching him, then turned off the light and closed his door.

Restless, she cleaned the kitchen, straightened the living room, started a load of clothes, brushed her teeth, then stared at herself in the mirror.

Why was she hesitating to take off her mascara and cover-up? Why instead had she freshened her light application of makeup?

Tristan hadn't said he'd come to see her. All he'd done was say they'd talk later. He could have meant the following day. He may have meant via phone after he was back in Chicago. He may have just been caught up in the moment.

No, he'd been telling the truth when he'd said he kept his promises. He lived by his own honor code and honesty ranked high.

Still, when her phone dinged at just after nine, her breath caught.

I'm in your driveway. Can I come in?

Yes, she typed back, wondering exactly what she was agreeing to. Was he there to talk or for a repeat of their last night together? If the latter, did she have the strength to send him away?

Obviously not, as she barely had her living room door closed behind him prior to his mouth covering hers.

Covering was such a mild word. Devouring. His mouth devoured hers.

When they pulled apart, Jenny's chest heaved with the need for air and her head spun.

"I've missed you."

"I—I missed you, too." It wasn't as if she were revealing some great secret with her admission. No doubt he knew, or he wouldn't be there. "But I just want to talk, not…not…well, you know."

"Have sex with me?"

She nodded. "I don't think we should do that again."

They shouldn't have done it to begin with and yet how could she regret what had been the most pleasurable night of her life? Too bad that pleasure had been followed by such anguish.

"As contradictory as it may seem for me to say, following what just happened, I'm not here to have sex with you, Jenny."

"That's good." Kind of. Another part of her immediately wondered if he no longer wanted her. Surely, he did. His kiss had been as hungry as her own.

"Is it really, my sweet Jenny?" He paced across the living room to stare at a photo of her and Sawyer. "I'm not so sure it wouldn't be easier to show you the things inside of me rather than try to put them into words."

"Why are you here, Tristan?"

"You knew I'd come."

"Yes." She had. "But nothing has changed since you left Chattanooga."

"Everything has changed since I left. At least, in my world, it has."

"I imagine Chicago is very different from my hometown."

"I'm not referring to where I lay my head at night." He snorted. "Or maybe that's exactly what I'm referring to. There's a nurse position that I've been looking at. It's here. I want to come back to Chattanooga, Jenny."

Her heart pounded so loudly its aftershocks could likely be felt miles away.

"I want to come back to you," he continued. "Before I sign the contract, I need to know if that's what you want?"

Fingertips digging into his clammy palms, Tristan waited for Jenny to say something. His declaration seemed to have shocked her, but she must have guessed how he felt?

"You're a grown man. You don't need my permission to move back to Chattanooga."

He ran his fingers through his hair as he searched for the right words.

"I'm not seeking your permission." Although, maybe he was. Maybe he wanted her to say all the right things to make this conversation easier. And maybe that wasn't fair to her. "Can we go sit on the patio?"

He'd been thinking about what he wanted to say to her for weeks, so why he'd stalled for a few extra minutes made no sense. But what about the things he did made sense these days?

He followed her out to her backyard. In the moonlight, he watched her sit in her porch swing and tuck her leg up beneath her.

Knowing he was too restless to sit, he paced across the stones.

"This should be easy. It's not as if I didn't know I'd be in Chattanooga this weekend, that I'd see you, and yet finding the right words seems impossible." He swallowed. "Roger offered me an out to my promise to jump with him, but I refused it."

"Why?"

"Because I hoped you'd be there."

"You aren't the only one who keeps their promises," she declared, lifting her chin.

"I played over how it would be to see you again in my mind what seems like a thousand times."

"Were you disappointed by the reality?"

"My eyes seeing you is never a disappointment, Jenny, but in my mind I'd imagined you running to me the way Sawyer did."

"He's a child. Life is less complicated for him."

"True. Tell me, were you tempted to run to me?"

"Only to look you in the eyes and ask how you dared to come there when you'd snuck away without telling me goodbye."

He walked over, sat beside her and took her hand into his.

"Had I awakened you, I wouldn't have left." There. He'd said it. "Not your bed and perhaps not Chattanooga."

Her forehead crinkled. "I don't understand."

"I'm in love with you, Jenny." Saying the words out loud weakened his knees to jelly, left him vulnerable and feeling as if he should protect himself. Instead, he stared into Jenny's wide eyes and left his heart's fate in her hands.

"You love me?" Her voice trembled with disbelief.

Lifting her hand to his lips, he pressed a kiss there. "Madly. Passionately. Completely head-over-heels in love with you. I'm in unknown waters, Jenny. I've never known what it was to look at a person and to see my future, to be with them and to belong. My heart is yours."

Tristan loved her? Surely, Jenny's ears deceived her. Because what he was saying seemed impossible.

"I—I don't know what to say."

His hand holding hers shook. He sighed. "Say you'll give me another chance to prove I can be the man you and Sawyer need me to be."

"You want to take the travel nurse position in Chattanooga so you can be with Sawyer and me?"

He nodded. "Not a travel nurse position. I plan to get a permanent job with the hospital."

"Even if I say I don't want to see you?"

"If you say you don't want to see me, then my heart will be broken, but I won't give up because I know you care about me. I am going to return to Chattanooga and will earn your trust and your heart. Meeting you and Sawyer has given me something I've never had before."

She waited.

"A sense of home. Leaving has always been easy. Since I've been gone from here, my heart has ached to return. I never understood what it meant to come home, but from the moment I saw you at the airfield today, I knew."

"Chattanooga is home?"

"You're home, Jenny. You are my home."

"Because home is where the heart is?"

He lifted her hand to his lips again. "My heart is with you and it's where the rest of me longs to be."

Everything he said sounded so wonderful, so like a dream, but fear clawed at the happiness she wanted to let fill her. "How do I know you won't leave again? How can I be sure?"

"You won't know, Jenny. Even I don't know what the future holds. All I've ever known is leaving one place after another, but not since I was a child have I wanted to stay somewhere. Then, I didn't have a choice but was at the mercy of those around me. Now, I have a choice, Jenny, and I choose you and Sawyer, if you'll have me."

What he was saying ran through her mind, jumbling as she tried to process what he meant. "You want to date me?"

He nodded. "I want everything with you, Jenny. To spend my life with you and Sawyer."

"He loves you so much."

Tristan cupped her face and stared into her eyes. "The question is, does his mother?"

"You know I do," she whispered back.

A smile spread across his face. "Then tell me."

"I love you, Tristan. With all my heart. That doesn't mean I'm not scared. Every man in my life has left me."

"I won't leave you, Jenny." He understood why she thought he would but, with clarity, he knew he wouldn't. "I'd rather die than hurt you and Sawyer. I'll finish out my contract in Chicago and when I come back to Chattanooga, I'm here to stay. My heart and my loyalty are yours as long as you want them."

Leaning toward him, she pressed her lips to his. "Then I want your heart, your loyalty, and all of you forever. Promise me."

Cupping her face, he stared into her eyes and he saw everything he hadn't known he'd wanted or needed reflected there. Without a doubt his next words were the easiest promise to keep that he'd ever made.

"I promise you my forever, Jenny."

And that was what he gave her. His heart. His love. His forever.

* * * * *

COMING SOON!

We really hope you enjoyed reading this book.
If you're looking for more romance, be sure to
head to the shops when new books are
available on

Thursday 16th February

To see which titles are coming soon, please visit

millsandboon.co.uk/nextmonth

MILLS & BOON®

Coming next month

SECRET SON TO CHANGE HER LIFE
Alison Roberts

'I tried every way I could to contact you,' Brie said quietly. 'But it was weeks after you'd left. Your phone was disconnected. You never responded when I tried to message you on social media. Nobody knew where you were.'

'So you just gave up?'

'It was during those weeks I found out that the baby I was carrying had spina bifida.' Brie's tone changed. She might deserve Jonno's anger but she wasn't the person he thought she was. She hadn't set out to lie to him. 'My priorities kind of changed at that point.'

That silenced him. Brie walked ahead and found another stick to throw for Dennis. Then she turned.

'I never expected to see you again,' she said. 'But when I'd had a bit of time to get used to you turning up out of blue, like that, I did try to tell you – the day I came to your apartment.'

She could hear the echo of what she'd said to him then, in spite of the background shriek of the seagulls. She knew Jonno could hear it as well.

I had to come…There's something I really need to tell you, Jonno…

They both knew why she hadn't ended up telling him that day.

'You could have told me well before then. Like when I asked you if you had any kids.'

'Oh… yeah… Right after you'd been telling me how thankful you were that you didn't have any dependents? How do you think that made me feel?' Brie's voice hitched. 'I was still trying to get my head around it myself. How was I going to tell my son that his daddy was back in town but might not want to have anything to do with him because he had better things to do with his time? That he wasn't even planning to be around long, anyway. He was going to get rid of the last tie he had here and then he'd be gone again. Forever. Probably on the other side of the world in Australia or New Zealand.'

'I said those things because I didn't know,' Jonno countered. 'Do you really think I'm someone who'd walk away from a responsibility like having a child? That I wouldn't care?'

Brie swallowed hard. Of course she didn't. 'Maybe I was hoping that one day, Felix would be able to find you.'

Continue reading
SECRET SON TO CHANGE HER LIFE
Alison Roberts

Available next month
www.millsandboon.co.uk

MILLS & BOON

THE HEART OF ROMANCE

A ROMANCE FOR EVERY READER

MODERN

Prepare to be swept off your feet by sophisticated, sexy and seductive heroes, in some of the world's most glamourous and romantic locations, where power and passion collide.

HISTORICAL

Escape with historical heroes from time gone by. Whether your passion is for wicked Regency Rakes, muscled Vikings or rugged Highlanders, awaken the romance of the past.

MEDICAL

Set your pulse racing with dedicated, delectable doctors in the high-pressure world of medicine, where emotions run high and passion, comfort and love are the best medicine.

True Love

Celebrate true love with tender stories of heartfelt romance, from the rush of falling in love to the joy a new baby can bring, and a focus on the emotional heart of a relationship.

Desire

Indulge in secrets and scandal, intense drama and plenty of sizzling hot action with powerful and passionate heroes who have it all: wealth, status, good looks…everything but the right woman.

HEROES

Experience all the excitement of a gripping thriller, with an intense romance at its heart. Resourceful, true-to-life women and strong, fearless men face danger and desire - a killer combination!

To see which titles are coming soon, please visit

millsandboon.co.uk/nextmonth